Islam

By

Johnny Jacks

Patriots and Infidels – Book 1

Copyright © 2017 by Johnny Jacks

Cover design and artwork by Hristo Argirov Kovatliev
https://www.facebook.com/hristo.kovatliev

All rights reserved. No part of this publication may be reproduced, distributed, stored, or transmitted in any form, including photocopying, recording, or other electronic or mechanical means, including information storage and retrieval systems, without the prior written permission of the publisher, except brief quotations embodied in critical reviews and certain other noncommercial uses permitted by copyright law. For permission, send email requests, to johnnyjacks@newamericabooks.com. Include "Permissions Coordinator" in the Subject. Published by New America Books, Cullman, AL 35056

This book is a work of fiction. Names, characters, plot, subplots, places, and incidents are the product of the author's imagination or used fictitiously, and any resemblance to actual persons, living or dead, is entirely coincidental.

ISBN-13: 978-1979584616
ISBN-10: 1979584613

Published in the United States by
New America Books
A Division of Partisan Prepper, Inc.
P.O. Box 2604
Cullman, AL 35057

ABOUT THE AUTHOR

Johnny Jacks was born in Alabama six months before D-Day to semiliterate sharecropper parents. His family lived self-reliantly the first ten years of his life off-grid, off city water, without indoor plumbing, and without assistance from the welfare state, which did not exist then. On his seventeenth birthday, he enlisted in the Air Force, later transferring to the Army, where he became a Special Forces soldier and began a career serving on Special Forces A-teams in Europe, Asia, and Central America, including a combat assignment to Special Forces A-team 102, Tien Phuoc, Vietnam, 1967-1968. He became proficient in guerrilla warfare strategies and tactics, radio communications, intelligence gathering, and guerrilla group organization and operations.

After retiring from the Army in 1982, Jacks worked for several government agencies over the next twenty-five years in national security and emergency preparedness programs. Those roles provided him with knowledge of the national security policy related to continuity of government and continuity of operations, with insight into what will take place with America's senior leadership when the Schumer hits the fan and the nation falls into a state of anarchy.

Jacks lives with his wife on their farm in the Appalachian foothills of North Alabama, where he enjoys gardening, animal husbandry, and writing. His hobbies include traveling, gold prospecting, hunting, and fishing.

DEDICATION

To the Green Berets – Active Duty and Retired

You know what we must do when the SHTF to organize those who survive the die-off to defend and restore America to her original constitutional foundation. DOL

ACKNOWLEDGEMENTS

To my wife, Kay, for encouraging me to remain focused on the manuscript, especially when the grass needed mowed or the bathroom sink unclogged.

To Mahala Church, editor and writing instructor extraordinaire, for not letting her head explode when my OCD brain continued to change, add to, and delete what she thought was settled, not to mention the chapters I deleted or moved around without telling her.

To beta readers, especially Chin Gibson, who provided unvarnished feedback and saved me from well-deserved embarrassment in several scenes.

To Hristo Argirov Kovatliev, master of graphic art, for adorning this book with its splendid cover.

To the personal and Facebook author friends who helped me solve several newbie-writer problems. I'm truly humbled at the high degree to which authors support one another. It's amazing.

To those who purchase and read the *stuff* that pours from places in my mind that I didn't know existed, you are my reason to write. If not for a strong desire to please you with stories that bring enjoyment to your lives and present you with prepper concepts that might someday save your lives, my work would be an empty endeavor.

Chapter 1

Irreconcilable Differences

Year 1

"I ask you for the second time, Detective Dean, you **purposely** shot those men between the eyes, didn't you?"

Grayson Dean scowled at the exceptionally adept Shannon Fisher, an ACLU lawyer he had done battle with before. He knew her objective was to malign his credibility. The tall, hard-muscled man had no intention of allowing her that satisfaction. It wasn't his fault this crazy woman chose to defend the lone survivor from a bank robbery that went horribly wrong—at least for the robbers. Determined to prove the charges of police brutality against Detective Grayson Dean, Shannon had been throttling the brash detective for two hours without breaking him.

A trickle of perspiration snaked down Shannon's spine as she stared at the unyielding man. She knew the odds were against her when she took the Delgado case, but she was single-minded in her efforts to get a short sentence for her client. To do that, she had to destroy Grayson Dean's credibility and gain the jury's sympathy. The outcome depended on the jury doubting the grim detective's morality and state of mind. She braced for his response.

"I happen to be a good shot with a handgun." Grayson's ice-cold retort hung in the thick air of the courtroom.

"So, it *was* intentional?" Shannon spoke directly to the jury and then reset her confident got-you-now gaze on Grayson.

"How hard-headed can you be, lady?"

Shannon spun to the judge. "Objection, your honor!"

The judge, all too familiar with the confrontational lawyer and the blunt detective, released a big sigh. "Objection sustained. Detective Dean, answer the questions without commentary."

"Sorry, your honor." Grayson's patience had left him hours ago.

He scowled at the frumpy woman in her baggy brown pantsuit. Obviously, she had a personal vendetta. Aware his answer might determine his future on the Houston police force, he struggled to tamp down his frustration.

Breathing deeply, he spoke in a measured, professional tone. "Of course, it was intentional, *counselor.*"

The hint of a smile tickled Shannon's lips and murmurs filled the courtroom.

Grayson timed a short pause and then spoke before Shannon could fire another debasing question.

"When criminals shoot at a police officer, his return fire is *always* intentional."

Low mumbles of understanding replaced the negative murmurs. Voices grew loud as the audience expressed mixed opinions, angry Spanish spilling rapidly from Delgado's family.

The faces of the jurors and the nods of their heads made it clear Shannon Fisher had lost her case. The brilliant and highly opinionated lawyer did not like to lose. In fact, she despised losing.

The judge banged his gavel. "Order in the court! Remain silent, or I'll clear the courtroom."

Order restored, Shannon tried again to discredit the detective and gain sympathy for José Delgado, the lone surviving thief. She pointed to him. "Look at Mr. Delgado, Detective Grayson. Notice that he's in a wheelchair, his legs useless because of the bullet you fired into his spine. Why didn't you offer him a chance to surrender before shooting him?"

Grayson's attorney objected. "We've already established that Mr. Delgado was holding a pistol and Detective Dean acted in accordance with proper police procedures."

"Objection sustained."

"No further questions, your honor." Shannon's voice betrayed her anger and defeat. She returned to the defense table, her eyes throwing a look of hatred at Grayson.

The judge called a close to the day. "Detective Dean, you are excused. Since it's after four, court is adjourned until 9 a.m. Monday."

The air in the room continued to spark with anger from both sides of the aisle as everyone stood for the jury and judge to exit.

There was no doubt that José Delgado was going to prison, but Shannon had begun planning how to make Grayson pay for paralyzing the man, intentional or not.

Grayson watched her retrieve her papers and shove them angrily into her briefcase. He'd never despised anyone, until Shannon Fisher entered his life.

My fate on the force lies in that liberal bitch's hands, and she doesn't give a damn.

Chapter 2

Urinal Turmoil

Year 1

Grayson stood at the urinal, wishing he'd not drunk that sixth cup of coffee. He flinched when the men's room door banged open. Shannon stormed in and marched within a foot of his side. She made the unfortunate mistake of poking him hard on the shoulder, causing his body to jerk and twist. Unable to stop the flow, he peed on his leg and Shannon's dull brown shoes before he got a handle on things.

She stepped back. "What the hell! You did that on purpose!"

"No. But I will if you don't get out of here."

She stepped towards him, venom dripping from her fangs. At five-feet-ten inches, she still had to crane her neck to look him in the face.

Grayson shoved his broad shoulder forward, attempting to turn away, his bladder too full to stop the flow. *Is there no end to this woman's audacity?*

"You're really proud of yourself, aren't you, Detective?" Her raspy voice dripped sarcasm. "You kill two men, paralyze another from the waist down, and it's just another day on the job. How can you live with yourself?"

"Are you nuts, lady? Get out of here and let me finish my business!"

"I don't care about your *business*! But I do care that you continue to shoot the citizens of Houston and aren't held accountable for it."

"Citizens!" Grayson's temper flared, his body struggling to avoid whirling towards her intentionally. "How dare you call those crud balls *citizens*! They're the scum of the earth! Your client and his gang were in the act of robbing a bank—a federal crime, and they shot at me first!"

"You should have let him surrender, or since you're such a good shot, just wounded him, asshole."

He lowered his voice and regurgitated anger. "They deserved to die, you ignorant excuse for an American! Ever look at his rap sheet? Did you consider the innocent people in harm's way when your *poor innocent* client and his buds began shooting? Ever wonder why *your* bleeding heart always champions the bad guys and ignores the good guys?"

Shannon's face filled with red fury. She never broke eye contact, sputtering as she searched for words that evaded her. She still had him at a significant disadvantage, but her mind thrashed for a retort.

"You don't give a damn about that scumbag client of yours! Face it lady, you're pushing your own agenda. You and your stupid anti-gun lobby use any tactic to try to confiscate firearms from law-abiding citizens. Otherwise, why did you accuse me of police brutality simply for defending myself against a gang of criminals trying to kill me?"

Shannon shook her head, as though awakening from a dream, and got in her last shot, looking down as his bladder finally emptied. Grayson's face grew red as he struggled to get his *business* retracted and safely zipped. Peering up at him, she turned her head sideways and telegraphed one of her sarcastic false smiles, grabbed a paper towel to wipe her shoes, threw it in the trash, and stomped out.

When the restroom door hissed shut behind her, Grayson heard a flush. Chief of Police Ramirez exited the nearest stall. His body shook uncontrollably, and a muffled wheezing snicker suppressed the belly laugh that wanted to burst from his gut.

"That is one of the funniest things I've ever experienced in my life. Definitely, the only time I appreciated a hole in the wall of a men's room stall. You know I'm going to have to tell this story a thousand times before I die, don't you?"

Grayson walked to the sink to wash his hands. "You got me, Chief. But, please wait until you're retired and out of the office…the guys…you know."

"Not a chance. Look, Grayson, you're one of the best lawmen on the force. Remember that. You are a *lawman*, no longer a Green Beret. This isn't combat where you can charge in headlong, killing everything in sight. As your commander in Afghanistan, I *know* your expertise with firearms, but that liberal do-gooder is right; you could've wounded that bastard. My sentiments are too close to yours, so I kept my mouth shut."

"Thanks. I appreciated your guidance in battle, and I appreciate it now. It's just that I hate seeing our society going to the dogs because bad guys have the run of the town. The damn liberal lawyers treat them as if they're Sunday school boys. For *your* record, I aimed to shoot the pistol from his hand. Unlike the others, he was shaking like a dog shitting peach seeds. The bullet accidently deflected off his gun, went through his guts, and into his spine."

"As much as it goes against your grain, sometimes it pays to let the bad guys go, catch them another day. The bad guys in that bank weren't the only ones shooting around civilians. As a police officer charged with public safety, you put innocent lives in danger."

Grayson felt the flash of heat in his face. Years of combat had desensitized him to civilian casualties, sometimes unavoidable to kill the enemy. It was the hardest lesson he mastered as a soldier and as a man. It required him to turn off his emotions temporarily to keep himself and his men from dying in battle. The result was a long struggle with PTSD that, although controlled, would be with him for eternity. In tension-filled situations, it sometimes resurrected its ugly head and fueled his anger. He argued with himself that this wasn't the case, but....

"I'll work on it, Chief."

"You'll do more than work on it, you **will** control your temper. Period." Chief Ramirez washed his hands and looked at Grayson in the mirror. "Don't make me send you to anger management class again. It's a good thing your *girlfriend* doesn't know about that, or she'd have used it against you today."

Grayson swallowed hard. A dressing down from the chief was worse than anything that ACLU lawyer could dump on him. "Don't you worry, Chief," the truth of Ramirez's statement sinking in, he took a deep breath, "I'll get it under control."

"Good. Because right this minute we have hot potatoes being tossed around like hand grenades at an anti-gun demonstration outside this building. Your ACLU lady friend has no doubt joined them by now. It's her pet project. I got a text while I was in the can. The demonstrators are demanding the state put you on trial for murder of the other two robbers. That's not going to happen, but it's best if you leave by the back door."

Grayson hesitated. He despised breaking contact with the enemy and running from a fight, no matter the odds of winning, but he didn't want to lose his job.

"Go home, Detective. **Now.**" Chief Ramirez's voice did not brook altering his exit plan.

Chapter 3

Sanctuary and Relief

Year 1

Grayson's anger morphed into a sour mood as he drove home. Despite the warm April day, a throbbing coldness settled into his bones. *Why do I let that woman get to me? When will I learn to tamp down my temper?*

He pulled into his driveway behind his wife, Margaret's, pink Mary Kay Cadillac and gave his son, Daniel, a thumbs-up. Daniel was a good kid, never a moment's trouble, tall and muscular like his father. The boy stopped the mower in the middle of giving the lawn its first cut of the year. Grayson only now realized April's fresh showers had brought out the new grass. Daniel beamed at his father, trotting towards him with obvious excitement.

"Pop, I received a scholarship check today for five hundred dollars for my essay on 'The Importance of Family.'"

Grayson grabbed him in a bro-hug. "Great news, son! At sixteen, you're becoming a serious young man. You make your old dad proud."

"Daddy! Daddy!" Grayson's daughter, Amanda, bounded down the front steps. Her short five-year-old legs churned across the lawn, and she jumped into Grayson's arms. His soul filled with love; Amanda's hug pushed the nastiness of his day into the background.

"How's my Little Angel?"

"Daddy, come see what I did in school today." Amanda wiggled down and pulled his hand with all her might toward the front door.

"Danny, I'll catch up with you inside when you finish the lawn." Grayson clapped his son on the shoulder, picked Amanda up and carried her inside. With his free arm, he pulled his wife into a hug with a quick kiss on the cheek, foregoing the usual double pat on the fanny.

"Amanda has something exciting to show me." Grayson halfheartedly winked at Margaret. He lowered Amanda to the floor, grabbed a beer from the fridge, and sat at the table to admire his daughter's animal drawings from school. "Something smells great! Barbequed chicken?"

"And scalloped potatoes. You'll be proud of me. I had a great Mary Kay party, and it put me over the limit to qualify for a new caddy."

"I'm always proud of you, baby, with or without a Cadillac."

"Did you talk to Danny?"

"Yeah, said something about a scholarship."

A smile lit up Margaret's face. "I'm proud of our son. He's a self-starter, just like his dad. He's well on his way to having enough credits to graduate next year as a junior."

"Daniel's a winner. I'm proud of him, too."

Grayson's affection warmed Margaret's heart, but the worried expression he was trying hard to hide warned her to walk softly. "How did the trial go?"

A frown slid across his face and his dark mood sprouted. His voice was flat. "Later." Grayson admired Amanda's pictures, slipped from the kitchen and into his large recliner in the den. Kicking off his shoes, he flipped on *Fox News* and stared at the screen, but his mind wandered. Amanda quietly crawled into his lap and snuggled for a few minutes before her mother called her to set the table.

A team, Margaret and Grayson openly shared their lives. She knew the kind of day he had the moment he walked through the door every day, knowing he would tell her what he was thinking once he settled. She smiled to herself and began formulating a naughty scheme to erase his gloomy mood and return him to normal. She knew her man well.

~~~

Grayson breathed a sigh of relief. It was a good night when he made it home to share a meal with his family, something police detectives often had to forego. He downed three glasses of iced tea before he washed away enough of the day to enjoy his dinner.

Margaret and he were childhood sweethearts, only fifteen when Danny was born. Margaret worked hard to become a first-class cook and mother while he was busy in the Army and then the police force. His precious family kept him afloat emotionally. At dinner, they discussed Daniel's scholarship and Margaret's thriving business. They enjoyed their meal, ending with peach cobbler and a scoop of vanilla ice cream, Grayson's favorite.

Whenever Grayson got home early, he read a bedtime story to Amanda, more, if she could con him with her dimpled smile. Tonight, Amanda asked Daniel to read to her. A typical teenager, Daniel ignored her until Grayson listed his choices. He could drive his rattletrap or Grayson's Ford F-250 pickup to meet his friends later.

"Come on, Mandy!" Daniel was suddenly in the mood to read. "Which story do you want?"

Once Amanda was asleep, Grayson tossed Daniel the keys to his truck.

"Thanks, Pop."

"Home by eleven, since there's no school tomorrow."

~~~

"Oh, baby, that feels good," Grayson rolled his head when Margaret came to the back of his easy chair and began to massage his neck and shoulders. She tilted his head back and gave him an upside-down kiss.

Usually when she gazed into Grayson's eyes, she saw the depth of his love and her heart filled with joy. Tonight, his eyes were flat, adding to her determination to put the happy back into them.

Grayson felt at one with Margaret; they had covered each other's backs since kindergarten. She brought peace to his soul. Sexy and smart, she made him feel like the luckiest man on Earth. Like all couples, they had disagreements, some small and some significant, but they remained faithful to their rule to never go to bed angry.

"Sweetie, let's get to bed early tonight," Margaret purred in his ear.

"Yeah, it's been a long day. I'm pooped. Mind if I shower first?"

"Have at it, baby." He missed her signal, but she knew there was time. "I'll finish the kitchen and lock up."

Grayson cranked the hot water to steam away the foulness of his encounter with his despised legal nemesis. He enjoyed remembering her ragged expression when it was apparent she had asked the wrong question. What did she think cops did when someone pointed a gun at them—ask for a timeout? Sure, he had overstepped the line with his sarcastic remarks, but the drab woman reminded him of the hippies in the sixties. People who turned on the country that had given them so much were a sore spot with him.

Grayson finished his shower and slipped between the fresh sheets, his tired bones aching for rest but honoring their wedding night commitment to go to sleep together. He looked forward to their pillow talk before drifting off to a peaceful sleep. It realigned his world.

When Margaret stepped out of the bathroom in a see-through red silk robe, he came to full alert.

She smiled, walked to the window, and opened the blinds. A bright full moon—a low-level spotlight—shined directly into the bedroom. She slowly twisted her head and gave him a come-hither look, before sauntering towards him. She stood beside the bed, allowing the soft moonlight to give Grayson the pleasure of seeing her sparsely veiled perfect body. Her beauty and the slight fragrance of her perfume filled his senses.

"Honey, it's apparent you had a rough day. Want to tell me about it?" Her voice was as soft and silky as her robe.

His masculinity stirred. He appreciated her gym workouts, which kept her body tight and fit. At thirty-one, she still had her schoolgirl figure. He considered not giving her a true answer. The last thing he wanted was that ACLU lawyer in their bedroom, their sanctuary, but he also needed to talk and release the pent-up pressure of court.

Responding to Margaret's flirtation, he tried to sound pitiful, so she would drag out her teasing. "I squared off with that holier-than-thou lawyer, Shannon Fisher, in court again. Would you believe she was astonished that a cop fires back at someone trying to kill him?"

She hesitated. He hadn't told her the robbers shot at him. She didn't like secrets in their marriage and turned her head away for a second to still her expression. They would deal with that another time.

Loosening her robe belt to let it open slightly, she cooed, "Oh, you poor darling. What did that horrid woman do to my precious?"

Her sultry, bedroom voice shifted his mood. Margaret moved her hips around provocatively and leaned over to kiss him on the forehead, giving him a close-up view of her *feminine charms*. Her robe dropped open and she stepped back before he could lay his hands on anything.

"You little vixen." He reached for his wife and she stepped closer to let him softly touch her in his special way.

Grayson's energy level surged as he described the court scene while distracted by his gorgeous wife. "I know this is chauvinistic, but the problems are exacerbated by her unattractive appearance. Every day, she wears frumpy, oversized pantsuits."

"You mean like Hillary Clinton?"

"Exactly. I swear I've seen her stupid black bun shift. It's obvious she wears a cheap wig. Like most women of her ilk, she's plain as mud and wears makeup smeared on with a putty knife."

Margaret moved her shoulders and allowed the robe to drop to the floor, but she remained silent.

Grayson whistled softly, "Oooh myyy!"

"You like, mister?"

"I like very much."

"And this woman. Does she look as good as me?"

"You are two different species of human. Heaven forbid she should show pride in her looks. She wears big ugly glasses like that girl on television, Repulsive Betty or something. Her raspy butch voice grates on my every nerve."

"My eyes are up here, sir," she teased.

He ignored her and continued to enjoy the view, but couldn't escape the day's events. His voice soared to match the anger festering in him. "The damn woman is trying to save the world and believes her opinion is the only one that counts! I'll be glad when this trial is over."

Margaret put a finger on his mouth. "Shush, my love. You're going to wake up Amanda. When you were in combat, you put yourself in harm's way to save others. You do the same as a cop. That woman sounds like someone hiding herself on purpose and needs understanding and support."

"Understanding and support my ass! Shannon Fisher needs a pop upside—"

"Grayson Dean, you don't mean that! You've never raised your hand against a woman and never would. Why don't you put yourself in harm's way, so to speak, and take a different attitude towards her? Maybe she'd respond to a positive approach. It might reduce your stress and give you more control when you deal with her."

"What in the world are you talking about?"

"Baby, it's obvious that she is concealing her true self. Focus on *her* difficulties instead of your disdain for her; you'll be a better man for it. Make saving Shannon Fisher your mission. Whether you're successful or not is irrelevant as long as you try."

Grayson's eyes flashed. "Right now, I want to save Grayson."

Margaret bent over, pressed her breasts to his chest, and gave him a deep kiss, quenching his hot anger. Unable to contain himself any longer, he reached around her waist and pulled her tightly to him.

"Thanks for letting me get this off my chest. You're the greatest wife a man could have. I love you."

"I love you, too," she sighed as they gave in to their desires.

Chapter 4

Unnecessarily Dead

Year 1

While the tow truck driver winched the disabled Jaguar slowly onto its flatbed, Grayson steamed at himself. He recognized the stranded motorist immediately. Even from a distance, she was hard to miss. His first impulse was to hit the gas and keep moving, but his inherent Texas gentleman instinct kicked in, and being a cop to boot forced him to turn on the hideaway lights of his unmarked car and pull over to offer the driver a ride to safety.

She signed the paperwork for the tow truck driver and plopped into his passenger seat, slamming the door as hard as she could.

His clenched jaw made it obvious he was not happy. Except for a few minutes in court earlier that day, Grayson had enjoyed a week of peace without her obnoxious presence.

Shannon Fisher's butch voice grinded on his every nerve. "Thanks for coming to my rescue, Detective Dean."

"Put your seatbelt on," Grayson growled. "Where do you want to go?" *I know where I want you to go.*

Shannon clicked her seatbelt in place, a self-satisfied smile on her colorless lips. She enjoyed annoying white cops. They were all lowlifes.

As the tow truck left, he pulled into the traffic on Cypress Creek Parkway with grim determination to get her out of his car as soon as possible.

"Home, if you don't mind. She gave him her address. I appreciate the ride. Larry, my husband, would have picked me up but he's out of town."

His lips maintained a stern line. *What man in his right mind would marry this witch?*

He stared straight ahead and remained silent. Her discomfort built until she couldn't take it anymore and goaded him into talking. "Grayson, you're still ticked off that I pulled your strings in court this morning, aren't you? Made you sweat, didn't I?"

Her sweet sarcasm lit a fire in his belly. "That's *Detective Dean* to you, Ms. Fisher. Yeah, you made me sweat, but I beat you and that scumbag, Sanchez, last week. Now, he'll rot in prison."

Fury replaced her sweetness. She twisted toward him and, waving a finger too close to his face, spoke with undisguised anger. "You **only** arrested him because he's an undocumented immigrant!"

"Get your stupid finger out of my face! He's an *illegal alien* dope dealer! Why can't you accept that *illegal aliens* should be forced back to their own countries instead of being allowed to screw up America?"

Her retort came instantly. "As a citizen of the world, Sanchez has every right to be here, and you have no right to take advantage of him! If you'd studied history, you'd know we stole this part of the country from Mexico."

"Evidently your history studies didn't go back far enough. Otherwise, you'd know the Mexicans stole it from the Indians. If not for liberal-ass lawyers like you, we wouldn't have this problem. Why in the world do you want illegals in America causing trouble?"

Shannon bit her lip. "Can we drop this for the rest of the ride?"

He thought of Margaret's sweet voice and her astute counsel. It calmed him and his temper moderated. He took a deep breath and compelled himself into a softer tone. "So, we have differences, so did Caligula and his mother. You believe in what you're doing; I believe in what I'm doing. That doesn't mean we have to…hate each other."

"I'm not your mother, Detective!"

No. Thank God, you're not. Grayson shook his head. "Let's bury the hatchet and get on with the business of getting you home."

"I'd rather be fierce enemies than have any type of business or other relationship with you or any other white racist cop!"

Grayson turned to speak, but Shannon cut him off. "Don't deny it, buster! Every study shows white cops profile and target nonwhites. It's despicable; you're despicable."

Grayson fought his instinct to defend himself and spoke through a tight jaw. "And every study shows white ACLU do-gooders profile and target whites, especially white men." Margaret's sensuous face flashed through his mind. He swallowed hard, lowered his voice a couple of octaves, and tried again. "Yet, I'd rather be friendly adversaries than deadly enemies, honestly."

Completely disarmed, her mouth worked to formulate a response. "You…you—"

"Attention All Units. High-Speed Chase. Unit in pursuit. 2015 Blue Dodge Ram pickup. Northbound Lane on I-45 at Highland Cross Drive. Subject Carlos Murtadha with one unknown passenger. Murtadha is Wanted. He's Armed and Dangerous."

The hairs on Grayson's neck stood on end. Turning on his hideaway lights, he slammed the accelerator. The tires squealed and smoked when he made a U-turn at Imperial Valley Drive and headed the opposite direction on the parkway.

"What the hell are you doing?" Shannon squealed.

"Dispatch, this is Detective Dean entering North Freeway Services Road heading north in pursuit of Murtadha." Grayson dodged cars exiting I-45 as he sped to find Murtadha.

Shannon held onto the edges of her seat in a death grip. "Stop this car right this minute! You take me home! I didn't sign on for a high-speed chase!"

"Afraid, counselor?" Grayson's eyes laughed at Shannon's pallor, visible even under her heavy makeup. *If I'm going to be fired, what better way than to scare the hell out of this bitch with an against-the-rules ride along.* "This is what catching bad guys is all about. Hang on for the ride!"

"Stop now, dammit! What's wrong with you?"

"Carlos Murtadha is Houston's most wanted man. I sent him and his brother to prison over four years ago for beating one of his drug dealers almost to death when the guy failed to pay on time. Can't believe you don't know him."

Grayson whipped his car around a gray Ford minivan and skillfully maneuvered through heavy traffic.

"The name sounds familiar." Her anxiety escalated as their speed increased. "Stop this insanity and slow down!"

Minutes later, Grayson spoke into the radio. "Visual on police unit and twenty-fifteen blue Dodge pickup."

He pulled in behind Joe Martin's patrol car at Parramatta Lane. He was now second in line behind Murtadha. They followed Murtadha's truck for miles when suddenly he careened left on the interstate ramp, Joe and Grayson on his tail.

Murtadha zigzagged across the lanes on I-45 north. He drove the way he lived: wild and wanton, the interstate his malevolent playground.

"So, the guy's a drug dealer. That's no reason to get us killed!" Shannon held her aching head and yelled at Grayson.

"Oh, he does a lot more than sell drugs!" Grayson's eyes never left the road. "A month ago, just after he was released and deported by ICE, Joe and I arrived at what we thought was a routine call and found a man bound with duct tape, a large crucifix shoved up his anus, and a butcher knife stuck in his chest. His head, frozen in horror, lay beside his body."

He jerked the car left and barely missed an elderly couple in a Lincoln. Entering a long stretch of open road, Grayson flung his words at Shannon. "Your friend and *citizen of the world* forced the guy to watch his wife and twelve-year-old daughter brutally gang raped, their throats slit, and their naked bodies tossed in front of him. We're still wondering about his motive. Nothing makes sense about the case."

"What do you mean 'my friend'? I don't know this guy!"

"You will, *Counselor!*" Grayson poured on the sarcasm. "This *poor, mistreated, illegal alien* took it a step further and decapitated the family's cat and beautiful German Shepherd, leaving her litter of newborn puppies to die of starvation. Yeah. He's your kind of client, all right."

"I don't believe you. I never heard about it."

"I'm not surprised. Your politically correct friends at the *Chronicle* refused to print the story. Seems the family was associated with one of the local mosques and the editor didn't want to insult the sensibilities of Houston's Muslim community. When I interviewed them, the editor and Imam both claimed First Amendment rights. Can't get anything out of either of them."

Shannon gave him a dirty look through her now sweat-drenched caked-on makeup but offered no retort.

"You don't want me to tell you about the children we caught him selling to pedophiles for their sexual pleasures. The DA wouldn't prosecute based on the skimpy evidence we had. You won't have to worry about defending him. If I catch him alone, he won't make it to court this time."

Bile rose in Grayson's throat as ugly images penetrated the mental barriers he kept erected to shield his sanity. Suppressed memories of the sights and rank odor of death in that house forced themselves into his dreams, dreams that made him fear for Margaret and Amanda.

Swerving erratically to avoid hitting a semi, the stench of vomit assaulted Grayson's nose.

"What the hell!" He shot a sideways glance at Shannon as she dumped the rest of her stomach on the floorboard.

"You okay?"

"Riding with a madman always makes me hurl."

Grayson's foot jammed the accelerator. "You're in this for the long haul, lady." *This bitch needs to understand who the men she tries to rescue really are.*

"How do you know it was this guy Carlos…whatshisname…that killed the family?"

"The home security cameras caught the entire grisly event, including *Murtadha* laughing on his way out of the house. You bring the popcorn and I'll show you the video."

Shannon leaned over the floorboard again.

"Open your window before we choke to death!"

She wiped vomit from her mouth with her fingers. "You're a twisted bastard!"

"Maybe, but not as much as the scumbags you protect."

Within minutes, Grayson almost sideswiped a silver Honda Odyssey as he tore down the exit ramp to the North Freeway Services Road behind Joe and Murtadha.

He grabbed the radio. "Joe, where the hell is our backup?"

"Racing to catch us on I-45."

"Radio our position so cars can head him off!"

"Roger."

Murtadha made a hard left on East Cypresswood Drive, barreling through vehicles at the traffic light, with inches to spare, and left behind a pile of crashed cars.

Lights blazing and sirens blaring, Joe and Grayson made a wide curve around the stalled cars and stayed on him.

Fighting through the chaos to apprehend Murtadha, Grayson was no longer aware of Shannon. He radioed the location of the crashed cars. *How loud does this siren have to be to get people to move out of the way?*

"Helicopter in the air," dispatch reported. "Your location in three minutes."

Grayson and his unwilling passenger stayed pinned to Joe's police cruiser. He clocked Murtadha at over 100 miles per hour. Closing in, he swore he smelled the murderous bastard's sweat oozing through the air.

Joe radioed, "We've finally got him, Grayson."

"Please let me out of here," Shannon moaned, startling Grayson with her presence.

"Don't lose him!" Grayson commanded.

Murtadha hung a left on Cypresswood Lake Drive and tore through the residential area. He disregarded every intersection and ignored lights, road signs, and traffic. A UPS truck crashed into a large water oak attempting to escape Murtadha's assault on the neighborhood.

Grayson caught a line of squad cars in the rearview mirror. Like an accordion, the patrol cars expanded to catch up, then contracted at intersections. Frantically avoiding traffic, Joe and Grayson stayed the course.

Joe warned him. "We're entering your neighborhood, Grayson. You have to call the chase off, man! Too dangerous for the locals!"

He snarled into the radio, "I know where I am! Stay on him!"

Grayson shifted into guerrilla tracking mode, fixed on his target. His dead stare unnerved Shannon. She screamed at a little boy paralyzed in fear at the edge of the road with his bike, Murtadha aimed right at him. He swerved at the last minute, barely missing the child, but collided with his bike, tossing it mangled and spinning in the air.

"Grayson, you saw that!" Joe barked into the radio. "We have to break it off! We'll get him another day."

"The hell we will! He's sold his last kid to perverts. He goes down, TODAY!"

"He almost killed that boy!" Shannon screamed. "For God's sake, stop!"

"Shut the hell—" Grayson's face paled. "Dear God…No!"

A familiar pink Cadillac edged into the intersection of Cypresswood Estates Run and Cypresswood Trace: directly in Murtadha's path.

"Oh, God! Margaret! Stop! Please stop! Amanda!"

God heard him, but Margaret didn't.

Grayson watched in horror—space and time suspended. Margaret glanced in her rearview mirror and smiled at Amanda, unaware of Murtadha coming in from her left. Amanda laughed and held her drawing high for her mother to see.

Murtadha's truck propelled itself forward, a bullet already fired and impossible to retract. His Dodge pickup smashed dead center into Margaret's door with a force that sent the heavy Cadillac flying sideways into a dump truck stopped at the intersection to her right. The passenger side of the car crumpled on the front of the massive truck, crushing Amanda.

Murtadha's Ram rotated dead in the middle of the intersection. A black Chevy Silverado, brakes screaming, slammed into the passenger side of the Ram and skidded it sideways twenty feet into a school bus. Three more cars, following too closely to one another, collided behind the Silverado, blocking the intersection.

"Grayson! Stop! Brakes!" Shannon screamed at the disoriented man.

He stood on his brakes, a screeching, spinning halt that turned his car ninety degrees. He jumped out running.

Shannon threw herself behind the wheel, stood on the breaks, slammed the gearshift into park, and struggled to catch her breath.

Bewildered, she stared at the twisted metal and chaos. The heavily bearded driver of the blue truck, whom she assumed was Murtadha, escaped from his seatbelt and airbag and crawled over the gearshift to his passenger. Stunned that any of them were alive, Shannon stared at Murtadha, his bearded face burned into her brain.

He frantically talked to his passenger, a man writhing in pain but apparently conscious. She gasped when a stab of hate for the evil man unexpectedly struck her.

Unaware of the danger, people began to exit their vehicles and move toward the intersection, some running in the belief that they could help.

Watching the chilling events unfold, Shannon jumped out of the car. She yearned to do something to help, but she had no idea what. She couldn't find Grayson in the crowd around the Cadillac. She started to run toward the truck, but a cop grabbed her and pulled her down.

"He's armed and dangerous! Stay down!"

Positioned behind the police cruiser, Shannon could see blood spurting in the air from the passenger's missing right arm.

Murtadha pulled the injured man's gun from its holster and placed it in his left hand.

"Buy me some time, compadre! Shoot the pigs!"

The man moved his lips and he stared at his right arm on the floorboard.

"That man is in shock," Shannon told the police officer.

"That's his problem. I ain't going near that loco."

"*Hermano*, Brother. Buy me some time!" he repeated. "I promise to care for your *mujer e hijos*, wife and children!"

The man nodded feebly. Life draining from him, he had nothing to lose.

"He's making a run for it! Shoot him!" Shannon grabbed the cop's arm and tried to stand.

"Get down! Can't shoot. Too many civilians near him!"

Shannon shuddered as she fell to her knees. *What the hell! I can't believe I wanted him to shoot that man.*

Spurting blood, the man trapped in the pickup aimed the automatic in the direction of the cruiser and blindly emptied the magazine through the truck's broken window before slumping over. Shannon screamed when a bullet ricocheted off the hood of the cruiser near her head.

She peered over the hood to see Murtadha stumble on his long legs to an orange Kia Soul. He jerked the door open, pushed his pistol in the woman's face and pulled the trigger. He hit her seatbelt release, threw her on the road, and jammed himself behind the wheel. With the door hanging open, he forced the car into a hard U-turn over the curb, yelling as he sped away.

"Did he shout 'Allahu Akbar'?" the policeman asked Shannon. "Isn't that what terrorists yell?"

"Couldn't have been. He's Mexican, a tall one, but he's Mexican nonetheless."

Shannon slumped against the cruiser, confused about her reactions and unable to believe Murtadha walked away from the severe wreck.

The officer leaned into her face. "You okay, lady?"

"Yeah. Thanks."

Wrecked vehicles and injured people blocked the intersection, preventing police from chasing Murtadha. More traffic began to cram the roads, quickly adding to the confusion.

Joe Martin got to Margaret's car first and turned to intercept his old patrol partner. "No, Grayson!"

Shannon heard his name and stood to see what was happening. She cringed as the events unfolded in front of her.

A big man himself, Joe skidded backwards against the force of Grayson's anguish. "Joe! Get the hell out of my way. They need my help!"

Other officers moved in to help restrain Grayson. "Let me go! So help me God, I'll shoot you all. I have to save my family!"

Grayson's left hook felled one of the officers, and Joe grabbed his Taser. The jolt sent Grayson to the ground. He lay in the dirty street and fought his knotted muscles as ambulances and fire rescue arrived on the scene. The emergency medical team covered Murtadha's dead passenger with a sheet, as emergency responders used the Jaws of Life to extract Margaret and Amanda.

When Grayson managed to stand, he made another run for the car, but Joe tackled him. It took a team of police officers to restrain him.

"Grayson, buddy, I'll Taser you again if I have to." Joe held Grayson's back tightly against his chest. "Listen to me! Margaret and Amanda are no longer with us. They…they're with God now. You mustn't see them like this."

Grayson twisted and fought to get away, but his fellow officers built a perimeter around him. Joe tried reasoning with him. "Slow down and think. You don't want your last memory to be this one."

Shannon flinched and tears poured when Grayson's primal scream washed over her. "I'll shoot every damn one of you! Nobody, you hear me, nobody keeps me away from my family!"

It was his family in the Cadillac. Murtadha had just killed Detective Grayson Dean's family.

When he reached for his Sig, Joe grabbed it and shoved it in his belt.

"You've been on scene at a lot of accidents like this one, partner. If our roles were reversed, you'd restrain me. Think Grayson! Slow down! Think!"

Grayson gradually stopped fighting. His body crumpled to the street, a torrent of primordial anguish billowing from deep within him sent chills through Shannon. Joe knelt beside his friend, never leaving his side, and crying with him.

"I know this is tough, buddy. Stay with me. Danny needs you to be strong."

Grayson covered his face with his hands. "My God. How am I going to tell him I killed his mother and little sister?"

Joe's jaw tightened and he spoke between clenched teeth. "You **didn't** kill them! That slimy bastard, Murtadha, did. We'll find him. I promise you we will find him."

Lost in guilt, Grayson couldn't hear his friend.

"They're in the ambulance. We'll follow them." Tears coursed down Joe's cheeks, as he helped his friend to his feet. "I'm so sorry, man."

Chapter 5

Don't Do It Grayson!

Year 1

Grayson stood stone-faced next to the sheet-covered body on the gurney. He couldn't remember arriving at the hospital morgue. He stared at his shaking hands reaching for the sheet.

"Detective Dean, you don't need to witness this." The coroner spoke in a firm voice. "Keep your memories of your beautiful wife unblemished."

Grayson clasped the edge of the sheet.

"Son, if you do this, it will haunt you for the rest of your days."

Grayson respected the heavyset older man standing across the gurney. His compassionate broken-veined face had patiently been with him when, with Joe at his side, Grayson identified Amanda's lifeless form over an hour ago.

The bear-of-a-man picked up his battered daughter and held her close as he slid against a wall to the floor of the morgue, rocking and crying. Rubbing his large grizzled cheek against her soft small one, now pale as tissue paper, he longed for her to say, "Daddy, look what I did in school today."

A policeman from the scene brought her drawing from the car, probably what Margaret and she were smiling about when Murtadha smashed the life out of them. Amazingly, the picture had no blood on it. He held the picture and talked quietly to Amanda before the officer eased it from his hand. "You're a good artist, sweetie. The water oak and squirrels are beautiful."

At the coroner's signal, Joe lifted Amanda from Grayson's arms and placed her little body back on the autopsy table. The coroner covered her gently with the sheet.

Now Grayson faced the biggest challenge of his life. His breathing grew deep and slow, like a heavyweight boxer before springing.

Frowning in confusion at the sheet-covered figure that, until a few hours ago, was his vibrant wife, the love of his life, his best friend, Grayson reached for the sheet but again pulled his hand back.

His absolute stillness, a wild cat poised for the kill, worried the normally indifferent, aging coroner. Years ago, his mind had spawned the survival tactic of indifference to corpses—an occupational necessity to salvage his sanity, but it was impossible to avoid sharing a colleague's torment and anger.

Prior to Grayson's arrival at the morgue, the Chief of Police had made an unusual visit to explain how the accident occurred and warn him of Grayson's murderous anger. When Ramirez's voice broke, it hit the coroner full force in the gut. Now, the deaths were a reality, causing his throat to tighten against tears.

After what seemed an eternity, while temporarily in control of his fresh anguish, Grayson looked at the coroner and slowly nodded, asking for help.

"Son, it isn't neces—"

In frozen tones, Grayson interrupted through clenched teeth, "Do it!"

When the coroner gently rolled the sheet back, Grayson's eyes narrowed. The color fled from his face. He transitioned from shock to rage, then profound sadness.

Margaret's long, silky blonde hair, smashed into the left side of her skull, was thick with her dried blood. A mass of ugly, pale-grey skin, with bone and teeth protruding and her left eye out of its socket, had replaced her once beautiful face. Her left shoulder hung loosely halfway to her waist.

Grayson reached to touch his precious wife when the air abandoned his lungs and his legs failed him. Joe grabbed him, and Grayson's bulk took them both to the floor. The coroner was right, but Grayson's heart had demanded to see his wife. He had to witness what he had done, a subconscious action that would feed his hatred of Murtadha for years to come.

He whispered, "I screamed at God to save them. Why didn't He stop her?"

Joe knelt by Grayson, his arm around his shoulders as he spoke quietly. The coroner watched the man fighting to gain control. He threw off his friend's arm as he rose from the floor and strode with purpose from the room.

Chief Ramirez, haggard with age and misery, met them in the hallway. He shook Grayson's hand and placed his arm around him, speaking privately.

Joe drove Grayson home in silence.

Chapter 6

Devoid of Love

Year 1

Grayson's house, full of laughter and love and noise a few hours ago, was dark and painfully silent. He led Joe to the kitchen and sat at the table, a slumped pile of despair. He spoke in hushed tones, "Joe, you go on home. I need time by myself."

Joe, fearful to leave him alone in his growing depression, ignored the sullen demand. "Come home with me. Belinda will fix you something to eat. You can sleep in our guestroom."

Grayson shook his head, stood, and walked out of the kitchen.

Joe sat at the table, uncertain what to do. After a few minutes, he followed his friend. He still had Grayson's automatic. He'd give it back when the time was right.

Margaret's intoxicating fragrance hung in the air, catching Grayson off guard in the great room. Shalimar was one of the few luxuries she allowed herself and it enfolded him. Instinctively, he scanned the room looking for her and spotted his daughter's pink jacket. Eyes of the *Frozen* characters embroidered on the pockets stared accusingly at him. Amanda was thrilled when she modeled the new jacket. "Daddy, look what Mommy got me!" echoed in his head and tugged at his heart.

Everywhere he looked, memories stabbed at him, mocked him.

From his leather recliner, Jo-Jo, Amanda's stuffed bear, watched him, indifferent to his existence. In another life, less than twelve hours ago, his daughter cuddled with him before school and then carefully placed Jo-Jo in his recliner. "We'll sit together tonight, Daddy, and Jo-Jo can tell us all about his day."

Grayson stared at the bear, transfixed by its lifeless, black plastic eyes gazing into nothingness. He slowly pulled the bear and the jacket to his chest, inhaling the clean smell of his precious child, dropped into his recliner, and sobbed uncontrollably.

The horrors of the day ricocheted through his brain, saturating his memories. A macabre video of the chase, a replay of Margaret driving into Murtadha's deadly path, and the gruesome images at the morgue played on a fast-forward loop.

Grayson raised his fists and yelled to the heavens. "God! Tell me! Has any man's ego ever paid a higher price for arrogance?"

"Grayson," Joe spoke from behind him, "this is not your fault. You were doing your duty as a police officer to get that bad guy off the street."

"That's not totally true, Joe," he mumbled. "Stop making excuses for my conceit!"

Grayson's malevolent brain drew him back to the chase when he smugly ordered his officers to keep at it, as they closed in on **his** prey. Evil at its worst, Murtadha was a force he had not been able to stop, as if protected by some evil entity. His arrogance cost him everything dear. He alone pushed the bastard, propelling him toward Margaret and Amanda.

"Joe, didn't God say something about vengeance belonging to him? I'm a conceited bastard, thinking I was His partner, doing His will."

Joe slid to the couch and laid his head back. He couldn't see Grayson's face buried in his hands, but he watched his body change, tense, tighten, turn to stone.

"Grayson, you can't do this by yourself. It will take all of us to bring Murtadha to justice."

Grayson drew his back straight and resolved to thrive on bitterness, make it count. Something ugly had infested his soul.

"I orchestrated the events that killed my family, but Murtadha is the bastard that destroyed them."

A bitter taste germinated from the sour pit of his stomach. Seeds of hate sprouted rapidly, their tentacles spread through his veins.

Without warning, his voice changed. "What happened to that bitch riding in my car?"

"There was someone in your car?" Joe, exhausted and confused, worried about Grayson's erratic behavior.

"Yeah. I was giving that ACLU lawyer bitch a lift home." Grayson saw her fear as he drove like a lunatic through the streets, his bravado sustaining him.

"That liberal lawyer, Fisher, was at the scene? Just what your career needed at—," Joe caught himself when Grayson pierced him with death rays from his eyes.

"Not her fault that I'm a jerk. Damn, Joe, how can a grown man act so childish?" Mindlessly, he flipped on the television. "Too bad *her* useless butt wasn't the one who died."

"Turn that damn thing off. It will be all over the news."

"I want to see if they got the jackass." Grayson flipped from station to station, found it on FOX 26 Houston. The reporter was describing the helicopter video of the chase and accident. "Huh. I didn't know we had helicopter support."

Joe gaped at Grayson in disbelief.

"A spokesman for the Houston Police Department says the manhunt was for Carlos Murtadha, one of Houston's most wanted criminals. He has eluded police since he and his gang raped and gruesomely murdered a family. Unfortunately, the police helicopter lost track of him when their fuel gage showed dangerously low levels. The pilot had no choice but to break contact and return to the airport. The HPD discovered the getaway car outside of the Islamic Society of Greater Houston."

"How the hell are we going to capture anybody if we can't even remember to put gas in the chopper?" Grayson slammed his fist on the arm of his recliner and leaped to his feet. "Murtadha has made fools of us for the last time!"

Joe watched in amazement as Grayson's personality made another quick shift.

"Where the hell is Danny?"

He grabbed his cell phone and tried to reach his son. The call went straight to voice mail. His voice softened as he pleaded with his son. "Danny, please call me the minute you get this message! I need to talk to you, son. This is an emergency. You need to come home immediately."

Grayson flipped the TV off and sent the remote flying at the stone fireplace, shattering it to pieces.

"Does Danny know?" He spun on a dime to face Joe. "Tell me someone is looking for my son! If Murtadha gets to him...."

Chapter 7

Farewell Beautiful Souls

Year 1

Outside of Prince of Peace church, Ramirez stepped to Grayson's side. "I'm sorry, Grayson. We've checked every street in the city and haven't found Daniel's car. It may be out of sight in a garage."

Grayson nodded and lifted his swollen eyes. "Thanks, Chief. I've waited as long as possible to start the funeral. I keep hoping I'll look around and he'll be there. This isn't like Daniel. He must know about the accident by now…and hate me."

"I feel certain he's safe. If Murtadha had him, he would flaunt it. Danny's probably hiding out with a friend. You want some company down front?"

"No, sir. I'll be fine." Grayson turned and walked to the side door of the church.

Mourners overfilled the church, but Grayson was oblivious. His eyes remained on the single casket at the front of the altar. Margaret and Amanda rested side by side in a white coffin covered in pink roses. Margaret's arm encircled Amanda; she held Jo-Jo in her little arms.

Continuously observing the line for the Eucharist, Mass concluded before Grayson accepted that Daniel was not there. He prayed that nothing horrible had happened.

As they prepared for the long procession to the cemetery, Joe approached Grayson. "Let's get in the limo, partner."

"Thanks, Joe, but I'd rather be alone for this ride."

"You don't have to do this alone."

"I wouldn't be alone if my son were here to pay his respects to his mother and sister. You ride with Belinda." He got in the limousine, a car designed for friends and family to share. It pulled away from the curb silently, following Grayson's wife and daughter on their last ride.

~~~

A slow ten miles later, the elegant white hearse rolled quietly to a stop, leading the long convoy of mourners to the final act in the age-old ceremony to honor the dead.

Ramirez rode behind the limousine that bore his old friend and comrade-in-arms. The line of cars snaked slowly through the streets of Houston. The officers were in dress uniform to honor Margaret, held in high esteem for her devotion and leadership assisting families of fallen policemen.

The procession stopped across the road from the vacant, timeworn chapel. Grayson lingered in the protective harbor of the limousine. If he dared move, it would be an admission it was real; Margaret and Amanda were dead. *Maybe if I wait, it will turn into a bad dream.*

The limousine driver opened his door, and Grayson's fantasy evaporated.

Expelling a long sigh and struggling with anger and disbelief, Grayson began the final steps that would forever detach him from his precious wife and daughter. Whimpering inside, he wanted to go with them and leave the insanity behind.

With Chief Ramirez and his wife, Grace, to his left, he stepped forward and began the longest walk of his life; each step lacerated his battered heart.

Unaware of the countless mourners moving to the burial site behind him, he vacillated between anger and pain. *Where are you Daniel? Please, God. Don't let Murtadha have him.*

The pallbearers, police officers led by Joe in full dress uniform, carried the precious cargo and placed it on the casket stand over the open grave. They marched to the side, and stood in formation at parade rest.

Grayson faltered slightly when he saw Louise, Margaret's elderly aunt, waiting for him. He didn't remember seeing her in the church. She sat next to him in the chair normally designated for Margaret's parents, who had passed several years previously. Louise was her only remaining relative. Had he called to tell her about Margaret? He felt her squeeze his hand lying on his knee. With the sign of the cross, she hung her head and prayed.

Soft weeping floated on the blue sky's cool, spring breeze. Oddly, Grayson was aware of birds singing, which brought him a modicum of peace. His beloved wife and daughter were in Heaven; of that, he was sure. His anguished soul stilled when the priest spoke of the loving spirits that Margaret and Amanda brought to the world. After acknowledging Grayson, he made the sign of the cross, opening the service.

"In the name of the Father, of the Son, and of the Holy Spirit, Amen."

"Amen," the mourners echoed.

The priest moved to the casket, said a prayer, and began blessing the grave and coffin with holy water, but he hesitated when the screeching halt of a car nearby ruptured the somber quiet.

Grayson and the startled mourners turned to see Daniel jump from his old jalopy. His twisted face and deliberate long strides amplified his anger. His hair disheveled and his eyes bloodshot, Daniel looked as though he had worn his clothes for days.

Grayson was happy to see his son alive, but anger pounded through his veins. How dare Daniel avoid the funeral of his mother and sister? He strained to deal with his reactions as his furious son approached.

"You son of a bitch!" Daniel cried, as he pushed his way through the mourners to stand in front of his father. Tears poured from his red and swollen eyes. Pointing at the casket, he screamed at his father. "This is your fault!" Grayson attempted to put his hands on his son's shoulder, but Daniel jerked away. Standing almost as tall as Grayson, Daniel jabbed him in the chest with his fingers. "I've seen the news reports. You just couldn't control yourself, could you?"

"Daniel, we're burying your mother and sister. Son, please show them respect." The air was dense with the awkwardness of a divided father and son, emotions volatile with a toxic jumble of grief and anger.

"We wouldn't be burying Mom and Sissy if you had the sense to control yourself! You always have to be the center of attention. The big, bad cop." Daniel's tortured face spewed hate. "Large and in charge! I'll never respect you again. Never!"

Daniel fought his way back through the crowd that opened a path, as he ran sobbing to his car. He peeled away, leaving the mourners in self-conscious shock.

"Folks, I'm sorry for my son's behavior. I...I don't know what else to say. I apologize. Father, please continue."

Grayson remained standing until the burial ceremony was over and only Joe and the priest remained. They stood at the edge of the tent and watched Grayson weep uncontrollably over the open grave.

When his anguish began to abate, the priest laid his hand on his shoulder and prayed: "Christ, bring comfort to the souls of Grayson and Daniel Dean in their hour of need. In your wisdom and mercy, give them holy rest and bestow your peace upon them. Amen."

"Thank you, Father."

They crossed themselves and the priest patted Grayson on the back. "Call me if you need anything. Daniel is reacting as many boys entering manhood would. I'll try to talk to him." Grayson nodded, and the priest strode sadly into the fading day.

On the walk to Joe's car, Grayson noticed a woman, dressed in black and wearing a thick black veil standing in the shadows of a small tree at the corner of the old chapel. She turned and rapidly disappeared behind the chapel.

What kind of weirdo stares at strangers in mourning?

~~~

Grayson found little comfort in the post-funeral meal at the parish hall. Completely drained, he didn't eat a bite and forgot to honor Louise's request to speak with him in private. Daniel's behavior at the cemetery had skewered what was left of him. He thanked everyone for their kind words and asked Joe to take him home.

Daniel's car, parked in front of the house, was loaded with his possessions. He stuffed a bundle of clothes in the backseat and was at the driver's door when Grayson approached him. Avoiding eye contact with his father, he jerked the car door open.

Grayson pushed it closed and looked straight into his son's face, a face bathed in pain. "What are you doing, Daniel?"

"I'm leaving! Isn't it obvious?"

"We need to talk, son."

"No way. I want nothing to do with you. Aunt Louise says I can live with her." Grayson reached to hug his son, but Daniel shoved him away. "You're no longer my dad. You killed Mom and Sissy. Get out of my way!" Daniel pulled at the car door.

Grayson stepped back. "I won't stand in your way, son. I hope and pray you find it in your heart to come back home. Louise will take good care of you, but I need you at home with me."

Daniel shot his father a venomous glare and started his car. "That's a joke. *You* don't need anyone. You killed everything that was important to me." The boy's voice caught in his throat. "I never want to see you again!" He jammed the accelerator to the floor and spun away.

The pain too fresh, Grayson let him go. He would be safe with Louise, while Grayson worked to repair their relationship. Abject loneliness descended heavily, and he wasn't sure he could make it to the front door.

"He doesn't mean what he said. The boy's broken into pieces, just like you. It's impossible to reach him right now."

"You know it's funny. I was worried about Murtadha hurting my son, but I was the bad guy all along."

"You're not a bad guy, Grayson. You're a guy who's had a bad stroke of luck."

"Joe, bless you for helping me through this past week. You're the brother I never had. I'd appreciate it if you'd hang around awhile."

The two friends entered Grayson's dark, empty house, flipping on the kitchen light. "Joe, Daniel's right. My damnable pride has finally killed almost everyone I love."

Chapter 8

Persecution and Transition

Year 1

The squad room was oddly quiet as Grayson made his way to Chief Ramirez's office. He nodded to a few of the staff but didn't linger. The chief shook his hand and shut the door. His distracted demeanor told Grayson the meeting would not bode well for him.

"Grayson, I know this is tough, the funeral only a few days ago, but policy dictates that I place you on paid leave, pending the outcome of the Internal Affairs investigation. I have to take your service weapon and badge. I was supposed to have done it the day of the accident, but I hoped they wouldn't notice."

Grayson, his eyes bloodshot and his body weak from lack of sleep and food, didn't object. He was surprised when Joe had returned his Sig that morning. His gun was a part of getting dressed, and strangely, he hadn't noticed it missing.

"I know the drill." Grayson placed his weapon and badge on Ramirez's desk, having left it with an empty magazine and the slide locked back the same as when Joe returned it.

"IA is all over me due to public sentiment over this incident. A police chase through a residential area and…uh…fatalities don't play well in the news. The liberal press is attacking, claiming police incompetence, endangerment of citizens. The teary kid with the mangled bicycle is all over social media. You understand?"

"Sir, we both know I'm screwed on this one."

"You aren't the only one who participated in the chase. Joe's butt and others are on the line."

Grayson shook his head. "But my family got caught in the crossfire because of my egomania."

"Listen to me. You weren't the lead car—"

"But I was the guy calling the shots…and had a civilian in the car. That ACLU bitch can destroy me." Grayson's limp body collapsed in a chair. "I'm responsible for the deaths of my wife and child. Period."

"Have you heard the rumor that the mayor and city council want you canned?" Ramirez asked.

Grayson nodded.

Ramirez rubbed the top of his salt and pepper brush cut. "The civilian ride-along isn't helping. They also recommend federal prosecution for civil rights violations."

"You gotta be kidding, Chief. On what grounds?"

"On the grounds that you chased Murtadha because he's Hispanic. They're calling you a racist. Passing it to the feds gets the problem off their plate. I imagine you can thank Shannon Fisher for that."

"Murtadha is a wanted felon. What the hell's wrong with them?"

"The department's been caught in unsafe car chases too many times, and this may be the one that nails us. Since you lost more than anyone, I hope they'll cut you some slack, but I honestly don't know."

"I should resign and not drag this out."

Ramirez gave Grayson a hard stare; his gruff retort left no room for argument. "That's not going to happen. Now, get out of my office. I've got a meeting to go to."

~~~

"Madam Mayor and esteemed select members of the Houston City Council, I appreciate you accepting my invitation to this limited-topic meeting." The council squirmed under Chief Ramirez's pointed gaze. Toughened by years of fighting terrorists in the Middle East and criminals on the streets of the United States, Ramirez had grown callous and calculating when protecting his turf. In J. Edgar Hoover style, he ruthlessly leveraged his position to keep the politicians in line.

"Cut the BS, Manuel," Mayor Edith Greenberg, a tough old bird herself intoned. "Get on with it!"

"I'm not difficult to get along with; my focus is on getting the bad guys off the streets of Houston, a focus that benefits your careers greatly. I have no interest in your activities except as they affect the police department. And we have a problem that does just that."

"No, Manuel. *You* have a problem." Councilman Ward Stein, Ramirez's most ardent political enemy, announced.

Ramirez flicked his comment aside. "Detective Grayson Dean must remain on the force, and you **will** assist in that endeavor. He is one of the finest officers I have the pleasure to command. The gang task force and other tactical endeavors require his leadership and expertise."

Coiled and waiting, they shot their venomous hatred at him. The grimy secrets the chief held on each of them surreptitiously hung in the air, as though thousands watched them intoxicated and naked. They cautiously avoided looking at each other. Ramirez held their attention.

"You will talk kindly of Detective Dean to the press, expounding on his record as a war hero, his brave law enforcement work, and that he works conscientiously to remove dangerous criminals from our streets."

A council member of metrosexual proportions started to speak, but shut up when the mayor's head snapped around and she glared at him.

"You might want to take notes. Diplomatically remind people that we all make mistakes. Sway Houston's citizens to take pity on a public servant who, while serving **them**, lost his wife and daughter to a foul criminal."

Ramirez leaned on the gleaming table, holding his firm position. "Remind citizens that Murtadha raped and killed a mother and her twelve-year-old daughter a few months ago while the husband was forced to watch, then stuck a butcher knife in the poor man's heart and cut his head off."

The Democratic mayor couldn't contain herself. "Pull the string, and it will follow wherever you wish. Push it, and it will go nowhere."

Ramirez bared his teeth in a grin. "Madam Mayor, you just quoted the great *Republican* president, Dwight David Eisenhower. At any rate, we don't want our boy to go rogue. You shortchange him, who knows what could happen in his grief-ridden state."

The hyper-liberal Democratic mayor's anger was unambiguous. "Is your perfect cop so psychotic he would go rogue? This is the upstanding detective you want us to save?"

Ramirez's ebony eyes drilled a hole in the mayor's blue ones. "No one's perfect. We both know that. In the Middle East, I saw him take on two Taliban fighters at the same time and kill them both with his bare hands. Detective Dean is the epitome of strength and integrity, a man you want on your side."

Edith Greenberg swallowed hard, adjusted her suit jacket, and regained her steel composure. "Heed me, Manuel. This is not over. That *star* detective is responsible for this mess, thanks—once again—to his infamous reactions. Let me be the first to deliver this piece of news. The ACLU is about to file a civil action suit against the City of Houston on behalf of Mr. Delgado. You remember; the man Dean shot in the spine?"

"If *Mr.* Delgado had not been fraternizing with the underbelly of Houston and in the act of robbing a bank, he wouldn't have been shot."

"If your much-needed detective is found to have been negligent and acted outside departmental policy"—she glanced around the table—"we all pay the price. And he **will** go down…hard."

Ramirez expressed a bravado he didn't feel. "This is a re-election year, Edith. I'll perform my job and…keep your and your cohorts' not-so-sweet photos locked safely away. You perform your job and stay out of mine, and we all keep our hidden transgressions."

He slowly scanned the table, refusing to forfeit his upper hand. "Questions? Hearing none, I declare this meeting adjourned. Have a good day."

Working to maintain their ravaged dignity, the city officials exited, ignoring Ramirez.

When the door shut, Ramirez grinned. Once again, he took the bunch of buffoons down a notch or two. He thanked Mark Twain for one of his favorite aphorisms: Politicians and diapers must be changed often, and for the same reason.

His grin faded. He sat down heavily. If the Delgado case found against Grayson, he doubted he could save him again. For now, he had to provide his surrogate son support and guidance, as he fought his way through the intense pain of loss and guilt.

"If I could just tamp down his damn temper."

Islamic State of America - 1

Cairo Egypt - Akeem's Mission For Allah

Year -4

Sheik Imam Omar Fadi warmly greeted Akeem Talal, a battle-hardened ISIS soldier for Allah. "Akeem, your cunning strategies and brave battles against the apostates in Syria prove you worthy of a very important mission for Allah."

Akeem's chest swelled with pride at the holy man's praises. Seeing that the revered man had more to say, he remained quiet.

"Thirty years ago, when I was a boy, the council sent a Muslim brother, Haider Murtadha, a descendant of Mohammed—peace be upon him—to the Islamic Culture Center in Monterrey, Mexico, to spread the seed of Mohammed—peace be upon him—and coordinate with smugglers to help our brothers cross the border and bring holy war to America. As instructed, Haider took a Mexican Muslim woman, Maria Baomi Murtadha, to be his wife. He planted the seed of Mohammed's bloodline into her, and she bore him two sons."

"Imam Omar, that means the sons are also descendants of Mohammed—peace be upon him." Akeem's excitement reflected in his grin and wide shining eyes.

His reaction pleased Imam Omar. "*Alhamd lilah*, thanks be to god, these descendants of Mohammed—peace be upon him—are the key to success for The Master Plan. Of course, whether their intended greatness comes to fruition, *faqat Allah yerf*, only Allah knows. Your mission is to determine the older one's ability, as is his birthright, to lead jihad on a large scale."

"How large is the scale?" Akeem asked.

"That is for later discussion, after you have reverted and educated him."

Akeem was intrigued yet still ambivalent. "I know nothing of Mexico. Where would I start?"

Imam Omar ignored his question. "You must ascertain the older son's ability to be trained to lead many soldiers of Allah in jihad against the infidels. As a descendant of Mohammed—peace be upon him—he is more than the average man but also illiterate and lacks culture. You will educate and prepare him for further training as a leader of the jihad against America."

His question still not answered, Akeem's brow furrowed as he struggled for the right words without insulting this holy man held in highest esteem. He did not want Imam Omar to think he was weak, but educating an uncultured, illiterate man into a jihadi leader, even a descendant of Mohammed, seemed an already failed task.

"I am honored that a leader and holy man of your stature would select me for such an important mission, but is it not the duty of his father to lead him in the ways of Islam and ensure his education? Certainly, his father is educated."

Imam Omar nodded. "Of course. Unfortunately, when he was only seven years old and his brother five a gang of robbers killed their father. Their mother moved the boys to Nuevo Laredo, Mexico, seeking work in a factory; she failed and could not earn enough to feed them. As happens in that part of the world, she left her young boys on the streets to fend for themselves."

Akeem was incensed. "This woman is an apostate for abandoning these descendants of Mohammed—peace be upon him. She must be put in a pit and stoned to death!"

"Your faithfulness to Sharia pleases me, Akeem. Perhaps you will have that opportunity. Be patient, my friend."

Akeem was still uncertain. "I speak English, not Spanish. It would be difficult for me to operate in Mexico."

Omar held up his hand. "There is more. We tracked their mother to a brothel in Mexico City and extracted important information from her. After their father died, she and his sons stopped praying and going to mosque. Because other children made fun of their Muslim names, she gave his sons Mexican first names, calling them Carlos and Miguel Murtadha."

Imam Omar led Akeem to a wall map of North America and drew a circle with his finger around Texas.

"We also learned that when these descendants of Mohammed—peace be upon him—were older, they left Mexico and entered illegally into Texas."

Akeem studied Texas a moment then studied the entire map. "Texas is a substantial area. What is the meaning of these dark lines surrounding large portions of America?"

"In four years, we will meet at the Islamic Social Center in Monterrey, Mexico. It is not for you to know until then."

Akeem quickly understood that he was to play a major role in an historic event, one that would please Allah, but self-doubt about his ability to function at such a high level played upon his psyche. "Where are these men now?"

"Through our information network of mosques, we located them in a Texas prison. A brother that works in the prison identified them. A judge recently ordered them incarcerated for four years for beating a man, almost killing him, which gives us the opportunity we need to revert them. The older one, Carlos, may be illiterate but he is a powerful commander.

"He quickly established himself as the leader of the prison's Mexican gang. You will go into the prison and revert them to Islam and educate them, instill them with culture, as should be the descendants of Mohammed—peace be upon him. Most importantly, you must assess Carlos' ability to lead an army of Allah's soldiers to destroy the infidels. It is his birthright and responsibility as the older son. The younger son will be his deputy."

Akeem feared the ugly things that happen to men in prison, and his concern was discernable, but his tone remained respectful. "You ask much of me, Imam Omar. Would it not be easier to revert them to Islam after they leave prison?"

Omar's eyes narrowed, his tone showed annoyance. "Your continued expressions of apprehension cause me to doubt your desire to serve Allah faithfully. Inside prison is the perfect place. There, Allah will call him to you. If we wait until the authorities release him from prison, he will return to his infidel's den in Houston and become impossible to approach."

Imam Omar paused and stared at Akeem, allowing his displeasure to sink in. "If you are not up to the task, Akeem, I will find another."

Shock at the revered holy man's expressed lack of trust made Akeem release his fears and embolden himself for the dreadful task. Contrite, he sought to appease the imam with flattery. "*Allahu Akbar,* God is great. Your wisdom is boundless and it will guide me as I do as Allah wishes. I will enter the prison with a glad heart and not fail you. *Insha'Allah*, god willing."

Still, Akeem had a practical problem. "How do I get into the prison?"

Imam Omar smiled and pointed to Houston on the map. "You will go here as a vacationer. We have many brothers in America, over three million. A policeman—a brother—will pretend to arrest you for a crime. You will plead guilty to another brother who is a judge. He will sentence you to four years in the same prison as these descendants of Mohammed—peace be upon him. It is prepared and they are waiting for you. You must revert Carlos and Miguel and any of their prison gang members willing to revert and serve as Carlos' deputies."

"When they revert to Islam, what will be their mission?" Akeem asked.

"Ah, yes, The Master Plan, *Allah's Plan*. That I will share with you in Mexico in four years, but only if you succeed in reverting Carlos to Islam and he demonstrates himself to be a worthy leader. You may only tell him and his men, that they will be sent to parts of Africa, the perfect training ground for the Master Plan, to conduct holy war for Allah."

"You can trust me. I will not let you down. *Insha'Allah*."

Chapter 9

Relegated to Nonexistence

Year 1

July was a time Grayson should be vacationing at Padre Island, enjoying the laughter of his family as they frolicked on the beach, not grieving in his voiceless house and enduring the constant hammering by Internal Affairs while waiting on the dreaded call from his boss.

"Hi, Chief. I guess you have the IA report. Give it to me straight."

"You know me, Grayson. What else would I do?" IA didn't shield you from their contempt. They weren't happy that your actions placed HPD in a negative light on the front pages of the *Houston Chronicle* and every local TV news outlet again."

Grayson hung his head and resigned himself to his fate. "So. That's it for me, I guess."

"Hold your horses! I *convinced* the mayor to countermand their efforts to remove you from the force. Come to my office and I'll give you the report. We have some issues to discuss."

Grayson perked up. "I'll be there first thing in the morning, sir."

"You'll get your ass in here NOW!" Ramirez slammed down the phone.

Grayson shook off the chief's gruff order. A part of him hoped the punishment would be harsh; another desperately needed to salvage some dignity from the horrible mess he created. Isolated at home, he was drinking too much, substituting beer for food; he bathed in self-pity and disgust as substitutes for soap and water.

Daniel still refused to talk to him, and he quit trying. Louise called every few days, said the boy carried his anger like a badge of honor. *Like father, like son.* At least the boy managed to keep himself in school.

~~~

When he entered Ramirez's office, Grayson's throat was dry and closing. Ramirez's hair seemed whiter, his shoulders stooped. Guilt hit Grayson in the gut. *How far had the chief gone to protect him?* He stood at attention in front of the chief's desk.

Handing him his service automatic and badge, Ramirez pointed to a chair. "I called you in to give you the official IA report before I release it to the press."

"Why didn't Internal Affairs take the usual, long drawn-out route with this investigation? It's only been three months, should have been twice as long."

Ramirez gave him a half grin. "Next month, the Delgado civil trial begins. Your *girlfriend* is his lawyer and she's demanding two million from the city, all based on your actions. You can't be a civilian with no skin in the game. Otherwise, when she puts you on the stand, you might testify in Delgado's favor and cost the city millions. The city council is scared shitless."

The dark cloud hanging over Grayson thundered. "Shannon Fisher is Delgado's attorney again? That makes my freaking day!"

Grayson's bloodshot eyes and unshaven face reminded Ramirez his surrogate son was in his own personal hell, still in deep mourning. "If you had been found culpable and discharged from the force, she'd have a field day with you on the stand. As an exonerated, model member of the force, you can at least decrease the city's liability, if not avert it completely."

"She'll have a field day with me anyway, Chief."

Ramirez's voice changed. "Not if you were dismissed from the force and went rogue, testifying for Delgado. The award against the city might be exorbitant. You have the administration by the short hairs." He kept his other ace in the hole to himself.

Lifting his head, Grayson showed some life. "Chief, you know damn well I won't testify to anything but the truth."

"I know you wouldn't, but the city council doesn't. It's an election year. Even if the city loses, your testimony that you followed procedures could sway the jury heavily in the city's favor and lower Delgado's award by millions."

"You're a tough son of a bitch, Colonel…sir."

Ramirez nodded appreciation. "Let's get back on track, soldier. IA found you not culpable of wrongdoing in the Murtadha situation, but the press will go nuts when they see this report."

"Because…?"

"Let's just say, they don't view you as a paragon of virtue."

"But I keep my job, right?"

Ramirez ran a hand over his gray brush cut, a sure sign he was uncomfortable.

"Not exactly. Given the uproar in the community over police brutality and recklessness, the mayor and I agree that it's political suicide to return you to the Gang Division…at least for a while. The council stood behind you—sort of. We need to return the favor."

Ramirez looked Grayson square in the eye. "I'm offering you the manager's position for the firing range and SWAT tactical training site."

Grayson's emotions erupted. "Let me get this straight. IA found me not culpable. The city council is *sort of* standing behind me. And I get bumped to a flunky job?"

Ramirez stood, pulling his shoulders back, his demeanor one Grayson knew well. He spoke with command. "Grayson, you're the best Gang Division detective I've ever worked with. This is a huge demotion, and I understand your annoyance, but the tactical site uses your unique skill-set to train and evaluate other officers. Would you rather be a paper pusher or crossing guard or return to passing out speeding tickets?"

Grayson's angry dragon readied to destroy him. He swallowed deep. "Am I stuck there forever?"

"That's up to you, son. Bottom line: take it or **leave**. Period."

Grayson's mind fought exhaustion. *Chief didn't say leave **it**; he said leave, period*.

"Sir—"

"Stay in control, detective." Ramirez warned and sat down. "There's more."

Inner demons demanded Grayson throw his badge and 40-cal on Ramirez's desk and walk out. He killed his wife and daughter. His son detested him. His life was over. The only meaningful thing he had left was being a Houston detective.

"Grayson, are you listening to me?"

"I'm with you, sir." He dangled by a thread.

"I need a highly qualified instructor to properly train the next generation of Houston's cops. You're a firearms instructor, have a master's degree in law enforcement with a thesis in special weapons and tactics, and you have practical combat experience chasing bad guys in urban environments. You have tactical training and combat experience in guerrilla warfare, which, I admit, has caused me plenty of heartburn in the past."

Grayson stared coldly at the chief. Was he being praised or punished? He clenched his fists around his badge and waited for the next bulletin.

"Your experience gives you a unique perspective on illegal aliens and gangs fighting to take over the city, especially that El Salvadorian gang, MS-13. This job is right up your alley."

"I have the expertise. That doesn't mean I'll like the job, or can force myself to put my heart into it."

Ramirez's anger ignited like a father confronting a recalcitrant, ungrateful child. He would not let Grayson continue to wallow in guilt.

Pointing his finger at Grayson, he blasted. "Mister, I saved your butt from being fired **and** referred to the feds for prosecution! Damn it, you owe me!" His voice lowered.

"There's something else."

"The last time you said that to me, you sent me on a mission that almost got me killed."

Ramirez released a belly laugh. "This is something much safer. You're going to become a prepper."

"I gave up booze ten minutes ago. And I'll go with Coke. I've never liked *Dr. Pepper.*"

"What the hell does...? Oh, I see." Ramirez again howled with laughter. "Wait until I tell the guys this! Grayson. We've got to clear those cobwebs out of your head. The prepper I'm talking about is a patriotic American committed to surviving a societal collapse that brings on a state of absolute anarchy, no police, no military, and no government; you're on your own and ninety percent of the people will die within a few months."

Grayson stared at Ramirez, trying to analyze what he said.

"You would probably think of a prepper as a survivalist," the chief clarified.

"I'm not interested in becoming one of those doomsday nuts," Grayson replied. "This is America. What could happen?"

"You know and respect a lot of preppers. And, *we* are not nuts."

Grayson's flabbergasted expression pushed a grin across the chief's face.

"We?"

"We. Unlike open prepper groups that accept all comers, ours is a clandestine operation and admission is by invitation only. We maintain a high level of OPSEC and invite nobody without vetting them first. We need you to be with us when the collapse occurs."

"What collapse?" *I'm not the only one who's losing it.* "I know I'm foggy from misery and no offense, but I'm pretty sure you've gone off the end of the pier."

"First of all, you're the kind of man who needs a mission in life, and I'm offering one to you. Second, you suffered a great personal loss and need something to fill the void until you can figure out what to do with the rest of your life."

"Being a cop is what I want to do with the rest of my life. What's this prepper crap? What do you do? Why should I—"

"Just hang on a minute!" Ramirez scowled. "You'll learn what you need to know from your assistant in your new job, Professor Mark Hamilton."

"Mark Hamilton, the guy that works part time at the range? Isn't he a college professor?"

"Yeah. Teaches economics at Houston Baptist."

Grayson shook his head. "It's official, Chief. I'm lost."

"Stop where you are! Mark is a prepper expert and can explain everything. If you find it's not for you, I won't hold you to any commitment. Just listen to him."

Grayson took a deep breath. "You've never steered me wrong, sir. But I reserve the right to opt out if it doesn't suit me."

"Take a couple of days to get some food in you and clean yourself up before reporting to work at the range."

"I took a shower and shaved this morning," he lied.

"Well, you didn't stand very close to your razor and either you didn't use soap or it's your messy clothes that smell like that outhouse we used in Iraq."

Feeling like a private who had just taken an ass chewing from his respected sergeant, Grayson looked at the floor. "I'll clean up and make you proud of my work at the range."

Ramirez put his hand out for Grayson to shake. "I can't ask any more than that, soldier."

Grayson hesitated at the door. "Thank you for trusting me, Chief." His flushed face stiffened to avoid tears, as he closed the door silently.

Chief Ramirez sat in quiet contemplation for a long while. Grayson had helped to fill the void in Grace and his lives after an ISIS sniper's bullet took their son from them. Just a few short months ago, Grayson was a man's man. Now, smacked down, his confidence diminished. If they could get past the Delgado civil case with a win, Grayson would be home free and on the road to recovering his self-worth. If they lost, his career would come to an abrupt end, his future uncertain.

"Thanks for meeting me for dinner, Joe. I just left the chief's office and need some company, somebody to help me put my ass back together."

Joe chuckled. "The chief's teeth are sharp. He's a tough old buzzard."

"He was the toughest commander I served under in the Army, but a straight shooter and the men loved him. Hope you're hungry."

"Yep. I never turn down a free steak dinner, especially at Ruth's Chris. You want to know all about being a prepper?"

Grayson gave him a questioning look.

"The group voted you in, and we knew the chief was going to tell you today."

"That's not why I asked you to meet me, but I do have a lot of questions about that prepper business. But tonight, I need help to figure something else out."

"You can save your money. Yes, you do need a bath."

Grayson chuckled. "So, I hear."

Settled at the table, Grayson hesitated over their drinks, so Joe took the lead. "When are you joining us for a prepper meetup?"

"You believe America is on the verge of collapse too?"

Joe took a sip of beer. "It was hard to wrap my mind around, but yes. Maybe not today, but sometime in the near future. Mark teaches our group with facts, not theories. This is some serious crap. We're not to the point of collapse, but I'm convinced it's inevitable sometime before the middle of the century. If you're like me, you don't remember a lot about history, but America began as a capitalist nation."

"I do remember that much, Joe."

"The executive branch got the power to regulate commercial enterprise in 1895 when Congress passed the Sherman Antitrust Act. That's when things began to change."

"The only Sherman I remember is Tecumseh. History is not my forte."

"Me neither. Mark taught us that since 1895, congress increasingly gave the president power to regulate commercial enterprise. Hundreds of federal laws followed the Sherman Antitrust Act. America gradually moved down the slippery slope toward socialism and fascism. Mark showed us the executive branch's power compared to 1895 and the difference is shocking."

"Joe, you don't honestly believe the United States is going to declare bankruptcy over some obscure act from the nineteenth century."

"This is more than a history lesson, Grayson, and I do believe it. That's why we need men like you in our group, strong leaders to help us weather the violent storm headed our way. The United States is at risk of failure."

"Okay, I get it," Grayson sounded exhausted and frustrated, "and I promise to come to one of your little meetings, but can you help me weather *my* storm while we cut into these delicious steaks?"

"Sorry I got off on a tangent. We'll talk more prepping later. In the meantime, discuss it with Mark. What do you need?"

"Maybe a lot, maybe nothing."

"Start anywhere and let's work from there."

Grayson's brow furrowed. "A short time ago, I was on top of the world. I had my dream job, a loving family, the best wife on the planet—no offense to you and Belinda."

"None taken."

"People looked up to me. First, I lost my family. Two hours ago, Chief Ramirez demoted me. If the Delgado case goes bad, I'll have to resign. I can't get a handle on things, where to go next. I don't fit in anymore, not on the force and not in my old life."

"Grayson, straight up…are you considering suicide?"

"Hell no! How could you…. Oh. I see. I was the guy others came to for counsel. Now, no one will even look at me. Asking for advice makes me feel weak."

Joe's derisive laugh annoyed Grayson. "You are anything but weak. Maybe a little vulnerable right now, but you've suffered a serious setback, one few men could weather successfully. Believe me; it won't stop you from going forward and building a new life." Joe screwed his face into a frown, leaned forward, and spoke gruffly. "Stop feeling sorry for yourself, asshole. You sound like a little pantywaist."

Grayson's emotions flamed. "I never feel sorry for myself, asshole yourself!" he hissed through gritted teeth.

Joe looked at Grayson over the top of his glasses. "Oh, yeah? Taken a look in the mirror lately?"

Joe's accusation hit Grayson like a Mack truck. He leaned back hard against his chair and stared at the ceiling. Slowly, he nodded acknowledgement.

"Look, man. You asked for my counsel; here it is. I know that I don't need to tell you what your family meant to you, the depth of your feelings for them, and the pain that nags at your soul. Those intense feelings are a large part of what's confusing you and throwing you off balance. But I think there's something else, something hidden within that's pushing you toward the brink of surrendering to insanity."

Keenly aware of his friend's wisdom and shocked at how well he knew him, Grayson focused on Joe's comments, pushing all other thoughts from his consciousness. Just as ordered several times in combat, he held his ground and awaited further instructions.

Joe paused to gauge Grayson's reactions to his comments. Feeling safe, he continued. "Your sense of self-worth, your manhood, is empty right now. Unlike the pajama boys of today, you're among what's left of the real men in Western Civilization. You have an innate compulsion, a primal calling, to provide and protect. Thousands of generations of men passed it down to you. It's what drives you, but the object of your calling has vanished. It will not return until you have another woman, and maybe, children to protect and provide for."

Grayson stilled in his chair, his jaw moving, as he absorbed Joe's words.

"Don't make any major decisions for a while, Grayson. Get back in the gym. Go to the range and work with Mark. You have more in common with him than you know. Relax. Let life run its course."

"Ain't gonna happen."

Joe spoke with discernable deliberation. "Grayson, if you are patient, the thing you seek will find you. You don't have to go looking for it."

Grayson rearranged his napkin. "How did I allow myself to sink this low? Margaret would be ashamed of me."

"Margaret was never ashamed of you one day of her life. And take note, my friend, this counseling session is costing you the most expensive steak on the menu, which I am enjoying."

"That's just like you, Joe. Treat me like crap and then make me pay the bill."

His profound grief would not allow him a glimpse into his future, but he'd cleared this first hurdle, thanks to his best friend.

Humph. Screw you, Joe. I'm a man, not a damn pantywaist!

Islamic State of America - 2

Texas State Prison

Year -4

Akeem followed Imam Omar's instructions and, as planned, a brother judge remanded him to Texas State Prison. He was pleasantly surprised to find that Islam had spread to all corners of America, including a low-ranking prison administrator who placed him in the cell across from the Murtadha brothers. After only two months, he had the hook dangling in front of their faces, their mouths open, and ready to take the bait.

Acutely aware of his target's interest, Akeem feigned indifference as he prepared for evening prayer. He firmly believed Allah gave all the lands of the earth to his chosen people and beloved servants, the Muslims. Occasionally, anger infiltrated his senses. He fantasized about cutting the heads off hated infidels who occupied the Muslim land, called America, and restoring Sharia, the law that pleases Allah. Until they killed or enslaved every *kafir*, unbeliever—Jew, Christian, pagan, Shia apostate—who would not revert, and established Sharia under Sunni domination, there would be no peace for the Muslims. It was Allah's order, clearly written in the pages of the Quran and defined by the Hadith. They must conquer all lands in the world through death or slavery and revert the lands to Islam, their original roots.

Every day, Carlos and Miguel sat on their bunks and stared unabashedly at Akeem as he kneeled on his prayer rug, shoes off, forehead on the floor, and sang his evening prayer. Carlos' faded memories of praying and attending mosque with his father were beginning to reemerge, bringing him to life.

Akeem's melodic tone and the words were faintly familiar; it soothed Carlos. He soon began to chant the sounds in his own mind, and the meanings of a few of the words returned to him. Akeem's incantations beckoned him, as the deadly flame lures the moth to its gruesome, certain fate.

Chapter 10

New Horizons

Year 1

Grayson sat in his truck and studied the small, concrete block building; its plain, ugly face stared back at him, indifferent and without beckon. He lectured himself on the drive to his new job, seeking confirmation that he would scrupulously perform his new duties. He didn't want to let the chief down, and he was curious about the prepper business, but entering the squat building had stopped him cold. He wasn't sure he could face police officers he'd known for years silently deriding or pitying him when they came through the facility for training and weapons qualification.

He'd been to the inconspicuous, beige building many times without giving it much thought, but today the tactical site stared back at him—boring and unfriendly—an insult to a man of his stature.

Who was he kidding? A man of his stature? He killed his wife and daughter, lost his son, brought shame on the officers in the Houston PD, suffered a demotion, and disappointed his mentor. Who the hell did he think he was? He stepped from his truck and entered his new inner sanctum.

"Hi, boss." A young man in his late twenties poured the first cup of morning Joe from a full pot. "Take this. I just brewed it."

"Thanks, and good morning, Dr. Hamilton. It's good to see you again." Grayson enjoyed a long sip of coffee.

"Please call me Mark."

"Call me Grayson."

The men shook hands.

"I enjoyed your class a few months ago on urban counter-ambush tactics, Mark. Great job."

Mark downed a slug of coffee. "Thanks. We have a group of four officers for annual weapons qualification due any minute. Everything is ready. All you have to do is observe and sign off on their qualifying scorecards. You know the drill."

"Did the chief give you a rundown on my latest woes?"

"Of course, he did; and I've seen the news reports. The liberal media has no principles, but I determine a man's make-up based on my own opinion. If you're worth a crap, we'll work well together. If not, I'll do my duty and treat you with the same respect you show me."

"Can't ask for more." He took an immediate liking to Mark, a straight shooter. The big smile permanently plastered on Mark's face was a refreshing change from the glances and dead-face stares he met at HQ the past few days.

"How did an economics professor become a weapons trainer and qualify for this job?"

"This is only a part-time position when I'm not teaching. My first real job was as an infantryman in the 75th Rangers."

Grayson's eyebrows lifted. "Iraq? Afghanistan?"

"Both. Sorry, but we'll have to hold off getting to know each other and discussing the Houston MAG."

"Houston what?"

Mark chuckled. "Mutual Assistance Group. We use the acronym MAG for prepper groups. Don't worry, Grayson, it won't take you long to get the hang of it. Right now, we need to get to the range. You know the officers here today, including Harold Weber. He can't hit the broadside of a barn."

"Yeah. He's a *choice* Houston police officer." Grayson's voice trailed off. *Just like me.*

~~~

After barely scoring to qualify with his service weapon on the third try, Weber complained loudly. "How the hell do they expect us to qualify with these new shooting time limits? One minute ain't enough time to aim and shoot a full magazine."

Yeung chided him. "Hey, Weber. Nobody else seemed to have that problem."

Mark lowered his voice to speak to Grayson. "I know he's a problem, but what's the real deal?"

"He's got an enormous inferiority complex and is only marginally competent as a cop. Word is they hired him because he was the previous chief's brother-in-law. During a major drug bust that included a high-speed chase, he accidentally wounded an undercover cop. If not for the union, he'd be gone...." As the words spilled from his mouth, Grayson's blood ran cold. His voice faded to a whisper. "They only assign him paperwork...so nobody has to clean up behind him."

"Grayson?" Mark withdrew his hand before touching him. Grayson's face forewarned him.

"What? Yeah, he passed, barely."

"Everybody qualified," Grayson spoke to the officers. "Please recheck your areas for spent brass. Mark will enter your scores into your personal training record on the computer and provide your certificates."

"Listen to the big *deetective* giving orders. How does it smell when you're relegated from the top of the rose bush to the compost pile?"

The other cops gave Weber disapproving looks and stooped to retrieve their spent brass.

Weber wouldn't let it go. "Must be pretty stinky."

Grayson clenched his fists, but he didn't take the bait.

Yolanda whispered a warning. "Back off Weber. You're playing with fire."

"Everybody knows the zero-tolerance policy for punching another officer." His sense of power building, Weber stepped closer to Grayson, cocked his head, and stared up at him. "I hear the traffic around your neighborhood is much slower these days, fewer cars on the streets."

Grayson's vision washed in blood red. In a matter of seconds, Weber was on the ground holding his bloody, snot-dripping broken nose and mumbling a final threat through split lips. "You just ended your career, *Detective* Dean."

Teeth gritted, Grayson responded. "It was worth it. You're a sorry excuse for a cop and a pathetic excuse for a man. Don't ever mention my family again, or it'll be the last words you utter."

Yolanda stooped to examine Weber. "Hey, man, that's a terrible fall you took!"

"Yeah," Yeung said. "Grayson warned us in the safety briefing about the top steps being wet and slippery. Too bad you lost your footing."

Samuel glanced at Weber. "You need to see a doctor, and complete an accident report to explain how you fell. Maybe you'll get paid time off for injuries received while on duty. Dickhead. Didn't you listen when Instructor Dean gave the safety briefing about the top steps?"

Weber pulled himself upright in stunned silence, watching the others walk to their squad car.

"Weber! You want to ride back with us?" Yolanda called.

He glanced at Grayson whose expression sent him running to catch the others.

Grayson gave the three officers a nod of thanks as two of them returned his nod and the other gave a small salute.

In the car, Pablo spoke first. "Keep your stupid mouth shut about this if you know what's good for you."

Still holding his nose, Weber glared at them but said nothing.

Yeung whistled. "Grayson hits like a jackhammer."

~~~

Mark read the post-combat-action look on Grayson's face: dead stare, false air of calm, and a need for reflection and recovery. Grayson needed room.

"I'll take care of the used targets and paperwork." You'll find sandwich-makings and soda for lunch in the refrigerator."

Grayson thanked Mark and walked back to the building.

Chapter 11

A Friend in Need

Year 1

Mark and Grayson ate lunch in silence and worked their way through other officers' evaluations throughout the day. When Grayson appeared approachable, Mark invited him to his favorite bar. "It's Friday, the sun is low on the horizon, and I feel like a burger and a beer. Want to join me?"

The thought of going back to his house, no longer a sanctuary but a grinding malevolence, hit Grayson. "That sounds like a great idea, Ranger Mark. Where's your favorite watering hole?"

"Funny you should ask that. It's called the *Watering Hole*."

~~~

"So, tell me, Grayson, when was the last time you got in a fist fight?"

Grayson took a sip of beer. "You have a knack for asking direct questions. I like that. It's been a long time. I was a senior in high school and some guy tried to get a date with Margaret, my wife. When she refused, he patted her butt. We were already married, but nobody knew. I busted the guy in the chops, knocked him cold. I got into trouble a lot for fighting before I joined the Army. To be honest, I've gotten into trouble more times than I can count for acting without thinking, going on instinct."

"Aren't your instincts what made you good in combat?"

"There may be something to the combat angle, but truth is, the news reports were correct. I didn't use good judgment when chasing Murtadha. The Delgado shooting was a fluke, but it may still cost me my job. I've gone on instinct too often in my life. Today was the last time. It was stupid of me to let that mental midget cause me to lose control."

"Maybe you've turned a corner. Still, don't expect your basic character to change overnight, but being self-aware is the first step."

Grayson considered Mark's comments and finished his beer. "Weber had it coming, but one of the last things my wife, Margaret, told me was to help an adversary of mine. It's time I heeded her advice and quit fighting the world."

"Sounds like a good start to a new life. Hey, barkeep, two more Heinekens."

"Not for me, Mark. I gave up over-indulging in booze last week."

"I don't see any tell-tale signs of alcoholism; you can start over tomorrow," Mark slapped Grayson on the back.

Mark and Grayson continued with small talk, comparing combat stories and sipping their way through half a dozen more beers and two burgers each. Their tongues loosened with each bottle.

"Tell me about your wife and kids…." Mark realized his error the moment it escaped his mouth and started to apologize, but Grayson stopped him.

"It's okay. I think it's time I discussed it with someone."

"You sure?"

Grayson shrugged. "We became sweethearts in kindergarten. Margaret was the love of my life; our love knew no bounds. She became pregnant and had Daniel at fifteen. Of course, both of our parents went nuts. I thought her dad was going to kill me. Once they laid eyes on Daniel, their hearts melted, and they helped us through the early years. They had no idea how tight Margaret and I were."

"It must have been tough providing for a family at that age."

"It was. Margaret never complained, but 'Tote that barge! Lift that bale!' got old fast. When I finished high school, I joined the Army to provide for my young family and get an education. As time rolled on, I became more patriotic and applied for Special Forces. They accepted me. You know how it went; I was away from home more than at home. It was hard on Margaret with me deployed in combat zones most of the time."

"It was hard on the married guys in combat, especially the younger ones."

Grayson studied the top of the table. "We had heated arguments before my last deployment. She couldn't understand my devotion to my A-team, why I'd feel like I would be letting the guys down if I didn't deploy with them."

"I know what you mean. For the rest of your life, you'd have felt like a coward."

"Exactly. She gave me an ultimatum: her and the kids, or the team."

After a moment, Mark looked questioningly at him. "Well?"

"Well…you know how hardheaded I am."

"Evidently you reconciled, but did she divorce you?"

"Almost. The day of her court appointment, Margaret's mother—smart lady—asked her why she hated me and how she would feel if I came home in a flag-draped coffin. It made her realize she would be devastated if I were KIA.

"Wrote me the sweetest letter. I sought Colonel Ramirez's counsel and he made me realize that I'd contributed more to America's security than over ninety-nine percent of the rest of the country's men; that it was okay to devote the rest of my life to loving my wife and kids; and that I could continue to serve as a lawman."

"Margaret must have been a good woman."

"You have no idea. She was the kind of woman that brings peace to a man's soul. She was as beautiful on the inside as she was on the outside. Margaret was a smart cookie, smarter than I was. She knew how to make me feel like a man without diminishing her own status. It made me want to do everything I could to give her a happy life. We had our ups and downs, like any couple, until I came to understand that she was in charge but cleverly maneuvered me into thinking I was. We had a never-ending, fairytale love affair."

"Where's Daniel now? You two have suffered a lot."

Grayson slightly shook his head. "Whole other story." His tone sent Mark a strong message to shut down that conversation track.

They finished a couple more bottles of beer and chatted about their similar life experiences, a mutual camaraderie growing.

Grayson jumped when Mark, now more than a little drunk, asked in a loud voice, "Okay, dude. Why do you hate Mexicans?"

"Who said I hate Mexicans?" Grayson growled.

"Everybody."

Grayson's protective armor dropped into place "It's something between me and the Devil."

Grayson learned watching his father struggle to take care of his family that every man has a personal shield and grips it tightly to maintain his dignity. Emotional shields were barriers that concealed closely held secrets. Ugly secrets men have difficulty confessing to a priest and fear that God may not forgive, even if his priest grants absolution. Grayson could feel Mark assessing him through his inebriation and knew Mark would never mention the topic again.

Comrades-in-arms whisper things never spoken to others, but they never divulge everything.

Islamic State of America - 3

Texas State Prison

Year -4

When noon prayers were over, Akeem's deputy, Qadir, called him to a corner of the prison yard. "Are you sure about this man, the chosen one? He is a strong leader within the domain of his gang, and he is ruthless, but other Mexicans we've reverted to Islam haven't been able to lead a camel to water."

"Trust me, Qadir. He is the one. He is ready to be cultivated. Unlike the others, who are squat and dark, notice he is tall with lighter skin, his brother too, certain to have the blood of the Spanish Moors. They are direct descendants of Mohammed—peace be upon him. Under my guidance and control, Carlos will lead other Mexican brothers to victory over the infidels."

Qadir revered Mohammed, but he wasn't convinced that Carlos Murtadha was worthy. Knowing Akeem's passions were as unpredictable as the Mexican's were, he expressed his thoughts carefully. "His emotions run hot then quickly cold, and he is illiterate. I respect your opinion, Akeem, but even if he is a descendant of Mohammad—peace be upon him—I worry we can't revert an ignorant man accustomed to being in control of all that is around him. Will he follow orders?"

Akeem stroked his long beard and breathed deeply, suppressing his irritation. "I managed a look at his file when I was cleaning the management offices. He is not school educated, but he has the IQ of a genius. He is an intelligent empty shell that I will fill with the passion of a pure Muslim, the passion deserved in a descendant of Mohammed—peace be upon him. We will teach him to read and write Arabic in the time we have left in this infidels' hellhole. Imam Omar was correct: if I recruit Carlos, *Insha'Allah*, others of his Mexican gang will follow him and become his deputies to lead their own cells. You are right in one respect. It is time I begin testing him. I'll not welcome him warmly as I did the others."

Qadir frowned. "Will that not cause him to reject your efforts to revert him?"

"On the contrary. His mentality now is that of a lowly gang leader. Only by manipulating him into a high state of emotion will I be able to bring him into awareness of a higher order, make him realize his Islamic roots, and understand his position as a great leader of Allah's soldiers."

Looking sourly at Qadir, he asked, "Will you help me in this effort or stand aside and remain pessimistic?"

Qadir shrank under Akeem's glare and became contrite. "I will help and pray that we are successful. *Insha'Allah*, god willing."

While Carlos' Mexican gang watched, stone-faced, Akeem subtly signaled to Carlos to move forward in the prison yard. Murtadha turned to his men and welcomed their gang sign of solidarity, and then he and Miguel eased their way towards Akeem.

Akeem's Muslim gang dominated the prison quietly and often with deadly results. Anyone foolish enough to tangle with the Muslims found himself splayed on the cold concrete of the restroom floor, his blood drained from his slit throat, his tongue beside his head.

Akeem had patiently observed Carlos' interest in his activities for several months, watching his curiosity build. Imam Omar was right; Allah called Carlos to him. The man relentlessly wielded power over his Mexican gang, but Akeem's objective was to teach him that it was important for men to follow not from fear alone but with a deep respect for Islam and the teachings of Mohammed.

Akeem knew Carlos' interest had reached the tipping point when he made a hand sign the previous night that he wanted to talk. Akeem nodded impassively and turned his back to conceal his joy.

Carlos saw Akeem receive numerous other inmates amiably and expected the same respect. Still, he moved toward the man with caution. His half-shuttered eyes subtly surveying the Muslims added to Akeem's interest in the Mexican. He wasn't surprised that he brought his brother. On high alert, Miguel walked beside his brother with the calm of a good deputy.

When Carlos and Miguel were within ten feet, Akeem began the test.

With a dead stare, he commanded in a gruff tone, "Stop there, infidels! What is it you want?"

The two brothers halted, unsure of the unexpected rebuff. Akeem's Muslim brothers hovered in the background and, as instructed, glared with menace from their alert stance. For a split second, Carlos lost his mental balance. Years of dangerous encounters from his childhood on the streets trained him to maintain his composure under pressure. His outward appearance must not reveal fear but project confidence, an intrepid readiness to take all comers regardless of the odds.

He met Akeem's challenge with a demand of his own.

"I see you praying alone in your cell and also with your musulmán amigos. Why do you pray so many times every day?"

"You are a Christian, an infidel; you cannot understand." Akeem turned aside, dismissing him.

"I ain't no Christian!" Carlos hissed with a low voice to avoid the attention of the guards.

"Don't lie to me, infidel." Akeem's sarcasm was calculated. "Your *Christian* father taught you to follow in his footsteps," he lied. "*Yalla imshi*! Go away!"

Carlos' eyes blazed. "I ain't got no father, asshole, and he sure as hell didn't take me to no Christian church!" Miguel nodded in agreement.

Akeem remained somber, ignoring the insult. "Then you are worse than a Christian. You have no god."

Carlos' eyes flashed, but his deep, resonant voice maintained control. "You waste **MY** time with your games, Arab!"

Akeem snapped immediately. "Why should I waste **MY** time with a godless infidel?" As he expected, the towering Mexican showed signs of readiness to pounce that he fought to control, and his brash attitude bore the seriousness of purpose. Akeem's rough talk had not intimidated him.

Carlos' face became hardened; his matter-of-fact tone changed. "I see you enjoy playing cat and mouse with me, Arab. I ain't got no time to play your silly games." He turned to walk away; Miguel moved in concert.

Akeem, impressed with the man's insight, changed to a conciliatory tone as he changed tactics. "Hold on! Perhaps I do want to talk."

Chapter 12

Indecision Time

Year 1

A brisk late-September breeze stirred the leaves in the chief's yard. Grayson hesitated at the door. What was he doing at a doomsday meeting? He felt like the leaves, first blown in one direction and then another, sometimes spinning in a circle before scattering in disarray. He should ditch this idea, get a contractor job with some CIA security outfit—Black Water sounded good—and escape overseas, back into a world filled with danger and adventure, his soldier's roots. That would place as much distance as possible between his torment and himself.

Turning to leave, he heard Joe's counsel echoing in his head to resist acting on impulse and explore prepping and its relationship to his love for America. What if Daniel needed him and he was halfway around the world? Indecision had never been part of his character; vacillating annoyed the hell out of him. He shook his head to rid himself of his irritating ambivalence and rang the doorbell.

The chief gave Grayson a hearty slap on the back. "Come in and grab a seat."

The ten members, including the chief and Grace, were there. He noticed Mark and Yolanda sitting side-by-side holding hands, but didn't say anything.

Everyone stood to greet him. "If I hadn't heard it from the horse's mouth—the horse being the chief—I never would've suspected any of you of being preppers. He looked at Samuel, Yeung, and Yolanda "No wonder you guys took up for me on the firing range that day."

"Would you like a cup of coffee?"

"Thank you. That would be great, Miss Grace."

Mark and Joe looked to Yolanda, who delivered an obviously planned speech. "To be honest, Grayson, your impulsive nature almost cost you membership in our MAG. It's not good to have someone with a short fuse under pressure in an outfit like this."

"You're lucky Mark stood up for you," Samuel added.

Grayson nodded at Mark. *So that's what our beer fest was about. It was an interview.* "I appreciate it. I'm in a much better place today."

Ramirez reassured him. "Relax. You're in. We're blessed to have you and just so you know, the vote was unanimous."

I'm not sure I want to be in, but it did feel good to walk into a room and not see eyes drop to avoid me. These people are friends, not just coworkers.

Grayson cleared his throat. "I looked at that *Absolute Anarchy* book you gave me, Mark. I understand the prepper movement a little better, but it's still hard to fathom there are millions of you."

Ramirez frowned but remained quiet.

"I agree with the argument that American society may collapse, and it could happen before Daniel has grandchildren. I just don't see the need to rev up for it now. With Republicans controlling both houses of Congress and the White House, things look good to me, even if the establishment Republicans are causing Congress to drag its feet on President Crump's agenda."

Grayson looked at the discomfort around the room and rushed to finish. "Look at me preaching to the choir. I appreciate you asking me to join, but I don't know if I'm a good fit…" Grayson smiled weakly, "temper or not."

"Grayson, do you understand that President Crump's efforts to reduce the size of the executive branch and turn power back over to the states have been thwarted at every turn?" Mark asked.

"Sure. But he's only been in office for little over a year, and his lack of political experience limits the insight he needs to know how dangerously large and powerful the executive branch is and how much the bureaucracy works outside of the Constitution."

Pablo chuckled. "I see that Mark has you well briefed. A major part of the problem is that none of the news outlets, not even *Fox News*, thoroughly covers the issues that will bring about a societal collapse. You hear reports every now and then on how an EMP could destroy the power grid and render vehicles useless, but that's about it."

Ramirez raised his hand. "Let's defer this conversation and get this meetup underway. Grayson, we'll bring you up to date on our MAG, so you'll know how you fit in. We're all lawmen, meaning that—"

Yolanda interrupted with a loud, artificial cough.

Ramirez laughed along with everyone else. "And *lawwoman*. Everyone stand and face the flag for the Pledge of Allegiance and prayer."

Ramirez opened MAG business. "Our police training will help with security when the poop hits the fan, such as crowd control when refugees start piling up. Although he defers to me to preside at meetups, Mark is our founding father and resident prepping expert."

Everyone applauded Mark, who stood and took a silly bow.

"We have two subjects for general discussion today: expanding the MAG and acquiring a bugout location."

Relieved that the pressure was off him, Grayson settled and surveyed the group, weighing what he knew about each of them.

"This is the sixth monthly meetup, and we're doing pretty well," Ramirez said, "but if we're to have adequate security, we must grow our numbers. With Grayson and Mama, we have only eleven members. Without more shooters, we don't stand much of a chance."

Whoa, Chief. You're getting ahead of yourself. I haven't thrown my hat in the ring yet.

Samuel looked concerned. "That's only about a quarter of the bodies we need for minimum security operations for our bugout location, if we ever acquire one."

Ramirez shook his head. "We've focused too much on things related to living in the woods, building improvised shelters, making fire without matches, etc. That won't get us very far without a BOL. We also need a variety of specialists to build and maintain our bugout location. Mark and Grayson are our tactical guys. Charles is our gunsmith. We also need medical, electrical mechanical, plumbing, gardening, construction, and farming experts to name just a few. Any ideas?"

Yolanda's optimism was infectious. "I've joined an organic gardening club and getting good at food preservation. I can help establish large-scale gardening."

"That's a good beginning," Mark said, giving Yolanda's hand a soft squeeze to show his pleasure with her contribution to their efforts.

Charles added his expertise. "Before becoming a cop, I was a gasoline *and* diesel mechanic and my electrician mentioned being a prepper. I'll check him out."

"Anybody else with skills to fill an important job? Backgrounds like Charles' that we don't know about?"

Yeung raised his hand. "I served a tour with the Sea Bees. I can operate heavy machinery and know simple carpentry, but can't build houses from scratch."

"Now we're getting a game plan," Ramirez said.

Grayson looked quickly at Joe before he spoke. "My father was a sharecropper. It's been a while but with a little time, I could work a small farm. I'd have to defer to Yolanda for growing more than corn, cotton, and watermelons though." *What the hell am I doing? So much for not making rash decisions.*

Samuel spoke next. "Joe, Pablo, and I have been cops all our lives. We could head security."

Ramirez looked at Grayson. "As you can see, we're getting off the ground but there're many holes yet to fill to be ready for the collapse. Any questions for us?"

"It's been a long time since I last pitched hay; other than training everyone how to move through the woods without getting ambushed, where do you see me fitting in?"

Ramirez didn't hesitate. "You are an expert at the art of guerrilla warfare. Just as we needed Mark's knowledge and skills on how to start a MAG, we need yours if we are to survive the die-off. Lots of bad guys will be out to take whatever we have. Their numbers will grow when people begin to starve."

"Your background is the same as mine, Chief."

"True, but look at this white hair and potbelly. I'm a headquarters puke, not a field trooper anymore." Ramirez stood. "Everyone take a couple of minutes to grab a fresh cup of coffee and hit the latrine before we move on to discussing a BOL."

~~~

"Joe, what did you learn on your recon of that hundred-acre farm for sale?"

"It's near the Trinity River, a short distance south of Palestine, Texas and is about as perfect as it can be, considering the population density for that region of the country. It's roughly a hundred and fifty miles north of Houston and far enough east of Waco not to be an immediate problem when the die-off begins. Crime rate is low. There's plenty of water, arable land, pasture, and woods loaded with deer and turkeys."

Joe turned to Grayson. "The locals are mostly church-going Christians, good folks. We've been visiting different churches and shopping in the area to get a feel for the people and environment."

"Joe, I don't want to be a pessimist, but I detect that you aren't giving us the downside," Yeung said.

"Good detecting skills, Officer Yeung. The total cost is outside our collective purchasing power. The price of the land is reasonable, but there's a big farmhouse and a large barn on it that drive the price too high. One of us has to hit the lottery to be able to afford it or else come up with some very creative financing."

"Sorry to make you waste the trip," Ramirez said.

"No problem. At least we know it's a good area if affordable land pops up, something where we can build on over time."

"Why not just bug out to one of the three national forests near Houston?" Yolanda asked.

Everyone looked at Mark for the answer. "Millions of others will have the same idea. Houston is the fourth largest city in America. After a few days, we would bump into too many desperate, starving people. They'll kill off whatever wild game is available in short order and then start on each other. Trying to survive long-term while living out of a backpack is impossibly foolish."

Grayson had a lot of respect for Mark, and it grew by the minute. The more Mark talked, the more he worried about the future of his country for Daniel and, hopefully, his offspring. He couldn't imagine where it would end. "How do you anticipate this die-off thing taking place? I read about it, but I want your personal take on it, Mark, before I make a decision on joining the MAG."

Stunned silence filled the room. *Well, guys. You assumed; you didn't ask.*

"In a congressional hearing a few years back, former CIA Director James Woolsey predicted that seventy to ninety percent of the American population will die if we lost electricity for a year due to an EMP. A concerted Islamist terrorist attack on the grid or a coronal mass ejection from the sun would do the same. Regardless of the reason for the collapse, that's three hundred million dead, leaving about thirty million survivors."

Yolanda's face turned white. "That scares me to death. We have to solve the BOL problem, and soon."

"I'm not trying to scare you, but we need to be practical. And you're right," Mark said. "It's incumbent upon the survivors to return New America to its constitutional roots. We can only do that if we have adequate security and food to keep us alive during the die-off and enough tools, seeds, and breeding stock for a sustainable food supply."

Mark looked around the room. "It really is important that everyone finishes reading *Absolute Anarchy*. It outlines all of this succinctly and is loaded with references for you to research in your areas of specialty. We've reached the point where this is an imperative if we're going to save ourselves, our families, and our country."

"Yolanda is right," Ramirez said. "Without a well-developed BOL, we won't be here to help build New America. That's priority one."

Grayson was confused. "That's the second time I've heard the term 'New America.' Can someone please explain it?"

All heads pivoted to Mark. *That's the first problem I see. Nobody knows what's going on but Mark and maybe the chief. These guys need to organize and develop a mission needs statement.*

"After the die-off runs its course, we'll return to horse and buggy days. Assume no electricity or fuel. Most, if not all the bad guys, liberals, and those who live off the welfare state will be dead and can't continue to screw up the country. I believe the survivors will rebuild a nation founded on solid Judeo-Christian principles and reestablish the original constitution, or New America."

Charles was clearly startled. "Mark, are you saying only Christians and Jews will survive?"

"It's logical reasoning, not a value judgement. Most folks who live in the countryside are Christian and have the means to survive, but only if they are ready for a collapse. Almost all non-Christians live in cities and are not self-reliant. Their chances of survival are slim to none. There are also over four million Muslims in the U.S. and most of them were not born here. Who knows what will happen with them?"

Everyone sat in silence, contemplating Mark's revelation.

Pablo finally spoke. "Regardless of what happens to those in other religions, there's nothing we can do about them. It sounds cold, but we must think of our own families. We need to acquire farmland ASAP, a bugout location where we can secure a safe place for our families, where we can produce food. It's a huge expense, but the alternative is unacceptable."

"How long do we have before the collapse?" Grayson asked.

Mark shrugged. "It could be tomorrow or twenty years from now, depending on the cause—EMP, super volcano eruption, coordinated terrorist attack on the grid, CME, tyranny, economic collapse. The one thing economists I deal with agree on is the country continues to inch away from capitalism and closer to fascism and socialism. Throughout history, all socialist societies have failed. Venezuela is the latest example. Once a thriving capitalist country, the strongest in Latin

America, socialism has made it one of the poorest nations on Earth. Their people fight over garbage and are starving to death on the streets."

Grayson turned Mark's reply over in his head. "So, you're saying that we have to be ready every minute for the next twenty years, maybe more?"

"Correct. If our education system, entertainment industry, news media, and liberal judges continue to bastardize our history and indoctrinate our youth into believing socialism is good and capitalism is bad, economic collapse will be sooner, not later."

If I die before the collapse, how will Daniel survive? I have to be a part of this.

"So. Where do we start?"

Chapter 13

Tribunals and Tribulations

Year 1

Ramirez wiped the sweat pouring down his face with his handkerchief. "I had to slice the air to get from my car to the courthouse. Still feel like I'm suffocating. Somebody needs to tell the weather lady that August was two months ago. You okay, son?"

"I'm upright. That's about the best I can say. You're in a dark mood, Chief."

"I can't believe we have to go through this bull. Grayson, if you lose this trial to Delgado because of your obsessive behavior and the city has to pay a bunch of money, I'll throttle you for good measure."

"Yeah, I planned this to make *you* miserable."

"Watch it, smart mouth. I won't be able to protect your job a second time. You'll be lucky to have fifteen minutes to clean out your desk."

In an equally dark mood, Grayson rubbed his hands together. "I understand. I'm prepared to live with the court's decision."

"You'd have fared better if you'd killed Delgado instead of accidentally paralyzing him."

"Honestly, Chief, even considering my tenuous situation and as loathsome as he is, I wouldn't wish death on him."

"You're too young to go soft on me, young man. Wait till you have gray hair before tempering your perspective on life."

"I'm a baby compared to an old fart like you."

"Show respect for senior citizens, boy. Don't you wonder in what world that Fisher woman thinks Delgado deserves two million dollars for robbing a bank?"

"According to her, I should have asked him nicely to put down his gun and surrender. I showed gross negligence, disregard for public safety, prejudice against aliens, and discrimination against Mexicans in particular."

"If he hadn't been holding a gun in a bank robbery, he wouldn't be paralyzed."

"When he aimed at me, I shot at his pistol, not his spine. I just wanted to stop the bastard from hurting anyone. The two working with him shot at me without a second thought, so I eliminated them, but Delgado looked like a scared kid."

"How many kids have shot our officers?" Ramirez snapped. "Too many to count."

"If he wins this, he kills me without firing a shot."

"Like hell he does! Your little finger is worth more than him *and* his wheelchair."

"Chief, this trial could get ugly quickly, and there's nothing I can do to stop it. Fisher's claws are sharpened; I'm the prey."

"Don't you let that woman get the upper hand in there. Hang onto your family jewels. You hear me, boy?"

Grayson knew too well that she had the upper hand. He had a gut feeling the hideous creature would emasculate him before the trial was over. She had a debt to settle for the ride-along. He blew out his breath through pursed lips when the lock clicked and the doors to the courtroom opened.

His future depended on his best game during this ridiculous waste of city money. Once again, Shannon Fisher was out to save the world from the big bad white cops.

Chapter 14

Shannon's Setup

Year 1

"All rise."
Shannon opened for the prosecution.
"Houston Police Detective Grayson Dean, disregarding public safety, fired the bullet that paralyzed my client, Mr. José Delgado, who will never walk again. The City's negligent policy to protect citizen safety created this situation." Shannon paused and scanned the jury.

"The primary perpetrator, Officer Grayson Dean, shot Mr. Delgado in the spine instead of affording him a chance to surrender in accordance with proper police procedures."

She paused again to let her words sink in with the jury.

"The defense will claim that the shooting was justified because Mr. Delgado was shot during the commission of a crime for which he was convicted. That does not relinquish Officer Dean from following prescribed procedures." She described how Grayson was demoted for failing to follow established procedures, and continued, painting him as a coldblooded, half-human with no respect for others and Delgado as a sacrificial lamb.

Grayson fought not to glare at the smirks she directed towards him.

"Officer Dean's obsession with arresting Mexican immigrants is a long-standing problem and a racial component of this trial. We will prove that Officer Dean, an employee of Houston's police force, breached all four basic elements of legal negligence." Shannon counted them, holding up her fingers in front of the jury. Several jurors took notes.

She assured the jury that she would prove beyond a reasonable doubt that Grayson's breach of duty directly caused the critical injury to her client, resulting in high medical bills and loss of income for her client's lifetime.

"The city failed in its responsibility to oversee their employee's conduct. The city did not ensure public safety. Officer Dean did not fulfill his duties in a professional manner."

Shannon walked to Delgado in his wheelchair, his face sad, head lowered. She whirled and pointed at Grayson with her right index finger.

"Officer Dean showed no sense of civic responsibility on that fateful day in the bank—a day that changed Mr. Delgado's life immeasurably."

She finished her opening salvo with dramatic psychological flourish, smearing Grayson as an out-of-control cop. Every juror condemned him as a monster before she was through.

"Officer Dean killed the other two bank robbers that day; then, filled with animosity towards Mexicans, he purposefully crippled Mr. Delgado. He breached his duty as a citizen of the United States **and** as a police officer of the Houston PD. Ladies and gentlemen, I trust you to listen to the testimony and find a verdict of guilty for the crippling of José Delgado. Thank you."

Makeesha Evans, Grayson's attorney provided by the police union, stood. "Good morning, your honor, ladies and gentlemen of the jury." She walked and talked.

"Ms. Fisher's emotional statements, designed to inflame everyone in the courtroom and place liability for Mr. Delgado's injury on the City of Houston and, in particular, on my client, Officer Grayson Dean, are not fact-based. And **facts**, ladies and gentlemen, are the touchstone of our judicial system. **You** were expressly chosen to hear the evidence that will enable you to make an informed decision."

Makeesha turned to José Delgado. "One **fact** is that Mr. Delgado was committing an illegal act when he was shot. Officer Dean responded to a call of bank robbery in progress, a very stressful and dangerous assignment."

Makeesha looked to the jury but pointed at Delgado. "Another **fact** is Mr. Delgado is a convicted felon sentenced to Texas State Prison for the commission of that robbery.

"A **fact:** Mr. Delgado tried to shoot his way out of the bank, leaving Officer Dean no choice but to protect Houston citizens.

"A **fact:** Mr. Delgado endangered bank patrons with his gun.

"A **fact:** Mr. Delgado pointed his gun at Officer Dean, resulting in his own paralysis."

Makeesha stared at Delgado for a full ten seconds and shook her head in silence.

"We will prove Officer Dean—a native son of our great city of Houston—a well-respected, exceptional police officer, a decorated Green Beret who served in Afghanistan and Iraq with distinction—operated within the bounds of proper police procedure when the incident occurred."

The jury studied Grayson as she spoke, and their harsh demeanor from Shannon's remarks relaxed, calming Grayson.

"Officer Dean has a pristine record with the police department and is a true patriot who **chooses** to protect the people of Houston. He is a brave man with a proven regard for the safety of civilians and police officers under his command.

"It is incumbent for law enforcement to make tough decisions under stressful conditions. Through extensive experience, Officer Dean deduced the best action at the bank that day. His decision to stop Mr. Delgado saved lives.

"Ladies and gentlemen, Mr. Delgado's suit is a grievous misuse of the judicial system for financial gain by a convicted felon.

"I believe *you*—the people of Houston that Officer Dean protects daily—will do the right thing. You will see that the **facts**, not innuendos, necessitated Officer Dean's professional actions during the bank robbery. His actions were in accordance with official Houston Police Department policies and procedures."

~~~

As the plaintiff's attorney, Shannon called her first witness, a professor of criminal law, to testify on proper police procedures in the use of force. She quizzed him about Grayson's use of deadly force against Delgado and the two men shot during the robbery. Her expert was adamant that Grayson used unnecessary lethal force.

Makeesha cross-examined Shannon's expert. "**Professor**, you teach criminal justice in a college classroom?"

"That's correct."

"**Professor**, have you trained or served as a law enforcement officer?"

He hesitated.

"Answer the question," the judge ordered.

"No."

"No, you haven't been trained or served as a police officer?" Makeesha clarified.

"Correct."

"Have you ever been in a gun fight?"

Shannon jumped to her feet. "Objection! Irrelevant!"

"Overruled. Answer the question."

"No. Actually, I hate guns."

"Is it fair to say your *expertise* comes solely from academic studies in classroom environments?"

"I've interviewed many police offi—"

"**Professor**, you're not answering the question." She looked at the judge.

"Answer her question."

"Yes. That's fair."

"No further questions, your honor."

~~~

After lunch, Shannon began calling police officers who'd worked with Grayson. Makeesha wrote and slid the pad to Grayson. "Here we go."

When Shannon asked the first officer what he would have done in Grayson's place at the bank, Makeesha objected, arguing the answer would be supposition. The judge overruled her.

Shannon designed her questions to make Grayson into a crazed cop with a vengeance-filled agenda. All the officers testified he acted appropriately according to the reports from the scene. They agreed it's difficult to make a firm call without being at the scene with a gun pointed at you. None had ever seen him disobey police procedures. Hours later, after a long list of police personnel and not getting the answers she wanted, Shannon grew frustrated.

She asked the last officer, "Have you heard Officer Dean make derogatory remarks about Mexicans?"

Makeesha jumped on it. "Objection! Irrelevant!"

"Your honor, Officer Dean's dislike of Mexicans is common knowledge in the precinct and pertinent to this case."

"Objection sustained. Ms. Fisher, who do you represent in this case?"

"Mr. José Delgado, your honor."

"As I understood your opening remarks, you would prove Officer Dean is prejudiced against persons of Mexican descent. If your proof is police department or community gossip, I assure you that I will methodically overrule each piece of so-called proof you bring before this court. Is that understood?"

"I assure you that I have proof."

"So, you **allege**. The only person of Mexican descent involved in this case—to my knowledge—is your client. I strongly suggest you deal directly with the matter at hand."

Shannon counted on the judge sustaining Makeesha's objection, and she achieved her goal. The seed that Grayson hated Mexicans was in the jurors' minds.

Makeesha elicited admiration and respect for Grayson and his professionalism from each officer.

Shannon left immediately when the judge adjourned for the day.

~~~

As Makeesha and Grayson reviewed the day, his indignation was palpable. "How did she come off the winner when all the witnesses said nothing negative?" He ranted and paced until he was drenched in sweat and dropped into one of the cracked leather chairs.

"Feel better?" Makeesha asked.

"Hell no!"

"We got a significant point when the judge admonished her for trying to use gossip to prove her claim about Mexicans. She got in a substantial point when she planted the idea that you hate Mexicans."

"You and I count points differently."

Makeesha smiled. "Okay, tomorrow. She'll question you about your attitude. Shannon undoubtedly has a card up her sleeve. Any ideas?"

"None."

"Remember. She pushes judges to the edge to make points with the jury. Since half the jury is Hispanic—"

Grayson growled. "That arrogant bitch never gives up. She pushes until she gets her way."

"Sounds like someone I know."

Grayson gave her a dirty look, then half-smiled.

"She has to work hard to prove you're the Devil Incarnate. My job is to interrupt her, take notes, and prepare the defense. I have to save your ass to protect the city's purse."

"The city can pay and move on," Grayson growled. "My loss will be permanent." He wiped sweat with his handkerchief. "This is harder than combat."

"It's combat of a different ilk."

"I've been in court with that woman too many times, and nothing prepared me for today."

"You've never been the one with so much on the line. Trials are a painful process and challenge the bravest and most stalwart of people. Don't throw in the towel on the first day."

Grayson's face was stern. "I never throw in the towel. Never!"

At the door, he looked back over his shoulder. "Thanks, Makeesha."

~~~

Ramirez and Joe were in the hallway. "Let's grab dinner."

"Not hungry. I'm headed for a hot shower."

"You, Bucko, are headed for an ice-cold beer and a steak," Joe said. "You need to replenish some of the blood you lost today."

At the Watering Hole, Grayson's anger transitioned to guilt. "I owe the guys an apology for dragging them through this."

Ramirez reproach came swiftly. "You've testified in their cases. It's part of the job. Let's not chew on the gristle. We're men of honor. We make decisions and live with the consequences. You're facing a formidable opponent, and you'll persevere until the jury makes the final decision."

When the last plate was on the table, Joe said, "It's amazing how good the steaks are in this little bar."

"Yeah, but there's something weird with the bartender tonight," Grayson said. "Did you see how nervous he is?"

Chapter 15

False Witnesses

Year 1

Grayson downed a quick cup of coffee and returned to the courtroom. Shannon had played cat and mouse all morning, tenderizing him for the grill.

Makeesha bolstered him. "You handled Shannon's remarks well this morning. I'll rebuff the small damage during our defense."

"Thanks." Grayson nodded to the door. "Here comes the judge."

Shannon called Harold Weber to the stand. As he took his seat, he avoided eye contact with Grayson. He braced himself for Weber to fire the bullet that would end his career.

"Mr. Weber, do you know Grayson Dean?"

"Yes, ma'am."

Shannon's hesitation told Grayson she expected more. "Have you worked with Officer Dean in the past year?"

"He evaluated my annual weapons test."

"Have you ever had an altercation with Officer Dean?"

"A word here and there, nothing major."

What the hell! I beat him to a pulp.

"Have you ever had a fist fight with Officer Dean?"

"I've never hit another police officer."

Shannon's body grew rigid. "No further questions, your honor."

"Any cross?"

"No, your honor."

Everyone in the courtroom wondered what they missed.

Jaw rigid, Shannon called Grayson, who walked confidently to the stand.

"Officer Dean, you heard the testimony of the expert on the use of force and your fellow officers on your actions during the robbery. Professor Stein confirmed you failed to follow accepted police standards for dealing with force; yet, your officer buddies stated you followed procedures. Why do you think there's such a difference in opinion?"

"You must have forgotten, counselor; your so-called expert is an academic who's never been a cop and doesn't have a clue what he's talking about. The officers of the Houston PD do know what it is to be cop. They follow professional police standards daily to keep this city safe."

"Officer Dean, answer the question, please."

"I thought I did."

"No, you avoided my question."

Makeesha rose. "Objection! Officer Dean answered the question. Can we move on?"

"Objection sustained."

Shannon paced for a minute, thinking. "Officer Dean, Professor Stein, an expert on the use of lethal force, confirmed that you did not follow nationally accepted procedures. You shot José Delgado without offering an opportunity to surrender. Is Professor Stein's confirmation of this fact true?"

"No, it is not."

"Are you saying that an expert in this arena is presenting false testimony?"

"You asked me a question. I gave you my answer."

Chuckles surfaced around the courtroom.

Shannon didn't flinch or lose her poker face. "Officer Dean, when you shot Mr. Delgado, were you aware he's a Mexican immigrant?"

"I know that he's an *illegal alien—*"

"Your Hon—" Grayson was too fast for her.

"*An illegal alien and criminal* well known to HPD."

"Officer Grayson, please confine your comments to the questions," the judge admonished.

"Detective…er…Officer Dean, please explain your hatred of people of Mexican descent."

"Objection!" Makeesha jumped to her feet. "Nothing has been introduced that Officer Dean likes or hates people of Mexican descent."

"Your Honor, Officer Dean's predisposition to loathe Mexican immigrants is pertinent to understanding his state of mind when he needlessly shot Mr. Delgado. Officer Dean's failure to follow established police procedures because of his prejudice toward Mexican immigrants is critical to determining Houston PD's liability. They knowingly allowed him to work with an attitude of hatred that led him to maliciously injure my client."

"Objection sustained. This is my last warning, Ms. Fisher. You have submitted no proof to this court that Officer Dean harbors hatred for those of Mexican descent."

Shannon pushed harder. "Your honor, may we approach the bench?"

"Make it quick, counselor."

Makeesha, Shannon, and the judge huddled at the bench. "Your honor, Officer Dean, fueled by his hatred of Mexicans, ruthlessly abandoned public safety the day he shot my client. His extreme dislike of Mr. Delgado's race drove his manic behavior. If not for Dean's mental attitude, my client would not be a paraplegic."

"Whether my client likes or dislikes Mexicans has no bearing on this case," Makeesha snapped. "Ms. Fisher, for some obscure reason, continues alluding to a dislike of Mexicans without producing evidence. I have no reason to believe the allegation, nor does the jury. The city charges their police department with removing criminals from the streets regardless of their race. Officer Dean protected innocent people caught in the bank that day."

The judge turned to Shannon. "Ms. Fisher, I understand your point, but I've not changed mine. Do you or do you not have substantiated proof that Officer Dean bears prejudice toward Mexicans as related to this case?"

"Yes, your honor, I do."

"I suggest, Ms. Fisher, you bring that information before this court today or do not mention it again."

"Yes, your honor."

Shannon returned to the witness stand. "I have no further questions for the witness at this time but reserve the right to recall."

"Call your next witness, Ms. Fisher."

"I call Russell Conrad."

A tall, lanky man in dirty jeans and well-worn cowboy boots strode to the stand.

"You know him?" Makeesha wrote.

"Arrested him several times for possession," Grayson wrote. Makeesha spoke to her assistant.

"Mr. Conrad, where do you work?" Shannon asked.

"Tending bar at the Watering Hole."

"Do you know the defendant, Officer Grayson Dean?"

"Not really. He's in the bar now and again."

"Were you on duty the night of June 25 this year?"

"Yes, ma'am."

"Did you serve Officer Dean?"

"Yep. Him and another feller. Dean seemed to be in a bad mood—"

"Objection!"

"Sustained."

"Please describe their conversation for the court?"

"Dean and that feller over there...." Conrad pointed to Mark Hamilton, "wuz throwin 'em back. Weren't long before they wuz drunk as skunks. Outta nowhurs that man yelled at Dean, 'Why do you hate Mexicans?'"

The jurors turned to Grayson for a reaction. His dead stare remained unchanged.

"Dean's cop's face twisted all up, and he yelled 'Who said I hate Mexicans?' 'Everybody,' the other man said."

"By the other man, you mean Mark Hamilton?"

"Yep. That Dean feller shocked the shit—pardon me your honor—out of me. He said, 'It's something between me and the Devil.' That Hamilton guy shut his trap quick. I moved on down the bar."

"So, Officer Dean scared you away?"

"He sure as hell—pardon me your honor—did."

"Thank you, Mr. Conrad. Your witness."

Makeesha remained at the defense table. "Mr. Conrad, how long have you worked at the Watering Hole?"

"Bout ten year, off and on."

"You drink while on the job?"

"Ain't allowed."

"How many customers were in the bar the night Officer Dean and Professor Hamilton were..." she looked at her notes, "drunk as skunks?"

"A few cops in and out as shifts changed."

"So, you just hung around my client and his friend, eavesdropping in between waiting on them?"

"Some."

"Are most of your customers police officers?"

"More'n a few."

"You must learn a lot by listening to their private conversations."

"Some."

"Ever try blackmailing one of them?"

Shannon jumped from her chair. "Objection!"

"Your honor, court records show Mr. Conrad spent a year in prison eight years ago for the attempted blackmail of Officer Alice White."

"Objection overruled. Answer the question."

"I reckon so."

"Mr. Conrad, how many times have you been arrested on illegal drug charges?"

"Objection, your honor!"

"Overruled, Ms. Fisher."

"Couple times."

"In fact, Mr. Conrad, you've been arrested eight times for possession and distribution of illegal drugs. Is that true?"

Conrad looked around as if trying to find an escape route. "Sounds right."

"Has Officer Dean ever arrested you?"

"Time or two."

"You testified that you didn't *really* know him, but in fact, Officer Dean has arrested you three times and you spent time in jail all three times. So you decided to use this opportunity to give him his comeuppance."

Shannon was on her feet again. "Objection!"

"Sustained. Jury will ignore the last comment."

Makeesha looked at the jury as she spoke. "Mr. Conrad, it's a **fact** you have a history of illegal drug use and prison time. It's a **fact** you eavesdrop on private conversations at work to gain information to use against someone, Officer Dean included."

She turned to Conrad. "That about sum it up?"

Conrad's irritation escalated rapidly. "That ain't true!"

"This morning, Mr. Hamilton, a professional educator and decorated Army veteran, testified he didn't recall Officer Dean saying he hated Mexicans that night. You're saying he's a liar?"

Conrad's face twisted, wide-eyed. "I damn sure am. I heard 'em talking 'bout Mexicans being evil like the Devil."

"Mr. Conrad, you are a drug user who drains society, a has-been blackmailer, and a man whose testimony is worthless. No more questions."

"You black bitch!" Conrad was on his feet. "You think you better'n me!" He grabbed the witness box to vault over it. Grayson was instantly on his feet, but Makeesha motioned him to sit. Two bailiffs restrained Conrad and dragged him yelling from the courtroom. "You ain't nothing but a mother f—"

Order restored, the judge looked tiredly at Shannon. "Ms. Fisher, are you through for the day?"

"No, your honor. I recall Officer Dean to the stand."

Chapter 16

The Ugly Super-Bitch

Year 1

Grayson walked to the stand on lead-filled legs. *That bum helped Shannon prove her Grayson-hates-Mexicans theme.*

"Officer Dean, what is the name of the plaintiff in this case, the man you shot and paralyzed?"

"José Delgado," Grayson replied.

"Is he a Mexican immigrant?"

"He's an illegal alien and also a felon."

Shannon ignored his statement.

"Officer Dean, please explain your hatred of people of Mexican descent."

"Objection!" Makeesha protested.

"If you'll give me a moment, Your Honor, I'll prove that Officer Dean harbors strong animosity towards Mexicans, animosity he's harbored since incarcerated in a Mexican jail. His response to shoot Mr. Delgado—rather than follow police procedure and give him a warning to lay down his gun and surrender—correlates to his personal dislike for Mr. Delgado's nationality. It is a pertinent factor that must be considered in this case."

The judge paused to contemplate his decision. "Objection overruled. You are on thin ice, Ms. Fisher. A question or two, and this **is** over."

There is no way she could have gotten that information! The Houston Chronicle barely mentioned it back then.

"Your honor, may I speak with my lawyer?" When Makeesha arrived at the witness stand, Grayson whispered. "I will **not** testify if she knows what I think she knows."

"The judge ordered you to answer the question."

"Then I'll be in contempt."

"Judge, may we have a fifteen-minute recess, so I can consult with my client in private?"

"Is that absolutely necessary?"

"Yes, your honor."

From the courtroom to the conference room, Grayson aged ten years. "What haven't you told me?"

"It never occurred to me." His voice grew deep and he stared at the wall. "When I was nineteen, I was home on leave from Iraq, and a buddy, George Walton, and I went to Nuevo Laredo to shop for Christmas gifts; Army pay goes a lot further down there."

Grayson drew a ragged breath. "I mouthed off to a Mexican cop, and he arrested us and threw us in a crowded cell with drunk Mexicans. The lowlifes roughed us up."

"Talk faster."

"I'll opt for contempt before telling this in court."

"Did you hurt anyone in the altercation?"

"Are you kidding? We couldn't do anything against that many."

"You got beat up. so what?"

"They ripped our pants down and threw us across a bunk, face down! You get the picture?" Grayson leaned a hand against the wall. "I…I've never told anyone."

Makeesha choked out, "Not even your wife?"

"No! It's humiliating. You're the only person alive that knows about it."

"Honestly, I don't think the judge will let this go. How did you get out of jail?"

"When I didn't show up, Margaret called my father and he came looking for me. One look at us and he bribed the jailer, didn't ask a single question. My dad was a wise man."

"What did Margaret say?"

"She chewed me out for mouthing off at the Mexican cop."

"Would it help to call your friend to testify?"

"George…he committed suicide two years later. I'm the only one that knows why."

The bailiff knocked at the door. "Time's up, counselor."

Grayson, drowning in black memories and sweat, continued. "George told his parents why he showed up the next morning with a well-beaten face, and they told the *Chronicle* so the article would serve as a warning to other teens."

"My guess is Shannon only suspects something bigger. She'll drag it out of you to prove your prejudice against Mexicans. Anything else I need to know?"

"Nothing."

Makeesha met privately with Shannon and the judge in his chambers. Grayson's refusal to testify forced her to plead without explanation. The judge ruled Grayson had to respond to it or be in contempt.

The judge spoke tersely. "Officer Dean, please take the stand and remember you're still under oath."

His mind frozen, his heart pounding, Grayson held his head high and walked to the stand.

If I go to jail for contempt, some lowlife I've arrested would get him. The case would be lost. If I divulge the secret, I might as well be dead. Grayson's stomach lurched and threatened to empty, marking his Rubicon. *That bitch is mine.*

Shannon now had Grayson by the gonads. Makeesha's behavior in the judge's chambers pointed to an embarrassing situation or worse. If Shannon could drag the information out of him, it would be her moment of glory.

With barely suppressed sarcasm, she began. "Officer Dean, I repeat my question. Please explain your hatred of Mexican immigrants."

"What makes you think I hate Mexicans? Everyone you've asked had no idea what you're talking about, neither do I."

"I repeat my question. Explain why you hate Mexican immigrants."

"You'll have to be more specific."

Shannon and Grayson had a brief staring contest before she rolled her eyes and took an exasperated breath for the benefit of the jury.

"Officer Dean, have you been to Mexico?"

"Yes."

"Have you been to Nuevo Laredo, Mexico?"

Sweat beaded on his forehead. "Yes."

"Have you been arrested in Nuevo Laredo?"

"Yes."

"Have you been assaulted in the Nuevo Laredo jail?"

"Yes." He braced for the blow.

"Please explain the details of the assault to the court."

He repeated what he'd told Makeesha, minus the graphic details.

"A few intoxicated Mexicans beat up you and your friend, so you hate the whole race. Seems a radical position to take, particularly with you in the military at the time." Shannon faced the jury. "Surely, there's more to this story. How many Mexicans did you assault in that jail?"

Grayson's granite expression held. "None. We were seriously outnumbered."

"Big as you are, you didn't get a punch in?"

"I was a kid in another country having fun with a friend when we got dumped into a dangerous situation. We got the shit kicked out of us."

She moved closer to her victim. "And you bear no ill will toward Mexicans, although you called them evil?"

"Objection! That witness' claim was discounted as a lie fabricated as revenge."

"Ms. Fisher, you have exactly five minutes to give us your **specific** and **exacting** evidence that Officer Dean harbors hatred against Mexicans. Clerk, begin timing, NOW."

Confident the jury suspected Grayson was withholding information, her mission was complete. But she couldn't resist twisting the knife.

"Your honor, if Officer Dean would simply give an honest answer to my question, we could move on."

"The clock is ticking, Ms. Fisher."

Relishing her manipulation, she turned to her prey and recoiled, drawing a fractured breath. She quickly stepped back from him.

Grayson's face had morphed into an ashen death mask.

It was obvious he didn't see Shannon, although she was squarely in front of him. With crystal clarity, she realized with horror that she had crossed an invisible moral line. She had pushed a witness into an ungodly place. His catatonic expression warned her it would be brutally inhumane to continue.

"Officer Dean, please answer the question," the judge ordered repeatedly, growing annoyed.

Shannon blinked several times, working to regain control. Finally, she blurted, "Your honor, I withdraw the question."

The judge leaned over his desk. "You *withdraw* the question?"

"Yes, your honor. I withdraw the question. I have no further questions for this witness."

Shannon was more stunned than anyone in the courtroom.

She spoke to Grayson softly. "Officer Dean, you may step down. There are no more questions." When she laid her hand lightly on his arm, Grayson's eyes slowly refocused. He jerked away from her and stood, a wooden soldier marching back to the table where Makeesha watched helplessly.

The flummoxed judge asked if Shannon had any more witnesses to call.

Her eyes following Grayson intently, she could not disconnect. "Uh...no...no more questions, your honor."

"Thank you, God," Grayson whispered. The color crept into his face as he sat rigid in his chair.

"You have further questions?"

"Your honor, I have no further questions for Officer Dean."

The judge threw up his hands. "I give up. Court dismissed until 9 a.m. tomorrow."

Shannon's face revealed her perplexed reaction, her eyes widened and suddenly morphed into a death mask of its own.

~~~

Makeesha presented a strong case in defense of Grayson and the city of Houston. She successfully discounted the testimonies of Conrad and Shannon's expert witness. She recounted Delgado's criminal trial, explaining why Grayson used lethal force, and questioned police officers on his professional and moral conduct.

Shannon appeared lost in another world and weakly objected a few times to Makeesha's points.

Nonetheless, the jury found the city of Houston guilty of negligence in overseeing their employee and awarded Delgado $300,000, significantly below the two million requested, but enough to let Grayson know his days as a police officer were over.

Mammoth doom engulfed Grayson as he heard the jury and judge's determinations that sentenced him to an empty and rudderless life.

He thanked Makeesha for her valiant efforts and stepped into the hallway, to speak with the chief. "Sir, I'm sorry. I hope you won't suffer because of this."

"There's not a man alive who hasn't made at least one major error while pushing to do the right thing." Chief Ramirez spoke with sadness. "If I'd been in your shoes, I'd have shot that scumbag myself and can't fault you for doing the same."

"The *ugly super-bitch* got me this time."

"You did as well as any man under the circumstances."

"I'm taking tomorrow off to visit Margaret and Amanda. I owe them an apology."

"It's your life, Grayson, but I suggest you make this your final apology. One day you'll be on the other side with them forever.

Kindhearted Margaret wouldn't want you to remain miserable on this side; it's such a short time."

"I hadn't thought of it that way, sir. Danny will be with us, too."

Ramirez's brow furrowed. "I'll hold off the wolves as long as I can to give you time to decide the actions you want to take about your future."

His words pierced Grayson's desolate soul. *Et tu, Chief?*

Islamic State of America - 4

Texas State Prison

Year -4

Carlos and Miguel paused and looked back over their shoulders. Akeem made a subtle gesture for them to return. They watched Akeem stroke his bushy dark beard while studying them, his expression calm, eyes alert. Seconds ticked while each man stood his ground in the silent enclosure. Every prisoner's attention was on them, itching for a bloody fight.

Akeem carefully considered the unusual, arrogant Mexican, the scarred face, thick gold loop dangling from his ear, and intricate tattoos inked on arms and neck. The man vibrated anger, a trait Akeem was prepared to exploit.

As they stood quietly in the prison yard, each waited for the other to make a decision. Akeem swallowed his pride; he had no choice. This first meeting must go well to open the door to the future. He could not fail his mentor, Imam Omar. He must be pragmatic.

Akeem motioned to a clear spot away from curious ears. "Why do you care how many times a day I pray?" Akeem asked, initiating the dialogue necessary to temper Carlos' juvenile bravado and lead him to the mature intellectual level he required to succeed as a leader of Allah's soldiers, assuming that was possible.

"I see you have peace after you pray. At night, you sleep without waking. I'm a violent man, the same as you. Even so I want peace and sleep, but it don't want me."

"You say you feel at peace when I sing prayers, even though it is in a language you do not understand. Perhaps Allah is calling you back."

Murtadha's eyes narrowed. "I understand more than you think, Arab! You don't know me. What's this *calling me back* shit?"

"Everyone is born a Muslim, and pure, but many are fooled into becoming something else. Islam is in your blood. You are a leader. If you learn of the one true god, Allah, accept his truth, and submit to him, I will teach you to become a mighty Muslim warrior, a leader over many men. Then, one day, you will lead hundreds, then thousands." Akeem wasn't sure of Imam Omar's plan but he made a play on Carlos' ego.

"I'm already a mighty warrior, Arab. I got my gang. Just teach me the prayers. We have time. We ain't leaving this casa del diablo no time soon."

Akeem's business tone remained unchanged. "Before I can teach you the prayers, you must first learn the ways of Islam and become a true believer. You must become a Muslim by reciting the Shahada and swearing allegiance and servitude to Allah. Then I can teach you the language and make you an educated man."

Carlos noted his comment on education but dismissed it as a fantasy, something he would never achieve. "What is this Shahada?"

"The Shahada is the first of the five pillars of Islam. You must say, 'I bear witness that there is no god but Allah, and I bear witness that Mohammed is the messenger of Allah.'"

"Easy enough," Carlos said. Miguel agreed.

"It is easy to say the Shahada, but you must believe what you are saying with firm conviction. You must be truly sincere and in compliance with the teachings of Islam and learn its language. Empty words make you an apostate and I would have to kill you."

Carlos eyed Akeem with suspicion. "What is this language I must learn?"

"The language of Allah is Arabic, as the angel Gabriel gave it to Mohammed—peace be upon him—to write the Quran. This was the first miracle of Islam. Mohammed—peace be upon him—did not know how to read or write, but Allah gave him the gift so he could teach Allah's way to the people and rid them of idolatry for all time. This gave them power, direction, and strength, as it does for me now. What you seek is the power of the sword and the peace and guidance of the Quran."

Carlos was frustrated with Akeem's responses. Except for vague memories of his father, something he often attempted to push out of his mind, he'd lived most of his twenty-eight years without religion. "Look man, I don't care what a Quran is. I only want to learn to sing your prayers. These other things I don't care about. That ain't what I want."

Addressing him by name for the first name, Akeem set in place the second phase of his test. It was time to set the hook before the fish got away. "It doesn't work that way, Carlos. You either become educated and a great leader of many men or go back to your useless little gang that, like you, will never amount to anything."

Carlos' triggered reaction to Akeem's insult overwhelmed good judgment. With closed fists, he leaned toward Akeem, whose men moved closer. He halted his strike when Miguel touched his shoulder and spoke softly in his ear in Spanish.

"Hermano, calm down. Don't you want to learn the prayers? Be patient and listen to him so you can be at peace and sleep. Imagine how it would be if he taught us to read and write. I want to be educated and read books."

Carlos jerked his shoulder from Miguel's hand. The Arab asked too much of him. He didn't want Akeem to know he couldn't read or write Spanish or English. How could he learn Arabic?

Akeem locked his hypnotic eyes on Carlos and he felt the fire go quiet in his belly. After a long moment, Carlos spoke in a dead tone. "I'm listening, musulmán."

Before Akeem could reply, the prison yard bell rang, ordering the prisoners back to their cells.

"We will meet in the library next week."

"What's wrong with meeting tomorrow?" Miguel asked.

"Be patient. You need time to think and to feel Allah's call."

"We'll be there, Arab." Carlos and Miguel gave their gang sign as a pledge, then turned, and walked away.

Sitting on his bunk that evening, Carlos listened closely as Akeem sang his prayers. Through clouded memories of a strange building and many men, one in particular, on their knees, shoes off, and foreheads touching the floor, he repeated familiar words and felt a connection. For the first time since finding himself and his little brother alone on the streets of Nuevo Laredo, Carlos Murtadha slept through the night without waking.

Chapter 17

Go Find Yourself

Year 1

Only the night crew remained when Grayson arrived at Ramirez's office. "It's taken a while, but I assume the hierarchy has come to a decision on my departure."

Ramirez smiled as he rose from behind his desk. "A decision is coming, but not today, not with Christmas in a couple of weeks and the union dragging its feet. No, I need your help with a new problem."

"I wondered why the after-hours meeting."

"I have a clandestine mission for you, something special."

"Chief, you've known since you saved my butt in Fallujah that I'm your man when you need something special. What's up?"

"January eleventh, the Department of Justice is conducting a seminar on their revised gang eradication policy and regulations. I'm up to my eyeballs in problems on the home front, and since you're my most qualified officer in that arena, and I trust you to pay attention to the presentations and not gallivant around, I want you to attend for me."

"Sounds like a free vacation. What's the catch?"

Chief Ramirez chuckled. "No catch. Sit through the seminar, take notes, and write the new departmental policy. I don't have time for that bullshit."

Grayson smiled. "So, you're sending me to sit through the boring bullshit."

Ramirez's face mottled. "Keep the trip to yourself. You understand the reason."

"I do, sir. It won't go over well if the liberal media think I'm back as a detective in the Gang Unit. HPD would be all over the front page again and not in a good way."

"You got it, son."

Grayson frowned. "We wouldn't be in this position if I wasn't so bullheaded."

"Stop with the self-deprecation. Every man pays the price for the bad and reaps the rewards for the good. Thanks to *that*...what is it you called her?"

"Who?"

"The ACLU lawyer."

"You mean the *Ugly Super-Bitch*?"

"That's it. The burrs you've stuck under her saddle over the past few years turned your situation into a public spectacle."

"I made the decisions, and I have to live with the consequences. Getting out of town sounds good. Where's it being held? DC?"

"Well…uh…." the chief teased.

Grayson feared the worst. He didn't like big cities, especially DC.

"It's at the convention center in a little place called the Entertainment Capital of the World, Las Vegas, Nevada," Ramirez grinned. "Soldier, you need some R and R. Do your job and keep a low profile, but enjoy yourself too. I set you up with a room at Caesar's Palace. After the convention, take a couple of days to rest. Rent a car and drive up to Death Valley. Visit Scotty's Castle, a marvelous place to relax. The weather is chilly but perfect in January."

"I've also heard Vegas called Sin City. I'll keep a low profile and get the job done."

"Son, no one should have to deal with the problems you've faced. Christmas will be difficult enough for you. I wish you'd join Mama and me for dinner."

"I appreciate your invitation, but I can't handle a family get together just yet. It's best I stay to myself this week. I'm clearing out the house some. I've been avoiding it, but it's as good a time as any."

The chief massaged his bristly gray hair. "I understand. Begin to forgive yourself, son, and face the New Year with a glad heart, or at least a heart that's at peace."

"I'll do my best, sir."

Ramirez handed him a folder containing the papers for the seminar and feigned being gruff. "Now, get the hell out of my office. Go find yourself, soldier."

Grayson offered his hand. "Thanks, Chief. It feels strangely pleasant to have this be my last official action."

Islamic State of America - 5

Texas State Prison

Year -4

The prying eyes and disquiet atmosphere of the prison yard were absent in the library, allowing the inmates to feel more at ease. Even so Akeem's hypnotic black eyes never blinked as he talked, which both fascinated and unnerved Carlos. Miguel was at ease and attentive, as usual.

Akeem began in a business tone. "There is a plan for you, one that will give you great power over many men, but first there is much to learn. I need to see your commitment and understanding. If you are serious, I will teach you. If you are not serious and waste my time, you will not like the taste of my shank when I shove it down your throat, cut out your tongue, and watch you choke to death on your blood."

As Akeem's words began to congeal and then crystallize, Carlos responded. "Don't worry about me, Arab. I find the words of your prayers…" his veil of control slipped away for a second, exposing his soul, "take away my pain."

Miguel snapped his head toward his stronger brother who never let down his guard.

Carlos recoiled at his own words; his eyes hardened and he morphed into an indescribable evil, sending a chill up Akeem's spine.

Carlos ruminated over their prison yard conversation and knew he wanted the power this Muslim man claimed would be his. First, he had to devise a way to get past the reading and writing problem.

Miguel eyed his brother with curiosity. He had never seen him this deep in thought.

Carlos had bluffed his way through life thus far; what was one more ruse. He spoke to Akeem with false conviction. "Yes. I want to be a leader of many men. I want to learn to sing your prayers. I'll do what you say, Arab, but if you play games with me…well," Carlos shrugged with a smirk, "I have a shank of my own, and you can't imagine how I'll use it on you." Pointing to Miguel, he added, "I want my brother in this too. We'll do our part, if you do yours. Comprende?"

Regardless of his words, Akeem knew Carlos had not crossed into full commitment. He moderated his voice and turned to Miguel to test his resolve and give Carlos time to settle down. "What about you? Does your brother speak for you or do you speak for yourself? Do you also desire to learn the ways of Islam and become a Muslim? If so stay. Otherwise you must leave."

"I'm with my brother. When I listen to you pray, it makes me feel the same as Carlos. It's like something I heard before, some memory I don't understand."

Akeem nodded and returned his attention to Carlos. "You are not fully convinced, are you?"

Carlos didn't reply.

It was time to push him over the line. Akeem narrowed his eyes and spoke in a flat tone, pointing a finger from one to the other. "Your father was a Muslim."

Carlos' muscles flexed like a panther ready to pounce. "Lying hijo de puta. I don't know my father, except that he is dead. I remember my mother enough to be annoyed when I think of her. You lie to me, musulmán. You ready to die now?"

Akeem remained calm as his dark eyes bored into Carlos' deep brown ones. "Your mother's name is Maria Baomi Murtadha."

Carlos and Miguel's mouths dropped open.

"How do you know this?" Miguel demanded, his nostrils flaring.

Akeem ignored the question. "Do you remember that you had Muslim names?"

Miguel shook his head, but Carlos acknowledged the truth. "I remember. What else do you know, Arab?"

"You are a descendant of the prophet Mohammed—peace be upon him—and Allah calls to you."

His brain struggling to process Akeem's revelations while fighting to push faint memories back into their dark place, Carlos casually surveyed the bookshelves. He had never been in a library. He saw books he couldn't read, computers that were a mystery, and a floor he was only capable of sweeping and mopping. He turned to Akeem, at the mercy of another man for the first time in his life. "I ain't heard nobody calling. What now, Arab?"

"First, you must study many things about Islam and learn the Shahada. I will lead you and your brother, but know that to learn Arabic and a few prayers doesn't make you a Muslim. Above all things, you must accept there is only one god, Allah, and Mohammed—may peace be upon him—is his messenger. You can be a part of it, *Insha'Allah*, but one thing at a time."

Miguel could not control his enthusiasm. "I can do it!"

Akeem ignored Miguel—special but not the first son, not the chosen one—and kept his focus on Carlos. "Allah is a demanding but generous god. Many hear the calling but answering it properly requires you to learn much, to take a new life, and follow Sharia, the law that pleases Allah, which I will teach you. I expect you to do as I instruct and follow the will of Allah. Do not betray me. Ever. We will see if you have the patience to master all you need to learn. Are you pledged to this?"

"Yeah." Carlos spoke without Miguel's enthusiasm. "We're with you." He was irritated that Akeem once again challenged him and made himself a promise: *We are with you unless you betray us. Then we will destroy you.*

Chapter 18

Merry Christmas

Year 1

Grayson shook his hand to release the cramp. He wasn't sure how long he'd been gripping the doorknob to Amanda's bedroom, his head leaning against the door, his eyes closed. She shut her door eight months ago, where it remained. As long as the door stayed closed, somehow, Amanda was with him. He heard her on the other side talking to her Invisible Friend and singing a school song to JoJo. The moment he cracked it open her voice would vaporize and his beautiful daughter would be gone forever.

Taking a deep breath and saying a prayer, he eased the door open and stepped into the hushed room. A cacophony of emotions slammed into him. He slowly walked to her twin bed, his heavy feet resisting every step, and gently sat on it, the sheets smooth and properly made, just as Margaret taught her. He stroked the pink blanket with its collection of fairies and unicorns and stared at the photo on her nightstand. She sat in his lap while he read *Goodnight Moon* to her.

He wouldn't be getting up before first light with Margaret on Christmas morning to watch Amanda run to check the empty glass of milk and plate of cookie crumbs Santa left from her offering, and no bits of grass beside the fireplace proved Santa took the hay she collected from last fall's grass cutting to feed his reindeer. His throat released a tiny whimper.

His father's advice to act like a man, no matter how hard life hit, prompted him to push off the bed deliberately. He slid open the door to the dark closet and turned on the light. It flickered, glowed brightly for a second, and burned out, blasting his brain with a flashback to a mortar round exploding nearby in a nighttime attack. It drained his resolve, and he collapsed to his knees, weeping loudly and cursing his father. He remained kneeling on the floor until no more tears would come, then forced himself to stand and shuffle to the hallway for a box to empty Amanda's closet. *Danny, come help me, son.*

Grayson's emotions sapped him well before he finished sorting things in the house into piles for the church thrift shop, trash, and the things he'd keep forever. Each door he opened reignited his pain. The master bedroom was exactly as Margaret left it, except for the night of the funeral when he moved his clothes to a pile in the dining room and began sleeping on the couch. He boxed her possessions slowly, caressing them with tenderness.

Guilt assaulted him in Daniel's room when he realized he was thankful his son had taken most of his things to Louise's house. He wondered if Daniel pitched the worn football haphazardly on his bed as a cynical reminder to him of the years the two tossed it to one another in the backyard.

Exhausted, his mind wandered too frequently to the new paths thrust upon him in the last eight months. What else did Satan have in store for him?

~~~

Absorbed with sorting the house and transporting boxes to storage, he left the heavy pieces until Joe could help. He didn't focus on Christmas until he dropped, dog-tired, onto the sofa. There would be no shopping for the kids with Margaret; no selecting the perfect tree and decorating it; no Christmas music playing throughout the house; no taking Amanda to see Santa; no driving through neighborhoods to see Christmas lights; no dressing up and going to Mass; and no Christmas dinner with all the accompaniments. Christmas was dead and so was he.

Christmas Eve, he took pink poinsettias to the cemetery, staying until the sun was low on the horizon.

Chapter 19

Viva Las Vegas

Year 1

The feds running the seminar handed out stacks of paper—*our tax dollars at work*. Grayson laughed to himself. He planned to stay off the radar, enjoy room service, and draft the chief's policy on his laptop during what he assumed would be a tedious, boring presentation. He wasn't disappointed. When the last speaker closed the conference, Grayson remained in his seat and rushed to put the final touches on the drafted policy before his laptop battery died. When he closed the computer and looked up, he was surprised that two thousand attendees were almost all gone.

He had a flash of recognition when a woman ten rows down turned sideways to reach for her laptop case. Oh, crap! It couldn't be. Shannon Fisher—no doubt learning new ways to twist the tougher regulations to her advantage.

He stood quickly and hurried to escape before she discovered him. Fumbling with his laptop bag and a stack of papers, he managed to drop everything. She turned to see what the noise was all about and their eyes locked.

I'm screwed. How am I going to explain my presence?

"Officer Dean?" Shannon's raspy voice notified his muscles to ready for attack; a hundred tiny spiders crawled over him.

"Ms. Fisher." *She must have flown in on her broomstick.* He busied himself collecting and packing the spilled items. *Move on, bitch. Move on.* He could see the headlines: "Rogue Cop Returns to Gang Department: Chief Ramirez Fired."

"I'm surprised to see you here. I'm glad this is over. I almost fell asleep from boredom."

Grayson was on high alert. His voice finally kicked in, and he spoke in professional tones. "I dozed off once myself."

Extending her hand, she smiled at him through her black horn rims and thick, smeared-on makeup. Her butch voice grated on him. "You headed back tonight?"

She can smile?

He stood to leave. "I'm hanging around a few days." *Walk away, bitch!*

"My flight leaves late tomorrow morning."

"Have a safe trip."

Shannon was all smiles. She had him by the cojones and she knew it. "I'm staying at Caesar's Palace. Would you like to have dinner at one of their better restaurants? The Old Homestead Steakhouse is very good."

He rummaged for a response. *I'd rather eat arsenic than sit across a table from you.*

"My treat." Shannon sounded strange; a sweet tone appended her guttural voice.

Grayson looked her up and down. *She'll nail my career to a cross before this is over.* What the hell? Maybe he could get in a jab or two before it was a done deal.

"My momma always told me not to turn down a dinner request from a lady." He managed a more sociable tone. *Momma just turned over in her grave.* Considering Shannon's liberal leanings, he didn't insult her by insisting he would pay the bill.

"Where are you staying?" she asked.

Damn! "I'm staying at Caesar's Palace, too."

Her smile broadened. "Let's meet at the Steak House at six-thirty. That'll give me time to pack and get some sleep."

No way in hell I'll make an entrance with this woman.

His conscience made him offer her a ride. They left his rental car with valet parking and walked to the bank of elevators. She punched the same floor as his. *What the hell!* They got off the elevator and walked in the same direction down the same hall, and when she stopped at the room directly across from his, he thanked the good Lord he hadn't run into her sooner.

Shannon was a revolting, anti-gun, leftist lawyer, someone he despised. Someone who currently held his life in her hands. He had dinner plans with a she-devil. A twinge of guilt hit his gut. *I've never had a dinner date with anyone but Margaret!*

~~~

He had a little time to contemplate how dinner would go as he showered, shaved, and dressed in casual slacks and a simple button-up shirt. There was no reason to put on a suit and tie to eat with the Brown

Frump. He rushed to get downstairs before Shannon and reserved a remote table in a dark corner, irrationally fearing somebody he knew would see them. He took a seat near the host stand to wait. It was the Southern gentlemanly thing to do, regardless of the situation. *My first dinner with a woman since losing Margaret, and it's with one of the homeliest and most annoying women I know.*

He had a perfect view into the open casino. It startled him that the ladies serving drinks in their very short, low-cut, and cleavage-revealing outfits caused a strong stirring in him.

Whoa, mule!

A gorgeous, leggy, perfectly figured redhead in a thigh-length, tight black-silk dress that plunged in the right places swayed down the hallway. Her flat stomach, followed by her perfectly rounded, tight derriere reflected in the full-length wall mirror behind her, fought for his attention. The curves of her firm, smooth breasts were deliciously on display. The redhead swayed down the hallway with that enticing model walk—one foot directly in front of the other. As the ravishing woman approached, he was aware of her faultlessly sculpted makeup. Margaret and her Mary Kay business had taught him well. Smoky eyes, sexy red lipstick, and matching nails. Her flashing diamond necklace and earrings adorned the woman with a sparkle any man would give his right arm to spend a night with. How did she escape from her millionaire boyfriend? *Lucky bastard.*

When the woman stopped two feet away and looked directly at him, he caught his breath and stood as if called to attention by a gruff drill sergeant.

"Close your mouth and extend your right elbow, please," came a soft, silky command.

"I'd love to lady, but I'm waiting on someone."

"Mr. Dean, *you* are waiting on *me*."

Grayson's eyes blinked rapidly while his brain processed the information at light speed. His elbow popped into position robotically and he stood tall and proud. The pride of an unchallengeable alpha male engulfed him, as he watched every man in the place stare at his prime female. He bathed in their envy. As counterfeit as it was, he enjoyed feeling like a man again.

Taking their seats, he soberly reminded himself he was having dinner with his arch nemesis. *What the heck is she up to? How…what…?*

He felt conspicuous in his casual slacks and shirt and as nervous as a cat in a room full of rocking chairs, and not the least stunned by the sexual tension at the table.

Shannon ordered wine without consulting him. Once the waiter left the table, they attempted small talk, until he could no longer restrain himself. "Ms. Fisher—"

"Call me Shannon," her sultry voice purred.

The sommelier appeared, decanted the wine, and moved the glass towards Grayson for approval. Shannon quickly reached and took the glass. She swirled the wine, checked the bouquet, sipped it, and gave her approval.

Grayson was not accustomed to a woman at the table taking the lead. He was curious about what was going one, but wasn't about to lose his manhood and dignity to this bitch, no matter how gorgeous she was. *She likes to pull the strings, so try this.*

"Shannon, let's get the elephant out of the room. You are an extraordinarily beautiful woman. Why do you dress like a…er—"

"Hag."

"Okay." He smiled. "If you prefer not to answer, I'll withdraw the question. I have to admit that I'm starting to believe in the Fairy Godmother."

"I object, your honor." She returned the smile.

"Objection sustained. No further questions." He held up his glass for a toast. They clinked glasses, sipped wine, and studied their menus as though editing the U.S. Bill of Rights.

Three glasses of wine during dinner and a brandy after dessert gradually loosened their tongues and allowed their personal histories to enter the conversation.

"Grayson, give me a few quick sentences that tell your life story."

He considered his options. "I will if you will."

"Okay. You go first."

"I grew up in a Central Texas farm community and married the love of my life. I'm a patriot, so I joined the Army and became a Special Forces soldier. I got my bachelors in law enforcement while on active duty and left the Army to complete my masters. Margaret and I had two children…."

His smile dissolved, and silence joined them at the table.

"I thought you were a simple-minded, Tea Party conservative who couldn't see past his bigoted nose," her voice was soft and apologetic.

"You were wrong!"

Shannon's face grew warm. "Sorry. I have a direct way of speaking after too much wine."

"Lady, you have a direct way of speaking before wine." Grayson forced a brief smile. "I don't agree with your politics, but I respect that you unabashedly fight for what you believe in. It's your turn. Who is Shannon Fisher? Where're you from? Siblings? Husband? Kids?"

She twisted her brandy snifter a few times, turned her head, and looked into a nonexistent distance before answering. "No kids."

Grayson waited for the awkward moment to pass, then gave her an out. "You a football fan?"

She held up her hand. "A deal's a deal. You told your story, I'll tell mine. I was born to Cajun parents in Louisiana."

That explains the fire in her soul and the swish in the caboose.

"I have a wonderful sister, Jillian. My husband, Larry, and I met at LSU then moved to Seattle for work. No luck having children. Larry's grown more distant over time. He suffers the love-making routine but doesn't have his heart in it anymore." *What the heck? I only share this stuff with Jillian.*

Grayson was stunned at her openness. "Shannon, that's very personal. I'm at a loss for words."

For a second, Grayson thought she was going to cry. Once again, silence dined with them. She swallowed and offered a half-hearted laugh. "I'm okay now. Saying that actually felt good. It's incongruous, but I trust you, even with our disparate histories and the wide gap in our political convictions. Could be the extensive research I did on you before the last trial. Damn you, Grayson Dean!" *Or, the alcohol. No! That's not it.* She tried to calm down.

Grayson flinched and debated whether to push her but decided against it. "Hey, what do you think about taking some of the casino's money?"

"Sounds like fun. What's your game, mister?"

"I like blackjack and play a little on the craps table every now and then. How about you?"

"Just slots and video poker on occasion. Let me watch you play blackjack, see what it's all about."

When the waiter brought the bill, Shannon reached for it. Grayson caught her hand and grew serious. He made it clear who was paying, then shifted to humor. *The last thing I need is an argument with the Ugly Super-Bitch.*

"Miss Shannon, darlin', it would be a deefault in me as a Southern gentleman and a threat to mah manhood if ah did not provide imbursement for this wonderful repast. It's not often that ah enjoy the company of such a charming lady in a fine dining establishment."

Shannon joined the game. Head slightly down, right hand on her chest just under her throat, and eyes tilted up, she fluttered her eyelids. "Why I do declare, Mista Dean. It would displease me something terrible if ah caused your manhood impairment. Ah submit to your petition, as ah received equal gratification from your company. Ah'm most grateful for your consideration, suh, and await the time ah can reciprocate with a special *reeward* for your generosity…in the very near future."

This woman is more dangerous out of the courtroom.

Grayson paid the bill in cash. When they stood to leave, the effects of the wine were evident. They laughed as they staggered toward the casino.

Shannon led the way, an exaggerated wiggle to her walk. She snapped her head and looked over her shoulder to catch him enjoying her efforts.

His face crimson, he laughed heartily. "I'm busted; but so is every man we've passed. You made that old guy stumble. You should be ashamed of yourself, ma'am."

She held her nose in the air and put on a sweet, innocent face. "Why, Mista Dean, ah'm sure ah don't know what y'all mean."

They both cracked up.

~~~

At the blackjack table, exercising his inherent sense of chivalry, Grayson paused for Shannon to sit first.

"I'll just stand and watch." She slid between the seats and closer to his right side. He swallowed hard and forced himself to ignore her revealing cleavage, inches from his face. Both ordered drinks, and he downed his quickly, thankful for an excuse to gulp, and ordered another. She followed suit. After a few minutes, she excused herself to go to the ladies room. She returned to find a voluptuous young blonde in the seat to Grayson's right, leaning toward him and flirting.

Shannon stood several feet back and watched. Grayson ignored the woman, but she didn't give up. Disturbed by an unexpected stab of jealousy, Shannon pushed between them. Her breast brushed against his arm. "Miss me?"

"Sure did," he half slurred. *What was it with this woman he thought he knew?* Grayson would swear the breast brush was intentional. *What am I doing in a casino with a married woman? Better yet, what does she want?*

Shannon watched Grayson play blackjack for half an hour, then with her breasts pushed well into his side, spoke in his ear. "This isn't my game. I'm going to play the video poker machines." He looked into her beautiful gray-green eyes and felt an intense, penetrating connection. *This is not right.* **Do Not** *ask her to stay.*

He cleared his throat. "I enjoyed dinner, Shannon. If we get separated, have a safe trip home."

"I had a good time, too, and you have a safe trip home as well."

He detected a slightly miffed voice but ignored it, and returned to his hand, the ace and jack of spades, the perfect blackjack hand. *An omen?*

Thirty minutes later, and a little more inebriated, he ran into her on the way to the craps tables.

"Hello, pretty lady. I won a hundred bucks. How'd you do at video poker?"

"A whopping ninety-five dollars."

"Let's put it all on the craps table and either win big or lose it all in a single roll and forget it."

"That sounds daring. How does it work?"

"We take a chance on one roll of the dice to build a good stack of chips. If that works, we bet it all on another single roll of the dice. We win it all and split fifty-fifty or walk away empty-handed. Are you game?"

She tilted her head and spoke softly. "I'm game." She interlaced her fingers with his.

They laughed each time they bumped into each other on the way to the cashier's window. Grayson added five dollars to purchase two one-hundred-dollar chips. She took his hand again, and he led her to a table with a lively party, evidence of a hot table with big winners.

At the craps table, the gentleman rolling the dice rolled a seven. The payout man retrieved all the chips from the table.

"Why did he take the chips?" Shannon asked.

"Because the guy rolling the dice threw a seven. That means you lose."

"I don't like to lose."

"Boy, do I know!" Grayson placed all of their chips on the number three.

The pit boss, stick man, and payout man looked at him as if he were crazy.

"I know what I'm doing."

Shannon squeezed his hand. "We're here to win big or give it all away."

The next person in line to roll the dice was an older lady. "Good luck, kids!" She rolled the dice and hit a three. The table erupted in cheers. The payout man took their chips and replaced them with three more.

Shannon looked worried. "I thought we won."

"We did. These are thousand-dollar chips."

"That's good, huh?" She giggled and swayed into Grayson's side.

He instinctively leaned back and put his arm around her waist to keep her from falling. She clung to him and placed her hand on his, sliding it down to her hip, where he left it.

"You said we would bet a second time. What else can we bet on?"

Grayson thought for a second. "Two or twelve."

"What would that give us?"

"With three thousand dollars at thirty to one odds, that would be ninety thousand dollars," the payout man said.

"Ninety...thousand...dollars! Let's do it!" Shannon nervously clapped her hands.

Grayson warned, "We can also lose the three thousand."

Her gaze left no doubt she was in, whatever happened. "I'm still game, one hundred percent. How about you?"

His passions, assisted by too many drinks, loosened his moral constraints, and he pulled her close. "I'm with you all the way, baby. Pick your number."

She turned to the stickman. "Put it on the...twelve...no...no...the two."

The stickman looked at Grayson for assurance.

"Place it all on snake eyes."

With shaking hands, the older lady rolled the dice. When they stopped bouncing on the table, one went straight to a single dot and the other spun on one of its corners for what seemed an eternity. When it finally fell, it revealed another single dot.

"Snake eyes!" The table erupted with cheers and high fives. Shannon jumped up and down shrieking like a teenybopper at a rock concert. She pulled Grayson's neck and gave him a big open-mouthed kiss, their tongues dancing happily.

When the long kiss ended, her eyes spoke her mind. "Let's cash out."

"Are you absolutely sure?"

Her smile and a kiss confirmed her reply.

An employee escorted them to an office to sign paperwork and receive their winnings.

They kissed again in the hallway between their rooms. "Give me twenty minutes then knock on my door."

Grayson nodded. "You got it." He took the quickest shower of his life, brushed his teeth, gargled, and dressed in record time.

He knocked on Shannon's door exactly twenty minutes later. When she opened it, Grayson stopped breathing. Her see-through baby doll jammies would make a Victoria's Secret model blush.

Stepping inside and closing the door, his eyes wide, he could not stop staring. "I've got to take this in." Holding her right hand high, he slowly twirled her, his eyes exploring every square inch of her body. *She's a real redhead and that black dress didn't have any pushup to it. Wow!*

Shannon wrapped herself around him and drew him into a deep kiss, then led him by the hand to her bed.

Chapter 20

Confession Is Good for the Soul

Year 1

The sun assaulted Grayson's eyes, intensifying the deleterious effects of the previous evening's over-indulgence. As consciousness pushed through the haze invading his brain, he sat straight up in bed, a major error. He grabbed his aching temples and moaned. Squinting, he surveyed the room for his cohort in iniquity; a running shower announced her location.

When the throbbing in his head slowed, he noticed the partially opened bathroom door. His brain's synapses fired wildly in every direction. He had made love to a married woman, a woman whom he had despised for years, and for some unknown reason carried a hidden identity. He rubbed his temples again and contemplated his options.

Would he be a jerk if he left unannounced or a wicked voyeur if he entered the lady's private domain unannounced? *What the hell happened here last night?* Speaking to Shannon through the door would make him feel adolescent. With no viable alternative, he floundered around the room holding his head and grabbing his strewn clothes and shoes.

As he bounced around trying to get a foot in his pants leg, he fell back on the bed. The shower turned off. After a few seconds, Shannon called to him, "Will you meet me in the restaurant for breakfast in an hour?"

He was on the verge of declining, when he realized her tone carried a plea.

"Yes, ma'am." He grabbed his clothes and shoes, got his key ready, peeked out the door, and shot across the hallway to his room in his birthday suit. *Grayson Dean, you are an idiot.*

~~~

When he entered the restaurant, Shannon was already sitting quietly at the same isolated table where they shared dinner. Dressed in black jeans and a fitted silk cream sweater, she had a cup of hot coffee and a shy smile. She was nervous, a state she rarely showed. He watched her finish doctoring her coffee and sip at the steaming brew. Underneath the tension, Grayson was sure he saw the look of a satisfied woman, a look that bolstered his ego. He wondered if Shannon detected the same in him and instantly felt the pangs of guilt.

Margaret would be so ashamed of me. My first date, if it could be called that, and it was with a married woman.

He removed his winter jacket and placed it on the back of his chair, ready for a cold January walk to help clear his brain. "Thanks for the coffee. I'm sorry about last—"

She quickly raised her hand.

"Grayson, you have absolutely nothing to be sorry for. But we've added a few more elephants that need to be cleared away."

He downed his coffee and a glass of water and called the waitress for a refill, then sat back and let Shannon have the floor.

"Last night, I didn't hold up my half of our deal. I wasn't totally open about my background. Our parents passed away several years ago. Jillian has always been my best friend, the person I confide in. Larry…is not a talker. He shirks responsibility…is passive, so with my…er…rather assertive…."

Grayson sat quietly and let her work it out. *The great Shannon Fisher is actually nervous and lost for words.*

"Anyway, being honest with you yesterday about my lack of children was quite cathartic. Naturally, Jillian knows…." She glanced up at the waitress.

Grayson waved her away.

"I awoke wondering why I told you things I have never shared with my sister. I believe I was right when I told you it's because I trust you, which is peculiar given our work relationship."

If what we have is a work relationship, I don't want to get on your bad side.

Shannon studied his face and finished quickly. "These are new feelings for me, but I think I like it."

Grayson was at a loss, so he bought some time with silence.

"Damn you, Grayson, say something!"

"I'm having a little trouble with the changes. Lady, there are *two* of you. Maybe more. What's the deal?"

"It's a boring story."

"Try me."

Shannon shook her head.

"Okay; how about this? Twenty-four hours ago, we hated each other." *Crap. Talk about throwing cold water on a hot flame.* "And now, we have a different history, and that's an elephant we definitely need to eliminate."

"Not today."

The irritated waitress returned to the table. "Sorry, folks, we've got a line. Are you going to order?"

Grayson barked an order and handed her a hundred. "Two buffets and bring a carafe of coffee and a pitcher of ice water. Here's a little something for your trouble."

He turned back to Shannon. "Okay. I'm glad *you* felt better, but I don't think it's a good idea for me to become your confidant; although, I might like it." *Where did that come from?*

"That's not what I'm asking of you. For the few minutes we have left, we do need to discuss last night. What happened was wonderful, but it can never happen again."

"You won't get an argument from me, lady. But I feel guilty as hell this morning. I'd like to think that going without making love for so long, combined with the alcohol, made me susceptible to your feminine wiles; but I'd be lying if I said there wasn't more to it. It's confusing."

She nodded, and then spewed words at him in one breath. "Regardless of your stupid right-wing politics, you are the most honorable and…sexiest man I've ever known."

Grayson's mouth fell open and he started to speak, but she cut him off again.

"Please. Let me finish. Last night…." Shannon hesitated and then looked him squarely in the face. "The love you carry for your wife and daughter is a mystery to me, but it's what I long for. There's something exceptional about your ability to work in a job fraught with violence, yet maintain your integrity…and love with such depth. You're an enigma."

"I'm an enigma? You talked to your other self lately?" He picked up the carafe and refreshed her coffee, added a heaping spoon of *Sugar in the Raw* and a tiny splash of cream.

She stared into the cup. "See what I mean?"

"Pouring coffee doesn't make me an enigma."

"We've been *friends* only a few minutes, and you know how I like my coffee. How can I *not* like you?"

"Shannon, I'm a cop. I'm trained to notice things. I appreciate the compliments, but I'm just an ordinary man."

"One thing is for sure; you are not ordinary! You are not a typical dimwitted cop."

Grayson's eyebrows reached for his hairline. "Thanks?"

"Yesterday, I planned to play a trick on a dumb cop. I teased you to make you think you were going to get lucky, intending to send you to your room frustrated."

Grayson shoved back his chair and stood. "Have a good trip home." *I must be bat-shit crazy to have anything to do with this vixen.*

"Wait. Let me finish. I used it as a strategy in college to get guys to stop asking me out. Please sit down."

Grayson sat. "You have one minute."

"Once I learned boys only dated me for sex, I devised a plan to set them up for a fall. It was a sure way to earn a bitch label, and get them to leave me alone. When Larry came along, he never pushed for sex, so I married him. I thought he loved me for more than my chest measurement. Turns out, he's extremely passive, a real mama's boy. All he wanted was someone to look after him."

"So, your plan was to lead the stupid conservative cop on and then dump me, play the high school prick-tease?"

She whispered. "It backfired on me."

Grayson's voice bore malice. "Let me guess. You fell madly in love with me."

"Yes…no…I mean…I honestly don't know what happened last night." She held her head with both hands, elbows on the table. "You don't have a couple of aspirin on you, by any chance?"

"Do I look like a man who carries around aspirin?"

"One thing I know for sure. There's more to Grayson Dean than I could imagine. Your self-control during dinner and in the casino made it clear you found me attractive, but you wouldn't act on it. You are not shallow or stupid, but rather a man to be respected."

"I'm flattered, but your minute's up."

"Oh, shut up and listen! When I left the blackjack table last night, you told me goodnight and didn't pursue me. Your senses of decency and self-restraint aren't the actions of an ordinary man, at least in my experience."

Grayson toyed with his coffee cup, feeling vulnerable and confused, and oddly aroused. *What is wrong with me? The woman is married!*

"I don't honestly know who seduced whom, but I had to tell you what I'd done." She hid her face in her hands.

Cop radar on high alert, Grayson sat quietly and gave her time to gather her thoughts, or courage.

"I *think* I controlled you from the dinner table to the bedroom, but you took over there." Shannon lowered her voice and leaned across the table. "You produced sensations in me I never knew existed."

It was his turn to blush. "Your delightful little screams undoubtedly peaked my performance. You are quite talented yourself. We both lost ourselves in passion."

She looked sadly into her coffee cup. "I'll probably never scream again as long as I live. I want to. But, we…this…can't happen again, and it's sad." Tears threatened to flow.

"Are you baiting me?"

"Just stating facts." The lawyer in her spoke.

Grayson dropped his head. "Honestly, I'm conflicted. Being with you was marvelous but I feel shame for what we did, you being married and all."

"Larry was supposed to come on this trip, but he had unexpected business to deal with. We always take an evening out on the town when we travel and I'd already packed my suitcase when his boss called. I didn't have time to repack. I've never been unfaithful."

"Do I sense an ulterior motive for telling me this?"

"I don't want you to think I take sexy clothing on solo trips to seduce men."

"The thought hadn't crossed my mind." He smiled, looking her up and down. "I think at least some part of you is a good woman. Liberal and weird, but good."

She laughed. "We're certainly on opposite ends of the political spectrum, but there's really nothing strange about the way I dress in court."

"Lady, there is something very strange about it."

"I have fewer social problems and make more money as an unattractive female lawyer. I'm a progressive, a feminist, and I believe women shouldn't be looked upon as sexual objects, but that's not totally the reason for the disguise."

"I'm listening."

"After passing the bar, I took the opposite approach from college. That venture was short-lived, the law firm not taking me seriously. I was one of their token female lawyers, a pretty face to maneuver into bed. They handed me the less-challenging and least-profitable cases. I'm a quick study. To make money you have to get into the courtroom."

"I *guess* I see your point, but you went off the deep end."

She laughed. "When we relocated from Seattle to Houston, I used what I'd learned. Men take less-attractive women more seriously and other women find them less threatening. As Ugly Shannon, the firm I worked for gave me important and lucrative cases, which I won. Respect followed. I maintained the ruse and shifted it into overdrive. I aspired to big-money cases while I paid off my school loans and bought expensive clothes and jewelry, including those diamonds I wore last night. Once I stashed a sizable amount and my legal reputation was solid, I did what I always wanted to do and joined the ACLU to fight for justice for those disenfranchised by society, enhancing my reputation as a very competent..." she grinned and stared into his eyes, "*ugly super-bitch.*"

Grayson blanched.

"The next time you talk about a woman in the court hallway, make sure it's not across from the ladies room."

"I'm sorry. I was blowing off steam and the name fit at the time."

"I laughed, took it as a compliment. I did my job well and made a *dumb cop* angry."

Grayson chuckled. "It's amazing how you camouflage that beautiful face, sexy body, and warm, passionate heart. Your secret is safe with me."

"I know all my secrets are safe with you. Damn you, Grayson."

"Why do you keep damning me?"

"Because you made me like you. We flawlessly meshed last night, and you made me feel like a perfect woman, a new experience for me. It scares me, and I can't get past it." Her voice changed to a whisper. "For a twinkling of time, I was in love."

"Shannon, I wish I could think of something brilliant to say, but I'm stone cold out of ideas and not a little flattered."

She reached across the table and took his hand. "I appreciate you more than you will ever know. We've pushed all but one elephant out of the room, but I have a flight to catch. They say confession is good for the soul, and my soul feels at peace this morning."

She retracted her hand, reached in her bag, and pulled out a tube of red lipstick, the same sexy deep-red from the night before. She blotted her lips on the cloth napkin, leaving a perfect imprint of her mouth, and placed it back on the table.

"Okay...what's the other elephant?"

"Our attraction to each other is palpable. Maybe it's lust, perhaps something else." Her voice dropped almost to a whisper. "Whatever the case, we must push it away and never let it back in. We dissolve it. Now."

He stood with her as she prepared to leave. "Shannon, I don't know where our separate paths will take us, but it would please me to know that you're happy. I hope you and Larry are successful in your quest to have a baby."

She walked around the table, put her arms around his neck, and pulled him down to give him a tight hug and big kiss. "I'm truly sorry about your wife and daughter. An officer I interviewed while looking for dirt on you said they were beautiful and happy, that you were a great husband and father. I saw the intensity of your pain at the cemetery and the encounter with your son. I'm ashamed, too, that I tried to force you to answer that awful question in the Delgado case. It's unforgivable."

Grayson's memory flashed to the funeral. "You were the stranger at the chapel."

"I wanted to honor your family, but I didn't want to intrude. How is your son?"

"Still not talking to me and he has some problems, but he's in good hands. Things will work out for us."

She smiled and walked away.

Still tasting her lips, Grayson sat down and watched her sexy derriere in tight jeans. She knew he was looking, and it pleased him. It didn't make sense, but he hoped she would turn and run back to him. When she disappeared, he felt unbounded loneliness for the second time in his life.

He picked up her napkin and, placing his lips where hers had been, kissed it softly to taste her again, carefully folded it, and put it in his winter jacket pocket.

Islamic State of America - 6

Texas State Prison

Year -4

As they walked with Akeem to an isolated part of the prison yard, Carlos saw the looks of concern on his men and offered their gang sign to indicate all was well.

"I am glad you pledged yesterday to become a warrior for Allah and devote your life to his commands," Akeem said. He studied the tall man before continuing. "First, you have to eject every man from your gang who will not revert to Islam."

Carlos' reaction was quick. "Nah, man. Most of my compadres are in this casa del diablo, a few left in Houston. I ain't giving up my control. Don't worry. They'll do what I say."

"You cannot lead jihad with Allah's soldiers if they are infested with infidels."

"Sure, I can," Murtadha bragged.

Akeem shook his head. "Your gang is a nest of infidels and idolaters, which is the Christian way. If you are to accomplish the important mission we have for you, your followers must submit to Allah, as you have done. Without all of you being pure, you will have no power and cannot say the Shahada."

"What's this mission you talk about? I ain't agreed to no mission."

Akeem glanced at the Mexican gang. "What did you and these men do to get in here?"

Carlos looked at his men and recalled their legal infractions. "Most for drug dealing, some for rape, others for robbing stores or burglary, and a few for assault, like me and Miguel, or murder. Why?"

"I asked so that I can demonstrate the power of Allah, the power you will have if you revert to Islam and follow the Quran. As a Muslim, Allah commands his people to commit those same acts against infidels and apostates, as they do not follow Allah, so they have no value; they are nothing. That is how we make the enemy weak and take his land, his possessions, and his women as our slaves to bear more children to become Muslims. It is the will of Allah and the teaching of Mohammed—peace be upon him. As a Muslim, the revered Imam Omar will make you the leader of many soldiers, and you can do with the infidels as you wish. Allah commands it."

Miguel's eyes widened. "*Hermano*, brother, I want to be a musulmán and have this power."

Carlos stood another moment in silent thought then raised his voice in unbridled anger. "If you and this Omar dude already had a mission for me, why didn't you tell me before now? You're playing with me, asshole, and I don't like that! What's your game, Arab?"

Akeem felt again that he was at the edge of the cliff with this pigheaded man and his vicious temper. It would take a significant shock to drag Carlos away from his small-minded gang mentality. But it must be done so that he could educate the man and bring him to a higher level of rational thought. He breathed deeply and asked Allah to stay his tongue, while he fought to ignore Carlos' personal insults.

"You have been chosen to be the great and powerful leader of all Southwest Province's holy warriors, to conduct jihad against the infidels and return this land to Allah under Sharia."

Carlos' anger turned to laughter. He looked around the yard. "You don't have enough soldiers to conquer a whorehouse." He looked at Miguel. "This Arab plans to conquer this big, powerful country with a handful of men. They dream big, eh Hermano?"

Akeem seethed. Through gritted teeth, he hissed, "Do you want to remain stupid all your life? I know that you can neither read nor write."

Carlos face turned crimson with shame that boiled into anger. Before his clenched fists reached Akeem, Miguel, a big man himself, jumped in front of him and held him back. "Hermano, not now! Listen to this man."

"I play no games with you, Carlos Murtadha. I offer you the opportunity to become a thousand times more than you are now or ever will be without me, and you do nothing but insult me. Either you want to become a leader of many men and prove your worth as a descendant of Mohammed—peace be upon him—or leave this prison to go back to your miserable and insignificant gang life in Houston and remain a nobody."

"Listen to him, Hermano," Miguel begged. "Akeem will teach us to read and write. It doesn't matter which language." Carlos seethed with rage and pushed against Miguel.

Akeem spoke quickly. "You think we are few. What you do not know is that there are over four million Muslims in America ready to support us."

Carlos registered that Miguel had never restrained him from taking action until now. Maybe it was time to listen to his little brother. "Suéltame, *Hermano*, let go of me, brother!"

Seeing the fire in Carlos' eyes diminish, Miguel stepped back to his side.

"*Quatro milliones son muchos*, four million are many. But the gringos are hundreds of millions."

"You must trust me, Carlos. Imam Omar, a holy man and our revered leader, has a secret plan to return America to Allah and make them Islamic states with Sharia for all, as pleases Allah. He is coordinating activities to revert many Mexican brothers for jihad, brothers that you will command. When finished in this hellhole, we will meet Imam Omar in Monterrey, Mexico where he will explain his plan to us. Until then, if you want to learn to read and write, learn about history, mathematics, and science, I will teach you. But only if you truly give yourself to Allah and learn his law, as given to us by his messenger, Mohammed—peace be upon him."

Miguel shocked Carlos. "Hermano, I'm going to become a Muslim and become educated. You do as you wish."

Unaccustomed to Miguel countering his actions, Carlos released himself from his anger to think about what was happening. His thoughts slipped to the spellbinding musical tones of Akeem and his father's prayers. He imagined the peace he would have when Allah gave him the authority to do what he wanted with the despised gringos.

He visualized himself a hero returning the lands stolen by the gringos to Mexico. Intoxicating images of power and control and great glory became a reality. It snaked through his dark, empty soul. He sensed his life begin to take on purpose. As Mohammed's descendant, he would save the world for Allah; for the first time in his life, he would be contented and sleep through every night.

Chapter 21

Parting is Such Sweet Sorrow

Year 1

A few weeks later, Grayson met Chief Ramirez at the Watering Hole to report on the conference in Vegas. "Two Heinekens, barkeep. Bottles. Not cans."

Russell Conrad's hands shook when he took the beers to the men. "Hey, no hard feelings about that there trial thing. Don't want you guys mad at me." Conrad squeaked a shaky laugh.

Grayson's expression didn't change. "Forget it." He ignored Conrad, turned to Ramirez, and handed him a thumb drive. "Thanks for meeting me here, Chief. The soft version of the policy and procedures are on here. I'll give you the paper version as soon as I dig it out of my computer bag." Grayson held his bottle up for a toast.

They clinked bottles. "Always available for you, son. Let's give the report a rest and socialize for a while. You amaze me, remembering I prefer Heineken bottles to cans."

"How could I forget? Remember that *clandestine* trip you arranged for me to Amsterdam to see Margaret? I'd just completed a rough mission, almost bought the farm. You sent me on a military flight as a courier with classified documents to deliver to the U.S. Embassy."

"I remember how you took a big chance to repay me. The penalty for bringing alcohol into an Islamic country is severe."

Grayson grinned. "The C-130 pilot didn't want me to board with the Heineken. so I took it into a bathroom stall in the terminal, packed my clothes around the bottles so they didn't rattle or break, pulled a few *special supplies* from my duffle bag, resealed the case, wrapped it in plain brown paper, and stamped it in red, 'Top Secret Scientific Instruments.' I used my courier credentials to get past airport security in Baghdad. That made it my problem, not the pilot's."

"You've got balls, Grayson."

"The pilot shook his head in disbelief when I arrived back at the C-130 with the *classified* package."

"Sergeant, I've dropped you guys from 20,000 feet over dangerous targets in the middle of the night more times than I can count. Fear weighs heavy on my soul wondering how many of you made it back alive. Bring your *Top Secret* package onboard."

Ramirez's face went dark. "My son was killed by a Taliban sniper a month prior. Your A-team medics delivered the bottles to me packed in a tub of ice. 'For medicinal purposes, sir,' one of them told me. It helped to ease the pain, Grayson, but I never thanked you."

"You've thanked me in more ways than I can ever count, sir."

Ramirez's mood morphed back into a more cheerful state. "I've told that story more than a few times. It'll be better now that I know how you pulled it off."

"You were ready to retire from the Army to become Houston's Chief of Police. I got my reward when you offered to hire me as a detective if I finished my masters."

Ramirez took a hefty draw and ordered two more. "I offered you the job because you were qualified, and I needed you. But what's the real reason you invited me to have a beer tonight?"

Grayson took a long pull before replying. "You told me to relax after the conference and do some thinking. I took your advice and spent a few days roaming around Death Valley, slept under the stars. It helped clear my mind and…well…I've made a decision to go in a different direction. I'm not sure which direction, but I know I can't continue to live in the past."

Ramirez looked over the top of his glasses at Grayson. "You know how decades of dealing with many different personalities gives you a certain feeling when you're not getting the full story? Spit it out, soldier!"

"Well, sir, I had an encounter at the conference that woke me up. In less than a year, I've lost my family, my job, and my trust in myself. I've had my ass kicked. It's time I regained control of my life, become more proactive."

Ramirez smiled. "An encounter, huh?"

"You wouldn't believe me if I told you. Let's save it for another day."

"Where do you go from here?"

"I'll turn in my resignation next week and work at the range while you search for my replacement."

"Mark can take care of the range. Set your timing to suit yourself."

"Sir, there are no words to expresses how much it's meant to me to serve under you in the Army and as a lawman. You've been an outstanding mentor, and I'm beholden to you for life."

"Which I hope will be a long time for both of us."

Grayson nodded. "And, there's something else."

Ramirez released a belly laugh. "There always is *something else* with you."

"Why did you become a prepper and how long have you been one?"

"I've been a prepper since retiring from the Army. When I ran into Mark, we began to talk economics, and one thing led to another."

"How did he get into prepping?"

"Econ professors with analytical expertise like Mark are the frontlines with knowledge of the impending collapse. He's a fount of information. He wanted to recruit me and start a prepper group. We've talked for hours about the future of this country, and I agree that if our economic, political, and societal systems remain as they are, America will succumb to its national debt and fail, all fed by the welfare state."

"Things are tough, but doomsday? Certainly, violence in America and race relations—God knows I've seen too much—but President Crump's economic recovery is off to a good start. I find it hard to believe you buy into the idea that a nation as powerful as America will fold. This country has absorbed many heavy blows and is still strong."

"Once I realized how vulnerable we are, I was onboard. The prepper movement needs capable men like you, Grayson, to step up and prepare to weather the brutal storm headed our way. Heaven help us if we ever elect another socialist like Obama. Those brainwashed progressive bastards will never give up their evil pursuit to convert America into a socialist country, with them as leaders, of course."

"Men like me?" Grayson's face went gray. "Murderers, guilt-ridden failures, hate-mongers, jobless bastards who wallow in alcohol and depression? Oh, yeah, the country needs a platoon of men like Grayson Dean."

Ramirez's anger was palpable. "I thought you were taking control of your life! Patriots, responsible leaders, men of integrity and faith, tactical experts, defenders—men like **you** are exactly what this country needs! This is not post WWII America when patriotism was at an all-time high."

"Yes, sir. But President Crump inherited a monster executive branch. It's bulging with two million employees. Add a million government contract workers, all buried in a thousand departments and agencies and that gives you an idea of the enormity of the problem. He needs time to clear out the excess."

Ramirez shook his head. "The excess is more than you think. The only thing that will prevent the collapse of our economic system is for Crump to eliminate seventy-five percent of the executive branch and turn the social welfare system back to the states, the way it was before President Johnson's so called *Great Society* programs. We both know that's not gonna happen."

"Hadn't thought of that. I doubt Crump has such insight. He's talking a twenty percent cut through attrition, but if you're correct, that's over fifty percent too little."

Ramirez nodded. "You're getting it. The executive branch is an army of bureaucrats fortified with laws that give them the power to regulate almost every aspect of our lives. That allows a president, like Obama, to rule like a king instead of a servant of the people. I agree that Crump is trying to do the right thing, but when the progressives regain power, they will destroy this nation."

"I guess I see why you're a prepper, but how are a bunch of off-the-grid doomsday nuts going to save the world?"

Ramirez, his jaws tight, twirled his bottle on the table a few seconds then focused his laser beam on Grayson. "Don't let me ever hear you say *doomsday nuts* again. You're showing your stupidity and about to get an ass-whupping."

"Yes, sir!"

Ramirez spoke in measured beats. "The world can end in many ways. Each would produce horrific results, but they aren't what keep me awake at night. Economic collapse is a given. Islamic terrorists infiltrating our country and getting a toehold is as threatening. You're a guerrilla fighter. If either of us led the jihadists, we could destroy America's electrical grid and oil refineries with a well-planned and executed guerrilla operation. Those bastards slither in like microscopic bacteria, infecting the native body and killing indiscriminately: babies, children, aged, women, men, you name it."

Grayson ruminated on the chief's prophecy from a previous discussion. "Nuclear war, super volcanoes, electromagnetic pulse, economic collapse, coronal mass ejection, and asteroids are old news, some millions of years old. I'm struggling to see the urgency."

"I was very skeptical, too, the first time Mark approached me. When you talk to Mark, he'll scare your balls hairless. Pay close attention to what he says about the Islamization of Western Civilization. It's already spreading rapidly across Europe." Ramirez slapped the table. "Enough of this crap. What are your plans for the immediate future?"

"It occurred to me when I was lying in my sleeping bag in Death Valley gazing at billions of stars, each with a different story, that my life needs a different story. I've decided to move on, but right now I can't see a fork in the road to take."

"Mama and I will pray for you, son."

"Thanks, Chief. Guess I'd better give you the paper copy of my report and get on home. Got a lot of packing and moving to storage to do tomorrow."

"Damned if I won't miss your ugly face around the office."

~~~

On the way home, Grayson mulled over random elements of his existence. Last year, his life's plan lay neat and clean in front of him. Retire after thirty years on the force, write a book or two, do some consulting, and travel with Margaret once the kids were through college. In less than thirty minutes, almost a year ago, that door permanently slammed shut. His sour mood rode home with him. Damn if he wasn't like Shannon and her multiple personalities!

Less than an hour ago, he was a new man, the chief's hero; now he was navel gazing again. He threw his jacket over a kitchen chair, dumped himself into his recliner, and kicked off his shoes. He needed to relax but his emotions roared in his ears. He slammed his fists into the recliner's arms. "You arrogant prick! Your life is an abyss. Sleeping with the enemy was another bad decision! You're a real winner, Grayson Dean!"

Lust had caught him unprepared in Vegas and traveled home with him. That infamous night repeatedly played in his tortured mind, mixed with abstract images of Margaret staring sadly at him.

Nights gnawed at him. He had to face the ugly truth. He killed his wife and slept with the wife of another man, a woman he still longed for. He had never felt so many opposing emotions in his life.

"Asshole, you have to get in a confessional booth and soon." *I can't go to confession until I'm 100 percent sorry for my sin and no longer want her.*

You never know when a snake will rise to greet you, and your life ain't worth nothing.

Chapter 22

Bug Out To Where?

Year 1

Ramirez led the MAG meetup in the Pledge of Allegiance and gave the opening prayer. "We closed the last meetup with the problem of finding a BOL. If we can't afford to buy a place, we'll have no choice but to start looking for a larger and more lucrative MAG to join."

Nine pairs of disbelieving eyes met his gaze.

"The future of our heirs and our country depends on people like us making the hard decisions."

Grayson looked pensively at Ramirez. *Here goes nothing, but then, what do I have to lose.* "What do you think about me purchasing the farmhouse Joe described last meetup, with a few acres, and the rest of you purchase the remaining land? The undeveloped land would be affordable for you as a group, and we could improve it together over time."

Everyone sat up straight and gave him their undivided attention.

"We're all ears, Grayson," Yolanda said.

"It's no secret my days on the force are numbered. Next month marks the first anniversary of Margaret and Amanda's deaths, and I prefer to resign before then. I've toyed with the idea of finding another job, but I wasn't sure what I wanted. Buying the farm is a good option for me…and for Daniel."

Joe smiled. "Partner, we want you as an integral part of our team, not our sugar daddy."

Grayson smiled. "No sugar daddy here. I pay for my part; you pay for yours. The land without buildings should be affordable to you. I'd like to check out the property, and if it looks doable, I'll purchase the farmhouse, and, say, ten acres to live on. You guys pool your funds and purchase the land around it. I'll be the caretaker, so to speak, and we'll share the cost of developing the whole property into our BOL."

"Where do we start?" Pablo asked.

"I'm not sure. We'll let a lawyer iron out the purchase details. You finance your individual rustic shelters, and we'll work together to obtain the other things over time. Mark, as I understand it, we'll be building a small town from scratch, so a lot will be needed."

"You're on the right track, Grayson."

"Stocking two years of food for each person by itself will cost a fortune," Yolanda said.

Samuel shrugged. "Forget food. The off-grid power and communications systems will eat up most of our money, not to mention a tractor and tools, a water treatment system. I don't want to back out, but I'm not sure a bunch of low-paid cops can pull this off."

Yeung, a chowhound, looked at Samuel. "*You* can forget food, but that tops my list!"

Mark called for quiet. "Do y'all want to continue talking about how we *can't* do this or do you want to figure a way we *can* do it? Developing a BOL piece by piece spread over a couple of years is easy if we apply our own labor to the task."

Embarrassed faces and silence followed until it became too uncomfortable.

"I say 'Hell Yes' to Grayson's proposal!" Samuel ignited an explosion of excitement.

Charles raised his hand. "I'm in. Course, Grayson, we may all be living up there, sleeping on the floor, as our savings dwindle."

Yolanda, ever positive and ready to do her part, added her thoughts. "We'll get our BOL in good shape with some elbow grease. Who knows what tomorrow will bring but with President Crump in office, we should have at least two years, and possibly six, before the progressives can regain a toehold and lead us back to the Obama days."

Yeung gave Grayson the thumbs-up sign. "If I can spread the cost over several years, I'm in. With that much land we can grow and preserve our two-year supply of food without having to get second mortgages on our homes."

Joe worried about Grayson's history of impulsiveness. "You're sure?"

Grayson nodded. "I need a new home and plenty to keep me busy. The farm is a great option."

Yolanda grabbed Grayson in a hug. "Thanks for solving our problem, big guy."

Ramirez quietly watched the scene between friends and coworkers play out. He and Grace exchanged a silent message. They prayed daily that Grayson would find what he truly wanted. Their unofficially adopted son had suffered immeasurable loss and insult and carried broad new emotional scars. They'd watched him carefully as he teetered on a precipice over the past eleven months and prayed he would regain his balance.

"I guess you can count Mama and me in, too."

"You guess?" Grayson asked, incredulous.

Ramirez frowned. "Why don't you take some time to think about this? Let things settle down then come back with a decision."

Eyes rolled, and a low groan rose from the group.

"Chief, settled hasn't been a part of my life for too long. I want a new life, new goals, and a place to belong. You guys are my family now, and this is what I want to do."

"Are you absolutely sure, son?" Miss Grace asked.

"Yes, ma'am." Grayson gave Joe a knowing look. "It seems the answer found me." He turned to the group. "Get busy and figure out how much money you have to spend. Won't do me any good to go shopping if I don't know what's in the purse. I'll ride up to the farm Joe looked at, see what the property offers."

"I'll ride with you," Joe said.

Grayson agreed and Ramirez took the reins.

"Everybody call Grayson and tell him the amount you can add to the kitty. Meet up adjourned."

Chapter 23

The Perfect BOL

Year 2

The first anniversary of the accident had come and gone. Grayson cleared the hurdle but not without the accompanying pain. It still rode high in the back of his mind, but his shoulders relaxed as they passed through the Texas countryside. It had a good feel to it. The friends took pleasure in the break from their chaotic lives. Grayson's new Ford F-250 floated over the newly paved highway and the May weather was perfect, making the drive to check out the farm pleasant.

"I like your new toy, Partner. Looks like you got every option they offered."

"Pretty much. I'm glad to have your company on this trip."

"It's a pleasure riding shotgun with you. It seems a lifetime ago that we patrolled the streets of Houston."

Grayson laughed. "Yeah. The chief wouldn't promote me to detective until I had my time on the streets. Joe, I was amazed that my *best friend* and coworkers were able to keep the MAG a secret from me. Of course, I did the same thing with Margaret when deployed on classified UW missions."

"UW?"

"Unconventional Warfare. You probably know it as guerrilla warfare. Operations security—they call it OPSEC in the Army—will be a vital element in MAG operations. What took you guys so long to invite me into the group?"

Joe stared out the passenger window. "You're right. Guerilla warfare is important."

"You've got something on your mind?"

They rode a few miles before Joe replied. "Since you respect the truth, that's what I'll give you. You can be a hothead. The chief was adamant that you become involved in the MAG, said you were the best special ops guy he knew. But it wasn't until Mark told us your transformation after the incident with Weber that we decided you might be ready."

The way Joe moved his jaw and stared straight ahead in contemplation told Grayson he had more to say.

Joe's voice bore an apology. "We wanted to bring you into the MAG much sooner. You're a great team leader and nobody matches your insights and problem-solving ability, but sometimes your anger gets in the way."

"Like the day I forced Murtadha to smash into Margaret and Amanda."

Joe caught himself just before spitting an annoyed retort. "You know that's not what I meant. Anyway, you're with us now. We really need your help, and I'm not talking about money. Hell, I don't think any of us knew you had two nickels to rub together. We need your leadership and the tactical skills you can teach us to keep our families alive."

"I understand the MAG's reluctance. I also know how far I've come in a short time. So much has happened this year. I've had trouble getting perspective on the future. I don't think I'll ever get past losing Margaret and Amanda," Grayson's voice tightened, "and Danny's rejection of me."

"I wouldn't expect anything different. You and Margaret were each other's better half. It's easy to see how losing her makes you feel like a ship without a rudder. Danny will mature and come around one day. Here's some unsolicited advice: Keep your eyes on the path before you. Looking back will do nothing but cause you to stumble and miss the good things in front of you."

They drove another half hour before Grayson's emotions let him break the silence. "Joe, you lived in other countries in the Air Force. What's your take on America ending up in the dust heap of history, just another scumbag country too miserable to contemplate living in?"

"America is the greatest country on Earth. Too bad most of our citizens don't appreciate what they have. We go about our lives unaware of the misery of billions of people living on the edge of survival, where, if you don't work today, you don't eat today. It terrifies me that my family could end up in that same dung heap."

"One of my greatest feelings is seeing the American shoreline from thirty thousand feet when returning from an extended tour in some soulless land, dog-tired from travel. It gave me energy and hope. Just hours before, my mind locked in a filthy shithole on the other side of the world, hell breaking loose everywhere, the end nowhere in sight, and then America comes into view. It's one of the strangest feelings I ever experienced, like I think entering Heaven will be."

"I agree and hope Mark's right about the remaining ten percent being mostly Christians, the ones who'll rebuild on the base our founding fathers created."

Grayson checked his watch. "We'll be at the BOL in about fifteen minutes."

"Get in the habit of calling it the farm. Our cover story with locals is we're purchasing the farm to grow organic vegetables, raise chemical-free meat, and have a place for hunting and fishing."

Grayson nodded. "Gotcha."

"We've been scrutinizing the area for the past year, traveling within a twenty-mile radius, each visiting different churches, restaurants, etc., to gather Intel. We received warm welcomes everywhere. Low crime rate. Neighborhoods are clean and well kept. It's a great part of the country."

Grayson laughed. "Sounds like a Special Forces operation. Chief Ramirez—the old guerrilla fighter—is still at it!"

"I think you'll like the BOL ideas we drafted before you came onboard. When you see all the features, it will curl your toes. The old couple that owned this property passed away, and their one surviving child doesn't want anything to do it. He's in debt up to his neck, so he needs to grab the money and run. We can get it all—tractors, farm machinery, implements, and livestock. A neighbor is taking care of the animals. It has a huge barn, and the farmhouse is something you see on a picture postcard. It needs minor repairs but is generally in great shape."

"After that build-up, I might make an offer today."

"Grayson, like the chief said, don't be impulsive. And if you don't mind me getting personal, how can you qualify for a mortgage without having a job?"

"You're my best friend, Joe. I don't mind you asking. Margaret and I saved enough over the years to purchase a farm outright, to get back to our roots and all that. With her passing, I received enough from life insurance to be set for life, paid double indemnity for accidents. After taking care of Daniel and Louise, I can still help the MAG survive the collapse. I want to use the money to help others. It's what Margaret would want."

"That's admirable, but you don't have to atone for the accident. It wasn't your fault."

Grayson's gritted his teeth. "Screw you! I'll feel any damn way I want!"

Joe didn't flinch. "It can take two years or more to move forward and accept the unexpected death of a loved one. If you don't drop that baggage you're toting, you'll be stuck in the past forever. Margaret would kick your butt."

Clenched jaws revealed Grayson's agony. "You a shrink now?"

"You're my best friend too. I'm trying to help pull you out of that hog wallow of self-pity you insist on rolling in."

"Is this that tough love shit your wife talks about?"

"Call it what you want. Sit up straight and be a man. Whatever was in the past was then, but this is now. Grayson, you've slipped from being one of the most confident, decisive leaders I've ever known into something I don't recognize, almost a self-pitying wuss. Remain pigheaded, and you'll find yourself forever on the outside of life looking in."

The veins in Grayson's neck distended from Joe's slap in the face and the truth of what he had become. His instinctive reaction was to counterattack, but it's impossible to retaliate against truth—a fool's mission. They drove in silence as Grayson clenched his jaw and fought to rein in his damnable anger.

"Self-pity, huh? How did you put up with me this long?"

Joe bumped Grayson's shoulder with his fist. "You've been an ass at times, but you're coming around."

"Margaret really was my other half. It's as if God sliced the core of my being in half and she took the good half with her to Heaven. How do I get it back and become whole again?"

"As I told you earlier, the answer will find you. Your job is to recognize it when it presents itself."

Grayson silently acknowledged Joe's advice and prayed again for guidance. They rode the last few miles to the farm in peaceful contemplation.

~~~

"Let's explore the property while we wait on the realtor," Grayson said. The two friends walked through the fields to the outer limits of the property, according to the plat they copied from county records. Returning towards the farmhouse, they waved to the real estate agent.

"Joe, let's stop here for a minute. Look around. What do you see?"

"Trees? Fields? Grass? Cows? Chickens? A donkey? A spring? A pond? A dilapidated old windmill? That's about it."

"Look again. From this prominence, the entire farm is visible. We could defend ourselves from here during the die-off with plenty of open space for shelter and excellent fields of fire. Between the fertile pastures and abundance of water, we could produce enough food to live on during and after the die-off and sustain our group indefinitely."

Grayson pointed to the lake at the rear of the farm. "There's food there. I saw fish rising to feed on bugs in the water. The creek running at the back of the property is deep and flows fast, ideal for hydropower. Timber covers the hill on the other side of the creek, giving us all the firewood we'll ever need. I bet it's loaded with deer and other game for meat. The elevation is high with plenty of wind to pump water, once we replace the old windmill. We can add wind turbines for power."

Joe chuckled. "From Mark's instructions, I noticed a few tactical advantages, but nothing like the scope you see."

"Where we're standing is the highest point with a good place for the rustic cabins we need to survive the die-off. We could easily arrange them in a defensive configuration to counter attacks. There's another big security advantage. Look on the map when we get back to the truck. The farm is on the inside of a huge curve in the Trinity River, a natural barrier that will help divert refugees and bad guys, providing us with additional security."

All Joe could say was, "Wow!"

They walked toward the farmhouse and Joe asked, "Have you thought of a cover story? He's bound to ask."

"I'll tell him the truth, for the most part. We want to produce our own organic food as well as hunt and fish for chemical-free meat. I'm a recent widower in need of a new home and change in my life."

"You're a smart man, Grayson."

"I appreciate your faith in me, Joe, but you're smart *and* wise. I can't thank you enough for the support you've given me during this terrible time. But you could back off the kicks to the seat of my pants a little." He clapped Joe on the back. "Let's go buy a farm."

~~~

Back home, Grayson settled deep in his recliner, his favorite place to talk to Margaret. "Hi, baby. I love you and miss you. What do you think of the farm? We both know my atonement bill is huge. Buying the farmhouse is a good way to give back. We can help Danny and others to survive so they can rebuild New America. I went from dirt-poor farmer to Green Beret to street cop to detective, and now full circle back to farmer—although not a dirt-poor farmer. I guess it'll catch up with me, but I'm not feeling it yet."

Islamic State of America - 7

Texas State Prison

Year -4

Murtadha heard his name from a distance and jerked away when someone grabbed his arm. "Carlos, are you okay?" Miguel asked.

"Suéltame, Hermano, let go of me, brother!" He stared at his younger brother who had just told him he would be a musulmán with or without him. Akeem's black eyes examined him. He flexed his powerful shoulders.

"I'm fine, *hermanito*, little brother. I was just thinking ahead to when I will be a powerful soldier for Allah." He spoke to Akeem with respect. "I will work hard to become a musulmán. I will talk to my men to follow me and become musulmán."

Akeem's cold eyes swept over the tall Mexican and glanced at his gang. "Once they step over the line, there will be no return to their past life. The same goes for you. Do you understand?"

"You said that already. What's the big deal if one of my men wants to go back to where he was before?"

"The Quran forbids it. Any Muslim who leaves Islam must die. If **you** go back, I will personally remove your head, very slowly as ordered by Allah in the Quran."

"Don't worry about me. I ain't gonna go back. I'm ready to be a musulmán."

Akeem turned his attention to Miguel for confirmation of his personal commitment. "Tell me, Miguel, do you think of Americans as your brothers?"

"If you mean the gringos, I hate them."

"Hate is a strong word. Why do you hate these Americans?"

Miguel slid his eyes to Carlos, still committed to his older brother's confirmation.

From his peripheral vision, Akeem saw a barely discernable nod from Carlos.

Miguel dropped his head to avoid eye contact with Akeem and spoke barely above a whisper. "Gringos that don't like women came often to Nuevo Laredo. When we were little boys, they tricked me and Carlos with food...." He fought his dry mouth to swallow, as a deep flush lit his face. "The hijos de putas made us do bad things before they would feed us."

When Miguel raised his head, the hate embedded in his face froze the blood in Akeem's veins. Miguel's venom-filled words hung heavily on the air. "I want to kill them all!"

Akeem thought better of explaining Bacha bāzī, boy play, a custom Western culture despised. Muslim men had enjoyed sex with adolescent boys for centuries, a customary and acceptable practice not considered homosexuality if the man did not love the boy.

Akeem spoke carefully to the brothers. "Mind my words. As you will see when we meet with Imam Omar in Monterrey, Mexico, you will be an important jihadi leader. Talk with your men. Let them know that the power of Islam can also be theirs. Tell them we will conquer the Western World and they will have much land and many wives as Muslims, but misery and death are their fates as infidels."

"Me and Miguel are ready to become musulmán. It's up to my men if they want to join us. I'll tell them about Islam the same as you told me. They ain't got no Muslim father like me and Miguel. Give me a few days to find those who want to revert."

"Be patient with your men and don't force them. To be pure, they must accept Islam within themselves. I will leave recruiting to you and not intervene. That will cause them to bond closer to you and accept your leadership."

"Let us meet in the library every day to study. I will teach you about Islam, to speak and write Arabic, and many other important things. I will teach all who revert, but you and Miguel, I will teach much more. You will be superior."

Carlos stood taller. He remembered Akeem's insults from the previous day and shook them off. He realized the man was right. He could remain stupid and return to being a miserable gangbanger with no direction when he got out. However, the thought of being educated and controlling men with his mind instead of his fists had seduced him past the point of resistance. He closed his eyes and released himself to the evil of Islam, sealing his fate for all eternity.

Chapter 24

Farmer Grayson

Year 2

Grayson yelled into his cell phone, "Damnit, Joe! If you were here, I'd kick your ass."

"You gone completely loco only six months out? What's wrong?"

"I was okay until I fell through the shower floor. You SOB! You told me the house needed only minor repairs."

Joe exploded with laughter. "You didn't damage the family jewels, did you?"

Grayson chuckled. "I'm fine, a few scratches, nothing major. Better than the house. The shower in the master bathroom has been leaking for years. The floor joists are completely rotted away."

"I can come up this weekend and help you patch it up."

"I'm just ribbing you, Joe. I found a good carpenter, Wayne Clauss. He's about my age and lives down the road. He'll have it repaired in no time. He's an interesting fellow, teaches English at the local high school, but prefers to work with his hands, owns a small construction company on the side."

"Whew! You had me going there for a minute."

"I really called to give you some Intel to pass on to the group. Wayne, and just about everyone else I've met here, are preppers to one degree or another. They feared what was going on with Obama, and even with Crump appearing to turn things around, they're worried the liberals and establishment Republicans will not allow him to turn things around. Two farms over, there's a guy who's been off-grid for the past five years, and there're a few more like him scattered around the local countryside. Quite a few have more guns and ammo than you could imagine and a store of canned food."

Joe's voice became tinted with anger and somewhat accusatory. "Grayson…you didn't discuss our MAG or the BOL did you?"

"Hell no! I was wearing a sleeveless tee shirt and he saw my paratrooper tattoo. He wanted to know about it. Once he discovered that I was Special Forces, he started discussing his prepper group with me. It's one of those open groups. Anyway, he invited me to their next meetup."

"What did you tell him?"

"I told him I wasn't interested in that doomsday stuff. But, Joe, I'd like to go to their meetup and become acquainted with some of the locals. I left the door open by telling him that I'd think about it. I wanted to discuss it with the MAG, see if everyone's okay with it."

Joe's voice didn't soften. "I don't know, man. That's a double-edged sword."

"I understand, but if the farmers around here are as prepped as they appear to be, and have a survivalist's mentality, we'll need their help with our own protection."

Joe remained silent.

"Trust me, Joe. A basic principle of guerrilla warfare calls for gaining the trust and support of the local community."

"I'll pass this on to the others and let you know. I'm not so sure they'll be happy with it, Grayson."

"Tell the chief this is a UW mission waiting for the right guidance. He'll understand. If he nixes it, I'll continue to pretend I don't believe in it and let Wayne think of me as a sheeple, naïve enough to believe the government will take care of everyone."

"What else are you up to?" Joe asked.

"I tilled the compost into the garden and it's ready for spring planting. Yolanda wasn't impressed with the size of our first garden. I need another year to expand and build the soil to meet our full survival needs. You guys get your butts up here next weekend to dodge cow pies and sweat with me."

Joe relaxed. "Will do. It should be a fun time even if hard work is involved. Some thick rib eyes, baked taters, and a number ten washtub filled with beer and ice will make it easier to get everyone up there."

"You got it."

"Sounds like you're adapting to your new lifestyle."

"It's taking some getting used to, but I'm enjoying the physical labor, helps me sleep. The quiet nights away from the city are great for reducing stress. The air is clean and the living is easy, as the old song says."

"We'll be up there in a few days to breathe some of that fresh air, but I can't sing worth a damn." The two friends hung up laughing.

Chapter 25

The Second Spring Planting

Year 3

Grayson toiled diligently all winter to expand the small, starter garden into the three acres Yolanda ordered, ready to plant by April. Everyone arrived eager to get the job done before the weather turned hot. While others planted seeds, Grayson parked the tractor and used a hoe to uproot clumps of grass the plow missed. He was close enough to hear the group's conversations but kept his distance.

Yolanda was elated. "Three acres of well-built soil makes a big difference. We'll need a ton of canning supplies this year."

Mark used a broken broom handle to make holes in the dirt, drop a corn seed in each, and cover them over with his foot. "Got to hand it to the first men who came to this part of Texas. They used hay-burners and muscle power for their main farming tools."

"Don't forget the women worked just as hard as the men…you male chauvinist pig!" Yolanda loved to give her man humorous jive—kept him on his toes.

Her feigned sarcasm caught Grayson in the throat. Amanda, as only a little girl can, used the same tone when sparring with Daniel, a tone no male can emulate. He was glad to have the team at the farm, but he didn't feel like talking.

Mark attempted to recover. "You're right, sweetie. The women actually worked harder. As they say, a man works from sun to sun, but a woman's work is never done."

Charles laughed. "Nice recovery, Mark. Give her a couple of beers, grovel some more, and she may allow you to sleep in the bed instead of on the sofa tonight."

Laughter covered the field but Grayson only managed a smile. He'd fought all day to keep his anger and grief at bay. Not understanding his reticence, the group left him alone.

"Isn't three acres a bit much?" Yeung asked. "What'll we do with the excess, and why so many varieties of everything? Who the heck eats kale, collards, and rutabagas?"

As usual, everyone waited for Mark to answer, but Grayson let it slide. "We're growing varieties to ensure they don't go extinct after the collapse. Whether we eat them or not, the locals do, making good barter items. We'll can a ton of them to survive the non-growing season and share with our neighbors if needed during the die-off. A big garden gives us extra seeds to share, so others can establish gardens and keep them from raiding ours."

Yeung made an ugly face. "Barter sounds better than eating these disgusting things."

"Cut the chatter and wrap this up," Grayson said, his voice flat. "By now, the chief and Miss Grace will have the steaks marinated for the grill and the potatoes baked."

"And cold beer to wet our whistles," Charles added.

Grayson looked at the ground. "Don't over-indulge. We have serious business to discuss at the meetup."

Mark whispered to Yolanda, "What's going on with Grayson?"

~~~

"That was a fine dinner, Chief and Miss Grace." Samuel patted his protruding stomach.

The group gave a round of applause.

"Thanks, troops. Let's get down to business so we can get back to Houston before midnight. Mama and I appreciate you young'uns letting us do the inside work. We wouldn't last long in that heat, but don't let anyone in Houston know I said that."

Grayson realized with a jolt that his mentor had aged a lot in the last few years, no doubt due in large part to his own stupidity. He took the last sip of tea in his glass to hide his sudden rush of feelings, the same feelings he had for his own father before he passed ten years earlier.

"Leave the dishes where they are. I'll take care of them after everyone leaves. Refresh your drinks, and let's get on with the meetup. No alcohol for drivers."

Joe gave Grayson a dead stare. "You receive bad news, Grayson?"

"No. But we've got a lot to cover."

"For a minute I thought I had detention."

The others looked at each other, unsure of what was happening.

They quietly moved to the living room, and Ramirez took the floor. "Grayson, we appreciate what you've done over the past year to provide us with this great bugout location. Yolanda, you've done an excellent job organizing our garden and supervising the planting."

Yolanda tried to soothe Grayson with praise. "Thanks go to Grayson for his hard work to get the field ready to plant. With all his other responsibilities, it was nothing short of a miracle."

Grayson nodded at her, but his sour expression didn't change.

"Grayson, you've been here well over a year," Ramirez said. "Bring us up to date on what you've put in place."

Grayson spoke tersely. "I'm no super-farmer, hired some of the work. I used the dozer to push a dam up below the big spring and stocked the new pond with a variety of fish; they're thriving. The new windmill is doing its job and the water is as pure as it comes. The pond water treatment system, our backup water supply, is complete and under budget. I've ordered a five-hundred-gallon water storage tank to place on the high point where we'll build our cabins. That'll make it easier to plumb to them. I replaced the old bull and added nine cows and three bottle-fed calves. We have—"

Yeung interrupted. "Why only one bull?"

Charles grinned. "Imagine two big dumb fellows fighting over the same girl, because she'll only mate with the one that beats the other to a pulp."

"So we'll need one rooster."

"Charles, you explain the facts of life to Yeung," Samuel said.

"I'm a city boy. How should I know?" Laughter spread around the somber Grayson.

"And that explains why your dating life is at an all-time low," Samuel said.

Grayson's brusque response killed the mood. "You have one rooster per about ten hens. An overly aggressive rooster that continually fights with the others goes in the frying pan."

"We need a big frying pan for Grayson," Mark whispered to Yolanda.

Grayson caught what he said and his anger bubbled.

"Wouldn't pay to be an alpha rooster around this farm." Samuel drew laughs.

"Why bottle-fed calves?" Mark asked.

"Makes them tame and easier to milk later on."

Grayson, looking funereal, returned to business. "The chicken and rabbit coops are completed, and a couple of neighbors are providing breeding stock next week."

Samuel asked, "Wouldn't some goats be good for milk?"

"Goats are a pain to deal with," Grayson clipped. "Sheep may be better. Research it everybody, and we'll decide at next month's meetup."

"I saw a donkey in the pasture. What's its purpose?" asked Charles.

Grayson sighed. "Donkeys are territorial. They protect calves by killing coyotes, and they're much louder than dogs when sounding the alarm if strangers or wild animals come into the area."

"We have plenty of sheds for the animals and plan to begin our individual cabins next month. Do you have plans for other buildings?" Mark asked.

Grayson's skin mottled. He rubbed the back of his neck and charged through a litany of information with no time for questions.

"I'm designing a large underground concrete storage space with a sizable two-story lodge above it, large enough for community meals, meetups, etc., and extra living quarters, if needed. The below-ground area will be cool and dry for storing our guns, ammo, two-year food supply, etc. It'll have space for a small medical facility, communications center, and a tactical operations center."

"Won't the locals question the underground storage?" Joe shrank back when Grayson turned his cold eyes on him.

"I've contacted a Waco company about building it. The local contractors won't have a clue that it exists."

"They'll notice all the heavy-duty equipment coming in," Charles said.

"I'm doing what I think is best, Charles. You got a better idea?" Eyes shot to the floor and a heavy silence filled the room.

Yeung was tiring of Grayson's attitude. "I thought this was supposed to be a team effort. Aren't we all part of the decision-making process?" He looked around the room for confirmation. Receiving none, his voice fell, "Maybe I misunderstood...."

"If someone asks," Grayson said, "I plan to say it's a tornado shelter and a root cellar to store my vegetables and smoked winter meats," Grayson said.

"I think you mean, **our** vegetables and meats," Pablo said.

"If anybody's unhappy with what I'm doing, just say the word." Grayson glared around the room. "Or better yet, spend more time up here working and you'll know what's going on."

Ramirez stood. "Let's take a short break. I need to hit the can."

Ramirez found Grayson pacing in the backyard. "You want to tell me what crawled up your butt? Or do you prefer to be rude until your temper gets the best of you?"

"I've worked my ass off for these guys, and all they do is criticize. They plant a few seeds and think they're gonna save the world!"

"If I remember correctly—and I'm sure I do—you volunteered to do this. If you needed help, why didn't you ask? Leading a team at the BOL is the same as leading a team in Afghanistan. The other members must first know what's needed before they can help. Look, son, you've had something stuck in your craw since we got here. Spit it out."

Grayson turned his head away and stared into the distant night. "Got a lot on my mind."

"Maybe being alone isn't good for you. Take a vacation. We can take turns coming up here for a week at a time and keep things going."

"Let's get this meetup over with." Grayson walked away.

Ramirez called the brooding group to order again. "Let's talk about the cabin locations that Mark and Yeung have been planning. Who wants to go first?"

Charles raised his hand. "Since we agreed at the last meetup to stick to rustic, single-room, two-by-four framing, plywood walls and floors, and metal roofs, the structures will be simple to construct. I'm ready to build mine."

Grayson, his sour mood discernable, intervened. "If we go about this piecemeal, it'll be a rat screw."

Pablo's face turned red. "Rat screw or not, we have an agreement and a plan. I'm ready to build, same as Charles."

Joe headed off an explosion. "Grayson is correct, and so are you, Pablo. We all want to get on with building our cabins, but we'll have a better chance of success and make it easier on everyone if we do it as a group project."

Mark picked up immediately. "Good thinking. Yeung, you're our Sea Bee guy. Can you bring a list of materials and tools we need and give us a cost estimate for each cabin ready for the next meetup?"

"Actually, since we decided to have individual shelters for each family, I've already prepared my own list of materials and a simple drawing. I can email the plans to everyone. If we buy in bulk, we get a discount at the building supply company. I'll be glad to manage that."

Ramirez jumped in. "All in favor say 'aye'."

All responded except Grayson, his face emotionless. Nobody said a word to him.

Yolanda spoke to Ramirez. "I've been rethinking the plan. It's too rustic for those of us with, or hoping for, children." She smiled at Mark. "A small log cabin with several rooms would be better."

"That *would* be more comfortable," Ramirez said. "Remember, we're an organic gardeners and hunting and fishing club in the eyes of the locals. We must make the BOL look authentic for those purposes."

Mark pulled her close. "When the poop hits the fan, we only have to survive a few months to get through the die-off. After that, with only about ten percent of the population alive, we'll have plenty of abandoned farms to occupy or open land on which to build our house."

"Okay. But I want to paint the outside pink and wallpaper the rooms."

Mark looked to Joe and sighed.

"Got you!"

When the laughter died, Charles asked. "Won't we be vulnerable to ground attack with bullets flying through the plywood walls?"

"Already thought of that," Mark interjected. "The cabins will be in a circle and the windows high on the walls. When the collapse occurs, and before the situation becomes critical, we'll use the dozer to push a berm up against each cabin's out-facing walls and the excavator to dig a deep, wide trench around it with a retractable footbridge. We have pallets of sandbags in the barn to shore up any place that needs it. That allows us to shoot out while still being well protected from incoming bullets. It's not possible to eliminate all incoming fire, but once attackers get a taste of what we send their way, they'll get the hint to not mess with us."

"Lots of good points," Ramirez said. "There's still a lot of prepping left to do, including completing the two-year food supply. The new solar and wind power station is adequate, but we need to add hydro and gasifiers for the gasoline generators and the old Ford tractors. It wouldn't hurt to do the same for our sixty-eight Ford if it's to be a functioning BOL vehicle when refineries no longer produce gas." He looked at Grayson. "Did I overlook anything?"

"We need more hand tools, enough to last a lifetime. We're still missing expertise in numerous areas, including medical and communications. The dual band, UHF/VHF radio repeater, small solar panel, and battery power setup are ready for our local area communications. Long distance shortwave radio is still a problem."

"What else is in the communications plan?" Charles asked.

Grayson's reply stung. "If you'd take time to read the BOL plan you'd know. When the collapse occurs, I'll place the solar-powered repeater at the top of the tall cell phone tower to the south. Other major projects pending include digging trenches to run the telephone wires between the buildings."

Charles ignored Grayson's insolence. "What happens to the repeater if we experience an EMP?"

Ramirez grinned. "Charles, you are officially the MAG worrier, but ask good questions. Grayson, it's apparent that we need to schedule a few folks at a time to come help you with these major tasks. Let's keep our eyes open for a good ham radio operator, somebody who knows more than just how to turn on a handheld radio."

Charles ignored Grayson. "I have a strong potential recruit, but still vetting him."

Grayson resumed his briefing. "We'll keep the repeaters—three so far—and the other survival electronics equipment in the below-ground Faraday cage that will be built into the lodge. We'll bring out a portion of the equipment, keeping spares secure until after EMP attacks are no longer a threat. You need to keep your personal handheld and mobile radios at home in your portable Faraday bags. How many of you purchased BaoFeng handheld radios with extra battery and chargers?"

Everyone raised their hand.

"How many of you have the ham license that allows you to use them legally?"

All hands but Mark's dropped.

"Study for the damn ham licenses and don't forget to bring your radios for the fall BOL activation exercise," Grayson barked. "You'll need them, especially for night patrols."

Yolanda broke the tension. "The chief and Mark are drilling us with tactical training and map reading in Davy Crockett National Forest."

"That'll help tremendously come fall. Everyone go on Google Earth and become thoroughly familiar with this area.

"I need a ten-minute break before going into the last order of business. It's very important, and we need to be fresh."

Islamic State of America - 8

Texas State Prison

Year -4

Under Akeem's watchful eyes, Carlos recruited fourteen of his men and placed them on the path to reversion. Akeem was impressed with his success and reported it to Imam Omar through his prison administrator brother. It was time for his initial discussion with the group.

Akeem greeted each with enthusiasm and, speaking softly, began his first lesson. "The first thing you must understand is that you were born Muslim." He knew they would question his assertion, but it got their attention.

He held up his Quran and pointed to it. "The Prophet Mohammed—peace be upon him—said, 'No babe is born but upon *Fitra*, which means as a Muslim. It is his parents who make him a Jew or a Christian or a Polytheist.' If you are willing, I will lead you to revert to Islam."

"My men are ready." They acknowledged Carlos' assertion with their gang sign.

Akeem looked stern and pointed his right index finger high into the air. "This is the only sign you must make. It is to honor Allah. One day, Allah will rule all of America and Mexico. Carlos will be your leader and you his deputies with men of your own to command. *Insha' Allah*, god willing. Everything the infidels have, their property and their women, will be yours for the taking."

"What's 'for the taking'?" Marco asked.

Akeem was glad to explain. "You will have the power to kill unbelievers, take their possessions, and make their women and children your slaves. You can do with them as you wish; they will be your property. Allah declares it. You can take up to four wives, even females as young as nine years old, as did Mohammed—peace be upon him—and as many concubines as you want. Allah gives you the authority. To earn that authority, you **must** first give yourself to Allah, say the Shahada, and follow the teachings of Mohammed—peace be upon him—and the hadiths, which I will explain later."

"I see you with your holy book and know it's the Quran. But what is this other thing you speak of?" Carlos asked.

"The Hadith is the record of the traditions and aphorisms of the Prophet Mohammed—peace be upon him—and is a foremost basis of Sharia and moral guidance, second only to the Quran."

Marco didn't understand. "We read and write a little Spanish and some a little English. We ain't educated in the university like you."

"Do not worry. While we are in this infidel hellhole, I will teach you to speak and write Arabic, about Islam, and our history, other things too. Work hard and do well, and I will take you to Egypt with me. There you will become immersed in the language and learn to be a holy warrior for Allah."

The thought of becoming educated and having the respect it would give them drew interest from all the men, Carlos in particular. "We study much hard." His men replied with great enthusiasm, pointing upward with their right index finger.

Akeem scanned his new apprentices, looking intently at each for a fraction of a second. His emotionless face caused some to pull back. "Are you afraid to die?"

Carlos cocked his head and looked around. "We ain't afraid a nothing!"

"That is good. After completing your training in Egypt, we will send you to Africa to lead other Mexican Muslims to fight infidels and establish Sharia. *Insha' Allah*. There, many of you will remain for years and gain much combat experience. You will become brave warriors. Any man who dies bravely in battle against infidels and apostates will go to Paradise, and Allah will give him seventy-two virgins."

A crooked grin lit Miguel's face. "Seventy-two virgins will be all mine?"

Akeem lowered his voice. "Yes. If you die a brave man. But, **Hell** is yours if you die a coward, running from the enemy of Allah."

Sticking out his chest and patting his brother on the back, Carlos bragged, "Miguel and me will die brave men and have many virgins."

Chapter 26

Guerrilla Warfare Ain't Easy

Year 3

Grayson scanned each face before throwing gasoline on a lit fire. "I'm going to suggest an OPSEC change of direction. I believe we need to open the MAG to the local militia, the SET Patriots."

His remark met a cold reception and not a few negative remarks. "Calm down! This is for discussion only—decision later."

Once they settled, Grayson explained. "So far, today we've talked about water, food, shelter, and communications, but not security. I have a proposal that I'd like you to consider. We are short on members and long on ideas. Many preppers are in this area and are open about it. Everyone is scared of what's coming. That presents us with the potential to add to our security force by expanding our operation into the local community."

Samuel, the cynic, jumped to his feet. "You've got to be kidding! We don't need anybody else in the MAG! The BOL can provide well for *our* needs. Taking on others, we stand to lose everything we've worked to achieve. Our families might end up refugees starving to death on some stupid roadside or shot by bad guys."

Yeung, his voice shaking with anger added, "I'm sorry, Grayson, but I agree with Samuel. We need to keep our operation a secret. What the hell good does it do if everybody knows why we're here? What would keep them from overtaking us and stealing everything?"

Mark agreed. "The thought bothers us, too. But Yolanda and I are willing to listen to your ideas. You're living here and getting to know these people. And you haven't steered us wrong so far."

Samuel was spitting mad. "It's stupid! Plain stupid! We would open ourselves to being overrun right away!"

Grayson prickled with anger. He was many things, but stupid was not one of them. *Let go of your ego and explain so this egghead can understand.*

"Samuel, calm down." Charles said. "Grayson brought it up for *discussion*. Give him the courtesy of listening. Nothing has changed."

Samuel hurled himself back into his chair and glared at Grayson.

"Correct me if I'm wrong, but at my first MAG meetup you talked about needing to grow the group, get other skill sets on board, court locals. What happened to that concept? Where are these members with the expertise we're missing?"

"We're working on it," Charles said.

Grayson sighed. "Working on it? For how long? I look around and they aren't here. Let's be honest, it will take years to find all the reliable preppers in Houston with the skills we need who would join us out here."

Dead silence met Grayson's remarks. *I don't know if I embarrassed them or pissed them off.*

Grayson started over. "Pablo, you haven't said anything. What are your thoughts?"

"Mixed, to be honest. Outside of police operations, you and the chief have knowledge and insight in the security arena that we don't—that guerrilla warfare stuff you told me about when you were a Green Beret. I'd like to think we can trust the locals to work with us, but like Samuel, I fear they would become desperate and overrun us. A man with a starving family doesn't have a conscience."

Joe nodded with each statement Pablo made.

Grayson briefed Ramirez earlier and he concentrated on the objections. Pablo opened the door for him.

"Pablo, you're right. What happened to trusting each other? Grayson and I have years of experience working with indigenous guerrilla bands and a damn good idea where our strengths and weaknesses are. Low numbers are a big security problem with no prospect for rectifying it. Charles, didn't you mention an electrician prepper you were vetting? What's his potential?"

"Sorry. He didn't work out. He's a boozer."

"Grayson is checking out the locals to see if they might be a good fit with our MAG," Ramirez said. "Here's the bottom line: No clandestine operation, which is what we are, remains secret permanently. The enemy eventually discovers your existence. If we are to survive, we must have the support of the local community. That's one of the primary concepts of guerrilla warfare. Without it, you're dead. Period."

"Then why the hell did we develop a cover story?" Samuel asked.

Ramirez spoke calmly. "It was a starting point and, as with all organizations, policies change to meet changing situations. Remember, we were going to bug-in initially to survive through the die-off. From what we know now, we'd have joined the dead in the die-off. We can strive to keep our operation a secret, but what happens when hundreds of desperate refugees or bad guys show up at two o'clock in the morning? Without community support, we and our families are dead."

Grayson tried again. "If we organize the locals to form a militia cadre—"

"Another new word. Damned if I don't need to get a notebook and start a list. What's a cat ray?" Charles asked.

Grayson spelled cadre and explained, "It's a specially trained group. We, as well-trained militia members, could lead untrained armed civilians and supervise their security activities, patrolling, guard posts, crowd control, etc. If we start now, we have time to get them ready for the collapse."

"What kind of training? I don't know how to train people," Samuel groused.

Samuel's whining and Grayson's patience slammed into a wall. "Damn it! Everyone step up to the table or this won't work! I never built a water treatment system, but I did it. Read a manual, research on line, but don't sit on your asses and wait for somebody else to figure it out for you!" Embarrassed eyes hit the floor again.

In the charged silence, Ramirez took control. "Grayson may not have been eloquent with his admonition, but he is correct. We've grown dependent on him living here and doing everything. To survive in the collapse, each of us must be able to take action and figure things out, just as our ancestors did."

The look he gave Grayson over the top of his glasses told Grayson what he must do.

"Look folks…Samuel…I'm sorry for being so blunt when a softer word was called for." He sighed heavily. "The locals have men and women with military experience, and plumbers, electricians, and other skills we can't survive without in the long term. By working with them, we limit the number of people we have to prepare for at the BOL. When we consider our spouses, kids, in-laws, etc., we could easily overextend our resources and become unsustainable."

Ramirez momentarily lost patience. "You need to examine yourselves carefully and make a firm decision to be in or out of the MAG. This is not a weekend camping trip. It's serious business. Take some time and evaluate your commitment to go forward."

Samuel flinched. "Chief, I don't think anyone wants out. Things are going in a different direction than when we started. I, for one, need time to digest this."

"How can we feed all those folks, so that they don't turn on us?" Yeung asked. "My great grandmother told me what happened in China under Mao. From 1959 to 1961, the famine killed forty-five million people. You wouldn't believe some of the things they ate!"

"Why do y'all assume these people won't have enough food?" Grayson sounded exhausted. "They're almost all farmers and ranchers, many of them preppers. Canning and curing meat are a routine part of their lives. Initially, we'll have to help them develop their food storage systems. We may even need to get food from them later."

Pablo spoke up. "My parents and I fled Venezuela as refugees when I was a kid. I returned to visit relatives a few months ago. I couldn't believe the number of people starving and the level of violence under their socialist dictator. Each of their generals now has a Cuban handler. It helped me visualize what the die-off might be like." He shivered. "It's too scary to think about. I believe we definitely need to work with locals to give us a better chance of survival, and we can do the same for them. It's starting to make more sense to me."

"What about lazy locals that aren't preppers, those who won't help produce food? Suppose they look at us as their food stamp program?" Charles asked.

Grayson's answered without hesitation. "Second Thessalonians, 3:10. 'For even when we were with you, we gave you this rule: If a man will not work, then neither shall he eat.'"

Mark whispered to Yolanda, "Something major is wrong with Grayson."

"If the locals are disorganized and unfriendly, their help certainly won't be forthcoming. If we remain secretive and things get tough for them, they may see us as a threat and be inclined to attack rather than ignore us. When the collapse occurs, everyone will be scared witless. I believe in sharing talents and skills to promote a convivial, cooperative atmosphere. We need their help with our security, and they need our guidance on how to prepare to survive."

Reality spread quietly through the room. Prepping as a faraway concept was one thing; prepping for an encroaching event was sobering.

"What the chief and Grayson are saying is beginning to make sense," Yolanda said.

"I agree," Joe added.

Grayson took a deep breath and reached out. "Samuel, you're right to be concerned. We need your help to make the right decision."

"I don't want to be an ass about this, Grayson. But I don't want to be everyone's savior, either."

Ramirez closed the meet up. "Okay, crew. Let's chew on this awhile. Study your Special Forces manuals for details on covert and overt operations. That will help you understand the concepts of working with locals to assist with our operations."

As everyone stood to leave, Mark addressed the elephant in the room. "Grayson, you look like you've lost your best friend. Are you okay with our decision for now? You've been out of sorts today."

Suddenly everyone noticed Grayson's drawn face, his eyes shadowed in gray.

"I know I've been difficult today. Tomorrow is the third anniversary of Margaret and Amanda's deaths."

"Oh, Grayson, I plain forgot. I'm so sorry," Mark said.

Grayson spoke softly. "It's like yesterday for me."

Grace, who'd been taking the minutes, moved to Grayson and gave him a hug, tears rolling down her cheeks.

"Forgive us, son."

"It weighs heavy. I'm going to Houston tomorrow to visit them. I just hurt all over."

Charles offered a prayer, and Grayson nodded approval.

"Please bow your heads. Most gracious Heavenly Father, You bring to us birth; Your providence guides our lives; You command us to return to dust. Lord God, those who pass from this Earth still live in Your glorious presence, We pray to You for our friend, Grayson, that You will give him peace in his time of sorrow, in the knowledge that You will unite him at a time of Your choosing with his loving wife and daughter. Amen."

"Amen."

Chapter 27

Talk To Me

Year 3

Grayson stopped by a florist on the way to the cemetery. When he arrived, the shadow of the abandoned chapel extended to the east across countless and long-forgotten graves. He stared at the ancient structure, its state of disrepair a reflection of his own miserable existence. He placed the vase of pink flowers at the base of the headstone and sat on the ground, staring at the names and dates of two people he loved with all his heart.

He closed his eyes, reliving happy family scenes, but it was a short reprieve before ugly images intruded, his grief and guilt consuming him. His throat closing, he labored to suppress his anguish.

"Hi, baby, and how's my little angel? I miss you both so much. I think of you every day and miss you in everything I do. Little Angel, I read *Goodnight Moon* last night and thought of you. I keep it on my bedside table at the farm. I'm going to talk to mommy awhile. You play with Jo-Jo."

Tears dripped on his shirt. "Sweetheart, I'm in pain. Guilt eats at me for what I did to you and our precious Amanda. She'll never share girl secrets with her best friend, feel her heart race with her first kiss, walk down the aisle, or know the wonder of motherhood. I robbed you of the joy of being a grandmother." He patted the grass.

"Everyone tells me to move on with my life, but how can I pretend everything is okay? Guilt vexes, draining me every day. Is it bad that I wish to be with you and Amanda? How I need you to tell me what to do."

Choked with grief, Grayson looked to the darkening sky and screamed, "God, please let her talk to me!" His voice echoed off the old chapel's moss-covered stone walls.

A sudden surge of strong wind replaced the gentle breeze, almost knocking him over. He flinched when the chapel's ancient bell began a gentle ring, pulling him toward it.

He jiggled the rusty latch open and exerted considerable pull on the door. The strong wind pushed back as if to say, "You're not allowed to enter." With a powerful heave, he wrenched the heavy oak door wide.

The fading light barely illuminated the obsolete contents. He stepped inside, and the wind slammed the door shut, howling its objection to his presence. Grayson brushed cobwebs aside to find dusty, empty pews. The stained-glass windows, dulled with time, filtered light, reflecting the chapel's lost significance.

The bell continued its beckoning toll, but Grayson hesitated. *Probably a kid trying to scare me.*

He stepped quietly to the faded white door, his tracks prominent in the dust of the forgotten floor. The rusty hinges creaking, he twisted the knob and pushed the door open quickly. The wild winds subsided; the bell stilled; and the frayed bell-pull lay on the floor in a dust-covered heap.

The setting sun reflected dully from the bell above his head, creating a halo around the bronze rim. A profound calmness cloaked him in warmth. He closed his eyes and felt Margaret's near to him.

While retracing his steps to her gravesite, a sentient peace touched him and he realized one day he would be with her in God's Kingdom and his grief would melt away. A warm, soft breeze caressed his face. He knelt and prayed for his misplaced family and thanked God for sending Margaret to him.

Chapter 28

The Blind Date

Year 3

Grayson sweated profusely under an unusually warm late August midday sun while replacing a broken fencepost. From the dust trail on the road, he knew he was about to have company.

Wayne drove up and got out of his truck. "Hey, Farmer Grayson, haven't seen you in a coon's age."

"Good to see you, Wayne." Grayson slipped off his leather glove to shake hands. "It's been a while. We need to grab a beer and grill a steak soon."

"Funny you should say that. I'm having some folks over this evening for a cookout. Hoped you'd join us."

"I'd love to, but one of my cows is going to drop her calf any time, and I can't abandon her baby to the coyotes. A pack has been hanging around lately, at least the ones I haven't introduced to my three-oh-eight."

"You might want to change your mind. There's a pretty widow lady coming; you two might hit it off. It's been over a year since her husband died. She recently decided it's time to get on with her life."

Grayson hesitated. *Would this be a date?*

"Please don't feel obliged, but I happen to know she's noticed you. She sat in front of you last Sunday at Sacred Heart."

A flicker of the pretty woman who turned to offer him the Sign of Peace put a smile on his face. Her pleasant look of surprise when they shook hands, her smile and the widening of pretty eyes were responses he'd experienced from more than a few ladies. He followed her to receive communion, yet it didn't register with him to strike up a conversation after Mass. Being single still felt new to him. There was something uncomfortable about approaching an unfamiliar woman, with the intent of potential romance being the outcome.

He remembered the woman's smile, the way she placed her left hand on top of his when they shook hands, and the intensity of her eyes. He casually dismissed her, the same way he did with all women since his encounter with Shannon.

"I remember her. I was glad I went to eleven o'clock Mass that morning and not my usual Saturday evening vigil, Beautiful smile."

Wayne's permanent smile turned into a grin. "There's more to her than her looks. She has great personality attributes that you'll appreciate. I can vouch for her character, absolutely, without doubt."

"Absolutely, without doubt, huh?"

The grin on Wayne's face broadened. "She's my sister."

Grayson's eyebrows rose and his voice took on a tone of interest. "What's her name?"

"Laura. Laura MacIntyre."

Grayson shrugged. "Dang. It's the heifer's first calf, and as you can see, it's coming late in the year. I guess I could check on her before I leave and spend a few hours socializing with y'all. Besides, I'm tired of my own cooking. What time should I be there?"

"Wise decision. We'll get started about six. With the sun low on the horizon, it'll be cool and the evening breeze will do away with the mosquitoes."

"Look forward to it. I'll see you at six."

~~~

While Grayson dressed for the cookout, he vacillated between schoolboy eagerness and fear tightening his throat. He would make sure tonight was different from the iniquitous one-night stand with Shannon. He had no real dating experience, and meeting Wayne's sister felt like something more than a casual encounter. A twinge of betrayal to Margaret stared back at him from the mirror. Meeting a woman that he might want to date or make a life with evoked apprehension he'd never faced as a young man. He wasn't sure he wanted to face it now.

"Margaret, I feel silly going on a date. I don't mind meeting a nice lady, and I know I'm supposed to move on, but you're my number one gal. There are times when I'm tired of eating alone, reading alone, and talking to myself, but dating.... I don't suppose you could send me a sign of some kind, tell me what to do?"

Grayson's nervous hands fumbled his cologne and the sprayer dislodged, dousing him in Margaret's favorite fragrance for him. "I get the message. Be polite and nice and get my ass back home."

After another quick shower so he wouldn't smother Wayne's sister in "smell good," he hurriedly dressed and headed to the cookout.

Stepping out of his freshly cleaned, red Ford F-250, Grayson felt confident sporting his best cowboy shirt, new jeans, and shined cowboy boots. He followed the sounds of happy chatter to the patio at the back of Wayne's home.

He spotted Laura at once. She looked lovely in a mid-thigh length, white cotton sundress sprinkled with small yellow roses and her Texas cowgirl boots. A bit of cleavage peeked from her modestly cut dress. Her long, natural blonde soft curls lay over her shoulders, creating the perfect picture of a Texas beauty any man would be proud to call his own. She was at the grill flipping steaks with one hand while holding a cold bottle of brew with the other.

A half-grown German Shepherd ran up to him with a stick in her mouth, tail wagging energetically, begging Grayson to play. He threw the stick as far as he could, and the dog tore up turf running after it.

"Grayson!" Wayne greeted him. "Glad you could make it. You know my wife Hellen. The other members of my family are Abner, Josephine, and Troy. I believe you met Laura at church."

Everyone focused on Grayson and Laura, anticipating the first awkward steps between boy and girl.

"Not formally. It's a pleasure to meet you, Laura." His heart pounded hard when she turned in his direction. Feigning confidence, he strutted over to shake her hand. He felt his masculinity stir, an involuntary primal reaction, when he connected with her flashing gray-green eyes. It pleased and disturbed him. He sensed her similar reaction from the little blush shadowing her face.

"The pleasure's mine, Grayson. How do you want your steak?" She asked in a deep Texas twang.

"Medium rare, more on the rare side, is my favorite."

"Yep, Wayne. He's a genuine Texan all right." The tenseness left Grayson when everyone laughed.

The German Shepherd puppy ran up with the stick in her mouth. Again, he threw it for her.

Grayson took a deep breath as he bent to the washtub. The hard part was over. He liked these people and felt a twinge of guilt about watching them with a cautious eye. *You may like them, bucko, but these people may be the MAG's best ally or worst enemy after the collapse.*

He joined comfortably in the conversation about crops and weather predictions, questions about growing organic vegetables versus using chemicals. They were curious about the hunting camp and his cover story for leaving Houston. He was pleased he could answer their questions about growing fruits and vegetables and killing garden pests without chemicals. *Remind me to thank Yolanda.*

The puppy wouldn't let Grayson alone. He enjoyed throwing the stick and petting her. Worn down and panting hard, she finally settled beside him.

Wayne was fascinated with the puppy's reaction. "Millie's taken quite a liking to you, neighbor. Do you have a dog?"

"No. I guess I should get one though. It would help keep the coyotes away. Millie's a nice name, and she's a beautiful puppy."

"She's the last of a litter, all yours if you want her. Does nothing around here but trip people."

"I'd love to have her, Wayne. That's very kind of you."

"Every man needs a dog, and if you noticed, *she* selected you."

Once the sun moved low in the sky, he apologized and explained he had to check on the impending birth, a situation they all understood.

"My steak was perfection," Grayson said. "I don't know how I managed it, but I filled my plate twice with grilled corn and fantastic biscuits. Once I get organized, I'll have y'all over."

Laura walked him to his truck with Millie in trail.

Grayson found Laura easy to talk to, a pleasure to look at, and she had a head full of sense. Somewhere in the back of his lawman's mind, he detected a well-educated lady. At his pickup, he cleared his throat until it was raw and finally got up the nerve. "Laura, maybe we could go to dinner sometime…if…ah…you're interested."

"I would like that." Laura handed him a piece of paper with her phone number. "Call me Saturday morning."

Grayson eyed the paper for a moment. *She's interested in me.* "Let me check on things at the farm, and I'll get back to you...Saturday morning."

"That's quite a pick-up line you've got there, cowboy." She smiled in the dusky evening.

"I'm a real charmer." A Harrison Ford grin grew on his face.

Grayson lifted Millie into the passenger seat and said bye. The grin remained plastered on his face all the way to the farm. The calf hadn't been born, but something had.

Chapter 29

Could She Be The One?

Year 3

Grayson pulled into Laura's long driveway. The house was a modest ranch in a neighborhood of homes with a couple of acres each. Walking towards her house, he was startled when an aged, half-bald man came out of the house next door pointing a 12-gauge shotgun at him.

"What are you doing over there?"

Grayson automatically reached for his 1911 .45 ACP, but he'd left it at home to prevent scaring Laura on their first date.

Laura opened a window and shouted. "It's okay, Mr. Becker! This is my friend, Grayson."

"Okay, Laura." Becker lowered his shotgun. "We're sort of protective of Miss Laura since she lost her husband."

"No problem, Mr. Becker." He was miffed the old man got the drop on him, but put on his best manners. "My name is Grayson Dean. I recently purchased the Smith place."

Becker placed the 12-gauge on his porch, walked briskly over to Grayson, and offered his hand. "Sorry for the shotgun, but you can't be too careful these days."

"I understand." They shook hands. "I'm sure Laura appreciates you looking out for her."

Mr. Becker lowered his voice. "Actually, she can outshoot me, but I can't help myself. Laura is like a daughter to us. If this were a few years earlier, I'd want to know where you're going, what you're doing, and what time you're returning."

"Sir, we're going to the Round Up to have dinner and do a little dancing, then to a movie. I'll have her home by midnight."

"None of that close and up-tight dancing, and you'll have her home by eleven, young feller."

"Yes, sir."

Their laughter lingered as Laura exited her front door and locked it behind her. A small boy, wearing pajamas and flip-flops, held her hand. "Grayson, this is my son, Austin. He's four."

Grayson took the shy little boy's hand offered him. "Hi, Austin. It's nice to meet you."

Austin looked wide-eyed and open-mouthed at the big man. "Are you my daddy?"

Grayson looked to Laura and she picked up the boy.

"No, sweetie. This is Mommy's friend. Now, go with Mr. Becker. I'll come over in the morning and get you."

She put him down and the old man took Austin's hand. "You kids have fun. Austin enjoys spending the night with us when Laura is on call at the hospital."

Under Becker's watchful eye, Grayson offered his arm and escorted Laura to his pickup. He opened the door and held her hand, as she stepped on the running board and up into his big pickup truck.

"Well, you're a gentleman, and that's a good thing. Take care and have her home before eleven. I don't want to have to come looking for you, boy!" Becker's gruff tone threw in a chuckle.

"Sir, I don't want you to come looking for me with that 12-gauge."

"Earnest Becker! Get yorself over here with the boy and leave them young'uns alone."

"I'm coming, Bertha," he grumbled. "See y'all later. Nice to meet you, Mr. Dean"

"Same here, Mr. Becker. Please call me Grayson."

Grayson and Laura drove out of sight before cracking up. "I told Mr. Becker about our date this afternoon. He knew who you were. An old Vietnam War veteran, he's seriously protective of Austin and me, but he also loves pulling practical jokes. That rusty old shotgun hasn't worked for years and wouldn't fire if loaded."

"Well, I guess Mr. Becker just made me an accepted member of the community."

~~~

The Round Up was the special type of restaurant rarely found outside the Lone Star State. They always offer steaks or barbeque and have a dance floor with a live Western band. It'd been a long time since Grayson entered one on a date with Margaret.

Grayson and Laura started their date on a fun note thanks to Mr. Becker, but once seated at the table, Grayson couldn't think of much to say. Laura stumbled to keep the conversation going. He refused to discuss Margaret, Amanda, or Daniel. She didn't offer any information about her marriage or dead husband. An old couple, also not talking, watched them. *Probably think we're an uncommunicative married couple, too.*

They both managed to drop their napkins on the floor and food in their laps. After Grayson asked her the third time if her steak was tender, she turned to concentrate on the people dancing.

Grayson decided it would go down in history as the most boring date ever and spread through the community with him as the butt of the joke. How in the hell had he dealt with Shannon Fisher in such an unflappable way and couldn't put ten words into a decent sentence with Laura?

As their silence grew too obvious, Grayson asked her if she knew how to do the Texas two-step.

"Do dairy cows give milk?" Laura shot back and blushed. "I mean yes. Do you?"

Grayson stood to take her hand and led her to the dance floor. He kept a respectable separation between them and danced like a robot. It was obvious she wasn't enjoying herself.

Laura checked her watch for the tenth time and noted it was time for the movie. They engaged in forgettable, stop-and-go chitchat over the half-hour drive. At the theater, he made an awkward attempt to let Laura select the movie, but she deferred to him. *Good planning, jackass.*

He selected a movie he guessed she might like. Ten minutes in, it was apparent his choice was a sappy attempt at a love story.

Laura leaned over. "Would you mind if we leave?"

"Are you okay?"

"Yes, it's—"

Somebody behind shushed them, and they slipped out.

Laura began laughing the minute they were in the lobby. "I'm sorry."

"Whew. That was hard to watch. What do you say to coffee?"

"I'd love a cup."

On the way, he asked about Austin.

"Sorry about his reaction. Mack was a big man like you, and you sort of look like him in a picture Austin has on his nightstand. He doesn't really remember him, so that photo is all he's got."

"Austin's a good-looking boy, sort of reminds me of my son, Daniel, when he was little." *But don't ask me any questions about him.*

It was almost midnight when they pulled into Laura's driveway. The easy conversation over coffee was gone and Grayson was back to edgy. "Laura, uh…I've enjoyed this evening with you and…." He stopped in midsentence and expelled a deep and long belly laugh.

"What the heck's so funny?"

"Me. I'm funny. Well, not *funny funny*."

"Okay?" She looked at him curiously.

"Laura, Margaret was the only girl I ever dated. We were together from kindergarten. This evening, I've been as nervous as a school boy on his first date."

Laura nodded. "Mack was the only man in my life, beginning with when I first took an interest in boys. You and I are like a couple of old fashioned sixteen-year-olds."

"Yeah. It sort of feels good in a way."

Grayson added a little tease with the deep voice of a narrator. "The boy's heart throbbed. He had never kissed a girl before. What should he do? Will she slap him if he tries? What will she do if he misses her lips and kisses her nose or accidently touches those bumps on her chest? How do you kiss anyway?"

"Does he like me?" Laura spoke in a girly voice. "Is my hair okay? He hates my hair. He hates me. Gosh, I hope he kisses me. I don't know how to kiss but maybe he does. I just hope he doesn't squeeze me and make me fart." She caught Grayson by surprise and he choked.

"Too much?" She laughed.

"Perfect end to a perfect evening."

Grayson walked around and opened her door. He lifted her from the cab by her waist and placed her gently on the ground. They walked to her door holding hands. She took her keys from her purse and was about to unlock the door when he put his hands on her shoulders and turned her towards him.

"He does know how, and he won't squeeze you too tight." She wrapped her arms around his neck, and they shared a short kiss, then a longer kiss. Taking time for a breath and a lingering, penetrating look, they wrapped their arms around each other and kissed passionately.

Grayson's thoughts rushed to the error he made in Vegas. "It feels good to hold you, Laura, perhaps too good. Couples relate differently today than they did several generations ago. What is taking place right now is as old fashioned and wholesomely Americana as it gets. The fellow walks his date to the door and gets a goodnight kiss. It feels good, but it needs to remain at the front door, at least for now. Is that too corny?"

"Considering that we're not a couple of kids, it's perfect, Grayson. Today's ethical standards and, honestly, our base natural instincts encourage me to invite you in and let the devil take tomorrow. You likely agree…and don't deny it, cowboy. You're holding me too tightly against you not to notice. But we both know it's not the right thing to do."

He took her keys and opened the door. "Let's keep this evening one to remember."

They kissed again before she entered and closed the door. He waited until she locked it before getting into his pickup and driving away.

Sitting in their swing on their dark porch and wrapped together in a warm blanket, Bertha and Ernest Becker held hands and smiled.

Islamic State of America - 9

Texas State Prison

Year -4

When Akeem arrived for his daily session, Murtadha was bragging about killing the infidels and getting his seventy-two virgins by dying bravely in battle. "...and when me and my men kill the infidels, they'll go to El Diablo, and everyone will know us as brave warriors who fight for Allah."

He addressed his men with the wrath of a god. "Leave now if you are afraid to die. I'll not have cowards for soldiers." Every man held his place, heads high as an indication of their resolve.

Akeem greeted the men and asked if there were any questions from the previous instruction.

"I understand who the infidels are you talk about," Marco said, "but who are the apostles?"

Marco was the one man in the group Akeem wasn't sure he trusted. "The word is 'apostates', not apostles, like the weak men who followed the prophet, Jesus." Akeem spoke with hardened disgust.

The men stared at him with blank faces.

"Understand, we are Sunni Muslims. We are Pure. Shiia are the apostates, the same as the unbelievers—the infidels—and must be eradicated. Allah commands it."

Carlos was confused and wondered how to ask his question without sounding stupid. He took a sidetrack. "Is Mohammed the same for both?"

"There was only one Mohammed," Akeem said then went into detail about the differences in Sunnis and Shiites. His effort ended in more confusion. He changed directions to avoid losing them. "As you can see, there is much to learn."

To regain his footing, he asked, "What are you thinking now?"

Miguel shook his head. "An imam is a Sunni holy man, but what is a caliph?"

"A caliph is a special imam, selected from a council of imams. He is the head civil and religious ruler of an Islamic state, which we call a *caliphate*. It can be a very large area of land."

"You mean like Texas?" Miguel asked.

Akeem stroked his long beard. "Yes, but it can also be larger."

Marco remained confused. "Akeem. I thought all Muslims were the same."

Carlos intervened. "Don't get too deep into it right away, hombres. Let Akeem teach us as he sees fit. We got *mucho tiempo*, much time. We will learn."

Marco started to say something but Carlos' glare cowed him into silence. Carlos was as confused as Marco, but he wanted to get to the killing of infidels and his seventy-two virgins.

Akeem gave Carlos a look of approval and decided to keep an eye on Marco by retaining him in Carlos' cell instead of giving him one of his own to lead. A decision he would come to regret.

☪ ☪ ☪

The jihadist recruits sat on the prison yard ground. Akeem's ploy to bring the group together in a cohesive bond was proving successful. "Did you know that we—you and I—all share the same blood?" Akeem asked.

Carlos and Miguel knew their connection. What was Akeem doing now?

"You are from Egypt; we are from Mexico. How can we share the same blood?" one of the men asked.

Akeem directed a question at the man. "You have Spanish blood, right?"

"We all do. Indian blood, too."

"Our Muslim brothers, the Moors, ruled Spain almost three hundred years from 711 to 997. During the Crusades, the Christians murdered the Moors they couldn't drive back to Africa and the Middle East. Ah. But our Moor brothers left their Muslim blood in Spanish children. You are sons of the Moors, and the Moors are descendants of my Egyptian ancestors. That, my brothers, means you and I share the same bloodline through our Spanish heritage."

Nods of understanding showed all around. The men were beginning to gain a sense of unity they'd never known in their gang affiliation.

"Those who live through combat will be soldiers for Allah. You will return to America, brave warriors, to make ready for the time to cut off the heads of the infidels and implement Sharia, the law that pleases Allah. Carlos will be your leader, and each who proves himself a worthy leader will be his deputy, with cells of your own."

"How will we know when it's time?" asked Marco.

"That is something to learn when we meet with Imam Omar." He wasn't privy to Imam Omar's Master Plan, but they did not need to know. Akeem described the training while in prison and how they would meet in Monterrey, Mexico to travel to Egypt for jihadi training, then to Africa to conduct holy war.

When their session was over, Akeem met with Carlos alone. "This man, Marco, who asks many questions, I am uneasy about him."

Murtadha shrugged. "That's the way Marco hangs. He asks more questions in an hour than most men in a year."

"He is trustworthy?"

"Mean as a toro. He never fails me. Always does what I tell him."

Akeem's hooded black eyes scraped over Carlos' face. "I trust you are correct. Tell me, brother, what are your thoughts now that you understand better about Islam?"

I would kiss a burro's *ano,* anus, rather than lose the chance to become educated and the most important man in Mexico. Traveling thousands of miles to learn about my new life and meet others who think and live as you do excite me."

Carlos had not told Akeem, but he was gradually memorizing the prayers as Akeem chanted them. Islam was taking him beyond anything he had ever dreamed. Woe be unto the infidels and apostates.

Chapter 30

Guess Who's Getting Married?

Year 4

Grayson relaxed in his recliner with two fingers of Maker's Mark in a crystal whiskey glass. A newly lit fire pushed a January chill from his man cave and the bourbon warmed his bones. Many evenings, he watched the sun slide behind the horizon through his bay window. Today's vista painted a soft blue-green background with orange and red hues reflecting off the bottoms of huge puffy white clouds.

He sipped his whiskey and contemplated the unopened letter from Louise. He worried about her health. She was more fragile since her heart attack the previous year. The unexpected call from the hospital put him in a panic that night, but the doctor assured him the bypass operation went well. She would recover well with proper care. but would need to slow down for a while. Grayson arranged for home health care and cardio rehab for her.

He hoped she wasn't writing about more of Daniel's drinking too much and crashing cars. He admired his son's determination to work his way through the University of Texas, but he wished Daniel would make things easier on himself and accept money from his trust fund. He and his son had one major thing in common: They were bullheaded.

Grayson pulled the single sheet of paper from the envelope, and a photo of a grinning Daniel with a beautiful young woman at his side dropped into his lap. His heart skipped at the sight of his grown son. He wished Louise was computer literate and sent frequent photos. Happy to see Daniel smiling, Grayson felt a glitch of sadness. Daniel's boyhood was over, important years lost to them both. The woman in the photo held the back of her left hand close to the camera to highlight an engagement ring. His son was getting married.

He looked forward to newsy reports from Louise. Her handwriting had grown spidery, and, as always, her lack of education unfolded in a charming way.

Dear Nefew,

I got some grate news fer you. Danny is engajed to be married to a wonderfull girl. Her name is Wanda and she is exactly what you and Margaret would want fer him. Ive been holding off telling you about her until I was sure she wasnt one of them silly girls he dated fer a short time. If you no what I mean. Hes a fine young man after all. Shes a Texas country gal from Comanche County and as smart as a whip. Never seen a girl with such common cents. Shes as pretty as a piture postcard, respectful, and likes to listen to Rush. The boy picked a girl just like his ma. Danny is sure head over heels with her. She takes care of my garden now that my heart wont let me do it no more and cans vegtables and makes jams fer me. She talks Danny into going on them backpacker walks and she shoots guns like Annie Oakley. Like you already no Danny finished hi school a year ahead an hes takin extry college class to finish it a year ahead to. Him and Wanda is gonna marry as soon as they graduate. She takes extry classes to finish early to. They go to church regular and aint said nothing to me but I thank theyre waiting to marry before they get into bed together. More likely than not its her idea not his. That's just so you no. They show me their reports and make reel good grades. Youd be proud of them. Wanda reads yor letters and Danny don't care that she does *but he wont read them. Hes stubburn like that. Just like you. I'll send you more on their doings in a couple of weaks.*

Love always,

Louise

Grayson laid back in his recliner, staring at Daniel's photo. Tears of joy and sadness pooled behind tired eyes. He considered calling Louise but dropped the idea. He'd heard Daniel in the background angrily disowning him enough to last a lifetime. She didn't need added stress or another heart attack. Daniel loved his great aunt and was attentive to her, a good thing for both of them.

~~~

While taking a sip of bourbon, Grayson's cellphone rang. It was Laura.

"Hi, sweetie."

Grayson's antenna went up. "What's up, baby?" He hadn't called her for several weeks and didn't know why.

"I miss you and can't get you out of my mind. How was your day?"

The tone in her voice told him he needed to get his act together. They'd been dating at least once a week ever since they met. His father's words sprang to mind: The worst thing a man can do to a woman is ignore her. His father also said it's okay, and sometimes prudent, to tell a little white lie.

"Sorry I haven't called. I've been a little under the weather, a cold, and didn't want you to catch it. I'm about back to normal now."

"You're full of it, Grayson! I have plenty of homemade chicken soup in the freezer. I'll be there in thirty minutes. You're going to eat every last bit, mister, and tell me what's really going on."

His father didn't always hit the nail on the head.

Grayson finished the last spoonful of chicken soup while he avoided conversation with Laura. "Great soup. Think I'll get sick more often."

Laura's eyes twinkled as she studied him.

"Okay. I don't have an excuse for not calling. Guess I've been too distracted, what with repairing chicken and rabbit coops, dealing with calves dropping all over the place, and this." He handed her the photo. "My son is getting married, and I'll miss it, just as I've missed everything else in his life since he was sixteen."

Laura looked quizzically at him.

Grayson's cheeks grew warm. "Oh. You don't know the whole story." He closed his eyes and his head dropped back.

"Grayson! What's wrong?"

"The short story: Against good judgement, I pushed a high-speed chase to catch a bad guy. He crashed into my wife's car, killing her and my daughter. My son blames me and has shunned me ever since; he hates me."

Laura sucked in her breath. "Grayson…that's terrible."

She took his hands. "I don't know how to help you. I can't imagine Austin and me separated. It would kill me." She regretted her words the moment they escaped her mouth.

His guilty conscience stabbed him. He understood her reaction.

"I'm sorry, Grayson. I didn't mea—"

"It's okay. Maybe I should force Daniel to see me."

"I don't know your son, but wouldn't that drive him further away?"

"I don't believe that's possible."

She made an attempt to remove the gloom that was choking the life from him. "Why don't we get away like a couple of young fools, head up to Vegas, recharge our batteries?"

"Why in the world would you want to go to Sin City?"

"It's Disney World for adults. I love going there."

"Never really liked it." Images of Shannon flickered before him.

A wonderful lady is sitting by my side and I'm thinking about the forbidden fruit. Daniel's right. I'm an egotistical jerk.

He offered an alternative. "Let's grab a flight to San Francisco."

Laura's smile told him they were back on solid ground.

Chapter 31

The SET Patriots

Year 4

Grayson's donkey, Jack, brayed a warning as Wayne walked to the chicken coop. "Glad to see you know to spread chicken feed so the alpha hens don't steal all the food." Wayne grinned. "Not bad for a city boy."

"Good morning." Grayson patted Jack affectionately and gave him a handful of chicken feed to quieten him. "I grew up on a farm. You know the old saying: You can take the boy from the country—"

"…but you can't take the country from the boy. I'm impressed," Wayne finished.

"You mentioned on the phone you wanted to discuss your doomsday group. What's up?"

"Laura told me about your time in the Army. I researched Special Forces and learned, my friend, that you have the answers to questions we've wrangled over for years. Thought I'd invite you again to a meetup. I'm not pressuring you to join, but if you'd clarify some things, maybe point us in the right direction, I'd really appreciate it."

Man, your timing is perfect.

Samuel had finally gotten past most of his objections to combine forces with the SET Patriots. At their last meetup, they asked Grayson to explore the feasibility of a merger. He needed to walk carefully, as his feigned reluctance to get involved could backfire once Wayne knew what the so-called hunting/farming camp really was. *I don't want to lie but I don't see a way around it.*

"You know, Wayne, I appreciate your invitation, but I watched a couple of shows on National Geographic about doomsday groups, and those folks don't have a clue what they're doing."

"That's exactly why we need help. You have the expertise to teach us the right way to do things. We know our plans need adjusting, but we don't know how to start."

"Tell me what you see as the problems before I jump in here."

"Great. You got time to talk now?"

An hour later, Grayson agreed to attend their meetup.

"You have no idea how much I appreciate this. We're having barbeque afterward. You'll like the cook."

"Is *she* one of your doomsday folks?"

"We have several women preppers. Laura is our medical person. Also, just so you know, the term doomsday has negative connotations for preppers."

"Good to know. Don't want to start on the wrong foot. So Laura's the nurse for your group."

Wayne slapped his hat against his leg. "I'm glad you didn't say that to her. Laura's a doctor and mighty proud of it. She has a family practice in town and pulls emergency calls at the hospital."

"Holy cow!"

"Next time you need a prostate exam, make an appointment."

"Get the hell out of here!" Grayson laughed. "I'll see you Saturday."

Wayne seemed locked on Laura being more than Grayson's regular Saturday night date. *Hopefully, our relationship will help with merging the two groups*

~~~

The 1911 .45 ACP strapped to Laura's left thigh and the skintight camo pants hugging her backside caught Grayson's full attention. The SET Patriots all wore camouflage uniforms and had exact models of M4 carbines and 1911 .45 ACPs, except one man with an old double-barrel 12-gauge.

"Those uniform pants aren't regulation, soldier!" Grayson's drill sergeant voice cut the air.

Laura spun, face pink. "Well, cowboy, your eyes are in good shape. Where's *your* uniform and is your *pistol* ready for action?"

A loud hoot erupted around them. *The woman can be direct and sharp. I like it.* He gave her a quick hug and kiss on the cheek. Almost everyone smiled as Laura made introductions; however, lack of eye-to-eye contact and weak handshakes from the sixteen members told Grayson some were less than enthusiastic to have him at their meetup.

Wayne placed the U.S. flag on a stand in a prominent position. Everyone stood and said the Pledge of Allegiance. Laura followed with a prayer.

Wayne took the floor. "This meetup of the Southeast Texas Patriots is open for business. Our special guest, Grayson Dean, has years of training and experience as a Green Beret and a Houston police detective.

I believe he can answer many of our questions to prepare for the poop hitting the fan."

Grayson cringed at the applause. He wished Wayne had kept things in a lower key. He didn't like duping good people. He'd lectured himself to keep his MAG's OPSEC firmly in mind at the meetup. He felt better knowing Ramirez and Mark approved his presentation outline.

"I asked Grayson to open with an overview of the main security considerations to protect our families and farms during a societal collapse. It's all yours, neighbor."

Grayson stood. The first thing he spotted was the suspicious glares from three men sitting in the back. "Thank you, Wayne. I'm not into doomsday prepping and—"

"We don't use the term doomsday." Laura's tongue was razorblade sharp, eliciting a frown from Wayne.

"Thanks for the reminder." *Be on your toes with this woman.* "In my Internet research, I was surprised to discover that millions of folks are preppers, but I'm sure that's not news to y'all."

"It isn't," Laura said flatly.

The man with the old 12-gauge agreed. "That's right, city boy."

"I'm sorry. I don't remember your name."

"Ahm Elmer Martel Bryant, and ah reckon you autta know up front, ah ain't got no use fer outsiders, specially city boys." The other two dissenters nodded agreement.

Wayne looked back. "You had your say, Elmer Martel. Keep your mouth shut, or I'll fire your asses. I don't care if you are my cousins. Sorry, Grayson. I should've warned you that a few Patriots aren't imbued with even the lowest social graces."

Never one to ignore a challenge and needing to refocus everyone's attention, Grayson— wearing the same emotionless face as when he had Taliban terrorists' heads in his crosshairs, ready to squeeze the trigger— spoke firmly. "Elmer Martel, I appreciate knowing where I stand with any man. Speak up anytime you have a question or comment."

Elmer Martel stiffened. His eyes widened. Grayson slowly looked over the crowd and stopped on Laura. She smiled oh so sweetly. *Lordy, she makes me nervous.*

"James Woolsey, CIA Director, stated that a nuclear bomb detonated high in the atmosphere over the middle of America would create an MEP…I mean EMP." *Damn that woman!* "Woolsey stated it'd destroy the country's electric grid, communications systems, and vehicle computer modules. The bomb wouldn't directly kill people, but throw America into a state of absolute anarchy. Ninety percent of Americans *would* die within a few months, due to the chaos. By that, I mean most people wouldn't have stored food or access to clean water, and no way to defend themselves."

Grayson rubbed the back of his neck and thought about Mark's lessons. "Those sobering numbers got me thinking. If Woolsey is correct, you have two primary considerations for survival. The first is to live through the die-off."

"I like that idea," Wayne said and got a few chuckles.

"Does everyone know what EMP stands for?"

"We know what an EMP is." Laura's sarcastic tone drew sneers from the not-so-friendly Patriots, aggravating Grayson. Wayne frowned at his younger sister again.

That damn woman is playing a game! You wannna play, let's play.

Grayson stared at Laura. "If you don't devise a solid plan and make preparations to survive the first three to six months after society collapses, you'll friggin die. The rest is irrelevant."

"What's the second primary consideration?" she demanded.

"Be prepared to establish long-term food production, which requires no less than a two-year food supply, lots of gardening hand tools, and plenty of open pollinated seeds on hand from the first day."

He repeated his warnings to the dead stares across the yard. "First, survive the die-off. Second, produce a lot of food without electricity or fuel for your tractors. What I mean by a lot of food is enough to eat and preserve to carry you until the next harvest **plus** provide seeds for the next planting."

The dead air held. *Surprise! The city slicker ain't no fool.* The piercing eyes drove him nuts. He covertly glanced to ensure his fly wasn't open. Determined to get it over with, Grayson forged ahead.

"The details on how to ensure security and the availability of clean water, shelter, and food are tied to those two considerations. If you only focus on surviving the die-off—meaning the security or the tactical side, you'll likely die of starvation." *Different tactic. Get them involved.* "Show of hands, how many could grow a year's food beginning today without electricity and fuel?"

Ground-staring and beard-pulling reflected back at him. He drove the point home. "Show of hands. How many have at least a two-year food supply to survive the die-off and can build a garden large enough to supply food for an entire year?"

Again, silence. *This is going well.*

Laura pierced him. "Did you learn all this from the Internet or in the military? Places you served? Things you saw? What other events cause societal collapse?"

This smart cookie has better radar than the Air Force.

"Using my guerrilla warfare experience, I analyzed the few things from the Internet. I focused on the EMP event today, because I found government briefings on it." He looked to Wayne. "If I understood correctly, surviving the die-off is where you had some questions."

"That's right," Wayne stood. "Any questions?"

The youngest member, Scott, sat up. "Damn, man! We've been working on tactical operations, improvised wilderness shelters, making fires without matches, and such, but if you're right, we ain't near ready."

Concurrence sounded around the yard, and then the naysayers got involved.

Grayson relished Elmer Martel and other naysayers devising ways to blow him out of the water. Elroy, thumbs under the straps of his bib overalls, spoke. "If yor sayin we don't know how to survive when we're bug'n out, what good is this other stuff? An ifn' yor so smart, how come you ain't no prepper?"

You arrogant ass! Maybe they aren't a good fit for our MAG. Okay, smart guy, talk to the yahoos. "Where're you going to bugout to?"

"Well...uh...Wayne read some books what says that's what we gotta do, bug out."

"You'd be better off right here. I found a great prepper guide on Amazon, *Absolute Anarchy*. I suggest y'all read it to get everyone on the same page."

"Anything you can tell us about militias?" A heavyset woman, wearing a flower garden dress, asked. "We call ourselves the SET Patriots."

"To organize a productive militia, first thing identify your mission needs."

Darnell, sitting by Elmer Martel, threw in his two cents. "We ain't in need of missionaries."

Scott looked irritated. "What'cha mean, mission needs?"

"What things do you plan to do with your militia?"

"Shoot bad guys," the big woman said and got a round of confirmation, several shaking rifles in the air.

Wayne shook his head. "Grayson, seems we need guidance starting from zero."

"We ain't need'n no help from no city cop," Elmer Martel said.

Wouldn't they be impressed if they knew I was fired?

"And no damn missionaries," Darnell said.

"Continue, Grayson." Wayne moved to the back and spoke quietly to his cousins. They settled but weren't happy.

Short and sweet and get out before the shooting starts.

"Your mission needs are things you need to do before and after the collapse. Examples include guarding critical facilities and protecting the community from outside forces, maintaining law and order, and long-term survival."

"Give us examples," Laura pushed.

"A mission need could be to prevent looters from stealing the drugs from your pharmacies."

Laura became more attentive. *Ah ha. The doctor's Achilles heel.*

"Another, guarding food sources, like Walmart and supermarkets, from looters. Another, blocking entry points from starving refugees. And maintaining civil order."

"Makes sense," Wayne said.

"What does a written mission needs document do for us?" Grayson was grateful for Laura's question.

"It keeps you on track with the primary things you need to do when all hell breaks out. Notice, I didn't say *how* you'd accomplish each mission need. Those details are recorded in a requirements document."

"I suppose you have examples of requirements, too?" Laura asked.

Grayson heard the dare. *What's up with this woman I kissed last night?*

"What's the first thing that comes to mind when millions of people are roaming the country, fleeing Dallas, Houston, Austin, Waco, etc., looking for food? When they arrive here, they'll be ready to eat anything—grass, snakes, bugs; you name it. For some, that may include the dead. They won't care what they have to do to obtain food."

*Their looks of horror say **point made**.*

"What was the first thing that came to your mind? Anyone?"

Laura, face pale, ventured an answer. "As much as it goes against my Christian beliefs, if we don't block them from entering, we end up starving to death, too."

"That, my dear, is where you start to establish requirements." *You pulled a Rhett Butler and put the woman in shock. Smooth, Grayson.*

Irritation flared in Laura's face. "So *now* we have to write a requirements document?" Her voice fell at the end as she realized her mistake.

Grayson was vaguely aware of heads pivoting between the two of them. *Hold your temper. Monitor your mouth. You care for this woman.*

"Exactly!" He smiled.

"And I'm sure you have a great example for us," Laura said, dripping scorn.

"Absolutely." Grayson looked around the group. "Let's say you decide the security mission need for the hospital requires round-the-clock double guards at each door during the day and an additional guard at night. Same goes for the pharmacies. Or, you may want to consolidate all meds in one location, which allows better control."

"What else?" Scott asked.

"You might define the mission need for a big store like Walmart requires ten guards per shift in eight-hour shifts. Roads must have physical barriers and roving patrols between them to maintain civil order and arrest criminals. You are limited only by your imagination."

Wayne began to laugh. "Your theory sounds good and probably works with a battalion of marines. We're small in number. As you were speaking, I envisioned at least ten mission needs. We're a tad short to even save Walmart."

"Speak fer yourself," Elmer Martel slung at Wayne. "Ain't nobody gittin by Old Bess and me." He held his granddaddy's 12-gauge high and gave it a pat on the barrel.

"The answer to your manpower issue is rooted in the fact that everyone in your community will be scared to death. They'll respond to those who know what to do, have a plan, and supply leadership. The better prepared you are, the greater the chance others will follow you and offer to help." He zeroed in on Elmer Martel. "You have to be quick, before the community goes into panic mode, running all over the place, shooting everyone that looks cross-eyed at them. Moving slow makes things ten times more difficult. That's why being prepared ahead of time is vital to the success of your mission."

"You can lead a horse to water but you can't make him drink. Some folks won't appreciate setting ourselves up as their saviors." The man in a back corner with his John Deere cap pulled low triggered the cop in Grayson. Patently territorial, his voice deep, resonant, he spoke with authority. He'd slipped in silently with two Sumo wrestler-sized men after Grayson started his presentation. *A monied man not used to being told what to do.*

Someone cleared his throat, and Grayson realized everyone was waiting for him to respond. He didn't break contact with the John Deere cap man.

"Your neighbors will follow anybody who exhibits leadership and has a clue what to do. Once the SET Patriots are a well-trained militia with well-defined mission needs and requirements, your neighbors will step up to the plate to follow and assist you."

"Do tell," Laura said. He pretended not to hear her.

"Each of you would be responsible for specific requirements. Establish yourselves within the community. Let them know who the Patriots are, what you're capable of, and why you're a blessing not a threat."

Side conversations filled the air. Wayne stood. "Let our neighbor finish."

"Quick example. The collapse occurs. You rush and pass out flyers to meet at the high school football stadium at 10 a.m."

Wayne walked towards Grayson. "The poop hits the fan, everyone is armed and scared to death, and we're going to pass out flyers."

Elmer Martel and his cronies got a good laugh.

Grayson smiled. "The flyer gives people a focal point. It's like an emergency hurricane plan, but in this case, you notify them to bring their weapons with extra ammo."

"Almost everyone will show up, but I honestly wouldn't know where to begin."

"Imagine the SET Patriots are on the high school football field lined up about ten feet apart when the people gather." He pointed to Lucas. "Let's say you're in charge of Walmart security and need thirty militiamen. Pick thirty folks and have them leave the stands and line up behind you. Do the same for each of your member's area of responsibility."

"If we do that, they'll come out in droves. We'd have folks left over. Can't leave them out of the action without hurt feelings." *Who gives a shit if their feelings are hurt? You're talking life and death. Cool it!*

Laura saved him. "They'll be the reserve to fill in for regular team members that can't make a shift and for a quick reaction team to reinforce trouble spots."

"Good thinking, Laura. Each team leader gives a quick training session. I know this sounds simplistic, but it gives you an idea of how to maximize your community's security."

"Grayson, you're a genius," Wayne grinned. Comments of agreement bubbled up from the group. Laura beamed with pride at the man she'd grown to like more every day.

"I appreciate it, but my background gives me insight, nothing more. You'll also need rules of engagement that explain the lawful use of deadly force, to keep folks from shooting everyone that crosses their path."

Elroy blurted out, "I'll shoot any SOB that messes with me and mine!"

Grayson saw a chance to emphasize his point. "Okay, Elroy. You see someone stealing food from your garden. What'd you do?"

Elroy threw out his chest. "Well, a man's gotta do what a man's gotta do."

"Are you saying you'd shoot the person?"

"Damn tootin!"

"The thief is a four-year-old girl. Do you shoot her in the head or the chest?"

The blood drained from Elroy's face.

"That's why you have rules of engagement."

"You'll also need to establish good rapport with law enforcement. It's essential that they think of you as an extension of their force. You pick up a criminal, turn him over to the sheriff or Palestine police."

"The sheriff ain't no problem. He's my brother-in-law and only arrests me when I'm too drunk to remember his name," George said.

Wayne closed the discussion. "Grayson, you haven't spoken more than thirty minutes but gave us more information than we came up with over the past four years. You're welcome to return and share your thoughts, even if you don't join us."

A round of applause told Grayson he had been successful establishing himself with the SET Patriots, but there was one more item to address.

"Take ten and then we'll practice tactical maneuvers."

Wayne looked at the troublemakers and pointed them to a place for private conversation.

Grayson moved to join them but Laura grabbed his arm. "Let Wayne handle this. It's not your place to interfere in local business."

"*I am* local business and I'm going to communicate with those boys in a language they understand. If I don't, I'll remain an outsider and continue to have problems. It's a man thing. Stay here," he ordered and walked away.

"Male chauvinist pig," she muttered angrily under her breath, and then was shocked at her primal sensual attraction for the man.

Wayne didn't pull punches. "What the hell is going on with you three? You acted like idiots. We asked a neighbor that can help us and you treat him like shit."

Elmer Martel looked up at Grayson. "It ain't nothing personal, mister. It's just that you ain't from here, and we don't need no outsiders butt'n inta our business."

Wayne started to say something, but Grayson held up his hand. "I'm the new dog in town, and you three don't want me pissing on your trees. As a man, I understand that. Respect it, too. What you forget is that I'm a Texan, same as you, and have my own tree. Don't think you can piss on it. As long as we have an understanding, we're okay."

Leaning his formidable presence slightly toward them and balling his huge fists, Grayson did something he hadn't done since high school. "You assholes interrupt me again, and I'll drag all three of your sorry asses into the woods." Giving each a dead stare, he finished. "You won't like what happens after that, but if you want, we can take care of this little problem right now."

They studied the bulk of the man.

"We ain't lookin fer no trouble. We just wanted to get our opines in," a cowed Darnell said. "No hard feelings, mister?"

Wayne noticed the rest of the group watching them and defused the situation. "You three have a choice. Join us for our tactical exercise or leave the SET Patriots. We don't have room for anybody that disrupts the organization. What's it gonna be?"

Without a word, the three men turned and walked towards the group, mumbling as they went. Out of range, Elroy boasted, "We could'a took him."

Elmer Martel grunted. "I ain't the best educated man, but I ain't no fool neither. Rekon he ain't all that bad."

"Grayson, I apologize for these idiots. Good men, but not the brightest bulbs on the Christmas tree. I hope this doesn't sour you on us."

"I come from a long line of rednecks and understand those boys. They'll be alright, now."

Wayne chuckled. "They may still cause a little trouble until their egos smooth down."

Grayson looked around, but couldn't find the man in the John Deere hat.

"What's the story with the guy who came in late, the one in the John Deere hat?"

"Don't know much, other than he's exceedingly rich—rumors are he's a billionaire—married to a Middle Eastern woman, and has an adult son. He bought a thousand acres ten years ago and built a huge compound in the middle of it. He comes to meetups but doesn't train with us. It's a short walk through the woods to his place. You're welcome to join us for training and the cookout after."

"I appreciate the invitation, but I've got a lot to do at home. Jack puts up quite a fuss when I'm late with his daily treat, and I have to get ready for my organic farming club. They'll be here tomorrow to slaughter rabbits and chickens to take back to Houston."

Grayson socialized with the SET Patriots for a few minutes and offered his hand to all, including the three dissenters. The group grabbed their rifles and headed toward the woods.

Laura took Grayson's hand and walked him to his pickup where she jerked his arm. "You're so full of it."

"What?"

"These guys may buy your BS about not being a prepper, but not me. Don't worry. Your secrets are safe with me."

"Laura, I don't know what you're tal—"

"Yes, you do know what I'm talking about, mister. I'm proud of you and glad you're here to guide the SET Patriots." She looked up into his blue eyes. "We need you…I need you, Grayson Dean."

"Then why did you give me such a hard time today?"

"I had you figured out before the meetup and wanted to give you some jazz to keep you on your toes, see if you're worthy of a good woman. You may want to move your prepper books into your office instead of leaving them in your man cave for everyone to see."

His face flushed and he chuckled. "Did I pass your…hmm…evaluation?"

Her answer was a big hug and kiss to send him on his way. Grayson appreciated the action of her slim, well-formed body jogging across the field. *Never seen camouflage pants fit so well.*

Laura didn't look back but held a finger in the air and wagged it at him, letting him know she was aware of his naughty thoughts.

A flashback to following Shannon into the casino sent an unexpected gush of deep yearning and an intense urge to see her. Their entanglement surged through him and a hot passion hit his nether regions. One night of illicit hot sex, and an archenemy overpowered him. *You'd better come up with some tactical maneuvers to get that hot-blooded woman out of your system.*

No matter how hard he tried, he wasn't able to convince himself she was nothing but a pleasant memory. It wasn't over, not by a longshot.

Driving home, Grayson contemplated the silent man in the John Deere cap and made a mental note to have Joe check him out.

Islamic State of America - 10

Islamic Social Center in Monterrey, Mexico

Year 1

Two months ago, the State of Texas released Carlos Murtadha. Unrecognizable as the illiterate, aimless gangbanger who entered four years earlier, he walked out an educated man focused on his new and depraved life's mission. His knowledge of history from the Islamist's perspective permeated his psyche, eliminating any conflicting truths.

The wickedness that invaded and controlled his soul imbued him with an evil presence that no longer required bare knuckles and a forged swagger to impose his will. Now, other men—the infidels—robotically sidestepped his path and averted their eyes for fear of making direct contact and becoming a target of his Islamic ire. Yet, with his own—his Muslim brothers—he was genial, his voice indulgent and hypnotic.

☪ ☪ ☪

Imam Omar had just arrived from Cairo and he was anything but pleased. He expected Carlos and his men to be ready for their initial briefing and training to build their team integrity and cohesiveness.

"Akeem, it's been two months since Carlos was released. You ordered him to report here immediately, to the Islamic Social Center. Where is he?" he demanded.

"He told me in an email yesterday that he is on his way from Houston and will arrive in four days," Akeem replied.

Imam Omar took a deep breath. "Houston is a dangerous place for him. Why did he disobey your orders?"

While Akeem understood Carlos, it was still difficult to explain the man's character to this holy man who only knew the Islamic ways. "After his father was killed, he was not raised as a Muslim as were we, but lived without direction and discipline. He has made much progress but it will take a little more time with this one."

Imam Omar was not pleased. "What has he been doing for the past two months?"

"After being deported, he re-entered America to search for and kill the detective that put him in prison."

"That was foolish and causes me to wonder if he is truly the chosen one, this descendant of Mohammed—peace be upon him."

Akeem's mind worked furiously to find a way to mollify the holy man's displeasure. "Carlos attended mosque in Houston, where he acquired several followers. He learned of a family that rejected Islam to become Christians. He led his soldiers to impose the will of Allah on the apostates and left behind an appropriate reminder to other of our Muslim brothers considering such foolishness."

Akeem thought it better not to tell about Carlos' narrow escape from the detective.

Imam Omar's face relaxed as he analyzed Akeem's statement and understood its significance. "He did as the law of Allah commands and killed those who turned from Islam, *Alhamd lilah*, thanks be to god."

Akeem had no doubt about Carlos' devotion to Allah and knew the holy man would be pleased with this descendant of Mohammed. "Carlos proved himself pure and will lead his soldiers of Allah to victory over the infidels."

Imam Omar allowed Akeem his time of glory for allowing himself selflessly to enter prison and accomplishing such an inordinate task. "You served Allah admirably, Akeem. Is your understudy ready to be tested on the battlefield?"

"Carlos Murtadha, a descendant of Mohammed—peace be upon him—is pure and ready. He serves Allah without question, without hesitation."

Chapter 32

The First Big Slaughter

Year 5

Profusely sweating in the cool November air, "I can't do it!" Yolanda screamed and let go of the beautiful snow-white rabbit's hind legs. She jerked its head out of the hooks, and held the helpless critter to her chest, caressing its floppy ears.

Samuel stepped in. "It's not that difficult. Watch me." He took the rabbit from her reluctant grasp, placed its head back in the hooks, held its dangling hind legs, and gave a quick, strong jerk to break its neck.

Yolanda yelped and gave Samuel a dirty look; tears washed her pale face.

The critter quivered for a few seconds and stilled. "See, there's nothing to it. Now, hand me the knife and I'll show you how to take out its innards and skin it."

Mark placed his arm around Yolanda's shoulders. "Baby, I told you not to pet it. You became emotionally attached."

She wiggled her shoulders out from under his arm. "Oh, shut up!"

Pablo walked from behind the barn to the rabbit processing crew, holding a headless chicken by its feet, the blood dripping from what was left of its neck. "The chickens' heads are chopped off, and they're hanging upside down, bleeding out. We'll need some help dunking them in the hot water pot and plucking them after the blood has drained."

Yolanda shot sharp daggers at Pablo.

"What?"

"Nothing," Yeung said. He spoke empathetically to Yolanda. "We city folks think nothing of going to the supermarket and picking out a packet of chicken breasts to put on the grill, because we don't see the process that got the chicken breasts in the packet in the first place. When the collapse occurs, and our survival is in our own hands, we must have the same attitude toward slaughtering animals as everyone else over the past tens of thousands of years. It will become an unemotional part of the daily routine."

"I don't want to learn how to slaughter animals," Yolanda said. "They're so cute. I'll let Mark do it."

"I know it's tough, but you and Mark may have children someday. They'll depend on you for survival. If Mark isn't there, and that is a possibility, you'll have to either do it or let your children starve." He eased another rabbit from the pen and held it out for her to take. "Be brave and try again."

Yolanda shook her head vigorously. "No!"

"You're a tough cop. I've seen you run toward the shooting while others ran from it. You can do this," Yeung said.

"But I never shot anybody."

Everyone's eyes were on Yolanda. Would she do what was necessary and carry through with the vile act to prepare herself mentally to help her family survive? Seconds passed as hours, but no one moved a muscle.

Yolanda looked at the rabbit, its sad pink eyes staring at her and its nose wiggling. She took a deep breath, let it halfway out, and held it as if she was ready to pull the trigger on the range. She slowly reached out with shaking hands, snatched the beautiful white bundle from Yeung, and held it at arms-length for a moment.

In one swift move, she hung its head in the hooks, grabbed its dangling legs, closed her eyes, and gave it a strong jerk, holding it for a few seconds longer than necessary. Then she flung her hands and body away from it.

Shocked faces watched to see what would happen next.

When the rabbit stopped quivering, Mark reached for it, but Yolanda pushed him aside. Tears pouring, she moved at top speed, released the rabbit from the hook, grabbed the knife from the table, sliced open its belly, removed the gallbladder, and slung the rest of the innards to Millie. Intensely focused, she cut off the rabbit's head and skinned it the way Yeung demonstrated. It wasn't the prettiest job, but Mark was pleased that she conquered her emotions and took a step closer to becoming his homesteading partner.

She slammed the knife on the table. "Satisfied?"

Everyone broke out in cheers and hugs while she held her arms with their bloody hands extended.

"I'm proud of you," Mark said. "You just became a bona fide survivalist."

Yolanda glared at all of them. There were no words for what she was feeling. Intellectually, she understood the act of killing animals as necessary to her survival. Regardless of her acquiescence to that reality, it didn't relieve her of the knowledge that a certain innocence she retained from childhood had just vanished in the flash of a bloody knife. She could no longer feel affection for the beautiful, innocent animals that would keep her alive.

"Okay folks, we're burning daylight," Ramirez said. "Finish skinning these critters and pack them on ice. We'll can them tomorrow. Grayson has a report for us on the local prepper group. Let's move it! This will be our first meal in the new lodge."

"Hand me another one," Yolanda said, her voice shaking.

~~~

On the way to the lodge, Ramirez pulled Grayson aside for a small chat. "It's none of our business, but Mama and I are concerned for you. We have a friend in Houston you may be interested in that we can bring for a short visit. A man needs a mate."

Grayson startled himself with his quick reply and the misgivings it stirred within him. "Actually, Chief, I'm dating someone local."

Ramirez cocked his head and squinted his eyes. "Did I detect a little hesitation, son?"

Grayson's reply spoke for itself. "She's a great gal, Chief, but...I guess...well...I can't seem to commit myself to her and don't want to jinx it by saying anything more...in case it doesn't work out...you know."

"This coming from the most impulsive man in the state of Texas," Ramirez said while shaking his head, releasing one of his famous belly laughs.

"Something keeps nagging at me, holding me back."

Ramirez patted Grayson affectionately on his shoulder. "Mama and I are always available if you want to chat. Now, let's get to the lodge. Just think, son, except for the cake, every bite of this meal was produced right here, even the cornbread."

~~~

After a quick meal of green salad, grilled chicken and rabbit, okra, squash, cornbread, and one of Grace's big caramel cakes, Ramirez called the MAG to order for their monthly meetup. "Great job today, guys, and we're especially proud of you, Yolanda. Survival entails performing unpleasant tasks at times."

Still pale, her eyes swollen from crying, she'd refused to eat any of the meat at supper. She nodded. "Thanks for being patient with me."

Ramirez motioned for Grayson. "Give us a quick overview of the new lodge."

"Glad to, Chief. The fireproof Hardi planks on the outside make it appear to be a wood structure but the concrete walls are thick enough to stop a 30-06 round. The second floor is for overflow sleeping quarters. It has cots but you'll have to use your own sleeping bags from your BOBs tonight. It also has gun ports for fending off attackers; ground level has the kitchen, dining, and general assembly areas. The belowground area is where we store our two-year supply of food, firearms, ammo, medical supplies, and Faraday cages with electronics equipment with concealed access through the kitchen pantry. Any questions?"

"I'm confused," Charles said, and he pointed to the back of the lodge. "I went downstairs through the stairway. Nothing secret about it."

"You entered the TOC," Grayson replied. "There's a solid concrete wall between it and the hidden storage area. Access is through a concealed door in the kitchen pantry."

"Do we have a tick for the tock?" Charles asked.

After the laughter died down, Grayson explained. "It's spelled T-O-C and that stands for tactical operations center. It's where we monitor and direct field activities, like security patrols, counter-attacks against bad guys, or send reinforcements to weak spots. We'll furnish the TOC with an off-grid power system, topographical and road maps of the area, military surplus field phones that connect to all the buildings, and short-range radios. There's a communications room, too. Keep your eyes open for a ham operator who knows how to operate shortwave radios."

"I'm starting to feel good about our secret BOL," Samuel said. "We'll be safe holed up here during the die-off."

Grayson almost mentioned again his desire to combine with the SET Patriots, but caught himself in time not to allow a shouting match to ensue. "It's been a great day, guys, but still a lot of work left canning meat tomorrow. Grab your BOBs and find a room. Lights out at twenty-two hundred hours."

Islamic State of America - 11

Islamic Social Center in Monterrey, Mexico

Year 1

Tired from travel, Carlos and Miguel stepped from the taxi with their recruits from Houston and entered the Islamic Social Center. Imam Omar and Akeem eagerly greeted them. "Welcome, brothers, *As-salāmu alaykum*, peace be upon you," the holy man said and gave them a kiss on each cheek, his eyes wide with awe at these descendants of Mohammed standing before him.

"*Alaykumu as-salām*, and upon you, peace," they replied.

Hearing of their arrival, Muslim brothers that composed Carlos' jihadi cell came pouring from the meeting room to greet their leader. Many were his former inmates but others he did not recognize.

After exchanging introductions, Imam Omar reminded them of their limited time. "We are scheduled to depart for Cairo in two days. Let us retire to the meeting room and I will explain the Master Plan."

☪ ☪ ☪

The men situated themselves comfortably and every eye focused on Imam Omar.

Speaking in Arabic, he began by praising them. "Akeem, you have done well, *Alhamd lilah*, thanks be to god." Looking over the group, he continued, "You have studied diligently and are ready for the next step, to begin training as soldiers to serve Allah in holy war."

Akeem and the group beamed with pride at the holy man's words.

"I and my men are pure. We give ourselves to Allah and are not afraid to die. We will continue to do His will until martyred in battle and enter Paradise, *Allahu Akbar*, god is great," spoke Carlos with pride. I have done the will of Allah. I killed the infidel wife and daughter of that gringo detective, a worthless woman that got in my way, and a family of apostates that turned from Islam. I will return to Houston and kill the detective."

Carlos' bravado showed no fear externally, but deep inside he knew Grayson Dean was also fearless and sought to kill *him*. The thought bore Carlos an unexpected shiver of fear.

"You are truly a descendent of Mohammed—peace be upon him," Imam Omar said and then gave Carlos a dead stare. "But be warned; do not return to Houston until the time is right. Your personal enemy can wait."

Akeem flinched and prayed that his primary understudy kept control of his emotions.

Carlos did not disappoint him. He now held control over his old instinct to retaliate immediately when attacked. For now, he thought of the chase and his narrow escape and conceded control to the holy man. "I understand, but one day I will cut the head from that detective. I will remove it slowly with a dull knife and listen to him squeal and beg for his life as I slice into the back of his neck, down to his throat, taking much pleasure in the moment his last stinking breath escapes from his lungs and sends him into hell."

Imam Omar was pleased with Carlos' response, but changed the discussion to his primary purpose for being there by asking questions. "When will there be peace?" he asked and waited for someone to respond.

Expecting instructions instead of a question, the men, caught off guard, looked around at one another. After a few seconds, Miguel spoke, "There can be no peace until Islam, through its holy law of Sharia, rules the world."

"Ah. Very good. Now what are we and our brothers doing to achieve peace?"

Marco answered, "Our brothers are conducting jihad against the infidels, killing them throughout Western Civilization through terrorism. We will soon join the holy war."

Imam Omar responded, "You are partially correct. It is not possible to kill all of them now. They are many and we are few." He gave them time to think about this dilemma before continuing. "The real battle is going on under the noses of the infidels without a shot being fired or a bomb being detonated. As long as we keep the infidels focused on terrorism, others work quietly in the background to overwhelm them. How will this take place?"

Carlos provided clarification, which pleased Akeem. "Allah will rule the world. As long as we are few, we cannot insist that the infidels eliminate their laws and follow Sharia. We will use the liberal politicians, the laws of the West, and their welfare system to establish Muslim neighborhoods where the infidels dare not go. We will breed Muslim children under Sharia. We will systematically take control of towns and cities until we become the majority, such as our brothers are doing now, and expand through immigration and high birthrates until we outnumber them. When we have control, we will bring Sharia on the infidels. They will become Muslims or they will die."

"Akeem has taught you well, Carlos," Imam Omar turned to the group. "As we speak, our brothers are invading and conquering Europe. In America, Canada, and Australia, we established communities where we ignore the infidels' laws and where they dare not go, the fools. Allah blinds them."

Marco raised his hand. "With much respect, Imam Omar, I am compelled to ask: Since it will take many generations to outbreed and conquer Western Civilization, is it not logical to conclude that we will be long dead before that happens? What then is *our* purpose? Are we to become jihadist and use terror tactics to slowly kill the infidels?"

Akeem felt uneasy and made temporary eye contact with Carlos but Imam Omar's response eased his anxiety. "You have directed us to the next item of our discussion, but it is almost time for evening prayer. We will continue tomorrow."

☪ ☪ ☪

After evening prayer, Imam Omar motioned to Akeem to follow him.

Chapter 33

Their Special Day

Year 5

"Laura, what a marvelous candlelight dinner. You've made the whole day feel special."

She gave him one of those looks that, as soft as it appeared and combined with a *certain* sweet tone, strikes fear in a man's heart. "It *is* a *special day*, sweetheart."

His face went blank and warning flags began popping up. *Crap! I'm in trouble. What did I forget? Margaret always gave me hints.*

Laura handed him a card and a small box perfectly wrapped in baby blue paper and tied with a matching ribbon. "Happy anniversary, love."

His ears flushed with embarrassment, he stared blankly at the gift and card but didn't open them. *Did we celebrate our first year? Who makes these rules, anyway?* His time in the Army taught him that immediately admitting to mistakes was the only way to correct them and, in some cases, avoid disciplinary action.

"Laura, I'm sorry. I completely forgot."

She didn't look at him and her voice was flat with a hint of irritation when she replied. "Last year, our first year, we went to dinner and dancing, so I thought this year, we would do something a little more intimate. Can't say I'm not disappointed that you forgot, but I suspect there's more to it."

The same doomed feeling he got when a teacher sent him to the principal's office hovered over him. The teacher sent a note outlining his current infraction and a recommended reprimand, making it a long walk to the office.

Laura's unopened envelope in his hand suddenly felt hot. He laid it on the table.

Grayson knew this feeling far too well. He'd spent his life as an alpha male. Letting someone down and being less of a man was foreign to him. He was accustomed to facing any foe or problem head on and without fear. When a teacher sent him to the principal, he got a lecture and a note sent home. His father counted on him to be the first in their family to go to college, and Grayson was determined not to fail him, but the little boy in him kept getting in the way. He welcomed the taste of the belt. It brought him restitution through penance and bolstered his resolve to walk a straighter line.

More than his father, he hated disappointing Margaret. Her lectures, even in elementary school, stung more in his heart than his father's belt on his bottom. They both helped him learn to stand strong and be a leader. Did losing Margaret, his partner in life, have that much of an effect on him?

"Stop worrying about it, cowboy. Every man, and frankly, some women fall victim to forgetting a special day sometime in their life."

"I'll make it up to you, baby. I promise." His hands were ice cold as he reached for her.

She teasingly pulled back and laughed. "Yes, you will, and big time, too."

"To quote Jackie Gleason, 'Baby, you're the greatest.'"

She tilted her head to the side and gave him a big smile. "Whoever Jackie Gleason is, I accept the compliment. You're an amazing man, Mr. Dean, number one on my list any day. Now, let's eat."

After dinner, they retired to the living room couch where Grayson pulled her to him. "Thanks for this great meal and thinking of me on this special day. I'm sorry I flubbed it."

She put a finger to his lips. "You didn't flub anything. Aren't you going to open your present?"

"I can't. It wouldn't be right. Let's do this over again, that is if you'll accept a dinner date with me."

"I look forward to it."

"Where do you want to go for dinner?"

She laughed. "You're not getting off that easy. Part of your make-it-up-to-me is to cook us a meal *from scratch*, the same as I did, and set the table with candles, have soft music playing in the background, and a fire in the fireplace."

"You got it. I'll cook you a meal to remember. Now, what did you want to talk about?"

Laura looked down at her hands twisting in her lap. "To be honest, I need *you* to talk to *me*, to tell me where we're headed. Everything between us seems perfect, but we're stuck in neutral. The bottom line is…I want to establish a family and I'm still young enough to have more children…if that enters the picture. I'm not sure that's what you want."

"So, you're saying that you're ready to get married?"

"That would be nice under the right circumstances, if we both feel it and want the same thing."

Grayson looked down in thought, then raised his head, looked into her beautiful eyes. "Laura, you're right. I'm the one that's been drifting along in neutral and that's not fair to you."

"Tell me your honest opinion, Grayson. Who are we as a couple and what do you see in our future?"

"Give me a little time to pray on it. Okay?"

"Of course, and, Grayson, determine what's best for you. Be honest with yourself. I'm not trying to pressure you into marriage. It would likely end in disaster for both of us if we don't want the same things out of our relationship."

"I agree."

"Give it some time and thought and ask God to provide you with the answer."

"Speaking of time, dinner will be served tomorrow at six p.m. sharp, and it's a dress-up occasion." *Smooth transition knucklehead.*

"You don't have to do this, *really*."

"I want to, *really*."

"Okay, cowboy, I'll be here at six sharp with a big appetite. And don't give me that freeze-dried stuff like you did on one of our tactical training exercises." Her face looked like she had sucked on a lemon.

"Hey, that was a gourmet dinner. It said so on the side of the package, right next to where it said, 'Add hot water and stir.'"

Laura grinned. "Remember the DVD we watched last month of *Crocodile Dundee*? Well, you can live on it but it tastes like shit."

On the way home, Grayson kept kicking himself for not marking this date on his calendar. He would put every bit of cooking ability he could muster into making it up to her.

~~~

Grayson spent the entire day working his way through online recipe books, gathering groceries, and preparing a special dinner for Laura. He had a lot of making up to do and committed himself to putting on a performance fit for his queen. He completed the finest meal he had every prepared in his life: chateaubriand with béarnaise sauce, oven-roasted asparagus, and chateau potatoes, all made from scratch and served with Pinot Noir, her favorite wine. For dessert, he created peach cobbler from Margaret's delicious recipe, and served it with coffee spiked with brandy. A little trickery to ameliorate his situation was okay, wasn't it?

The meal was in warm serving dishes, candles lit, and his suit on just before Laura knocked. That's when it hit him. He focused on the meal and forgot about a present! No need to panic. He had already placed her present and card to him on the table and she was at the door; he had no choice but to answer it.

Grayson opened the door to find Laura in a deep-purple silk dress that fit every curve perfectly. Looking her up and down, he whistled. "Hellooo, lovely lady. My but you look stunningly beautiful tonight!"

"Thank you, Mr. Dean. Your invitation stated that this is a dressy occasion. I must say, you are as handsome as Prince Charming in that well-tailored suit. Hmmm, something smells great."

Grayson took her wrap, hung it in the coat closet near the door, and escorted her to the table. He pulled her chair out and she sat at the table. Instead of sitting, he said, "Pardon me a moment. I'll be right back," and walked away rapidly.

Laura sat admiring his efforts but curious about why he was running from room to room throughout the house.

There are times to panic, and this was one of them, but he had to keep his cool long enough to come up with a present. Nothing in the guest room. No, that picture's been hanging on the wall for years. He almost passed the prepper library but backed up and started quickly going through the books. *Maybe, just maybe. Anything would beat returning with empty hands. No! No! No! Oh, yes. Thank you, God.* Grayson pulled the book from the shelf and placed it inside his jacket, holding it under his arm.

"Sorry for the delay but I forgot where I put something important." He deftly allowed the book to fall into his hand from under his suit jacket, placing it on the floor, not as subtly as he would have liked.

"Prince Charming, that silly grin on your face tells me you are up to no good."

"Oh. This is *good*, my Princess, but for now I think I hear a grumbling stomach on the other side of the table that needs to be fed."

"So, feed me, my Prince."

~~~

"Are you sure you didn't have a French chef come in to prepare this meal? It was amazing. You never cease to surprise me, Grayson Dean."

"It was just a little something I threw together for my special lady."

"You didn't just throw that masterpiece together, cowboy, and you can rest assured that I loved it!"

"Thanks, m'lady."

"I've been dying to know what you laid on the floor before we ate."

Grayson's mood became serious as he leaned down and picked up the book and slid it onto his lap, hidden from Laura. "I'm really sorry that I forgot the anniversary date of our first meeting. I have something for you. It's practical but I hope you know that it comes from my heart." *I'll have to go to confession over this one.* "It's not wrapped because I'm not any good at that."

He eased the book up and slowly passed it to Laura, concentrating on her face for a reaction. She took it with both hands and read aloud, "*The Survival Medicine Handbook* by Joseph Alton, MD and Amy Alton, ARNP."

She slowly flipped through the pages and kept turning them for what Grayson thought was too long, afraid that she was stalling to form a response and let him down easy for his stupid gift.

After several minutes, Grayson cleared his throat. "Well?"

"Grayson, this is wonderful! I'm in family practice and perform some work at the hospital emergency room, but I'm not a trauma doctor and never thought about many of the things I see here. This is the perfect gift."

She got up and walked around the table to Grayson, who quickly stood. She gave him a big hug. "Thank you, sweetheart."

Dumfounded, he thanked God for looking out for him. "Dr. Alton and his wife, Nurse Amy, have a great website, *Doom and Bloom*. They address potential medical emergencies we might encounter after the collapse."

She reached up on her toes, kissed him on the cheek, and released him from the hug. "I'll be spending lots of time on that site, for sure. Now, it's your turn."

"My turn?"

She picked up his present and handed it to him. "Yes, silly, open *your* present."

Grayson slowly untied the ribbon and removed the baby blue wrapping paper to reveal a small jewelry box. It contained a gold Saint Michael the Archangel Medal and chain.

"The warrior against Satan. Perfect for *my* warrior." Laura put it around his neck and latched it, adding a short sweet kiss. She didn't mention the absence of his card for her. It wasn't important now and he would notice it soon enough.

Grayson prepared coffee and led Laura to the living room sofa.

She took a sip of coffee and placed her cup on the end table. "What do you think about us, where we've been, and where we're going?"

Grayson's brain fought unsuccessfully for an answer. *Give me some time, lady.*

"We have lots of fun when we're together. We've traveled to fun places, except Las Vegas. I still don't know why you won't take me there."

Grayson moved on quickly. "I really liked the Panama Canal cruise. Going through the water locks and watching the howler monkeys making such a racket in the jungle was crazy."

"You started that racket by howling at them. I liked shopping in Colon, all those stores loaded with interesting things from around the world." She gave him that *special smile* and a kiss on the cheek. "I don't regret us having broken our vow of celibacy on that cruise. How about you, lover boy?"

Grayson kissed her cheek. "I've never regretted a minute of our *special times* together. I loved the time we climbed to the top of that mountain near Lizum, Austria and looked out over the Alps."

"We've had a ball, Grayson. Big trips are fun but, you know, dancing at the Round Up and family cookouts are my favorite."

"Remember when I helped you deliver that baby in the broken-down car on the side of the road? It was about the most exciting thing I've ever done. Man, I hated wasting that good whiskey on sterilizing my knife to cut the umbilical cord."

Laura gave him a gentle poke in the ribs. "You have a great sense of adventure. I love being with you."

"I love being with you, sweetheart."

Laura looked at her watch. "I'm sorry to cut this short but I have to take a shift in a couple of hours at the hospital for Dr. Addison and need to go home and get ready."

"I'm an old soldier and understand the call to duty."

"I'll call you tomorrow when I'm rested. Thanks again for the great meal. It really was special." They hugged and held a long kiss before she got into her car.

Grayson could have sworn Laura had tears in her eyes when she waved goodbye in the car.

He changed clothes, put on his old winter jacket, and lay on the grass. Millie ambled over and lay beside him. He petted her and gazed at the stars, searching for Margaret and Amanda and contemplating his situation with Laura. She was clear about wanting to marry and have their children but, thankfully, she was willing to give him time to think about it. He never considered remarrying. Margaret, Amanda, and Daniel were his family.

It wasn't fair to Laura. He had to make a decision, and soon. It shouldn't be a part of the decision, but how would their breakup or marriage, whichever way it went, affect Austin and the relationship between the MAG and the SET Patriots?

Islamic State of America - 12

Islamic Social Center in Monterrey, Mexico

Year 1

After Morning Prayer, Carlos and his men entered the meeting room and wondered at the map of America attached to the wall. Akeem recognized it as the one he saw in Cairo four years earlier.

Everyone settled in quickly and Imam Omar reminded everyone of Marco's question from the previous day and began his briefing. "To understand your mission for Allah, you must first understand what is happening in Western Civilization. Many of our Muslim brothers are educated in the ways of the infidels and we know their weaknesses. It is obvious that their governments are becoming socialist and will eventually collapse."

The men looked questioningly at the holy man.

"No socialist society has ever succeeded. They all come to a point of economic, political, and societal collapse. It is inevitable," he explained, and went on to describe how hyperinflation takes place and deliveries of survival goods, especially food and fuel, cease. "When that happens, those who live in cities will begin to riot. What Osama bin Laden said many years ago still holds true. 'We will defeat America and bring it to its knees, financially.' That is also true for the rest of Western Civilization."

"Imam Omar, these stupid gringos riot all the time, but they end quickly. It goes nowhere," Carlos said.

"That is true when considering riots that happen in only a place or two at any given time. I tell you that there will be riots in every city across America, all at the same time. Once every city in the entire country is burning, delivery trucks won't drive into them. Within a few days, all of the people living in cities will have no food or fuel and no driver will deliver them. What do you think will happen then?"

Carlos considered the options before speaking. "They will leave the city to find food. If not, they will starve to death, just like the people in Venezuela today."

Imam Omar leaned back and opened his hands in a gesture indicating that Carlos' answer was correct. "That is when America goes into a state of anarchy. There are not enough police and military in America to control such widespread turmoil. The police will run home to protect their families and property. Local governments will collapse. In a few weeks, the infidels will begin to starve to death. Without America's protection, our brothers in Indonesia will invade and conquer Australia and Canada."

A sly grin slid across Carlos' face. "Will we not also be hungry and starving to death? How will we stay alive?"

Imam Omar was pleased to see the Chosen One's rapid analysis. "Very good. Your quick thinking will help you to win in battle. What do you think you will do to stay alive?"

Carlos looked into the distance, his grin deepening. "I will lead my men to attack the rich gringos. We will kill the men, take their food, and have their women and children as our slaves. Allah declares it."

Imam Omar replied enthusiastically, "Within three months, most of the infidels will be dead and you and your soldiers for Allah will kill or enslave those who survive."

The lights were beginning to come on for Miguel. "I see. There are two strategies. The one, we outbreed the infidels and conquer them over generations. The other, if their own evil governments collapse, we soldiers of Allah conquer them with the sword."

"Miguel, you are a true descendant of Mohammed—peace be upon him," Akeem said.

The men began to show excitement for the challenges they faced. Akeem led them to become pure Muslims and this special holy man brought them to full realization of the power of Islam, given to them by Allah.

Imam Omar, having explained the Master Plan to Akeem the previous night, turned the remaining portion of the briefing over to him. It was important that the men see Akeem as an authority figure.

Directing their attention to the map, Akeem explained, "Notice the outlines of different portions of America. They will become Islamic provinces. Imam Omar is developing Islamist cells in each of these regions. Together, these provinces compose the Islamic State of America, or ISA, a caliphate of the West." Pointing to the Southwest region, he continued, "This is our province. When the time comes, Carlos will lead you to conquer it."

"Akeem, I understand how most of the infidels will die of starvation, but how can we conquer the many that will be left?" Marco asked.

In the presence of Imam Omar, Akeem fought to restrain his contempt for Marco. "The answer is simple but also demanding of every man here. Allah will test your devotion in ways you cannot now imagine. Paradise is the reward for those who prevail.

"When we arrive in Egypt, you will have uniforms and weapons and you will train to be great holy warriors. We will push every man to his limits. Afterward, I will escort you into combat in Africa. These events will prepare you with the heart of a pure jihadist and make you capable of conquering your enemies and returning these lands to Allah; it is his will.

"Select men who demonstrate bravery and leadership will be assigned to a cell of their own, twenty-five men per cell, with an Imam for each."

The seriousness of their mission and the demands Allah would place on them began to settle into the men's psyche. Their mission was no longer a theoretical concept, but rapidly becoming their reality.

Chapter 34

Surprise, Grandpa!

Year 6

Grayson almost tripped and fell returning from the mailbox. He kept looking at the name in the top left corner of the envelope, Wanda Dean. His daughter-in-law had written him a letter. His heart pounding, he hurried inside and plopped down quickly in the first available seat. His hands shaking, he roughly opened the envelope, careful not to destroy the return address, and began to read:

> Dear Father-in-Law,
>
> It is with great regret and sadness that I must inform you of the sudden and unexpected passing of Aunt Louise. She had a heart attack yesterday and the EMT medics couldn't revive her. By the time you receive this letter, she will be interred. I would have called but don't have your number. You have my condolences.
>
> The return address is a post office box and you can use it to write to me directly. I'll continue to keep you informed on conditions and activities here in Austin. Danny is okay with us communicating as long as you don't send mail directly to our home, including email. I know that's silly, but I have to be honest with you; after first hearing from Danny about

what happened with his mother and sister, I didn't care for you either. That changed when I started reading your letters and discussing you with Aunt Louise.

I've begun following the prepper and BOL information you sent Aunt Louise. I saved the map you sent her with alternate routes.

I'm a prepper now too and belong to a MAG here in Austin. It's a rather weak MAG. We don't participate in survival activities as you've explained, just the usual how to can food and make fire without matches sort of stuff. I fear these folks won't make it through the die-off.

I've managed to get Danny involved in extended backpacking trips and hunting. He enjoys shooting and is into reloading his own ammo. He sees it as a chemical engineering project. We'll be prepared to bug out when the time comes; he just doesn't know it. I don't like keeping secrets and plan to tell him about my prepping activities when the time is right.

When the SHTF—bet that makes you smile—I'll have to confess our plan. I'm sure that, after the initial shock, he'll agree to bug out to the BOL. Danny is a *good man. He'll provide the best for us, including his son. Yep, you're going to be a grandpa. Our baby boy is due October 11th, your birthday, and his name is Gabriel.*

I'm so sorry for not being able to inform you about Aunt Louise in time for you to attend her funeral.

*Love always,
Wanda*

P.S. My cell phone number is 512-555-1212. Call me if you have an emergency.

Grayson read the letter several times, running the emotional spectrum between sadness for Aunt Louise and joy for his daughter-in-law, along with anger with himself for forgetting to provide Louise with his cellphone number. His affection for a daughter-in-law he had never met filled his heart. Daniel was a lucky man.

He set about writing a response letter, his head spinning with information. She needed updated information on the BOL, especially the radio frequencies. I'll send her radios, too. She'd need photos and a better map with additional alternate routes. He wondered if he could get her to send him sonogram images.

I'm gonna be a grandpa. Crap! Am I too young to be a grandpa? Wait until the guys hear about this.

Chapter 35

Weber Returns

Year 7

   Grayson exploded before Charles fully exited his car. Weber stayed in the car and eyed Grayson nervously. "Charles, what the hell are you doing bringing that SOB to the farm?"
   "He's our newest MAG member and—"
   "Newest member! Are you nuts? I sure didn't vote him in."
   "Slow down, Grayson. There's more to his story than you know. You weren't there for the vetting and vote to let him in the MAG."
   "Since when does one part of the group make decisions for the other part?"
   "Since one part, namely you, refuses to come to the meetups in Houston. You don't have a right to dissent. Right now, he wants to talk to you but he's afraid to get out of the car."
   "I'll talk to him all right. Bring him around back of the barn."
   Charles looked Grayson in the face and nervously shook his big shoulders to get his full attention. "Listen to his story. That's all I ask."
   "What good is he to the MAG if he's too afraid to get out of the car? He's an idiot."
   Charles's voice dropped several octaves. "Now you listen to me. Weber is not an idiot. He's one of those smart guys who bumbles his way through normal life but excels in a specific field."
   "What specific field?" Grayson growled.
   "He's skilled at ham radio, uses shortwave radios to talk around the world, including preppers all over America and other countries. He's our key to knowing what's going on worldwide after the collapse. He's also a super-nice guy, once you get to know him. Remember how he backed down from testifying against you in the Delgado trial?"
   "Yeah. I remember. Odd," Grayson said a bit calmer.
   "Keep that in mind, let your hackles down, and go talk to him."
   Grayson trusted Charles, but why didn't Joe or Ramirez warn him about this? Grayson took a deep breath and walked over to the car.
   Weber stepped out, his voice a little shaky. "Hi, Grayson."
   Unable to muster more than a flat tone, Grayson managed, "So what's up?"

"You want the short story or the long one?"

"Short's fine."

"I owe you an apology for talking badly about you and your family at the firing range."

"That was settled at the time."

"Not exactly. You see, I...I was approached by one of the city council members before that. The council wanted you fired. They knew if you punched a fellow officer, the chief would have to can you, no choice. I didn't count on the others covering for you. I humiliated myself and got a broken nose for nothing."

"That doesn't make any sense. Why would you take a beating for such a stupid thing?"

Weber pulled at his shirtsleeves. "They offered me a promotion to get you fired, and I needed the money for special education for my son, Ethan. He has Asperger Syndrome, and I worry about what'll happen to him when my wife and I are no longer on this earth. How will he support himself? I'm sorry, Grayson, very sorry, and hope you can forgive me."

"You had a second chance at the Delgado trial but didn't take it. Why?"

"At the last minute, I realized you were a good and moral man, also, about as down as any man could go. I couldn't live with myself if I did such an awful thing. It would make me a reprobate, worse than I'd already become, and bother me every day of my life. I had to put right what I did to you that day on the range. I'm sorry, Grayson."

Grayson was shocked at his abrupt change of attitude toward Weber. It took as unexpected a turn as it had with Shannon in Vegas. His voice mellowed. "How's your son?"

"He's very smart but has trouble analyzing things. We're struggling with his social skills training. He won't be able to do more than janitorial work or stock store shelves but eventually he can become self-reliant with the right training."

Grayson grabbed Weber's right hand and shook it firmly. "Let's start over, Weber. I have some resources that will make sure Ethan gets the training he needs."

"What do you mean...resources?"

"Come in the house. We can talk about it over lunch. Welcome to the MAG." Grayson left Weber and Charles staring at each other, speechless.

Sitting alone on his porch that evening in his old winter jacket with Millie curled up at his feet, as Grayson watched the stars sparkle against a black sky, a moment of self-awareness, the turning of a corner, came over him. Ramirez's conversion over the years from a tough, exacting Army commander into a compassionate elderly gentleman was beginning to make sense. Not every event in his life had to be a battle. He looked deep into the night sky and felt Margaret's touch and knew that she was proud of him.

Islamic State of America - 13

Islamic Social Center in Monterrey, Mexico

Year 1

Akeem used a pointer to identify each of the new cells' mission area on the map. "Carlos will be here in the Houston area and every cell that composes the ISAC Army of the Southwest Province will be under his command. Other cells will be here in Texas, New Mexico, Arizona, Oklahoma, and the southern parts of Nevada and California."

"Excuse me for interrupting, but how long will this take. When will we go into action?" Marco asked, seeming eager to get on with it. "Why can we not attack now?"

Carlos was becoming irritated with Marco but refrained from reacting and taking control away from Akeem.

Akeem's response left no room for misunderstanding. "You are not to worry about time. Focus on the process. The more years we have to build and train our secret cells, the stronger we will be when the time presents itself. Our concern is to do the will of Allah without regard to time."

Imam Omar, unaware of Akeem's distrust of Marco, interjected, "Western economies will fail. *Insha' Allah*, but that must not happen before we establish all cells throughout America, perhaps, fifteen years or more. We are Muslim; time is nothing to us. As Akeem said, focus on the process." He motioned for Akeem to continue.

"After initial training in Egypt, we conduct holy war and bring Sharia to other parts of Africa. Those who succeed in combat will be rewarded with many wives and concubines. The bravest will have first pick, as young as nine years old, as it was with the wives of Mohammed—peace be upon him."

"Each of us can be Carlos' deputies and lead a cell of our own and have many wives. Allahu Akbar!" one of the men exclaimed, almost in disbelief and barely able to contain himself. His excitement was infectious. The other men sat up and gave Akeem rapt attention.

"Others of your countrymen are reverting every day. Over time, many Mexican brothers will join our cells and infiltrate the Southwest as laborers."

Marco realized he was in a tough spot with Akeem and Carlos and took action to placate them. "Please forgive me, Akeem, for being so curious. Questions come to my mind that I believe may be helpful as warriors for Allah. I have only one more, if you will be patient with me, and then I will remain silent." He paused to give Akeem time to digest his peace offering.

Imam Omar gave Akeem a subtle sign to accommodate the man.

Akeem bit his tongue and yielded to the holy man's silent directions.

"Of course, Marco. What is your question?"

"The cells are hundreds of miles apart. After the collapse when telephones and satellite phones are useless, how will the cells stay in contact with Carlos?"

Akeem admitted to himself that Marco asked good questions but still couldn't bring himself to trust the man. "We will use shortwave radios that transmit long distances. Select members of each cell will train as radio operators," he replied, without further explanation.

"Let us take time to pray and eat. Akeem will then present the last of your instructions. Then, you can prepare to travel to Cairo," Imam Omar ordered.

☪ ☪ ☪

Pointing again to the map, Akeem directed their attention to the other provinces scattered across America. "Each of these has a leader from his province, someone who blends in with the local populace."

Miguel sat up. "Like Carlos and me."

"Exactly. Brothers experienced in combat will return to their provinces and live regular lives incognito and under the guidance of their imams. All will continue to train in our hidden camps in America. Cell leaders will remain in combat zones until it is obvious the collapse is close. They will also return at times to conduct jihadi exercises with their cells."

Carlos, as a good leader should, remained quiet until the end, taking in all information before responding. "One thing is still missing. Who will be the leader of all the provinces?"

Akeem looked at Imam Omar and beamed. He paused until all eyes followed his to the holy man. "As we discussed before, we will make America one Islamic caliphate that follows Sharia, the law that pleases Allah. Imam Omar will be our caliph, the leader of all. *Insha' Allah*, god willing."

Carlos led them in vigorous applause. With the men comprehending and accepting the seriousness and dangers of the tasks before them, the trap closed tight. Akeem's mission for Allah was a complete success.

Standing, Carlos addressed his men. "Tomorrow we depart for Egypt. There we train as holy warriors then go into battle for Allah. Surely, some of us will die, perhaps even me. Those who survive will return to America when the time is right to restore Sharia, the law that pleases Allah. Any man afraid to face the infidels and die in battle must stand and leave now."

Their resolve etched in their faces, not one of them moved.

"Allahu Akbar!" Carlos shouted.

"Allahu Akbar!" came their spirited response.

Imam Omar and Akeem exchanged a knowing smile.

Chapter 36

Laura's Big Gamble

Year 8

Grayson gave Laura a peck on the cheek. "Thanks for letting me come over. I've been worried about you ever since you turned me down to go dancing with the chief and Miss Grace last week." *Why is it that a man doesn't know something's out of kilter until he feels a need to apologize?*

She led him by the hand silently from the door to the living room sofa and gave him a hug before sitting down. She leaned her head against his shoulder. "Straight up, Grayson. I'm not a woman a man can take lightly. I care about you but I won't play second fiddle to *anyone*. I treat you with the same respect."

Caught by surprise, he remembered his dad's advice that a smart man knows when to nod, keep his comments short and sweet, and then shut his mouth. "Laura, you have my utmost respect."

"I have something important to discuss with you." Trouble tinged the edge of her tongue.

Grayson grinned broadly. "You're pregnant!"

"No, but it's nice to see you have a positive reaction to that prospect." Laura smiled for a few seconds before returning to her somber mood. "As we discussed before, we seem perfect together, yet we're going nowhere. We enjoy our times together, but we're spinning our wheels. We've dated for four years and I love you, Grayson, but I need more. I don't know how to say this other than to come straight out with it."

Sounds to me like you already have. Hold your tongue, cowboy.

She looked down and released a sigh, then raised her head and made deep contact with Grayson's blue eyes. "I have a dinner date tomorrow evening with Marvin Rapose."

Grayson laughed. "Okay. I have a date with J-Lo. She's getting on in age but still hanging in there."

Laura's eyes never left his and she spoke softly, "I'm serious, Grayson."

She was not kidding. A stab of jealousy hit his heart; it hurt. Incredulity replaced his gleeful attitude. "You mean the banker at Wells Fargo? He's a good guy but—"

"He asks me out every time I see him, and I decided to take him up on his offer."

Grayson was stunned into silence.

"My biological clock is ticking and I have to get on with my life. I would welcome a brother or sister for Austin. I often fantasize having a daughter to share girl things with. It's obvious that's not what you want. It's become something of a practical matter with me."

Grayson's mind raced, analyzing the situation, a rapidly changing firefight and the enemy now outflanked him. They sat looking at each other for a minute.

"Laura, I admit I understand what you're saying. I wish I could explain it, but—"

"If I didn't know better, I'd say that you had another woman."

"There's no other woman, and you know it!" He threw it out too quickly and angrily.

Laura remained calm. "I know. In this tight little community, it would be the gossip of the day. Yet your actions tell me I'm competing with another woman. If it's not a woman, I don't know what it is."

"You are perfect for me. We have a great relationship, and I love the things we do together. Oddly enough, I especially like our time together with Austin."

Her reply gave him no room for escape. "Then why can't you commit permanently to us?"

Grayson leaned back and contemplated the question for a long time, too long. "I don't know." The lie pushed too deep in his subconscious to be apparent, or for him to admit to.

"Maybe you're still mourning Margaret. I could understand that except it's been too many years since she passed."

"Laura, I care for you. You're the greatest thing in my life."

"Sometimes you have to *let* the bull throw you to live another day. Who is she?"

His anger showing, he spoke with exhaustion. "I swear I'm not seeing another woman. Certainly, you know that."

Laura remained composed but with eyes beginning to glisten. "Yes, I know, you have to face yourself and admit that your mind is with Margaret...or...another, perhaps. Either way, I'm competing with a ghost."

Grayson looked confused, then his eyes widened. He thought Laura had helped him push it deep enough that he could tamp it down if it tried to resurface. Obviously, he was wrong. *Why did you do this to me, Shannon Fisher?*

He tried hard to keep Shannon hidden in his subconscious but she was tucked securely in his heart, slipping out every now and then when he least expected it. He struggled to refute the enormity of his desire, but the truth was staring at him in Laura's precious face. If he were to have a normal life, he had to rid himself of her. He had to kill the beast before it killed him. Laura also deserved a normal life.

"You're a smart lady, Laura MacIntyre." He kissed the tears on her cheeks. "I'm sorry, so sorry."

She sat in his lap, her head on his chest, and cried softly. He enveloped her in his big arms and laid his cheek on the top of her head, rocking her like a child. Inhaling the sweet fragrance that was *Laura* caused him, for a moment, to doubt his resistance to commitment. *Shut the door on Shannon and ask Laura to marry you at this very moment, you idiot.*

"She is a mistake from a past indiscretion, a mistake that I didn't think mattered. I've been a fool and messed up your life."

"You haven't messed up my life; you've added to it, helped me to get past Mack. And, yes it does matter," she whispered. "I love you and will not share you with any woman, even a mistake." She pulled back to look at him. "You have to go and take care of whatever it is that draws you to her. If you can't erase it completely, we can't continue."

"I can't go anywhere. I love you, Laura. You are the per—"

"I know you love me Grayson, in a good way but not the *special* way you love the other woman. I loved Mack in a special way that I can never love another man. That's not a lick on you, just a fact. You have that same unique feeling for someone else. It's strong. *It* controls you; you don't control it. If Mack were able to come back, I would dump you for him."

"Laura, that's callous."

"It's also true. You'd do the same if Margaret could return. There is no room for dissent, not in my heart. After all, you have to admit it isn't fair to have someone else on your mind when you're with me."

"No…it's not. But until you pushed it, I hadn't faced it myself." Before he could fully commit to Laura, or any woman, he had to reconcile his passion for Shannon, if that were possible.

Grayson took a deep breath and hugged her tighter. He struggled against her conclusion, but she had him in her crosshairs and just pulled the trigger.

"You have great insights, Laura MacIntyre. I wish you and Marvin or any other man lucky enough to win your heart, all the happiness this world can bring."

As he drove away from Laura's home for the last time, his old familiar friends, Emptiness and Loneliness, rode with him. A grown man isn't supposed to cry.

~~~

An April cold front had moved in. Grayson reached into the closet, pulled out his old winter jacket and walked outside with Millie. They lay in the grass, and gazed at the Milky Way. The big German Shepherd placed her head on his leg and licked his hand. "I gazed just like this at the night sky when fighting ISIS and thought of my family. I hate loneliness, girl."

Millie, tuned to her master's emotions, released a small whine.

"It gnaws at the soul and will consume a man if he lets it. I hate to admit it, but before tonight, even when I was alone, I used Laura as a security blanket. I honestly didn't know that's what I was doing. She brought me joy and kept my emotions stowed and even. I hope I brought her happiness. I realized today that she was my first thought every morning and last thought at night. How can I let such a wonderful woman who gave me reasons for rising and taking on the day go away so easily?"

Millie lifted her head and her ears pricked up. She got up and went on reconnaissance.

Laura and Grayson lived almost as a married couple. They talked about everything under the sun, spent time with Austin doing things as a family. He loved them both but maybe not enough. He wondered with an aching heart what she would tell the boy about him and pictured her at home crying herself to sleep. His overwhelming sense of guilt bedeviled him relentlessly for hurting someone who treated him with nothing but love and respect.

"I've done it again, Margaret, disappointed someone I care about. I have a gut feeling that I'll never learn, and it worries me that our son has trouble with his emotions." *You're a piece of work, Grayson Dean.*

Several times, he impulsively reached for his cellphone to call Laura, to ask if he could come over and hold her, love her, but he retracted his hand each time. That was pure selfishness on his part. "Margaret, I have to tell you that Laura reminds me of you. She's sweet; she's lovely; she's a strong woman. I've made a mess of this, darling. I'm wondering if the similarities between the two of you are the core of the problem and not Shannon." The minute he said it, he knew he was lying to himself.

Shannon and his illogical desire to be with her had a stranglehold on him. He kept running scenarios through his head on what course of action to take. Should he go straight to her? No. That would only make matters worse. He could not inject himself into her life and be the cause of any conflict between her and her husband, assuming she was still married. He had to remain at a distance and observe, but he **had** to be close to her, to be able to see her. His drive to be near her was like an addiction only someone hooked on cocaine would comprehend.

He placed his cold hands in his jacket pockets, to warm them. His left hand felt something soft, perhaps a handkerchief. He pulled it out, and there was the napkin from Las Vegas, a bright full moon illuminating the imprint of Shannon's luscious red lips calling to him. Millie, returned from her security patrol, nudged his hand and sniffed at the napkin. "No, Millie, you can't have this." He scratched the dog's ears, arguing with himself and circling through his life until he lay limp in the grass. Millie snuggled against him. He petted her. "Tell me, girl, why is Shannon's lure so powerful? Why can't I simply ignore her and make a life with Laura?"

Millie licked his hand.

"Margaret, I need you!"

He awoke in the wet grass, Millie's cold nose in his ear. He pulled himself up and went to his bed. His dilemma re-emerged, tormenting him. The moonlight peeked through the blinds and carried him to his last sweet night with Margaret, giving him a short respite from his quandary. In the twilight of consciousness, just before slumber conquered his body, Grayson Dean listened to Margaret's soft, sweet voice and made his decision.

Chapter 37

A Change of Plans

Year 8

Grayson was pondering the reason for Ramirez request to visit ahead of the meetup when the no-nonsense man went straight to the point. "We have a special favor to ask, son."

"Something wrong, sir?"

"No. Everything's fine." He started to say something, but deferred to Grace. "Mama, you take him on. Any man's a sucker for a sweet-talking, pretty woman."

Grace reached over from her chair beside Grayson and placed a hand on his arm. "After all these years, Papa has finally agreed to retire. We're going to move to a quiet place, maybe travel and enjoy life while we're still active."

Grace's soft voice and easy cadence had a calming effect on Grayson. "So, you want my help finding a retirement location?"

"We want to buy an acre or two from the MAG, somewhere away from BOL operations, to build a cabin."

"Buy my ass! Oh. Sorry Miss Grace."

Ramirez chuckled. "Believe me; she's heard a lot worse than that from this old boy."

Grace smiled lovingly at Papa and rolled her eyes in agreement.

"There's no way you'll pay for any of this land." Grayson said. "Remember, I own the house and ten acres outright." Abruptly, he became solemn, pensive, his mouth half opened. "No!"

"No?"

Grace became panicky. "You change your mind?"

Grayson didn't hear them. He remained in deep contemplation. Ramirez and Grace stared at him until the atmosphere became uncomfortable.

"What's going on in that thick head of yours, son?" Ramirez, sounded more than a little peeved.

Grayson suddenly became as excited as a boy with a new bicycle for Christmas. "I have a better proposal and you're gonna love it."

The pressure off, Ramirez expelled another of his famous belly laughs. "Son, I can see mischief and some wild, grand escapade written across your grinning face. I can't wait to hear this."

"I'm moving back to Houston. Instead of you having to construct another house, I'm offering you the farmhouse with the ten acres. You can have it for a dollar, just to keep it legal. All I want is my man cave set aside, where I can have a bed and leave my gear."

Ramirez and Grace were speechless.

"You'll also have to take Millie. She wouldn't adapt to city life very well."

"Other than Papa, you are the most unusual person I've ever met."

"Mama, this boy is a Green Beret. His soul yearns for the next battle, and he doesn't put a lot of emphasis on material things. He can't help himself; it's in his blood."

Grace chuckled. "You have that same yearning, Papa, but you're ancient and can't do anything about it."

"The missus is a good woman and doesn't mince her words, a comfort in my old age."

"When are you submitting your papers, Chief?"

"I still have another year, but we thought we'd need the time to build a cabin. We'll stick to the schedule. That'll give you time to find a new place."

Grace looked perplexed. "It's personal, but I'm curious to know why you want to move back to Houston."

"Yes, ma'am, it is personal. I've gotta remove a burr that's been under my saddle for too long."

Ramirez eyed him carefully. "Any burr under a young man's saddle likely involves a woman. Be careful removing that burr; it could leave permanent scars."

"I'll heed your advice, sir."

Grace tilted her head down and looked at him over the top of her glasses. She spoke as a mother scolding a child. "Papa and I have been around long enough to know when young folks are doing things against better judgement."

"I respect your concern, Miss Grace, and know that what I'm about to do, logically speaking, isn't necessarily the best thing for me, or Laura for that matter. But, if I don't take care of it now and get it out of the way it'll haunt me the rest of my life and destroy my prospects for a peaceful soul."

Ramirez studied him closely. "You aren't going after Murtadha by yourself, are you? You do know that he disappeared years ago and we have no idea where he is."

"I'd like to get my hands on him, Chief, but this is different; it's personal. Since you brought it up, if you find Murtadha, I want first crack at him."

Grace panicked. "That could be dangerous. We've already lost one son."

Ramirez patted her hand. "He's made up his mind, Mama. Let's leave the boy alone and pray for him. Grayson, we'll gladly take you up on your generous offer and would love to have Millie stay with us."

Grayson looked at Ramirez then dropped his gaze to the floor. "I could use an update on anything new going on in Houston."

"Anything in particular?"

"Is that ACLU lawyer still giving you problems?"

Grayson's attempt to sound casual fell flat. He detected the slightest change in the chief's left eyebrow. Nobody could fool the old man. He knew Grayson was fishing for something, but went along to see what he had up his sleeve.

"Ms. Fisher? She's always a pain, a little nutty if you ask me, had some sort of coming out thing she did in the courtroom some years ago."

"That's one butt-ugly woman. I think she was getting a divorce about the time I left Houston."

Ramirez gave him the, I'm-on-to-you look. "Haven't heard. She used a disguise to hide a beautiful face and pretty figure. She's quite attractive."

"You've got to be kidding. If she's pretty, she must have changed a **whole** lot." He sat silently, hoping Ramirez would give him more information.

Laura's right. I must have closure, and I can't get it anywhere else. Please, God, forgive me.

Ramirez looked at Grayson over the top of his glasses. "Son, you know you can always come to me if you have anything you need to discuss…man-to-man."

"I see Joe and the gang pulling in for the meetup," Miss Grace said, looking out the window.

Glad to have her yank his grits out of the fire, Grayson jumped to his feet. "Let's make our way over to the lodge."

Ramirez winked at Grace and they followed.

Chapter 38

The Intel Report

Year 8

Ramirez opened the meetup with the Pledge of Allegiance and a prayer.

"We're skipping the normal order of business. Joe has a contact in the FBI who has access to Top Secret information on Middle Eastern intelligence matters. His contact provided some disturbing Intel on Murtadha. After Joe's briefing, Grayson will review the pros and cons of joining the SET Patriots."

Every eye fell on Samuel and a few members released low groans.

Ramirez waited until attention resettled on him. "It's time to act. Today, we'll take the final vote and either we're in or we're out. Regardless of how the vote falls, this is it." He gave Joe the nod.

Joe stood, opened a folder, took out several large photos, and handed them to Mark to pass around.

"I have to warn you some of these are grizzly. They show dead bodies with their heads cut off. The ones with the sheep, donkeys, and men wearing dresses were taken in Egypt at a jihadi training camp. The ones with the dead bodies were taken in Africa."

Mark's mouth dropped open. "Something's not right about this. Joe, these men aren't Middle Eastern."

"Good call. They're Mexican Muslims. The tall one in the middle is Murtadha. After he escaped the…uh…accident, he went back to Mexico and disappeared down a black hole. That black hole was Egypt. According to my FBI contact, after their training he went somewhere deep into Africa with his brother and the other Mexicans to conduct holy war with ISIS."

"The psychiatrist's report at the prison—what little we could access—revealed that a Muslim inmate, Akeem Talal, converted Murtadha, his brother, and some of his gang members to Islam."

"Reverted," Grayson said.

"I'm sorry. I don't understand."

"Muslims believe that everyone is born Muslim but are fooled into believing in something else. When infidels become Muslim, to them, they are reverting to Islam, not converting. They also believe that Allah gave them everything on earth. That's why they have no qualms about stealing or taking welfare fraudulently from the infidels; it's already theirs as far as they're concerned. Infidel women are free game. To Muslim men, raping them is not immoral, but the will of Allah."

Everyone stared at him with blank faces.

Grayson shrugged. "Sorry for the interruption, Joe."

"Actually, that's good to know. It tells a lot about why Muslim refugees in Western countries act the way they do. It also gives us something to think about if we run into them after the collapse. Prison records show major changes in Murtadha after he…reverted to Islam and his Muslim inmate friend taught him to speak Arabic and learn enough to consider him educated. He experienced a euphoric awakening or some such shit. The bottom line: His violent temper and deep-seated hatred of Americans will be a major problem if he and his gang return to Houston."

Charles wasn't convinced. "Murtadha and his gang aren't that many. Certainly, we can handle them. Besides, why would they come here?"

Grayson rubbed the back of his neck. "If they're in Africa with ISIS, that means they're raping and killing, making his gang as evil and emotionless as Murtadha himself. Africa or not, my gut feeling tells me there's something big going on. We'll see. What else do you have, Joe?"

"Notice the man on the left side of photo number three. My contact wouldn't explain, but told me there was something special about him, that we'll learn why when the time is right. That's all I have, Chief."

Grayson didn't want to begin his spiel immediately. "Take ten." He walked outside the lodge to gather his thoughts.

Chapter 39

It's Now or Never

Year 9

Grayson paced as he practiced how to open the topic of joining the SET Patriots. President Crump's aggressive actions to stabilize the economy and shore up national security provided additional time to prepare for the coming collapse. Unfortunately, after the establishment Republicans screwed up Crump's agenda, the Democrats regained control and began to re-establish the Obama socialist agenda.

For too long, some in the MAG had given their approval and others only tentative thumbs-up to merging with the SET Patriots. Stubborn Samuel was the biggest holdout. If they couldn't get unanimous approval tonight, he and Ramirez had decided to stop pushing the issue and hope for cooperation between the two factions when the collapse occurred.

"Okay, back to business guys. I'm not going to pussyfoot around with you. I've—"

Ramirez and Mark began to laugh and others followed suit.

Grayson looked confused "What's so funny?"

"Sorry, Grayson, but you've never pussyfooted around in your entire life," Ramirez chuckled.

Grayson put on a pompous expression, held his nose in the air, and faked a good British accent. "Well, ladies and gentlemen, perhaps I'll fool you and pussyfoot around sometime…just to let you know that I can."

His response was so out of character, it evoked a hardy round of hooting and laughter that made him more at ease about his next sentence.

He took a deep breath and studied the faces around the room before speaking. "We have to decide on whether or not to combine resources with the SET Patriots."

Groans and eye rolls replaced the jovial mood.

"Now, just wait. These are serious folks and straight shooters. They have a few dissenters just like we do. They're receptive to instructions, which means we can mold them into an effective cadre to lead their relatives and friends to seal off the area during the die-off exactly what we need but can't do."

He went on to describe the details of their meetups, but kept his relationship with Laura to himself.

Ramirez opened for discussion. "The floor is now open to anyone who wants to address the MAG. As always, every voice carries the same weight."

They all remained silent, expecting Samuel to speak. He looked down, studying the photos of the Mexican Muslims Joe passed out earlier. They sat quietly while he took the top photo and placed it on the bottom until he had reviewed all of them several times.

Samuel cleared his throat and spoke quietly. "Everybody knows that I've been adamantly against letting anyone know about our MAG. I've given it a lot of thought, and we've talked it to death. I pondered Grayson and the chief's information and researched the Special Forces Operations manuals, even did online research into guerrilla warfare. The logic of it sounds good and it seems feasible."

Grayson heard Samuel's words, but his somber tone did not bode well for a positive decision. He held his breath.

"I came here today still prepared to vote against combining into a single unit. My family's security, for me, meant keeping our BOL an absolute secret. Alice and I see the bits of news on the Muslim refugee invasion of Europe and Africa, but we haven't given it much more than a passing thought. After looking at these photos and pondering what Joe told us, something deep inside tells me there's more to this Murtadha situation than first meets the eye. Can't put my finger on it, but there's something strange going on there and it's a little scary."

Samuel, still looking at the photos, paused but nobody spoke a word. After a few seconds he continued.

"When the collapse takes place, for weeks we'll be faced with an overwhelming number of refugees starving to death within walking distance of the BOL. City gangs and other desperate people would kill us for our food without a second thought. I've always believed that we could keep our operation a secret forever. Now, this Muslim crap pops up. We may have to contend with a combat-experienced gang of zealots hell-bent on killing us because of our religion. It's obvious to me now that, without the SET Patriots, we don't stand a chance. I'm in."

Grayson let out his breath and plopped into his chair. "Thanks for your vote of confidence, Samuel. I believe you're exactly right. You made a wise choice, made even wiser by your effort to gather and analyze all of the complexities of the issue."

"So, what do we do to get this merger underway?" Charles asked.

Grayson had been considering his approach for months. "I'll discuss it with Wayne in private. I have no doubt he'll see the benefits of combining our resources. I'll verify with him and then attend their next meetup to explain the plan and address their concerns and schedule a joint meetup at the lodge to make it official."

"Let's have a formal vote." Ramirez said. "Those in favor of combining forces with the SET Patriots say *aye*."

Everyone replied with a resounding *aye*.

"Those opposed say *nay*."

The silence sealed the deal, as far as Grayson was concerned.

Ramirez made his retirement announcement, and their plans to relocate to the farm, but didn't provide details. He then asked Grayson, "Any more business?"

Grayson considered announcing his return to Houston but decided against it, at least for the time. "No, sir. We may adjourn."

"I like the sound of *SET Patriots*," Mark said.

~~~

After everyone left, Grayson filled his insulated cup with coffee, put on his winter jacket, and lay in the grass to enjoy a star-filled black sky. A few puffy clouds lazily floated by, hiding a full moon now and then. A cool fall breeze and an owl hooting softly in the distance cleansed the cobwebs from his mind and soothed his soul. Millie came over and nuzzled his hand for a rub behind the ears. While analyzing his ambivalence to commit to Laura, his thoughts drifted to Shannon. Was she still trying to save the world and eliminate guns from the earth? He hoped her efforts were fruitless. There would come a day when they'd need every gun they could get their hands on. He felt it deep inside.

Chapter 40

The Merger

Year 9

The lodge was loaded with the full contingent of SET Patriots and MAG members. Using his strong command voice, Ramirez opened the joint meetup. "Settle down troops and let's get this meetup underway, lots to cover. Please stand for the Pledge of Allegiance and prayer."

Grayson spotted the man in the John Deere cap sitting, as usual, at a back-corner table, near the rear door. He drove to the meetup in an armored military vehicle with a machine-gun turret, but without the gun attached. Two men in camouflage and full kit with M4s accompanied him but waited in the vehicle. For the first time, oddly, the man nodded at him, but he didn't smile.

After the opening ceremony, Ramirez pointed to Wayne.

"We're gathered today to finalize a proposal to combine our forces with the Houston folks, our *organic farmer* friends."

After the laughter died down, Wayne continued. "I've got to admit, your attention to OPSEC had us fooled. You wouldn't believe the city slicker jokes that went around. We're glad to know you're well organized and disciplined. We believe our combined forces will complement each other's security and survival when the time comes. We took a vote last meetup and, now, officially invite you to join the SET Patriots. What say you?"

Wayne sat down, and Ramirez took the floor for a prearranged quick word. "Thank you, Wayne. We are proud to join with you and call ourselves SET Patriots."

His arms outstretched to sweep around the lodge and encompass all present. "Our combined forces will present **all** of us and **all of our families** with a greatly enhanced chance to survive a societal collapse and begin New America as a single community. To ensure that we are all of the same understanding, I'll turn it back to Wayne to explain the protocols that we agreed to at the leadership meetup."

"A quick overview is a good idea, Chief." He directed his attention to the SET Patriots, "Notice that I referred to Mr. Ramirez as *Chief*. He is a distinguished retired military commander with years of combat experience as a Green Beret and currently is the Chief of Police of the

Houston Police Department. As of now, he is our senior leader with command over our two divisions, the Headquarters Division and the Tactical Division."

Elroy interrupted. "We voted to join forces, not turn ourselves over to them city boys."

"I'll get to that, Elroy. For now, let's keep this simple. If anybody has questions or comments, please hold them until the end.

"From today forward, I am the Tactical Division commander and Scott is my lieutenant. Our primary mission is security and preparing the local community to survive by working with our friends, neighbors, and relatives to produce their own two-year food supply and seed banks. We'll also make them aware of our mission needs and requirements.

We also furnish medical, construction, plumbing, electrical, and other expertise the Headquarters Division lacks. Our alternate responsibilities are to assist the Headquarters Division to gather and preserve food." He looked at Elroy. "The Headquarters Division has already helped a few of our group to eat well and stay off food stamps. I'll now turn the floor over to Grayson."

Laura gave Grayson a faint smile. "I'm the Headquarters Division commander and Mark is my lieutenant. Our primary mission is to produce food, a lot of food, and preserve and distribute it to you for storage at your homes, with excess going to others in the community for their two-year supply. We furnish the central control point for tactical operations, the TOC, and communications for the entire SET Patriots. Our alternate mission is to provide standby reserve to reinforce the Tactical Division when necessary. We also provide guerrilla warfare, security guard, and crowd control training and expertise." Grayson looked at Wayne. "I believe we've covered the basics and should leave it at that for now and get into the details as time progresses."

Wayne took his cue. "These are the basics but we must be flexible enough to make adjustments as needed. Questions?"

A few folks mumbled in the back of the lodge but no one spoke up. "Elroy, did I address your concern?"

"Yep."

"Chief, you do the honors, sir."

"Let's make this official by unanimous vote. Either we all agree or all bets are off. One single nay vote and we remain separate entities. All in favor of the Houston MAG joining the SET Patriots say *aye*."

"*Aye*," sounded in a roaring response.

"All opposed to the Houston MAG joining the SET Patriots, say *nay*."

Noticing that Elmer Martel and his cohorts remained silent, he paused longer than necessary, staring directly at them. The silence hung heavy for about five seconds before Ramirez exclaimed, "Hearing none, I hereby declare us SET Patriots, each and every one!"

Grayson and Wayne shook hands and all but the naysayers cheered and walked among each other shaking hands and giving bro hugs.

When they finally settled down, Wayne acknowledged Ramirez. "Chief, I think it's time for you to take the floor again and continue with the regular meetup."

They had agreed the day would be one of celebration and not deal with the difficult issues facing them. The days ahead promised to be busy with new responsibilities and work required to help them all survive.

"Fellow Patriots, we are here today as a cohesive group because we love our God, our families, and our country. We will work in unison to defend against the ugly evil that will inevitably befall us. God bless the SET Patriots and God bless America. Now, let's enjoy the feast prepared for this celebration."

Grayson sought the man in the John Deere cap, but he was gone, sneaked out again before anyone noticed. *Is the man a damn ghost?*

Chapter 41

Chain of Command

Year 9

"I shot you first!" Samuel was in Elmer Martel's face.

"Bullshit. I shot you first!"

"Next time we have a training exercise, let's use real bullets instead of blanks to settle these who-shot-who first disputes," Wayne joked.

"No way." Yeung laughed. "That'd take the fun out of arguing; but it would present us with first aid training opportunities."

Darnell leaned against a tree. "I've had enough field rations for the day. I'm ready for a beer and real food."

Tired from predawn to early evening target practice, sneaking through the woods and lying for hours in ambushes, the group released a loud roar of whoops and backslaps in agreement.

"Let's head for the lodge, troops. The chief and Miss Grace promised burrito makings and homemade chili." Grayson's order didn't need prompting.

~~~

Laura's sad eyes made Grayson self-conscious as he stood to address the group. He steadied himself and began, "I have a big announcement to make." He hesitated, as conflicting thoughts raced through his mind. *Drop this before you lose everything again. Laura is a good woman. She'll make a wonderful wife.*

"The chief and Miss Grace are retiring and moving to the farm." Grayson paused, wishing he'd warned Laura of his next statement. He choked back his emotions. "And I'm returning to Houston."

Laura's expression didn't change, but the blood drained from her face and she wavered slightly; her hopes of establishing a life with him had just vanished.

You gave me my freedom, and I'm going to follow your advice and bring this mess with Shannon to closure one way or another.

Laura pushed Grayson away and he owed her no explanation, but he felt heavy guilt when all eyes in the room shifted in her direction. He had a strong desire to go to her and wrap her in his arms to comfort her.

Silence added a palpable tension to the air. The reaction from the group was not what Grayson expected. *Arrogant SOB. Of course, they're going to reach out to one of their own...and to a woman.*

"There are times in your life when change is in order. My reasons for returning to Houston are personal."

A few whispers were the only sounds in the room.

Ramirez came to his rescue. "Grayson, without you, we wouldn't be where we are today. The Houston MAG and the SET Patriots would still be fumbling in the dark trying to find our separate ways instead of working together to ensure our mutual survival."

Laura blinked to fight back tears, making Grayson want to crawl into a hole. A blast furnace of anger tossed him to a different place. He hadn't grasped until that moment that Laura had used a feminine ploy to get his commitment. Taking her at her word, he'd agreed that he must deal with the other woman issue. Laura hadn't figured on Grayson's feelings for Shannon being so strong, certain he would see her as the better choice. The bull threw her hard to the ground and bruised her severely, but she *would* live to see another day. It wouldn't be anytime soon, but it would come her way.

Obviously confused, the group stared at each other. The chief had provided them with their principal guidance but the man they had come to depend on most for leadership was abandoning them. In one sentence, he had shaken their world.

Wayne, glancing from Laura to Grayson, was furious. He demanded an answer for the question on everyone's mind. "Does this mean you're dumping the SET Patriots?"

Grayson scowled. "Absolutely not. I'll continue as the Headquarters Division commander, help work the farm, attend meetups and training, and, of course, when the poop hits the fan, I'll be here."

Grayson looked to the chief for assistance and realized he was on his own. *Damn, he should have talked this out with Wayne, not just the chief. He had avoided telling him because of Laura and that was a big mistake.*

"I apologize for not meeting with the full leadership group prior to this announcement, but it came up suddenly and has to be dealt with now." Wayne glared at Grayson, not accepting the apology.

Chief Ramirez, ever the skillful strategist, saw the opening he'd been waiting for, one that could prevent an upset of the entire applecart and place Grayson in a better position to assume overall command in the future. "I have a proposal I think you will like and agree with. Mama and I are getting along in age and, to be honest, I'm having some issues with my heart. We can't take part in the physical demands of tactical activities but we can feed the chickens and rabbits, weed the garden on cool mornings, and other simple tasks."

Grayson thought he saw where Ramirez was going. "You can call me for the more strenuous jobs, Chief."

"I'll help, too," sounded throughout the group.

"Thanks guys. Mama and I know we can count on you, but I have a slight realignment proposal. Good friends, you've given me the privilege of guiding you through these developmental stages. But it's time for someone else to take the reins and lead the SET Patriots."

Everyone sat silent for a moment. Grayson's announcement was shocking enough. Now this.

Yolanda spoke first. "Chief, you're our leader. We'd be lost without you."

"Those are kind words but it's really not true. You have many leaders among you, and it's time for me to pass the baton to one of them, now that Mama and I are retiring."

Slightly calmer, Wayne spoke. "There is only one man, other than you, fully qualified to lead this group and that's Grayson."

Grayson was humbled. "*You* have great leadership skills, too, Wayne. If not for you, the SET Patriots wouldn't exist."

"Maybe so but I don't have the military background you have that gives you the innate ability to analyze strategic situations, the subtle things that, if missed, could explode out of control and get people killed. You have knowledge and an uncanny ability to perceive problems I often miss."

Elmer Martel had to have his say. "Ah gotta be honest, cousin. Ah don't like this one bit, you making yorself secondary to Grayson. Yor from here'n he ain't."

Elroy and Darnell made noises of agreement.

Wayne's no-nonsense reply came quick and sharp, "You three knock off the crap and listen closely; we're talking survival for our families. This is no time for egos to get in the way. I want my wife and kids to survive what's coming. That means putting the best man in charge. I recommend Grayson."

The man in the John Deere cap began to clap in approval. Others joined in a loud round of applause and cheers, especially Laura.

Ramirez began expelling another of his belly laughs that caught everyone off guard, wondering what was so funny.

He paused a moment to regain control. "Good folks, remember I said I have a proposal. Your conversation leads right into it. Military units have a commander that provides overall guidance and an executive officer, an XO. The XO controls the day-to-day operations under the guidance of the commander. Mama and I have retirement plans. If you want me to remain as your commander in an advisory role, I'll accept, but under certain conditions."

Miss Grace looked worried. "What Papa is saying is that we're going into retirement and plan to travel and take life easy as long as our health holds out."

"If you can accept that, I suggest that Grayson take the XO position and handle the details," Ramirez said.

"When Grayson moves up to the XO position that leaves the Headquarters Division commander's position open," Charles said.

"True," replied Grayson, "and we have the perfect man for the job."

Everyone's head turned toward Mark.

Yolanda gave him a quick kiss on the cheek. "It appears you've been silently selected, sir."

"Wayne and I have a great rapport. I would be proud to serve as the Headquarters Division Commander," Mark said.

"I agree," Wayne said.

Miss Grace was uncharacteristically humorless. "We just want to be free to travel, to go and come as we please without restrictions."

"Mama, they're saying that we'll be free to enjoy our retirement. I won't have to do more than conduct meetups every now and then and be available to provide guidance as needed, right guys?"

Samuel confirmed it. "That's right, Miss Grace. Not to worry. You two lovebirds can come and go as you please."

Her face relaxed and Ramirez smiled and looked at Grayson. "What's next on the agenda, XO?"

The applause and cheers reflected the SET Patriots' approval.

The turn of events seemed to have mediated Grayson's turbulent opening of the meetup.

To establish his new position, Grayson closed the meetup. "Okay, SET Patriots, having no further business, I hereby declare this meetup closed and order everyone to grab a beer for the social."

Laura slipped out the door quietly.

Chapter 42

What to Do?

Year 9

Grayson stopped by his climate controlled storage unit in Houston and verified all was well with his old furniture, then set up housekeeping in an extended stay hotel. He took a few days to visit Joe and Ramirez and reorient himself to the bustling life in Houston, and then settled down to find Shannon and begin setting his life straight; at least, that was his intent.

Finding Shannon's address was easy but determining her marital and work status wasn't. According to the *Houston Chronicle*, she was still active in the anti-gun movement and defending scumbag illegals. He hoped she had put aside her brainwashed liberal mindset, at least to some degree. *Yeah and I voted for Hillary. That's not likely.*

He couldn't find any records that she had divorced, so he drove by her house occasionally to see if her husband was there and maybe catch sight of her. He felt like a stalker but pushed the feeling aside.

One Saturday morning with little to do, he called the real estate agent whose sign was in the front yard of a nice-looking house in Shannon's neighborhood and made an appointment for the next day. After hours of researching houses for sale online and watching the Houston Astros play baseball on television, he drove to the cemetery to visit Margaret and Amanda.

The sky was clear and a warm July breeze made the trees sway to a soft waltz of their own. His visits could become routine now. He prayed that Daniel would forgive him and that his son would find peace. He remembered Shannon standing by the old chapel the day of the funeral and shook his head, contemplating the irony that he could not touch the three beautiful women in his life. As darkness crept across the cemetery, he made a call and headed to the Watering Hole.

~~~

Conrad, in a sleeveless shirt and as derelict as ever, was still the bartender. He visibly tensed and stepped back when Grayson walked up to the bar. "Look, officer, I don't want no trouble. That lawyer lady tole me I'd go back ta prison if I didn't do what she said. I didn't have no choice but talk bad about you."

Grayson was surprised that Conrad recognized him. "That's old news, barkeep. Just do your job and we'll be cool." He laid a hundred on the bar. "Bring me two bottles of Heineken and hold the change until I'm finished."

He stepped over to his favorite table just as Mark walked through the door. The friends shook hands. "Thanks for meeting me here. Want a burger?"

"I'll take the beer but pass on the burger," Mark said. "You sounded like you were in trouble. What's up?"

"I need to share some thoughts with someone I trust, and I'd appreciate your perspective on a personal issue. I know you'll keep it confidential and not beat around the bush with your advice."

Mark cut his eyes at the bartender. "And you want to do it here?"

Grayson suppressed a laugh, leaned over the table and whispered. "He's scared shitless of me. We won't talk when he's around."

Mark didn't like giving advice on someone's private life. He opened the door to that prospect, however, the first time he invited Grayson to the bar. More than that, Grayson had become a good friend and was asking for his help. "It's your dime, but it sounds like you need a priest, not me. Besides, I'm a Methodist."

"We're all Christians, Mark. Besides, you know my life has been out of kilter since I lost Margaret and Amanda. I can't seem to get my feet back on the ground and everything points in one direction, a sinful direction."

Mark leaned back in his chair. "Stop right there! You *do* need a priest. My minister is a great counselor, too." His voice rose just as Conrad delivered the beers. "You're not gay, are you?" he teased loudly. Several heads turned to look at them. "Is that what happened with Laura?"

Conrad leaned over and whispered angrily, "Listen, you two, this is a *straight* bar. You can stay but none of that funny stuff, like kissing and touching. It drives out the regular customers."

Grayson and Mark looked at each other and burst into uncontrolled laughter. Conrad's face turned crimson and he muttered to himself all the way back to the bar.

Grayson finally recovered. "No, that's not what happened with Laura."

"You two are like two peas in a pod. What happened?"

"We're…we…that is; I met someone, years ago. It was under unusual circumstances, before Laura, and I can't get the other woman out of my mind. I have to reconcile my feelings or Laura and I can't go forward."

"So, what's stopping you from dating the other woman to see what happens?"

"She's married," Grayson stated flatly.

"Damn, Grayson! Not good."

"It gets worse. She's married to a loser, and I'm hoping she'll dump him. I wish I didn't feel this way. It's just not right…and sinful as all get-out."

"You might want to get on your knees and crawl into the confessional. I sure as hell won't tell you to go after her. That would make me a co-conspirator in your sin and give you a false sense of having permission."

"I'm not asking you for permission. Sometimes I solve problems by discussing them with someone else, and you and Yolanda seem to have a good thing going."

"Here's some advice anyway and remember you asked. I think you're a fool not to commit to Laura. Are your feelings for your…paramour that strong or are your feelings for Laura too weak?"

Grayson twirled his bottle on the table. "Yes and no."

"You're confused, alright."

"My feelings for Laura are very strong, and I think we might be happily married. You'll think I'm nuts but I'm willing to wait for the other woman. She draws me in to her in a way that defies logic. I can't be married to one woman while another is constantly on my mind."

"I know you well, Grayson, and you're not nuts. You're apparently in love on a level that few men attain. I know. It's what I feel for Yolanda. If you want to wait completely on the sideline and not interfere with this woman and her husband, I think that's half okay, but coveting another man's wife is wrong, no matter how long you wait."

"I shoved this thing down so deep, I thought it was over. I've tried for well over seven years to turn it off. You're right, Mark. I can't do anything to bring about the separation between her and her husband. Not one single thing."

The two sat in worried silence before Grayson spoke. "If their separation was by my hand, it would dilute our relationship and haunt me until I died."

Mark studied his surroundings, the table, his bottle, and finally faced Grayson. "Is this why you're back in Houston?"

Grayson nodded.

Mark pointed the bottom of his bottle toward Grayson. "Then you may have already made your decision. You here to see her?"

"I'm between a rock and a hard place. I can't leave, and I can't see her. Maybe after a few years, I'll view her in another light and move on. For now, I have to do this." Thinking of what Laura had told him, he continued. "It controls me, I don't control it."

"Are you really willing to wait, perhaps for years, maybe forever, for her to become widowed or divorced and forego your happy relationship with Laura? You're taking a big chance if you see her. It'll place you right in the middle of something ugly."

"That's exactly why I needed to talk this out. Hearing it out loud makes me realize how much trouble I'm in and may get into...or cause others."

"Grayson, don't make me lose faith in your integrity and be disappointed in you." Mark hoped his challenge would stick with Grayson and help him to stay on the straight and narrow.

"I won't disappoint you."

"You're notorious for breaking the rules, Grayson."

Mark's bite at his character stung Grayson. "I'll toe the line; don't worry about me. There's something else, something I can't put my finger on, like a force pushing at me that has nothing to do with the woman."

"For your sake and hers, I hope you resist the urge to break your own rules, to say nothing about Jesus' teachings. You're on thin ice." Mark shook his head and blew out hot air. "Welcome home to Houston, my friend." He held his beer up for a toast and Grayson followed suit. "Here's to success in the resuscitation of your love life."

"Hear! Hear!" Grayson exclaimed.

"All this talk has made me hungry," Mark hinted jokingly.

Grayson got Conrad's attention. "Hey, barkeep! Two more Heinekens, please, and a couple of thick T-bones, medium rare, with loaded baked potatoes. The guy looks like a scumbag but cooks the best steaks in town."

Chapter 43

What Am I Doing?

Year 9

"Mr. Dean, we've toured every home on the market in this neighborhood, but none are to your liking. Many homes in similar neighborhoods in Houston meet your specifications. I'll take you back to your hotel, and if you are amenable, we can check out some of those tomorrow."

No other neighborhood would put him close enough to Shannon that he could casually monitor her long enough to determine his next step.

"I told you before that I'm not interested in other neighborhoods." *It's time to dump this ignorant jackass.* "I'll continue to search the Internet and call you if I find what I'm looking for."

Grayson had plenty of time; he would wait until the right house came available in Shannon's neighborhood. After meeting with Mark and Father O'Brian, he established rules for himself, some not in accord with the church. Get close enough to observe her, keep a safe distance, stay hidden, and avoid interfering with her life. He would gather information on her personal situation over time. If she was happy, he would sell and move on, wherever *on* might be.

As he drove to Gatlin's BBQ, he tried to convince himself that he wanted a house in *that* upscale neighborhood to conceal his research on Murtadha. "If you're going to talk to yourself, at least be honest. You love another man's wife and wish she would split from him. How are you going to hide from Shannon if you live in her neighborhood? Maybe you can get a disguise like the one she used to wear. Fool. Daniel's right; I'm a raging egomaniac. I'm an asshole who always has to have my own way."

A delicious pulled-pork dinner and three glasses of iced tea later, he mulled over his situation and took a leisurely drive through Shannon's neighborhood. Maybe he would be lucky enough to get a quick glimpse of her. As he passed the cul de sac where Shannon's home was located, he saw a real estate agent hammering a for-sale sign in front of the property to the right of her house.

Was it an omen? Is it against the rules? How could it be against my own rules? I'll regret it forever if I don't at least check it out.

He parked in the driveway and approached the agent. "Hi. I'm Grayson Dean. I've been looking for a home in this neighborhood."

"Hi. I'm Gloria. Buy this house tonight, and it'll be the quickest sale I ever made." She gave him her best real estate smile. "I just got this listing a half hour ago. It has five bedrooms, each with its own bath. Do you have a large family?"

"No, I'm a…a widower and live solo."

"Sorry. You have my condolences."

"Thanks, but it was a long time ago."

Her curiosity peaked, she had to ask, "Why do you want such a large and expensive home for just one? Wouldn't a small bachelor pad be more practical?"

"Upscale homes bring a better return when you sell them. And what if I marry a woman with ten kids?" he joked, to keep Gloria from asking him additional personal questions. *Stay off the radar, dummy.*

She laughed. "That would be a hoot. You'll like this deal then. It's a bank repo, marked down for a quick sale as is. They will not make any repairs or negotiate the price. You want a quick tour?"

Gloria pointed out the features, and Grayson fought the conflicts bouncing from one corner of his head to another as they walked through the house. He knew he should run away as fast as possible, but he couldn't budge. Damn Mark and his warning not to break the rules. They're my rules, not his. I'll do whatever the hell I please!

After going through every room and checking everything that could be a problem, and there were many, Grayson did not hesitate. "Well, Gloria, this house needs a lot of small repairs. That'll keep me busy for a while, but that's okay. Let's make this the quickest home you've ever sold. Put the sign back in your car and let's work up a contract."

"Are you always this impulsive?" Her tone told Grayson she thought he was shining her on, didn't have a dime to his name.

"I've lived my life mostly in impulse mode. It feels right to me but drives others crazy."

"I hope you don't think I'm prying into your personal business too much, but I have the feeling there's more to this." Grayson was enjoying talking with the easygoing stranger. He liked her straightforward approach. Other than Shannon and Laura, he'd never had a personal conversation with a woman other than Margaret.

"Of course there is. For one thing, I'm a prepper and—"

"Sorry for interrupting, but do you mean one of those doomsday guys I saw on the National Geographic channel?"

Grayson laughed. "We don't use the term *doomsday*." Repeating what Ramirez told him years ago. "It carries negative connotations that real preppers don't care for."

"So, you're willing to put big money in a home that may become useless and have no value some day?"

"Think about that for a second. I have the money to pay cash for this house. Suppose the country experiences a collapse the day after closing and everything's in a state of absolute anarchy. This house and everybody's money will be worthless. so why should I not enjoy life today? Worrying about the future is wasted energy for those of us prepared for it."

He could see Gloria's wheels turning. *My man, you've confused the hell out of this woman.*

"I'm sorry, but I don't see what you mean. Why will money be worthless?"

"If the world as we know it collapses, every one of Bernie Sanders' millionaires and billionaires will find themselves as poor as any homeless person and at risk of dying of starvation along with the rest of the population. It won't matter that they could pay a million dollars for a loaf of bread or a can of beans. Money can't buy what doesn't exist."

Gloria's eyes widened. "Go on."

"So, I might as well live in a big expensive home and enjoy it while I can."

"I'm not sure I fully buy the collapse thing, but I do agree that we should live while we can. Follow me to the office, and we'll work up the contract. I'll hand-carry it through the process and it'll be yours within a few days."

Grayson was in near panic mode all the way to her office. His good side versus bad side had a fierce argument that gave him a headache, and he had to envision Shannon in Vegas to keep him driving.

Thirty minutes later, Gloria pointed to the signature line on the purchase agreement. "Sign right here, Mr. Dean, and give me an earnest money check for a thousand."

His hand shook slightly as he signed. *What the hell am I doing? Just like jumping from an airplane at twenty thousand feet, there's no turning back now.*

Chapter 44

Knock Knock – Who's There?

Year 9

Grayson had many talents, but he admitted home decorating was not one of them. Miss Grace helped him furnish the farmhouse, but he wanted to do something entirely different with his first solo house, although he didn't know what. His initial attempt got off to a shaky start.

He moved in some furniture from storage, including Daniel and Amanda's bedroom furniture. Leaving Margaret and his bedroom suite in storage, he shopped for a king bed for the master bedroom and a new recliner for his man cave. Looking at his old recliner for the first time since placing it in storage, images of his precious Amanda crawling into his lap to snuggle hit him hard. He swore never to sit in it again. Closing his misting eyes, he could smell her favorite shampoo and hear her giggles.

He furnished the sunroom with a patio table and chairs set, and turned one of the bedrooms into an office. Another bedroom became survival preparation, including firearms, ammo, water filtering systems, a stock of freeze-dried and canned foods if trapped at home for any reason, and a bugout bag. Hidden by the privacy fence, he added rain collection barrels to the backyard gutter downspouts.

From there he was lost. He convinced himself he would hire a decorator, hoping to impress Shannon if the day ever came. He wondered why he hadn't inadvertently run into her yet and figured that she must be participating in the anti-gun rally in Washington.

When the few pieces of new furniture were in place and the delivery truck gone, he put the king bed on a frame and hung a few of his clothes in the closet, not fully committing—an annoying new habit. Afterward, he settled into his new man-cave recliner with a pen and pad and surveyed his new domain. Daniel and Amanda would have loved the new place and his new toys, especially the big movie theater-size popcorn popper.

He relaxed, looked around, contemplated his next major step and began to make a list of things to do: buy tools to replace the ones he left at the farm, doorknobs, painting materials and paint…. As his list grew, his sense of wellbeing leveled out and he became stimulated by the challenges. A man needs a mission in life. He'd have the place in tiptop condition in a few months. Finishing his list, he flipped on the television and stared in amazement as his eighty-inch flat screen came to life.

Fox News had footage of a battle going on in a small town in the north of Iraq on the Syrian border. A group of ISIS fighters was repelling a contingent of Iranian soldiers. The Iranians' intent was to wipe out the Sunnis and reunite Iraq and Iran, under Shia control of the Iranian Ayatollah, of course. The footage included bearded fighters, one waving an ISIS flag. Oddly, they looked unlike Middle Easterners. Grayson spent enough time in that part of the world to notice subtle differences. Recognition slowly creeped into his consciousness. He grabbed the chair arms and sat forward, eyes wide. *It can't be.*

He backed the clip up on his new DVR and reviewed it several times before he was certain. "Carlos and Miguel Murtadha. Well I'll be damned." *Bless Joe for obtaining those photos from the feds.* Even with their beards. He stared at their ugly faces. "Damn!"

Grayson ignored the doorbell, twice, too engrossed in the image frozen on the screen. His concentration broke when it rang a third time. Perturbed and expecting someone trying to convert him to another religion, he jerked the door open.

Shannon, looking lovely in a pale green, thigh length, spaghetti strap sundress, stared back at him. She carried a Welcome Friends gift box in her hands. They stood in shocked silence, mouths open, waiting for the other to speak.

Grayson opened the door wider, stepped back, and swallowed hard. "Please come in. You live around here?"

Shannon took a step inside and gave him a skeptical look. "So it appears." He saw the anger hit her. "What the hel...heck are you doing here?"

"I got tired of farming."

"Farming? You're no farmer. You know what I mean; damn you, Grayson."

His impulsive reaction was sarcastic. "Thanks. It's good seeing you too."

Shannon briefly closed her eyes and shook her head. "I'm sorry, but you have to admit this is quite a shock. And don't try to convince me this is a coincidence...*neighbor!*"

A little head with beautiful long red locks peeked from behind Shannon. "Mommy, can I give the gift to our new neighbor? Can I? Huh?" The little girl held out a card to Grayson.

Grayson, mouth agape, looked down at the pretty child. His heart clenched. "Amanda," he whispered.

Placing her little fists on her hips and employing the most profound sarcasm a little girl could muster and with her nose in the air, she announced, "My name is not Amanda. It's Marcie and I'm six."

Shannon looked at Marcie, then at Grayson. She blinked her eyes and managed to croak at her daughter and hand her the gift box. "Marcie, this is Mr. Dean, our new neighbor. Show your manners," she scolded.

Grayson took the card and gift box from Marcie and shook the little hand extended to him, which now bore a pleasant smile and accompanied with a little curtsy. "I'm pleased to meet you, sir. Welcome to our neighborhood, Mr. Dean."

"I'm pleased to meet you too, Marcie."

She looked at Shannon. "Did I do it right, Mommy?"

Shannon smiled, "You did great, sweetie."

She refocused on Grayson, who was still staring at Marcie. "As you can see, Larry and I finally got our wish. This is our beautiful daughter."

Grayson returned his attention to Shannon. "Yes. She's a beautiful girl…just like her mother…who hasn't changed a bit." He raised his eyebrows and flattened his voice. "She seems to have inherited her mother's demeanor, too."

Shannon flashed a quick smile that just as quickly turned to a frown. "I never expected to see you again. Been farming, huh? Married?" *Damn, I can' believe I asked him that.*

"Well…counselor, the short story: I'm single." *Flash of the eyes. She likes that answer.* "I sold the old house and bought a farm near Palestine, but it didn't work out as expected. So here I am. And you?"

Marcie peeked around Shannon to check out the house. "Are you poor, Mr. Dean?"

Grayson chuckled. "No, Marcie. I just haven't had time to decorate the house yet."

"A farmer. Interesting choice for a detective. My practice slowed, taking care of a little one absorbs much of my time. But, I'm as engaged in my favorite project as ever."

"I'm not little." Marcie poked her lips out in a pout. "I'm in first grade, and I can read."

Grayson heard Marcie loud and clear, but Shannon's sudden change to a friendlier temperament kept him talking. "You mean eliminating the Second Amendment and confiscating all the guns?" he teased.

"Oh, how I wish," she teased back. "Larry will be home soon, and I need to get dinner started."

"It's good seeing you again, Shannon. I'm glad we're neighbors."

Shannon offered a handshake as she took her first look around the house, scrutinizing its meager settings. "Same here, Grayson. One day soon, we'll have to explore how this *coincidence* happened. You have a lot of work ahead of you. The people who lived here before partied a lot. Feds busted them for selling drugs, bigtime. I imagine the damage is extensive.

"Actually, this is probably it for a while. Not sure how long I'll be staying."

Shannon gave him a half smile. "Come, Marcie, and help me prepare dinner."

"Thank you for the card and gift, Marcie."

"You're welcome, sir. Do you live all by yourself?"

"Yes," he replied, wondering at her curiosity.

"Mommy, we should ask Mr. Dean to eat dinner with us, so he won't be lonesome."

"That's okay, Marcie. I have plenty to eat right here in my house."

"Grayson, dinner is at six. Don't be late."

"Shannon, that's not necessary."

As she led her daughter by the hand across the porch and down the steps, Shannon turned her head and spoke emphatically, "Marcie has spoken, and you know that girls always get their way. Besides, it's the proper thing to do for a new neighbor." Curiosity got the better of her. *What has this man been doing and what is he up to now?*

"In that case, I accept your invitation."

"Yay! See you later, Mr. Dean."

"See you later, Marcie."

While helping set the table, Marcie looked up at her mother. "Know what? I like Mr. Dean."

Shannon's broad smile lit her face. "Me, too, sweetie, me, too."

Larry looked up from reading his paper and frowned. "You don't mean Grayson Dean, our new neighbor?"

"Yes. Do you know him?"

"I saw him moving in and recognized him from the news reports several years ago. You used to hate him, complained about him all the time. When did that stop? Better yet, why did it stop?"

She forced a false smile. "I caused his resignation from the Houston Police Force, one of my grandest achievements. Once he left, I haven't thought about him and there's no reason for me to be enemies with him now." She bent her head to the cobbler she was taking from the oven to hide the guilt filling her.

"Interesting he moved next door to us and now you're old buddies?"

She snapped her head around and glared at him. "Stop it, Larry! I admit it's strange, but it's been years since I got him fired. If anyone should hold a grudge, it's him, not me. Please be nice at dinner."

~~~

Grayson smiled at Shannon. "Dinner was delicious. You're a great cook. Thank you for inviting me."

"You're welcome. I'm glad you enjoyed it."

Marcie beamed. "Peach cobbler and vanilla ice cream was my idea. I rolled the dough."

A quick flash to his last dinner with his family burned, and he found Marcie staring at him and waiting for a response. "Peach cobbler is my favorite, and I haven't had it in years. Larry, you are one lucky man to have these two sharing your life."

"Yeah, I guess so."

This guy is weird. He watches Shannon and me like we're monkeys in a cage. I need to walk cautiously. He's guilty of something or suspicious of me; it's subtle, but it's there. Maybe, the new alpha male in the neighborhood threatens his metrosexual manhood. Tough shit.

Shannon gave Larry a dirty look. "Gentlemen, retire to the living room while Marcie and I clean the dishes."

Larry walked ahead to a loveseat and motioned to an overstuffed chair for Grayson. As they settled with a brandy to top off dinner, Larry spoke blandly. "So, Grayson, I'm curious. When you were a cop, Shannon hated your guts, and I doubt you particularly liked her. Now, you seem like long-lost best friends. What gives?"

Grayson pegged Larry as a class-A metrosexual. The bleach-blond permed do and the thin strips of hair along his jawlines that blended with his well-groomed goatee were indications of his struggle to hide his subconscious sense of masculine inadequacy. *The pretentious ass craning his neck to look up at me doesn't help. We're as different as a tiger and its prey. The question at this point: which was which?*

"There came a time after I lost my family when I realized *hate* consumed more energy than…any other sense I had for people." *Accepting this dinner invitation was not a good idea.*

"You mean a sense like *love*…for example."

"And other feelings that fall in between. I lost the desire to hate when my wife and daughter were killed." Larry seemed satisfied for the moment. *I need to get the hell of here!*

"I remember Shannon telling me about that wild car chase and the accident. My condolences."

Grayson changed the subject quickly. "You have a beautiful daughter, and it's obvious she's an extrovert."

Larry's face turned to stone cold marble. "She's a lot like her mother."

Shannon entered with a glass of wine and sat beside Larry. "Marcie's playing with her Barbie dolls, her favorite before-bath-and-bed ritual."

Holding his brandy high, Larry proposed a toast. "Here's to our new neighbor. May your presence enhance our community."

"Hear! Hear!" Shannon raised her glass. *What a dick I married!*

They engaged in small talk for a few minutes before Grayson excused himself and left.

~~~

Halfway down the sidewalk, he heard Larry's angry shouts about never inviting that SOB to his house again.

Grayson hesitated, fists clenched. He forced himself to continue to walk, ignoring his innate male instinct to protect Shannon. His anger accelerated as his thoughts flew to his conversations with Father O'Brian and Mark. Mark's hopes that Grayson would not forfeit his integrity over a forbidden woman came back to smack him in the face.

Way to go, dumbass! You successfully broke **ALL** your rules in one day! And look at the result."

He went straight to his newly stocked refrigerator, grabbed a bottle of Heineken, and looked at it as if viewing another world through the green glass. He was a protector, a sheepdog, but tied with an invisible chain to a tree. Unable to protect his female, the volcano erupted.

He threw the bottle against the kitchen's tile wall, where it burst in a torrent of crushed glass. He grabbed another beer and repeated the action, then fell to his knees in the scattered glass, looked to heaven, and screamed, "Father O'Brian, you'd be ashamed to call me a man of God! I have failed in every way!"

~~~

At first light, Grayson awoke in the wet grass and felt around for Millie. Finally realizing where he was, he rolled over and struggled to stand. His knees were hot with a hundred bee stings and his pants were stuck to them. He could barely crack his swollen eyes. What happened?

He saw the light in his kitchen and memory assaulted him. He'd screwed up royally. He remembered promising Mark, Father O'Brian, and God it would never happen again. He couldn't escape the fact that he had lied to all of them, especially God.

Shannon's reaction to him yesterday had stroked his ego, but the fact remained that she was married and had a child. Hurting that little girl or Shannon was not his intention. He questioned what he would have done if a *Grayson* had come sniffing around Margaret and Amanda.

He staggered into the house through the kitchen door to find glass shards and beer scattered everywhere. "Dear God Almighty, will I ever get control again? Please forgive me."

His body aching, he walked stiff-legged to the bathroom where he was startled at the image of a broken man staring back at him through the mirror. Eyes red and swollen, crusted with sleep, he gazed at the blood spotting his face. He turned on the shower, allowing it to warm while pulling off his filthy shirt. He stepped in with his pants on to soften the bloody cloth stuck to his knees. Finally stripped, he let the steaming hot water wash away blood and glass slivers. Soap set him on fire, but he scrubbed with the punishment he felt was warranted.

Over the next two weeks, Grayson picked glass out of his face, arms, and knees and stayed inside, showering on occasion as his beard grew. He contemplated his lost family, his lovely Laura, his lust for Shannon, and his life in general. He ordered pizza and Chinese delivery and ate canned soup as substitutes for real food. He deliberated what to do about the trashed kitchen, a reflection of his own life.

Margaret and Laura were constantly on his mind, and he missed Millie and visits with Wayne. He decided telling Mark and Father O'Brian about Shannon was a mistake. He'd set himself up to fail on all fronts. Annoyed that Murtadha was out of reach, he again fancifully toyed with the idea of going back to the Middle East to kill the scumbag, but logic caused him to forfeit the idea altogether. By the end of the second week, he had made concrete decisions.

He had a responsibility to the Set Patriots. As the XO, he was the de facto commander and had to keep them motivated and trained. He also had to determine what to do differently to prepare to fight organized gangs, especially MS-13 and Murtadha with his hardened jihadist fighters, assuming they ever returned.

They would have years of combat training and experience. If the Intel was correct, he was no longer a street fighter with limited skills but combat ready, trained and experienced, which somewhat leveled the playing field. He and Mark must turn the SET Patriots into a military fighting machine capable of defending against attacks from these enemies. He also had to help Wanda prepare Daniel and Gabriel for bugging out when the time came.

As time passed, he started to become accustomed to his new surroundings and his new life. The pizza deliveryman's recoil at the inside air when he opened the door told him it was time to destroy the evidence of his beer bottle tossing battle. After removing the signs of his emotional eruption and a good scrubbing of the kitchen, he showered, shaved, dressed in clean clothes, and went shopping for a Texas-size steak to put on the grill.

Arriving at the supermarket, he noticed a small gym in the strip mall. He stepped down from his truck, glanced down at the results of inactivity, pizza, and Chinese food, to his waistline and walked directly to the gym. A buff young man in a foot cast greeted him and presented workout options and costs. He apologized for not having an instructor on hand. "I just purchased this place and getting started is more difficult than I imagined."

Grayson rubbed his chin. "Hmmm. I'm looking for a job and have years of experience with the Army Physical Fitness program. Hire me and I'll start a military-oriented program for you that'll bring in customers."

"Sorry. I don't have enough customers to pay for employees yet."

"Don't worry about it. Put a sign in the window, 'Green Beret Fitness Program,' and I'll be here in the morning at eight to start the program. You can pay me as a consultant when I start making money for you. In the meantime, I'll pay you for my workouts. How does that sound?"

The young man stuck out his hand. "Damn. I can't argue with that deal. My name is Brandon."

"I'm Grayson."

Before Grayson left, they made plans to advertise the new class.

~~~

Grayson grilled his steak and, for the first time, took his meal to the table in the sunroom. Looking through the huge glass enclosure, he became aware of his unobstructed view of Shannon's home. Mixing the butter and sour cream into his baked potato, he contemplated his situation with her. Cutting into his steak, he looked at the small row of yellow knockout roses on the border of their properties and drew a thick mental line along it, resolving never to cross it until the time was right, if it were ever to be.

Chapter 45

Douchebag Larry

Year 10

"Thanks for coming over, Jillian. I don't know what I'd do without you."

"Baby sister, we are the only ones left in our family." She handed Shannon a tissue to wipe her eyes. "Other than some distant cousins, we don't have anyone to turn to but each other."

"Thanks, Jillian. You're my sister *and* best friend. It's good to have someone to unload on, but it's a one-way situation lately. I have a guy friend but, because of Larry's insane jealousy, I can't have anything to do with him."

Jillian cocked her head sideways. "Oh, Sissy, you've been holding out on me."

"Not really," she lied.

"You said that too quickly and dropped your eyes." Jillian filed it away for later ammunition. "What's the douchebag up to this time and where's Marcie? I have a birthday hug for her. She's very tall. Hard to look at her and think she's only seven today."

"She's playing Barbie dolls with her friend, Melodie. Larry has his issues, but he's doing well in his job. I was so happy when I discovered that we were pregnant and—"

Jillian scolded Shannon as though she were a child. "*We! We* were pregnant! *You* were pregnant, not *him*. Stop with the politically correct crap. He was conspicuously absent most of those nine months and you know I'm not talking about his stupid job."

Shannon stood her ground. "Down girl! I'm starting to accept that you've drifted completely away from our liberal roots, but, the fact is, a married couple is considered *we* for pregnancy."

"Mom and Dad were brainwashed…and by extension, so were we, but that's for another day." Jillian giggled. "Let's talk about your guy friend."

"I haven't told you this before, but when **I** discovered **I** was pregnant, it was the happiest day of my life. I couldn't wait to tell Larry. I rushed home from the doctor's office and cooked a special dinner, put on a pretty dress, used the fine china, put candles on the table, the whole shooting match."

"You *must* be upset Miss I-Hate-Guns."

"Touché. Anyway, when I told him, he stared at me for the longest time, his face turned purple, he became extremely angry, and he barreled out of the house. He went to the club and got drunk, something he continues to do, and quite frequently."

"He's always been a douchebag loser who runs to hide rather than deal with real life." Jillian threw up her hands. "I know! I know! You thought he would change, but they never do. He's a douchebag mama's boy."

"Stop calling my husband a douchebag."

"No! Admit that you agree with me. Divorce the bastard."

"We're Catholic. Divorce is out of the question. I discussed annulment with Father Flannery, but I have no grounds acceptable to the church."

"He's well over thirty and older than you. When is this maturity supposed to kick in?"

"Will you listen?" Shannon begged.

"Sure. As soon as you tell me the latest irrational thing he's done to you and get on to your guy friend."

"I can take whatever Larry throws at me, which isn't much outside sex, and he's pathetic at that." Shannon looked away from Jillian and bit her lower lip. "Do you know I've only had an orgasm one time in my entire life?" Shannon dropped her head and shook it. Expelling the air from her lungs. "I can't believe I said that!"

"TMI!" Jillian was in shock. "I'm glad you've gotten at least one in."

"Yeah, lucky me. Marcie craves her father's attention, but for the most part, he ignores her, and the rest of the time, he treats her with pure meanness. I honestly don't know why. Maybe it's his way to avoid responsibility for her. Maybe he wanted a boy."

"Ask him."

"He refuses to talk about it or get professional counseling. I sometimes wonder if he has another woman but feels unable to escape from us."

"I can't see it. The douchebag doesn't have it in him."

"You enjoy demeaning him, don't you?"

"With good reason. He's destroying the lives of my baby sister and niece."

Shannon's tears began to flow and she blubbered, "She tried to climb into his lap this morning for her birthday hug. He stood up, dumping her on the floor. I wanted to kill the bastard."

Jillian's mouth fell open. She held Shannon the way a mother holds a traumatized child, stroking her hair while Shannon sobbed. As Shannon calmed down, Jillian abandoned her sisterly bantering.

"I *would* kill the bastard, or at least I think I would. Then, I've never been married, or loved a man or a child enough to want to lash out. I can be a sounding board, but that's about it."

"That's what I need the most, someone to listen."

"Well then, let's talk about you. I've watched you go through some changes over the past few years, but you've not lowered the volume on your tough, liberal positions. You mellowed in some ways after Marcie was born and don't belittle cops so much now; yet you continue to fight for that stupid gun control ban and push the Progressive Movement's agenda. What gives?"

"I had some experiences…awakenings I suppose, that gave me pause for contemplation."

"What experiences?"

"It started with that high-speed chase I was involved in years ago. I wanted to do something awful to a criminal. And then—"

"What kind of awful?"

"I actually wanted the cops to shoot Carlos Murtadha. The detective I was riding with had just told me some horrible, evil things he'd done."

"Oookay. What else?"

"I was harsh—beyond all reason harsh—with a witness." Shannon shuddered. "Later, I realized…I'm still conflicted. Give me a second."

Shannon struggled to say what was on her mind. Without warning, wrenching sobs tore at Shannon's body. Jillian gave her the room to purge whatever was torturing her. Shannon wound into a tight ball of pain and she wouldn't look at Jillian.

"I saw myself…saw what I had become…a…hard-hearted bitch. I didn't give a damn who I destroyed as long as I won the case. It was a moment of perfect clarity. I hated myself and barely made it through to the end of the trial!"

"Oh, Shannie, you're not hateful. How could you hate yourself? Was the witness a woman?"

"It was the detective I rode with when his wife and daughter were killed in the accident. I tormented him on the stand, belittled him mercilessly. He looked like I had killed him."

"Shannie, baby, that must have been horrible."

"It was. The poor man couldn't breathe."

"No, honey, I mean horrible for you."

"I've never hated myself more than at that moment. What happened to me? Where was the compassion I thought I had?"

Shannon began to feel relief sharing her torment with her older sister. She wanted to tell her about Las Vegas but held back. How could she tell her sister that, for the first time in her life, she experienced the marvelous feelings of being in love? Even if in the throes of passion, it felt real.

It took months to admit to herself that her tryst with Grayson was more than a fantasy. Then the guilt set in. Telling Jillian about Grayson would serve no purpose and might create big problems with him living next door. Jillian saw the world differently than she did.

"Let's just say that I've done my penance and received absolution from Father Flannery and let it go at that."

"No way, baby sister. What have you done besides confession to deal with the changes in yourself?"

"I took a hard look at the clients I was representing, talked to Father Flannery regularly, that type of thing. Along the way, I became pregnant and Marcie has been the best thing that ever happened to me. I adore spending time with her and less time on cases."

"I'm happy for you and adore spending time with Marcie, as well. So now you've seen the light and become a Tea Party Republican."

Shannon, temporarily relieved of her burden, giggled. "Have not."

"Have too."

Shannon rolled her eyes. "Abandoned my trust in the Democratic Party and our efforts to stop gun violence and fight for social justice? No way!"

"Seriously, Shannon. You've seen the explosion of Hispanic gangs and influx of Muslims that won't assimilate in Houston and other parts of the country."

"I know that Islam is a religion of peace and every time there's a lone-wolf attack by some guy with a beard, the conservatives show their hate by blaming all Muslims."

"Good Lord! Open your eyes. Islam is not a religion of peace."

Jillian realized that, continuing the conversation would only end in a heated-argument. "Oh. Never mind. Let's not go down that path. If having a child's safety to consider caused you to look at the world from a different perspective, I'm glad."

"It's a crime, the unconscionable way conservatives treat migrants. Every human has a right to live wherever they want, anywhere on the planet."

Jillian held her tongue and grabbed her purse. "Baby Sister, do you realize that you mentioned that detective more than once in the last twenty minutes?"

"Have not."

"Have too. Love you."

"Love you too, Sissy."

~~~

After Jillian left, Shannon caught herself peeking through the kitchen window at Grayson working in his small backyard garden. Her desire for him delivered a stab of guilt. She was truly sorry for her indiscretion, but it was comforting to know a real man lived next door.

Why did you return to haunt me, Detective Dean?

Chapter 46

The Babysitter

Year 13

For the second time in her life, Shannon rang Grayson's doorbell.

Having distanced himself from her for the past four years indicated that he was not there to inject himself into her life and cause trouble. As she waited for him to open the door, she wondered where he disappeared to on cue every month, and why he hadn't moved away. *Please don't move away.*

She jumped when the door opened. Grayson's heart skipped a beat and he went on alert at the worry in her strained face. "What's wrong?"

Her intense embarrassment and sense of urgency revealed themselves in her shaking and rushed speech. "I have an emergency meeting this evening with an important client. I absolutely can't miss it. Jillian, my sister is, on a date and can't get here in time. Would you mind watching Marcie until I get back?"

Grayson hesitated but he saw Marcie looking up at him with her beautiful grey-green eyes and his heart melted. He was tired of an empty house, the aching loneliness that hovered over the kids' bedrooms. "Sure. I'd be glad to. Where's Marcie's father?"

"Out of town on business. I'll be home by eight. I really apologize, but she hasn't had dinner."

"No problem. I haven't eaten either. I'm more than happy to babysit Marcie this evening."

Marcie, characteristically, balled her fists and put them on her hips. "I'm ten and I'm taller than the other kids in my class. I'm not a baby."

Grayson chuckled. "I see her mother's character is well rooted. Tough kid you have there, lady."

He spoke to Marcie. "On the way to eat, we'll talk about the meaning of the word *babysit* and the proper attitude children use to address adults. Be nice, and we'll go to your favorite restaurant."

"Chucky Cheese!"

Shannon relaxed and gave him an approving look, one that included a smile and nod that gave him permission to tutor Marcie on proper etiquette. "Thank you, Grayson. I'll pick her up by eight."

"Give Mom a hug and get in my truck. Be careful and put your foot solid on the running board to step up into the cab. It's pretty high." He took his keys out of his pocket and used the remote control to unlock the doors.

"Yes, sir." Marcie hugged Shannon. "Love you, Mom."

"Love you too, sweetie."

Marcie shot down the steps and headed for his truck.

Shannon's voice was uncomfortable and she was embarrassed to break Grayson's no-contact rule. "Larry's not very helpful even when he's home. I hate to impose, but I'm in a bind." Her tone betrayed a vulnerability Grayson remembered in Vegas. Perhaps her ugly Shannon disguise covered more than her physical identity.

"I'm glad to help. Now, relax and go take care of your emergency. She'll be fine and, honestly, I look forward to her company."

~~~

"Your truck is big! I can see down in the cars! I've never been in a truck before."

"Be a good girl, *and respectful*, and I'll let you ride with me lots of times." *I can hope.*

"Yes, sir."

"Showing respect for adults is a good start. Turn on the radio and let's listen to some music."

"My BFF, Melodie, thinks I'm crazy to like old country and western music. This is fun. My Aunt Jillian is always busy. Do you like pizza? You're nicer to me than Daddy. He left town again, so he wouldn't have to take care of me."

Do not say one word. Not one word.

~~~

Grayson, half-asleep on the sofa, jumped at the sound of the loud chimes and ran to open the door. Shannon, obviously flustered, with dark circles under her drooping eyes, her shoulders sagging, began talking ninety-miles-an-hour. "I know it's almost midnight, and I'm so sorry for being this late. I stupidly didn't have your phone number. We need to exchange numbers. Where's Marcie? I'll take her home now."

Grayson held up his hand. "Slow down. Everything's fine. Walk softly and follow me."

Grayson led her to a bedroom and eased the door open. Marcie was sound asleep in Amanda's bed, wearing one of Grayson's tee shirts for a gown and holding onto a big purple teddy bear.

He quietly closed the door. "You can sleep in Daniel's bed if you want."

Tension visibly left Shannon's face. "I appreciate that and again apologize for being so late. I think I'll take a shower and crash at home. I'll return early in the morning with her school clothes and backpack."

He walked her to the door and stood aside for her to leave. Shannon gave him a tight hug and he lost his breath. He eased his arms around her shoulders. When she slowly released him, he strained to let her go.

She patted his chest. "Thanks, neighbor."

He stood on the porch and watched her sluggishly make her way home and lock herself safely inside. Confounded at the emotions surging through his body, his feelings of protectiveness overwhelmed him. Obviously, something was wrong next door, but it was up to Shannon to tell if she wanted him to know. She and Marcie had thrown tidbits of information his way, but the only thing he knew for sure was that he loved her, and he needed to stay away from her.

~~~

Marcie raced to open the front door. "I'm making blueberry pancakes, Mom!"

Still wearing Grayson's tee shirt—pinned at the neck so it wouldn't fall off and tied in a knot on the side of the bottom—she pulled Shannon to the breakfast nook.

"Good morning," Grayson beamed. "The chef is preparing your pancakes, madam. Please take your seat, and I'll serve your coffee." He pointed to the purple teddy bear sitting in the chair next to Shannon. "This is Mr. Purber."

Marcie giggled. "Get it, Mom? Purple bear. Mr. Purber. Bet you can't guess which one of us named him."

Shannon smiled at Grayson. "Pleased to meet you, Mr. Purber."

Grayson added a heaping spoon of Sugar in the Raw and a tiny splash of cream to Shannon's coffee, stirred and set it on the table in front of her. "Hmmm. Perfect." Shannon looked down at the mug of coffee and back at him with her eyebrows raised.

"I have a good memory. So what?"

She shook her head and smiled. "Well, aren't you two quite the pair of chefs."

"Mom, we made popcorn in Grayson's big machine and watched *Alice in Wonderland* on his great big TV after we got back from Chucky Cheese. We played games, and I won so much I earned Mr. Purber. Isn't he cool? I'm going to put him in my bed. Grayson played every game with me. Can you believe that? I can see everything from way up in his truck. It was great."

Shannon marveled at the difference in the subdued child that normally moped around her house but now bubbled with delight. Shannon beamed at Grayson. "Looks like you have a new fan."

"I'm glad you had a good time, sweetie. Don't forget to take Mr. Purber home."

"Why?"

"You said you're going to put Mr. Purber on your bed."

"Yes, ma'am. My bed here."

Shannon looked at Grayson, her emotions running wild.

"Thank you, Shannon, for loaning this beautiful child to me for the evening. She's a joy to be with."

Shannon turned off the logical side of her brain and took a calming sip of coffee. *This man is back in my life. What have I done?*

"The way things are going at the office, I need a full time bab...adult to watch Marcie. My schedule is erratic at best right now, but finding reliable, safe sit...adults is a challenge."

Marcie focused her eyes on cooking pancakes but her ears were wide open. "Mom, you can say *babysitter*. Grayson explained how it's an in...in...noc...u...ous term and how I want to be mature but act immature. That's called irn—" She looked to Grayson.

"Irony."

"Took me a while to get it, but I'm going to use those words at school today. Don't you think that'll surprise the teacher? Mom, did you know I'm self-centered? Well...I was, but now I focus outward and think of others first and that makes me happier."

Marcie took Shannon a plate of pancakes with a side of bacon and gave her mom a hug, then skipped back to the stove to make more pancakes.

Shannon gave Grayson a thumbs-up while drowning her pancakes in maple syrup.

"It's not like I haven't had years of experience. Eat your breakfast and we can talk about it tonight. You two need to get to school and work and I have to report to work."

Shannon looked surprised. "Where do you work?"

"It's just part time at the gym."

"Detective. Farmer. Trainer?"

"It keeps me in shape…you know, in case I have to carry you over my shoulder if the house catches on fire."

Shannon shook her head and smiled as Grayson and Marcie laughed.

Grayson hadn't felt so good in ages. "Tell you what; I'll grill us some steaks tonight, and y'all can come over to eat while we talk."

"You may tire of us quickly." *Is this cheating with Larry out of town? Do I care?*

Marcie looked worried. "You won't get tired of us, will you, Grayson?"

"I'd never get tired of you, sweetie."

"Grayson, Marcie is supposed to refer to adults by their title and last name."

"We'll talk about it."

"Yes. We will." Shannon smiled at him. She knew she'd already lost that battle.

"Here's a refill on your coffee, ma'am."

"Just the way I like it. I'm amazed you remembered."

"Remembered what?" Marcie asked, pouring pancake batter on the griddle.

Grayson spoke quickly. "Marcie, remember to sprinkle the blueberries in the batter while it's still soft on top and keep your hands away from the stove top…*and* the griddle."

"Yes, sir."

Grayson had an immediate need to talk to Mark and Father O'Brian. *Smart guy, you didn't listen last time. Do you really want to spill your guts again?*

Shannon's demeanor clouded. "Let's finish breakfast and get you dressed for school, sweetie. Your father will be home later tonight."

"Daddy will get mad if he knows we had a good time while he was gone."

"You may be right. Let's keep it to ourselves."

"Yes, ma'am."

She didn't like telling Marcie to keep secrets, but the girl was wise beyond her years. Still, she kept her eyes low, avoiding Grayson's steady gaze, letting him make the decision.

"I just remembered the grill isn't working. We'll save that for another time."

Chapter 47

Ambushed

Year 14

First light was over an hour away when Grayson placed his travel cup in its holder and connected Mark and Wayne in a three-way conversation on his cellphone. "Okay, guys, let's initiate the SET Patriots annual activation training exercise. What are your first actions for phase one, Mark?"

"Initiate the Headquarters Division's notification plan, reminding everyone to tune their ham radios to channel one, grab their bugout bags, and leave immediately for their assigned positions."

"Good. And you, Wayne?"

"Initiate the Tactical Division's notification plan, open the lodge, simulate installing one of the repeaters on the cell phone tower by placing it near the top of the BOL windmill, give the prepared briefing to the troops as they arrive at the lodge, and perform a 100% radio check with each member. Oh, and assign someone to the TOC to monitor the radio nets."

"Good. Okay, guys, remember it's a walk-through drill. Don't overdo it. Make notes on what went right and where we experienced problems. I'll see you at the BOL. Let's do this. Grayson out."

On the way to the BOL, Grayson mentally reviewed all of the topics he'd taught the group since they combined. It was all basic to him, but the troops thoroughly enjoyed the adventure his training brought them. They commended him on his realistic classes and practical exercises. The neighbors did a great job as desperate refugees, almost overwhelming the guards and bringing to light the need to reinforce blockades to avenues of approach. They were coming together as an effective guerrilla band.

Getting close to the farm, Grayson was pleased to see the SET Patriots had moved into action. Small colored ribbons tied inconspicuously to tree limbs at what would be roadblocks during the die-off were in place. The militiamen had camouflaged themselves with tree bark uniforms, dark and light camouflage face paint, and vegetation to hide their presence inside the woods. It was important to train as realistically as possible, but they obviously couldn't block actual traffic without irritating the public and the sheriff.

Laura was the only Tactical Division militiaman in the TOC. Grayson dropped his bugout bag, rifle, and tactical vest. "Good to see you, Laura. What brings you to the TOC?"

She flashed a smile. "Silly boy, you ordered an activation exercise." Her voice, soft and silky, stirred him, but he didn't bite.

"It's been months since I've seen you. How've you been? How's Austin?" *Slow down. You sound like a kid who knows he's in trouble.*

He couldn't help but notice her tight camo outfit, exposing her trim figure. With her 1911 Colt strapped to her thigh, she presented a stimulating vision that would stir any man's loins. *I must be a fool to avoid this woman.*

Maintaining eye-to-eye contact, she sauntered over and gave him a tight hug. The feel of her firm, ample breasts pressed hard against his chest took his breath. She'd ambushed him, but it felt too good not to respond. He closed his eyes and immersed himself in her. *Let her go now. Don't get drawn in. Friends, we're just friends.*

Laura unclenched and gave him a backside view as she went to the desk.

"Austin and I are great. It's good to see you, too. Between tactical training exercises in the field and sick patients who kept me from attending meetups, it has been awhile. I've missed you. What have *you* been up to and how are Daniel and his family?"

He moved to his BOB and jacket and pretended to be searching for something, then fiddled with the coffee pot. He needed to recover. Laura's little reminder of what he was avoiding left its mark.

"I've missed you, too. Danny and family are doing well. I spend most of my time researching the Quran, studying Arabic, and renovating my house."

Wayne entered the TOC just in time to hear his last statement. "Need a good carpenter?" The men shook hands and engaged in small talk.

Laura clapped her hands to get their attention. "Hey, guys, we have an exercise to run! Let's get with it."

"Good idea, Sis. I came in to report that all of the roadblocks and guards are in place. The civilian auxiliary squad is passing out information sheets and notifying neighbors who volunteered to participate. As soon as Headquarters Division reports in, we'll send security patrols to the wooded areas."

"You're doing a great job, Wayne, as good as any militia leaders I've ever known."

"That means a lot coming from you. The little military training I received in high school ROTC but mostly the guidance you provided has helped tremendously. Okay, I'm off to do my rounds and check on the troops. Oh, Sis. Just a heads up, Marvin told me he has the tickets to the Cowboys game and…be ready for that big date next week. Thanks for volunteering to monitor the TOC radios." Wayne rushed out when he realized his screw-up. He'd seen Grayson's head snap toward Laura and her face flush.

Laura hurriedly began making radio checks in the silent room.

Let it go, man. You have no right to ask her anything. She volunteered to be the radio operator. The lady does not give up easily.

He switched the TOC to solar power, took his position at the table in front of the wall maps, and thumbed through the activation plan. It was going to be a long twenty-four hours stuck in the TOC alone with Laura. *She felt so good against my chest. Jealous? Me? No way. To thine own self be true, Grayson…Damn! Let's give the lady something to chew on.*

"Laura, your idea to have medical in the TOC on a permanent basis in case of a medical emergency is a good one."

Laura smiled at his back. "Since the medical facility is in the adjoining room, I can keep up with activity on all channels, have things ready by the time they get here. Glad you approve."

They conveniently ignored the fact that the medical facility had radios for all the channels, and she had her handheld radio with her at all times.

Grayson gazed at the topographical map on the wall unaware of anything he was looking at. "Make that part of the Standard Operating Procedures."

"WILCO, sir," she cooed.

Chapter 48

Man Talk

Year 14

Ramirez was digging weeds out of the garden when Grayson arrived. "Hi, Chief. It's good to see you so active and losing weight."

"I feel better than I have in twenty years. Country life and retirement have been good to me, Mama too. How've you been, son?"

"Busy as a one-legged man in an ass-kicking contest."

"Mama's in town on her Wednesday ladies church social and shopping trip. Gives us some time for man-talk. Says it mellows me out. I think she uses that as a trick to get you to visit more often. Let's grab a beer and sit in the gazebo."

"Miss Grace is a smart lady. Chatting with you makes me miss the days our A-team sat around campfires. Nothing like a relaxed non-tactical training event for shooting the breeze, telling tall tales, and passing gas. Remember Bobby Stein? He could fart on command."

"Yeah, everybody fought to get a position upwind from him. I enjoyed pulling rank on some poor team member."

Ramirez and Grayson immersed themselves in reliving old days and predicting the future, a bond that only comrades-in-arms appreciate.

"Feeling good about the Patriots, Chief. The last full training day went smooth as a school girl's silk drawers. Wayne and Mark had everything in order and we only ran into a few hitches. We built a winning team."

"It took us long enough to get there, but glad to hear it. Wayne pays us a visit about once a week. Brings Laura every now and then. She usually sits quietly, looking around. I trust everything is going well for you back in Houston."

"Everything's fine, sir," he lied.

"Joe dropped by the farm couple of days ago to tell me his FBI contact reported that Murtadha has been traveling back and forth between Mexico and Africa. Apparently, he sneaked across the border into different cities in the Southwest several times."

"That's odd. Why don't they grab the SOB? What's your analysis, Chief?"

"He's probably using a fake passport to get in and recruit more fighters for ISIS. They're tearing Africa apart. It doesn't bode well, whatever it is. Murtadha and his gang could give us problems if they're in Houston when the collapse occurs, but I'm not concerned about his little group of scumbags."

Grayson started to disagree but held off. *I wish I agreed. But I can feel that bastard looming.* "I'd love to have a few minutes in an empty room with Joe's Intel source. My gut feeling is we're only getting a piece of the picture."

Ramirez shook his head. "I'm more concerned about how things are moving since the lefties retook control of the government and put us on a downhill slide toward socialism. They've destroyed everything President Crump did to restore our capitalist markets. The assholes reinstituted their socialist agenda of tax, borrow, spend, and regulate, forcing millions who were working back on welfare. The borders are wide open again, Muslim refugees are coming in by the tens of thousands, and businesses are closing left and right."

"There's a tension in the air America hasn't felt since Obama was in office. Only, it's worse now. With inflation creeping up and the government's credit rating diminishing, it makes me wonder how long before the collapse hits. It's clear to me, unmistakable."

"Clear as a bell to me, too, son."

Ramirez sat back and looked out across the pasture for a while.

Grayson sipped his coffee and waited.

"There's a question, something personal that's niggled at me for decades, a curiosity. You don't have to answer if you don't want to. I won't be offended."

"What is it?"

"There's no doubt in my mind about your hate for Mexicans. I'm of Mexican descent and so are Yolanda and Pablo, yet your attitude toward us is genial. It's odd, and something I'd like to have the answer to before I die."

Ramirez frowned when Grayson laughed.

"Chief, I have no problem with true Americans of any race or skin color and families that come here legally to work, learn English, and assimilate into our culture as genuine American citizens. Muslims and major areas in the U.S, solely populated with illegal alien Mexicans who give us the finger, suck the welfare teats dry, and demand that we allow them to destroy our American culture intentionally, that's a different story. The thing that gets under my skin is the liberals that promote it and folks like you and me that can't do a damn thing about it without becoming wanted men."

Ramirez's reflected on Grayson's sentiments. "The collapse and die-off will take care of them. Truthfully, I thought your feelings were more personal, after your reaction in court when Fisher pounded you. Most of the Mexican-American families I know have been here a long time, some for centuries, true Americans that feel the same as us. Most put aside speaking Spanish generations ago."

Grayson looked down. "I had a personal reason; but, like that bartender said, it's something between me and the Devil. I let go of it a long time ago…but I haven't gotten over that bastard, Murtadha."

"That's understandable. Just don't let settling your score rule your life."

Chapter 49

Rush Limbaugh! *Fox News*!

Year 15

Shannon entered Grayson's house without ringing the doorbell, a common practice now that Marcie was with him almost daily.

After Marcie had such a positive reaction to Grayson, he relaxed his rule to stay away from Shannon. The child bonded to him quickly and openly admitted it was because he paid attention to her and she was afraid of her often angry and drunk father.

At first, Shannon objected to Marcie spending so much time with Grayson, but changed her mind after coming home to find Marcie alone repeatedly and Larry at the club getting drunk. She was relieved to no longer worry about her daughter.

This day, Shannon arrived home from work earlier than usual, and what she saw shook her to her liberal core. "What the hell are you watching?"

Grayson and Marcie looked away from the TV to find Shannon's face the color of her flaming red hair. "Hi, Mom. It's *Fox News*. We watch it after listening to Rush Limbaugh. Grayson gets Rush on the Internet without all the commercials."

Through squinted eyes and clenched teeth, Shannon ordered Marcie to her room, not realizing the irony of her directive. Marcie hated being excluded adult conversation. "Yes, ma'am," she said, acid dripping from her mouth.

For Marcie, there were her mother's expectations about sending her to her room, and there were her expectations. She closed the door loudly while still in the hallway, eased off her shoes, and sneaked near the open doorway where Grayson and Shannon engaged in verbal combat.

When they heard her door slam shut, Grayson stood and braced himself for Shannon's onslaught. "What does she mean, you listen to Rush Limbaugh and watch *Fox News*?"

"Shannon, it's not a big deal. We—"

"Of course, it's a big deal! I don't want my daughter brainwashed by that…conservative compost. You do it again, and I swear I'll send her to boarding school."

Grayson shook his head and held up his hands in surrender, but a hint of his anger reflected back at her. "I've been taking care of *your* daughter since she was nine, almost four years. All the while, her so-called father sits on his sorry ass or leaves her at home alone." Trying to regain control, he softened his voice. "Shannon, you know I love Marcie and losing her would not be acceptable. I don't appreciate you using my feelings for her to try and control me."

"I'm her mother and have a right to do as I please with her."

He wouldn't let her pivot to a different subject. "I thought you liberals respected all points of view and encouraged kids to watch the news."

"No, Grayson! She's not just watching the news; she's watching that stupid conservative propaganda, *Fox News*! Rush Limbaugh…ugh! I thought he'd be dead by now."

"Give me an example of *conservative propaganda* you've heard from either of those news sources—just one!"

Her anger intensified at his challenge. "I've never wasted a second of my time with either of them and never will."

Grayson smirked. "Let me understand this. You're a lawyer. Someone presents a case to you. You analyze it before you determine its veracity. Right?"

She huffed frustration. "Correct."

"You're prejudging *Fox News* and Limbaugh without due diligence. You're accepting hearsay for known facts. You'd never allow that in court. I challenge you to join us and analyze what they say."

Shannon hated when Grayson or anyone out-maneuvered her. Off balance, she worked her jaw but couldn't muster a rejoinder.

"What is it you fear? Marcie learning there are two sides to a discussion?"

"I don't need to take you up on your challenge. There are plenty of other news outlets."

"Can you prove they're telling the truth? Are you afraid to learn they make fools of millions daily?" He gently taunted her. "You're afraid to analyze their reports, aren't you; to learn the facts?"

"I know the facts! And I don't want my daughter exposed to that conservative crap."

Grayson knew the drill. He'd seen it repeatedly in others. Her liberal wall automatically rejected information that challenged her entrenched emotion-based progressive convictions. He wanted her to understand how shallow it was to dismiss conservative positions without analysis.

His deep, mellow voice, softly laced with a delicate passion, reached out to her. "I love her, Shannon. I love Marcie the same as I love Amanda. She's like a daughter to me. I would never expose her to anything harmful."

In the dark hallway, Marcie grinned and covered her mouth.

Shannon paced the room, the pressure diminishing with each step, until a book caught her eye. She picked it up. "*Absolute Anarchy! Prepper Study Guide.*" She slammed the book back on the table and glared at him.

"I'm a prepper. so what? I have guns and store food. Is that so bad?"

"Guns!" She closed her eyes and refocused. "We'll discuss that later. Let's get back to the subject at hand."

"Shannon, I'm not a perfect man, but there's one thing for damn sure; I want to help Marcie grow into an informed woman. If I stepped outside the bounds of my authority, please discuss it with me in a rational way. I'll do my best to abide by your wishes."

An unexpected warmth saturated her. Grayson took the time to instruct Marcie patiently on many life lessons, helping her to mature and make good choices. He'd instilled in her a sense of responsibility and evolved into Marcie's protector and teacher—a father figure. *I knew this subconsciously. What was I thinking? This man cares about my daughter.* Shannon's face softened and her eyes penetrated deep into his.

Grayson tensed for the next attack.

"Damn you, Grayson," she whispered affectionately. *Why couldn't Larry be like you?*

Marcie stepped into the room and walked to her mother. "Sorry for eavesdropping. Mom, I see through the conservative deceit. I know you teach me the truth. Sorry, Grayson, I didn't mean to mislead you."

Marcie gave Shannon a tight hug while sneaking a conspiratorial look at Grayson over her mother's shoulder and winked at him.

Whoa! I gotta watch this kid. She's too smart for her own good.

Mustering energy to sound rejected and humble, he followed her lead. "You're right to listen to your mother. I hope I didn't mislead *you*." Grayson put his hand over his beard and squeezed hard. *That's my girl. Wait! What the hell am I doing? I'm teaching this child to lie to her mother.*

He'd known Shannon's politics, but it never occurred to him that she wouldn't allow Marcie to consider other points of view. Without malice, he'd planted his conservative political seeds. Other than gun control and her ACLU hogwash, he'd never considered her political point of view. He should have seen the signs. *Would I have allowed someone to plant liberal seeds in Amanda and Daniel?*

The answer was obvious, but the conflict growing in his brain was out of control. With the calamitous situation brewing in America, he had to prepare Marcie and determine how to save Shannon. Not unlike Shannon in the Delgado trial, Grayson had unwittingly stepped across a moral line; but he couldn't drop it, as she had.

Regardless of what took place from this point forward, it was a done deal. She had attained critical thinking skill, something devious brainwashing based on emotional reaction could never erase. Marcie would never share her mother's perception of normalcy.

Chapter 50

Adios Hubby

Year 16

"Thanks for helping me with the party, Jillian. The kids had a great time, and Marcie will never forget her thirteenth birthday."

"I'm happy for her. You too, sis. By the way, where's the douchebag?"

Shannon shook her head. "He's at the club getting drunk."

"Sorry I asked. Let's grab a cup of coffee and talk about the douchebag."

Shannon went straight to the heart of what was on her mind. "I've run out of ideas. Larry gets more distant every day. He skipped her party. No present, nothing. I don't understand a parent who doesn't love his child. Yesterday, she showed him her report card with straight A's. He looked at it in her hands and grunted, then went back to reading a book. I wanted to slap him."

"Maybe you should slap him from time to time."

"You can't fix stupid."

"Baby sister, I saw his extreme passiveness when you were dating. He wears his self-indulgent, mama's boy attitude like a medal of honor. He's short and has a Napoleonic complex, hungering for attention and adoration. Men like him show their masculinity in absurd ways. Marcie's thirteen and she's at least an inch taller than the cretin. That's got to be a rock in his shoe."

"She's going to be tall like me, maybe taller."

"The man—not that he deserves that title—doesn't care about anyone or anything but himself. His sense of responsibility is lower than whale shit." Jillian patted Shannon's hand. "Back in college, you had to choose his classes. I should've spoken up back then."

"I would've rejected your argument. It's just so odd. It took years to have Marcie, and he acts like a dipshit. She'll do anything just to get a smile out of him."

"That right there is a good reason to dump him. He's not healthy for her. You and Marcie would be better off without him."

"He's the only man I've ever loved."

"I'll reserve comment on that."

Shannon didn't argue her point. "Marcie needs him. He's the one that made her. If he'd go to family counseling, maybe he'd realize what a gift she is."

"Where in God's great name do you get these ideas? You're one of the strongest, smartest women I know, but you have a blind spot when it comes to that piece of crap. Mom and Dad were proud of you, and so am I. Larry's not capable of seeing outside himself. I still say you *and Marcie* would be better off without him."

"For Marcie's sake, I can't give up on him. Me? I don't care anymore. Father Flannery says they'll bond as he matures and mellows out."

"Larry may become ripe and rot, but mature to a healthy state, never. But then, I keep hoping *you'll* become a Republican."

Shannon pushed Jillian's knee. "That, sister mine, will never come to fruition. Anyway, being strong and smart *and* a Democrat is no help when it comes to the stranger I married."

"All engineers are strange. The problem is his maturity...and his manhood...or lack thereof."

Shannon looked at her watch. "I hate to run you off, but I need to get him home before he drinks too much."

"You're more mommy than wife. One last thing before I go. Why didn't you tell me about the hunk living next door? How long's he been there?"

"You just saw him?"

"I'm not exactly a frequent visitor, thanks to the cretin."

"He moved in a few years ago. Marcie invited him to dinner, but Larry got jealous and was rude. I never invited him back."

"He looks like the cop who was driving when you got caught in that ride-along. Don't you despise him?"

"He is that cop; and I don't despise him. It's all in the past. He left police work years ago."

"When I drove up, he was cutting his grass in gym shorts and a sleeveless tee shirt, sweating deliciously. You've got to introduce me."

"Except for a wave and hello in passing and the conversations Marcie has with him, Grayson keeps to himself. He disappears a few days every month. Maybe a job. Who knows?"

"*Grayson,* is it? And you know his schedule. Baby sister, you're smitten. Look at your face!"

"Am not!"

"Are too! And Marcie likes him?"

"Weirdly, they hit it off, like they have some spiritual connection." Jillian got up to find her keys and looked through the kitchen window. "Mighty close, Sissyyyy."

"He often sits in his sunroom, reading or working on his laptop. Marcie goes over and chats with him. He seems to enjoy it, and I can watch her from here. I'm sure he misses his daughter. Remember, the poor baby died in that dreadful accident. He gives Marcie the attention she doesn't get from Larry. She likes it when he occasionally babysits her when I'm caught short."

Jillian cocked her head, sisterly sarcasm in gear. "First, you said Marcie talks with him. Now, you say he's babysitting. Isn't it dangerous to have a strange man babysitting your daughter? Is Larry okay with this?"

Shannon snatched her purse from the counter. "Larry couldn't care less." Shannon broke eye contact. "I trust Grayson."

"So, you sit here where they can't see you and watch them bonding, and trust the man without question. Next, you'll tell me you get a glass of tea and pretend to be with them."

"Shut up!"

"No I won't! So now you don't hate cops?"

"They're the scum of the earth."

"You need to work on your acting skills. I never understood your animosity toward cops, and I sure as hell don't understand this reversal."

Shannon flinched. "You aren't around cops. Most of the white cops I see in court are arrogant racist asses. They use their power to treat people of color like trash. The 'Black Lives Matter' movement started because a white cop killed a young black man with his hands up shouting, 'Don't shoot!'"

"Love you, sis, but, like Mom and Dad, you're brainwashed with liberal junk. We'll research the facts one day. Right now, tell me why you changed your mind about the hunk next door."

Shannon flipped off the lights. "He's changed since I knew him. It is peculiar, though; he's become one of those doomsday idiots. I let him know in no uncertain terms not to discuss that drivel with Marcie."

"I've read about the prepper movement. There're millions of them, regular people worried about what they see coming down the pike. Maybe I'll introduce myself and ask how it works."

Shannon opened the kitchen door. "Free world. As if you needed my permission."

Jillian tossed her keys back on the counter. "Get the hell out of here and find your not-so-adorable husband. I'll stay with Marcie until you get back."

"He's probably smashed by now."

"Take your time. I'll hang out in the kitchen in the dark, get a glass of ice tea, and watch your oh-so-adorable neighbor."

"Don't go causing trouble. Stay away from him."

Jillian smiled. "I'll not take him from you, Sissy. But another woman might if you don't dump lily-livered Larry and wiggle your fanny on the front porch instead of hiding it behind the kitchen window."

"Take Marcie with you when you go over there. And don't tell me you weren't going to. She's on Melodie's porch with her girlfriends."

~~~

Grayson opened the front door to find Marcie with a woman he'd noticed at Shannon's house on occasion. "Grayson, this is my Aunt Jillian, Mom's sister. Mom told her about you being a prepper."

"Nice to meet you, Jillian. Come in, please. Let's get you two something to drink and sit in the sunroom to chat."

~~~

Shannon held Larry up on one side and the bartender on the other as they walked him to the car.

"Shtop! I...gotta...baaarrrff."

Experience had taught them to step back when Larry threatened. He fell to his knees on the sidewalk and emptied his stomach. George lifted him as he was about to fall into his own vomit. "Come on, Mr. Fisher, just a few more steps."

"I'm sorry, George."

"Don't worry, Ms. Fisher. I'll hose the sidewalk. Part of the job."

"Lucky you." She handed George a nice tip after he clicked Larry's seatbelt.

"I wanna deevorsss."

"You're drunk, Larry."

"So wat. I shtill wanna deevorsss...bich, filing tomoorow."

When he was drunk, Larry stated what his sober mind didn't have the guts to speak, so she knew he meant it.

Grayson and Jillian had just finished discussing prepping basics when they noticed Shannon struggling to get Larry out of his seatbelt.

"Jillian, stay with Marcie," Grayson ordered and ran to help.

"Alpha male, one hundred percent," Jillian whispered under her breath.

"Grayson's cool, isn't he, Aunt Jillian?" Marcie glowed.

"He's something, all right."

"Looks like you need help."

Shannon's face crunched with embarrassment. "Thank you."

He hauled Larry out of the car and upright on his wobbly legs.

Larry swayed back and forth a few seconds, squinted at Grayson, and grew vicious. "You sss...na...bich. Think you're better man'n me...ash...ol?" His weak swing glanced off Grayson's chest.

Grayson threw him over his shoulder, hauled him inside, and dumped him not so gently on the sofa.

"I'm sorry, Grayson."

"If it's okay with you, I'll keep Marcie tonight."

"Unfortunately, she's used to this."

"Not tonight, she isn't."

Shannon didn't have the energy to argue. She closed the door behind him. When she turned around, Larry was stumbling toward her. "I wanna deevorsss."

"Fine. I'll agree to a divorce on one condition."

He attempted to stand straight. "Con...di...tion. Whoopy do."

"Look at me, Larry. Try to focus."

He steadied himself against the wall with his arm.

"Here's the condition for a divorce. Explain why you treat Marcie the way you do."

His face dropped, his voice as serious as a drunk can marshal. "Ssits not 'portant."

Shannon was not about to let him off the hook. "Tell me the truth if you want your freedom. It's your call."

"No...you calling ssshots. Always have." He swayed dangerously.

"Come back to the sofa and sit down before you fall."

He plopped down and looked around confused. "Whassa quesshion?"

Shannon enunciated carefully. "Listen. To. Me. Why don't you treat Marcie as a father should treat his child?"

"Memer we first gaged? I went to Mex...co?"

"You went with your brother on a fishing trip before we were married. What does that have to do with Marcie?"

His head shook, then bobbed up and down. "I lied...yep...lied."

"About going to Mexico?"

Larry became pensive. "Shannie, I'b sorry not...the man...for you. Didn't...want kids...scared me."

"Focus Larry and get to the point. Mexico."

"Oh. I had a vasss...ec...tomy. Oooh! But you...." He shook an accusatory finger at her. "But you...you had sex with men...bich."

"A vasectomy!" Anger burned within her. "I haven't had sex with other men! How dare you!"

"I caaan't make ba...bies. You bad, bad bich."

"Your vasectomy must have failed, some do."

"I check...ed. No swimmers. No little spermies. I caaa...n't make baaa...bies," he repeated.

Larry's statement crashed into the room with a thud.

"Then how...what...? Oh, my God!" She stared at the floor. *This damn fool! I'm a fool! Grayson and Marcie must never know.*

"I hate you!" She attacked Larry, beating on his chest with her fists. "You bastard!"

"What's wrong, Mom?"

Shannon whirled to find Marcie staring at them in shock.

"You're supposed to be with Grayson and Jillian."

"They're looking at Grayson's guns. I came to get some of my birthday presents to show Grayson. What's wrong?"

Gaining a little more control, Larry shouted, "I'll tell you waaat's wrong, misssy!"

"Don't you dare!" Shannon grabbed him by the shirt. "She's a child, you idiot!"

"Not *myyy* child!"

"Larry, no!"

He spit out the poison that had infected him for the past thirteen years and nine months. He pointed an accusing finger at Shannon. "Your mo...mother's...a whore!"

"Mom, what's he talking about?" Marcie sobbed.

Shannon reached for Marcie, but she ran to Larry and wrapped her arms around his waist. "Daddy! Daddy! I love you!"

"I don't looove *you*. Neeever have. Neeever will. You're n...not *myyy* kid." Years of amassed ugly anger spewed at the symbol of his failed primary mission as a man. He twisted her arms away. "Let go mee, little bich. I haaate you."

The disgust pouring from Marcie's face ripped Shannon's heart open. Overwhelmed by guilt and shame, she opened her mouth but nothing came out.

Marcie ran up the stairs and locked herself in her room; her wails filled the house. Shannon ran after her and knocked repeatedly on the door. "Baby, please let me in."

"Go away! I hate you! You're not my mother anymore!"

"I love you, Marcie! I've always loved you. Ignore your father. He's drunk and doesn't know what he's saying. Please, open the door."

Marcie threw another spear into Shannon's heart. "Who is my father? Do you even know?" Shannon looked over the rail and saw Larry passed out on the sofa. For the slightest streak of time, she considered killing him right then, right there. She closed her eyes and slid against the wall to the floor. *No mother should ever experience the look I saw in my daughter's face tonight. Happy birthday, sweetie.*

Chapter 51

Relationships

Year 17

When Grayson finally opened the door to the insistent pounding, he found Marcie glaring at him with pouty lips, her fists balled on her hips. Adolescent sarcasm reprimanded him. "You aren't in the sunroom! I left my key to the stupid door in my school locker! It's time for our visit, and I've got something important to tell you!"

"You're definitely Shannon's daughter, Little Miss Caustic. Get the glasses from the cupboard and fill them with ice, and I'll get the lemonade."

Grayson allowed her to pout until they entered the sunroom. He grabbed a bag of popcorn from the movie-sized popper and sat. "What's the important thing you have to tell me?"

"Mom told me to tell you the church finally approved the annulment. She told me not to tell you that she told me to tell you. But you told me to be truthful with you always. This having to tell and not tell is confusing."

"You did fine. Let's not over-analyze this. You feel caught in the middle, right?"

"Duh."

"Watch your mouth, kid."

"I'm okay, I guess. I hate her and won't talk to her except when I have to, like when I'm going to Melodie's."

"Marcie, that's not an appropriate way to treat your mom. This has been going on for almost two years. It's none of my business what happened, but it's time to make amends. She loves you."

"I don't care. What she and Larry did to me wasn't *appropriate* either."

"You're not speaking to him?"

"I don't know where he is."

Didn't see that coming.

"All I ask is that you try to be civil with your mother." He suspected Marcie's anger was why Shannon kept her distance and communicated through her daughter.

"I'll try but don't expect much."

"Let me tell you a story about a man I once despised who is now my friend." Grayson shared a modified version of his experience with Weber.

"But that's what I'm saying. If she'd tell me what I've a right to know, we might work it out."

"See, that's the thing. That man made a decision to try with me because he didn't want to hate himself later. He almost did something mean and selfish that would've been devastating to me. Because he didn't, and because I learned more about his situation, we worked it out."

Marcie laid her head on the table and mumbled. "I'll try."

"Thank you. Let's get supper going. Jillian's eating with us. She'll be here any minute."

Marcie didn't move. "Where do you guys go when you disappear on weekends? Is Aunt Jillian your girlfriend?"

"Heavens no, child! We're good friend, that's it."

"But, she comes over a lot, and you don't tell me where y'all go."

"It's not a big secret. Do you remember the farm I told you about where I used to live, the one my old boss and his wife own?"

"Sure."

"Our organic gardening club goes there to do our share of work. It's like the one we grow in the backyard, but much bigger. We hunt there, too."

Marcie sat up, rolled her head to the side, and offered an unvarnished observation. "I can smell bullshit from a mile away. You don't need your guns when it's not hunting season, and you don't need camouflage uniforms and backpacks to work in a garden."

He was abruptly aware, and saddened, that Marcie was shedding her little girl self. "Do you realize that you're becoming a young lady? I'm proud of you, sweetie, but lose the profanity."

"Whatever."

Jillian entered the kitchen just as Marcie said, "I want to go to the farm with y'all next time."

"Hi, guys. What's this about the farm?"

"Hi, Jillian. Marcie, run home and get some spend-the-night clothes."

Marcie frowned. "Shannon's working late, again? Her precious illegals mean more to her than me, not that I care. I've got clothes here and you know it, but I'll give you time to decide about the farm."

Grayson's reprimand was swift. "Stop calling your mother by her first name! You can't continue to do that and think of yourself as a young adult. Got me?"

Stung by his reproach, the sarcasm in her voice vaporized. "Yes, sir."

After Marcie left, Grayson brought Jillian up to speed. "She's on to us. I think it's time to bring her into the fold, make her a MAG member. What's your take?"

"Shannon will have a fit if she finds out."

Grayson nodded. "But Marcie has to be prepared. Did you see where the S&P downgraded the government's credit again yesterday?"

"Makes me proud to be a financial analyst. Economic growth rate has stagnated below one percent for the last three quarters, propped up by the Fed dropping billions monthly into the economy. No wonder prices are going sky high."

"When the time comes to bug out, Shannon will be a problem. Her brain is too entrenched in the liberal mindset to sway her. She may delay us getting out of Dodge, and I don't like the idea of walking to the BOL. It'll be no less than two hundred walking-miles by the time we maneuver around dangerous areas."

Jillian poured a cup of coffee. "My gut feeling says you're right, but the relationship between Marcie and Shannon is extremely fragile. Sissy won't discuss it with me, and that's strange."

He busied himself with dinner. "If you can't get her to open up, nobody can. Marcie is so much a part of my life, I want her involved in everything I do. We must take action, and soon."

"Interest rates will be out of control before long. I give us a year, two at the most. The collapse is creeping up on us, Grayson, and I'm nervous."

He sighed and peppered the chicken. "I don't want to live the rest of my life riddled with guilt because I could've saved them and didn't. If Marcie's to survive, she needs training and a warrior's mentality."

"I've been a SET Patriot only a year and know that Marcie must be trained if she's to increase her chances for survival. Think of what'll happen if we're not available, and she has to go it alone, dragging Shannon as an anchor."

"They'd be raped and killed or die of starvation for sure."

"Bingo, big guy!"

"I'm not comfortable keeping it from Shannon, but I can live with it."

The door slammed. Marcie was back. Grayson and Jillian glanced at each other.

"Well, guys?"

Chapter 52

Prepper Marcie

Year 17

Marcie shot through the door, leaving it open. "Mom's outside in her car and wants to see you, Grayson!"

Shannon shouted at Grayson through the car window. "I'm sorry for dumping her on you, but I forgot I had to be in D.C. this weekend."

Call it what it is, Shannon. You intentionally forgot. "Don't tell me you're going to that stupid 'Coalition to Stop Gun Violence' demonstration at the Capitol?"

Clearly pissed, she flung words at him. "It's a march, not a demonstration! And it's none of your business. Gotta go, catching a flight in two hours."

"I can't keep her. I'm leaving in an hour to go to the farm."

"Damn!" She whacked the steering wheel.

He didn't like this side of Shannon, but Lady Luck had given him an opportunity, and he wouldn't throw it away. "I'll take her with me."

"Why do you have to go so often?"

Exasperated at having to repeat himself for the umpteenth time, Grayson sighed. "I've told you. The chief and Miss Grace can't handle the farm by themselves. I'm working in the garden and taking care of the farm animals this trip." *And I'm taking your daughter up there to make her a prepper.* "Have fun at your stupid march. Marcie will enjoy seeing a working farm. She can help shovel cow pies."

Shannon stared through the windshield and relented. "I suppose you're right. I'll be back late Sunday evening." She waved and sped away.

Thanks, Shannon. You made our decision for us. While you're opposing guns, your daughter will be mastering the use of one.

"What was Mom shouting about?"

"Get your bag. Add a change of clothes and a dress for Mass. We're going to the farm."

Spinning around, she started at a dead run. "All right!"

Ramirez eyed Grayson suspiciously while shaking Marcie's extended hand. "Welcome, young lady."

Miss Grace gave her a hug. "Hi, Marcie. It's nice to meet you. Tomorrow we'll go shopping in town and have lunch while the others have their meetup."

Marcie looked to Grayson in confusion. "Oh, I thought we'd be farming and stuff, but shopping sounds fun, too. Is it okay, Grayson?"

"It's very okay, sweetie." *Odd. She didn't ask what a meetup is.*

~~~

The sun had been up two hours and warmed the September morning. Grayson and Marcie were in the gazebo eating oatmeal and blueberries with Jillian when other SET Patriots began to arrive. Everyone ignored them, except for Austin. He stared at Marcie all the way to the lodge door, almost tripping at one point; his face turned red but he didn't lose focus. She giggled and smiled.

Ramirez passed them on his way to the lodge. "Mama's excited to have you accompany her to town today, Marcie. She'll be ready in a few minutes." He spoke brusquely to Grayson and Jillian and kept walking. "See you two in the lodge."

"Go find Miss Grace. Jillian and I have to go to the meetup. Have fun!" He handed her a wad of bills.

"Yes, sir. I will. But I want to get army clothes and guns and come to the meetup next month, like everybody else."

That kid needs to yell, "Switch!" so I can keep up.

~~~

After the Pledge of Allegiance and prayer, Grayson stood. "Today, we're—"

"Some of the folks, including me, want an accounting of why you brought that girl here. I picked up a few things last night, but it wasn't the right time to ask questions with Mama talking to her. Who is this kid and why is she here?"

Grayson became aware of staid faces staring at him, a few glaring. Jillian looked at the floor and lightly bit her lower lip.

"Marcie's the daughter of my next-door neighbor, a single mom. I've been babysitting her several years. Her mother's out of town, and I couldn't leave her by herself."

His reply barely left his mouth before Laura asked, "Who is your next-door neighbor?"

Grayson cringed at her tone. "Her name is Shannon."

"Shannon what?" Laura shot back.

"Shannon Fisher."

Mark's expression spoke volumes. "That liberal, anti-gun, ACLU lawyer?" He shook his head at Grayson.

"That's her." *Once again, Grayson, you've stepped in it.*

Headquarters Division members raised their protests while the Tactical Division looked on, confused.

Grayson froze when he saw Ramirez's maroon and white mottled face and neck. Sweat beaded across his forehead. *He looks like he's going to blow a gasket.*

Ramirez raised his arms, palms out to stop the chatter, swallowed hard, and spoke in a strangled voice. "You owe us the full background and don't spare any details."

Grayson was searching for words when Jillian spoke. "Shannon is my sister. She and Marcie are somewhat estranged. Grayson's been Marcie's surrogate father since she was ten years old. Her thinking is the same as ours. She is conservative through and through, a *Fox News* girl."

"How old is she?" Austin's voice cracked and sounded worried. "Kind of tall. Looks about eighteen."

Grayson wasn't sure he liked Austin's question. "Almost fifteen."

Laura didn't take her eyes off Grayson. "Tell us about her ACLU mother."

Grayson was pissed. His answer made her sorry for asking the question. "Marcie's mother is my girlfriend."

Joe didn't hide his anger. "Grayson, you're as dumb as a sack of rocks! Why the hell would you date *her*? She's lethal with a capital L."

Grayson's muscles twisted into knots. "That's my damn business!"

"Partner, you made it our business bringing her kid here."

"Look, Shannon went through a bad divorce and carries the effects of a bad marriage. Marcie's father is an alcoholic, a not-so-nice guy who mistreated her. The whole affair traumatized the child and…well…I love her the same as I love Amanda. That's it."

Laura flinched. "*Affair* is an interesting word."

You sent me hunting and I bagged something special.

"I brought Marcie here so you could meet her. I'm asking you to let her join the SET Patriots. She can carry a heavy backpack in the mountains all day, slaughter and dress a rabbit, and make a fire without matches to cook it. She can also outshoot half of the men in this lodge."

Elmer Martel grunted loudly. "Lettin' in kids ain't a particular ah favor."

Wayne stood and surveyed the room. "The SET Patriots is an open group and, to be fair, Marcie's the same age Austin was when we accepted him two years ago. He's as much a member as any of us, and I see a few other young members here today, too."

Laura looked like she could beat her brother senseless. Wayne shrugged.

Grayson's stress level dropped a few levels. "Thanks, Wayne. Marcie would be a good addition to the MAG. She's a conservative, one of us."

The lodge filled again with loud chatter. Grayson asked for quiet.

"Here's the deal. Marcie and Shannon **WILL** bug out with me when the shit hits the fan. Let there be no doubt. Shannon can sit in a corner by herself and sulk if she wishes, but Marcie must be capable of helping us—*as one of us*—to survive the die-off and rebuild New America."

In the silence that followed, Jillian spoke softly. "Shannon is curious about the farm. It's a blank spot in her mind."

Laura couldn't help herself. "Maybe you should bring her here, so we can judge her for ourselves."

Shock and anger resurfaced. Grayson didn't want the two women on the same turf at the same time.

Ramirez, oblivious to the implications, sealed the deal. "Okay, Grayson. We'll vote for admitting Marcie. If she's in, then we'll put on a dog and pony show for her mother. Otherwise, both are out. Remember, one nay will nullify the aye votes."

"We gonna show that ACLU lawyer everything?" Mark asked.

"No." Ramirez commanded and gave them a few seconds to think about it. "All in favor of Marcie Fisher joining the SET Patriots say 'aye'."

"Aye," came weak votes. Some remained silent and glared at Grayson.

"All opposed say 'nay'."

Elmer Martel grunted.

"Was that a nay vote?" asked Wayne, and gave him a hard look.

"Ah wuz just a clearing mah throat."

Ramirez repeated, "All opposed say 'nay'."

Austin's grin zoomed ear-to-ear at the silence that followed.

"No nays; she's in. Get on with regular business," Ramirez ordered Grayson.

"Thanks everyone for your vote of confidence. Joe has a short Intel report for the managers. Everyone else retrieve your rifles and ammo from the armory and go to the range for target practice. Charles, please take charge."

And let me bandage my kicked ass.

Grayson returned Laura's sweet smile with a numb frown. *This thing with Laura is not over, not by a long shot.*

~~~

Joe was all business, and Grayson felt the sting to their friendship from the meeting.

"This was too sensitive to share with the entire group. My FBI contact told me Murtadha is in Mexico recruiting Mexican Muslims, taking them to ISIS-controlled zones in Africa for training and then into combat. Once they are combat-hardened, they return and cross our border masquerading as cheap laborers. They have no idea how many there are, but the numbers are certainly mounting. It doesn't appear to bode well for us."

"Were you able to obtain more information on that fellow in photo three?" Grayson asked.

Joe paused a few seconds before answering. "I have a current photo of him, but my contact told me to not share it."

Joe doesn't trust me. "Time's starting to run short, partner. Economic output is going negative and inflation is picking up. What's special about this guy?"

Joe looked at Ramirez. "My contact told me not to share it and I'm not."

Ramirez's voice didn't bode debate. "We're professional men who've killed and could be killed in the near future. We're in charge of this shebang. If you don't share it with us, who the hell are you gonna share it with?"

Wayne looked around the table. "Gents, you have me at a disadvantage. This Mur…whatever, SOB is your bailiwick. I'll leave this decision to you four."

Mark spoke quietly. "We're all a little sensitive after the meetup. Let's get down to it. Joe, why would your contact give you a photo for your eyes only? You sure that's what was said?"

"Damn straight, I'm sure! I don't want to shut down my Intel pipeline."

Ramirez's fuse was getting short. "So, don't tell your contact. Pass the photo and tell us what you know. You may not be here when the time comes, and we need to know if there will be a Muslim problem to contend with!"

Joe passed the photo to Ramirez reluctantly. "He's a CIA operative. Couple of decades ago, the agency received word that an important group of imams in Egypt targeted Murtadha for…reversion to Islam. They inserted this guy into prison to join Murtadha's gang and find out what was what. He uncovered something big that caused him to remain with Murtadha."

Grayson spoke, his voice flat. "Does he have a name?"

Joe's face flushed. "His code name is Marco. That's all I have."

Grayson had never seen Joe so nervous.

"If this gets out and he's discovered, I'll be responsible for them torturing and killing him. It'll be on me."

Grayson understood. "We'll memorize his face and I'll store the photo in the gun safe. You know, Joe, it's tough on an operative that spends half his good adult years serving America under those conditions. The chief and I have worked with a few on clandestine operations. Marco is a patriot. You did the right thing."

Ramirez nodded. "He right, Joe. Thank your contact for us."

Chapter 53

The Ride Home

Year 17

After the managers' meetup, Ramirez started into the house, but paused. "Grayson, take Marcie on a tour of the farm; check out the animals and the garden."

"Good idea."

Marcie, suddenly excited, could hardly contain herself. "I want to see the rabbits and chickens."

"Let's go to the barn first. There's something I want to show you."

When Grayson opened the barn door, three just-weaned puppies, two females and one male, tails wagging wildly, welcomed them. Millie remained on her hay bed, her days growing short. She looked longingly at them and whined for Grayson. Everyone was amazed when she became pregnant.

Grayson knelt by Millie and scratched her behind her ears while he talked to her. The females stayed with Grayson and Millie, but the male jumped around Marcie excitedly and licked her legs.

"Why do you keep them in the barn? Wouldn't they be happier outside?"

"They might be happier, but the coyotes and hawks might get them."

Fear covered her face. "Oh."

She has a lot to learn about the real world. It can be cold and cruel.

When they stepped out of the barn and Grayson closed the door, a high-pitched sorrowful wail came from inside. Before Grayson could stop her, Marcie flung open the door and out popped the male, jumping for joy. She picked him up and held the puppy against her chest. The energy he put into licking her face and wagging his tail almost made Marcie drop him. She couldn't quit giggling.

Grayson knew immediately he had a problem on his hands. He also knew the outcome and resigned himself to it.

Marcie gave him that begging look that he couldn't resist.

"Okay, sweetie. What do you want to name him?"

To his amazement, she replied immediately, "Maverick."

"I like it. Why 'Maverick'?"

"He reminds me of you. In our woman-to-woman talk, Miss Grace told me a lot about you and your adventures, all good stuff. She said you and the chief are both mavericks. I'm glad you're not like all my other friends' fa...." Her voice faltered. She snuggled into Maverick, her face crimson and eyes misty.

"May I take Maverick home with me? I'll train him to be a tactical dog, like the ones the Army uses in combat, and he'll protect us."

Like any man confronted with a forlorn female, he melted. "There's a small cage in the back of the barn. We'll put him in it for safe transport back home. We don't want him to jump out of a moving truck."

She looked at him questioningly. "No, sir. But—"

"He can't come up front until he's clear of fleas and mites. The ride's too long. I'll get the cage."

Marcie put Maverick down and jumped into Grayson's arms with a big hug. "You're the greatest...friend."

He heard her unspoken word. *If only it were true.*

~~~

Grayson put Maverick in the back and Marcie, pensive and quiet, held her new pet rabbit, Bubbles. They entered the highway to Houston early in the afternoon with plenty of time to ease back into civilization.

After a few minutes, he asked, "Did you have something you wanted to discuss?"

"Aunt Jillian said it's a secret between the three of us."

Oh Lord. I'm not sure I like this.

"She talked to me about being a prepper. I knew you're one, but I didn't know she was. I can't let Shan...sorry...Mom know I'm a prepper too, but I don't care. She keeps a secret that's important to me. Course, she may not know the answer."

Grayson almost drove off the road. "What do you mean, you're a prepper?"

"I read your prepper books and the activation plan you left on the coffee table once. That, and what you've taught me about survival when we go backpacking, helped me to become a prepper."

"How did you find my prepper books?"

"Duh. I clean the house for my allowance. You never said not to clean your office. I wasn't being sneaky."

Grayson smiled at her. "You're honest with me, but a little booger nonetheless."

"I keep my backpack ready to bug out with you. Sometimes I wish Mom were a prepper and other times I don't care."

"How many of my books have you read?"

"All of them. I like the ones by Angery American and Franklin Horton. Steven C. Bird's stories have lots of bad guys that get killed and that's cool. In Horton's *Locker Nine*, you're like Grace's dad; you make sure I'm safe and that's comforting to me."

Grayson was floored by her revelation and bursting with pride, but her comfortable acceptance of killing people, bad guys or not, was worrisome. "I guess there's a good reason you were placed in the advanced program at school. You do know that in real life killing someone has serious religious and moral implications and consequences, to say nothing of legal ramifications. Killing someone can scar a person mentally for life."

"You killed people."

"That was in war and as a cop. I still suffer from after-effects."

"When the collapse comes, we'll be at war with bad guys. We must have a warrior's mentality to survive. That's what I read. Isn't that true, even for me?"

"Your logic is impeccable, Marcie, and what you're saying is true, but remember, preppers kill only to protect ourselves or others."

"Yes, sir. I know that, but you being in war before makes it more real to me."

"I'm hungry. How about you?"

She turned her head sideways and grinned. "Chucky Cheese?"

"We'll be there in thirty minutes."

"What about Maverick and Bubbles? It's too hot to leave them in the truck."

"We'll drop them off at the vet's on the way and pick them up tomorrow. They need shots." Marcie softly rubbed Bubbles' head. "You're a country rabbit, Bubbles. I'll plug in the iPhone and play George Jones for you."

Bubbles wiggled his nose in response.

Chapter 54

Time for Reflection

Year 18

Grayson couldn't wait to open the latest letter from Wanda. He felt the photos through the envelope and knew she'd sent more pictures of his grandson.

> *Dear Father-in-Law,*
> *As you can see from the happy faces in these photos, Gabriel's tenth birthday was a festive event. He's really into dinosaurs, so that's the reason for the wild decorations. I know you saw them on Facebook, but I wanted you to have a hard copy of some special ones that have Daniel in them.*
> *I tried, but Daniel still wouldn't allow you to attend. He's stuck in his cocoon of animosity but softening as he matures and bonds with Gabriel. He becomes irritated, but no longer very upset, when I compare his relationship with Gabriel to his relationship with you when he was a kid. That's my way of making him think about the good times he enjoyed with you. I sent him into shock when I told him that Gabriel needs a grandfather, and since my dad is no longer with us, it's you. He didn't like it either when I told him that love and forgiveness are both voluntary.*

At 32, Danny's not the same kid I met in college. He's matured and mellowed like you, something I've noticed through your letters over the years. I told you last month about Danny's promotion to lead chemical engineer. He enjoys the increased responsibility and that will help him mature more.

I'm glad things are going well in Houston and happy that you're still active in the MAG, as I'm counting on you to help save us when the collapse happens. The BOL sounds wonderful and so do the people. I wish we could visit, but Daniel won't hear of it.

I pray for your reconciliation with Daniel. Have faith that God will make it so.

Love always,

Wanda

The pictures of Daniel always caught him off guard. The sixteen-year-old boy he remembered was now a man. He'd filled out and looked like Grayson at that age. He reclined his chair, closed his eyes, and began to reflect on the considerable changes that had taken place in his life when the doorbell rang.

"Jillian! This is a surprise."

"I apologize if I bothered you. I'm meeting Shannon, but she's running late. Can't find my dang key."

"So, you thought you'd swing by and aggravate me. Coffee?"

"Sounds good. Thanks."

Jillian threw down the gauntlet on the way to the sunroom. "When are you going to make a move on Shannon?"

Warning bells reverberated between Grayson's ears. "That's what I love about you and your sister. No subtle fishing; dive in with both feet. What makes you think I'm interested in her?"

Jillian laughed. "Look, big boy, you're the one that announced she's your girlfriend to a none-too-happy audience. Anyway, you two have a secret that's not so secret, at least not to me."

Grayson chuckled. "Well, you know more than I do then. We have no secrets. Shannon avoids me. Maybe she has someone else. Maybe I should marry Laura, a good woman who loves me."

"You pissed her off in spades with the Shannon admission, but the way she looks at you and wiggles her fanny to get your attention hasn't changed. I admire the way you mask your feelings. Do *you* love Laura?"

"Well, yes, some." *Careful.*

"But Shannon is the one you desire, the one you can't stop thinking about. What a dilemma that must present you."

Walk VERY carefully. This woman could track and take down a grizzly with one hand.

"Jillian, some things don't make sense. Laura is perfect for me, but you're right. Shannon has a hold on me I don't understand. I want her to be mine, but she's erected an invisible barrier."

"You're just the man to break it down, a man who understands the old English adage, 'Faint heart never won fair maiden's hand.'"

"Thanks for your confidence. If you know how to get over the most daunting task, her liberal brainwashing, and save her from herself, tell me and I'll make her heart mine."

Jillian shook her head. "She's been a progressive too long. It'll take a traumatic event to make her see the light; but her heart is yours."

"Guess I have to face it, Shannon won't be onboard until Houston is engulfed in flames and maybe not even then. If she doesn't accept the collapse before the roads are jammed, we're screwed."

"She'll be in denial to the end, expecting the government to come to the rescue."

"You think she'll be in a state of normalcy bias?"

"I do."

"Rest assured, Jillian. I won't abandon her. I'm counting on you to get Marcie safely to the BOL, in case I'm not around."

Jillian glanced out the window. "She's home. I'd better run. For whatever it's worth, I won't bug out without you guys. Something else, big boy, you have to take action soon. Do something unusual to get her attention."

"Like what?"

"Maybe flowers with a 'thinking-of-you' love note. Add a box of gourmet chocolates."

"Hmmm. If you think it'll work, I'm game."

Shannon saw Jillian leave Grayson's sunroom and felt a stab of jealousy at their closeness. There was something curious about them, as if they were keeping a secret from her. Her jealousy turned to fear when it occurred to her that Grayson might have lost interest in her.

Chapter 55

Shannon's Quandary

Year 18

Shannon began joining Marcie and Grayson for meals. She didn't mention why, just showed up one day with a big smile, giving Grayson a knowing look. Her presence annoyed Marcie but pleased Grayson, who knew why, even if she kept it to herself.

"Grayson, you've become quite the grill master," Shannon dabbed her lips. "The chicken was delicious. How about the three of us enjoy a steak dinner Saturday night at Ruth's Chris, my treat?"

"Do I get the same dessert as the last time you offered to pay?" Grayson wiggled his eyebrows.

"You guys are weird," Marcie frowned. "I'll stay home if you're going to act like that."

"Why don't we make a picnic lunch and go to Lake Houston Wilderness Park, instead?" Grayson offered.

"You're on, mister." Shannon turned to Marcie. "Last chance, in or out?"

"Out!"

Shannon looked questioningly at Grayson.

"She's sixteen, old enough to stay by herself for a few hours," he said, not daring to tell her that Marcie's 9mm was handy and she knew how to use it.

~~~

Settled across from each other at a picnic table by the lake, Grayson and Shannon watched the canoes gliding quietly across the water and ate roast beef sandwiches, chasing them with root beer. Finishing their sandwiches, Shannon removed a box of Godiva chocolates from the bottom of the picnic basket. "I saved these to share with you. I thought you had given up on me."

"Given up?"

"After the divorce, you didn't ask me out. I thought you didn't care anymore, but your flowers and these chocolates—"

"You isolated yourself. I thought you didn't want to be bothered."
Women! Hints! Men need hints!

Grayson popped a chocolate into his mouth, and mumbled as he chewed, "You have something else on your mind?"

"What makes you think I have something on my mind?"

Grayson lowered his head, looked at her through the tops of his eyes.

"I hate it when you read me. I'll have to change tactics." She smiled.

"That won't work, and you know it."

"Damn you, Grayson! I wanted us to enjoy this evening, but there is an issue we need to discuss."

"Elephant in the room?" Grayson looked around, "Or I should say the park?"

"Something like that."

"I'm all ears. What's the elephant?"

"I'm concerned about some aspects of your influence on Marcie. She wrote a school report on how prices can skyrocket and cause the American economy to collapse. She discussed a state of anarchy with cities burning and people fighting and starving to death, all of which reek of that doomsday stuff you believe. It's ridiculous and we know that's not possible in this country. The government ensures price stability."

And there it is. Normalcy bias. "What was her grade?"

"What?"

"Her grade on the report; what was it?"

"She got a D. Her teacher said it was well written and argued, but it was science fiction, and the report was supposed to be non-fiction."

Grayson felt like the time he was trapped in a minefield in Iraq. Combat engineers cleared an escape path for him back then. Today, he was on his own.

"First, the teacher should be fired and a conservative teacher hired that has a clue. Second, you made it perfectly clear you didn't want me to interject my idiotic opinions—your words, not mine—into Marcie's studies, which is virtually impossible because she's with me all the time. Third, I haven't seen the report, but the details you mentioned are true."

"That's preposterous! America's too strong to have a failed economy."

"It failed in 1929 and caused the Great Depression."

"Yes, but it didn't result in anarchy, thanks to President Roosevelt."

"True; but FDR was a socialist. He caused the economy to suffer."

"Are you nuts? FDR was not a socialist!"

"He implemented socialist programs the Supreme Court ruled unconstitutional, at least, until he packed the court with progressives. Do your research, counselor. World War II and the economic boom that followed masked FDR's failed presidency. He was good at making people *feel* like he was saving them with his handouts, convincing them government was the answer to all their problems."

"Sharing of wealth to the less fortunate is a good thing," she retorted.

"Shannon, FDR's actions caused the Depression to extend longer than it would have if he'd not soaked up the available cash for socialist programs. It kept companies from accessing the funds they needed to start new business or expanding to provide the jobs needed to restore the economy through capitalism."

"America's economy has always been and is now capitalist."

The romance went right out the window or drowned in the lake. Here goes.

"No, it's not. Our slide toward fascism started in 1895 with the Sherman Antitrust Act when Congress gave the executive branch the power to regulate commercial enterprise. Hundreds of laws since added tremendously to the problem and created the current outrageous oligarchy we call The Establishment. America has a fascist economy, with socialist elements supported by what's left of the capitalist element."

"That's bull crap."

Nothing like a little sweet talk with the woman I love.

"Veterans Administration hospitals, Amtrak, Conrail, and Legal Services Corporation are all socialist entities. LBJ's Great Society program and Obamacare are perfect examples of fascist programs."

"You are seriously mentally ill. Where do you get these dumb ideas?"

"Listen. VA hospitals and Amtrak workers are government employees. Both are failures due to poor management, and cost taxpayers billions of dollars a year. That's socialism, plain and simple."

Shannon paced next to the table. "Define capitalism, socialism, and fascism," she challenged smugly.

"You want the drawn-out textbook version or my abbreviated version?"

"If you can't do it in a couple of sentences, let's go home."

"Capitalism permits citizens to own property, acquire wealth, and engage in commercial enterprise with little or no interference by the government. America had that before the Progressive Movement started at the end of the Nineteenth Century."

"Grayson, you know as well as I do capitalism during the American Industrial Revolution created monopolies and child sweatshops and most definitely did not protect workers."

"But you don't kill a cockroach with an atomic bomb. Question is, at what point does government control become tyranny?"

"You're pontificating, but go on." Grayson was now on his feet.

"Socialism does not allow citizens to own property, acquire wealth, or engage in commercial enterprise. Under socialism, the government owns everything—housing, factories, farms, transportation systems, you name it—and every worker is a government employee. Have you checked on Venezuela and Cuba lately to see the awful results?"

"And fascism?" she spit at him.

"Fascism allows citizens to own property and engage in commercial enterprise, but only through autocratic government regulation and oversight, again, like the Great Society program and Obamacare. It's how the Nazis ran their end of WWII."

"You're saying America's economic system is the same as Hitler's. You're certifiably insane!"

"Technically, America's economic system is fascist. Business has to toe the government's line. If the shoe fits, wear it."

"Obamacare gave thirty million people healthcare who didn't have it. What do you say to that, mister?"

"Shannon, over five million families lost healthcare the day it was implemented. Twenty million don't have it now and another ten million can't afford the premiums or co-pays. Nothing changed. Oh, wait, the price of medical care skyrocketed."

"Where do you get your numbers? *Fox News?*"

"From government websites. For Pete's sake, educate yourself."

Shannon's red hair glowed with indignation. "You and your *Fox News* crap!"

Bucko, tiptoe out of this minefield before you lose everything.

Grayson softened his voice. "Shannon?"

"What!" She stopped and they faced each other across the table.

"I respect that you have another political perspective, but understand this: America's kids need both sides of the story explained if they're to develop critical thinking skills. For too long, our education system has taught our kids *what* to think, not *how* to think. That's why I let Marcie see both sides. Certainly, you understand that."

Her anger boiling, Shannon had to get in the last punch. "She's *my* child, not your...." The blood drained from her face. She sat hard on the picnic table bench.

Grayson hurried around and kneeled beside her. "Are you okay?"

"Sort of."

"I thought you were going to pass out."

He moved to sit beside her, pulling her close. Once her breathing stilled, he tilted her head up and gave her his best disarming smile. "There's one other thing."

"What?" she sniffled.

"I love you with all my heart, Shannon Fisher, and I want to be with you all the days of my life."

Without a moment's hesitation, she replied. "I love you, too, Grayson Dean."

His arms enfolded her and they converged in a deep kiss. She rested her head on his chest. "This is the first time I've felt alive since Las Vegas. It seems a dream; it was so long ago. Damn you, Grayson Dean," she whispered.

"Regardless of our differences, Shannon, I've got to know where we stand on taking the next step. I'm ready."

"I can't make any promises, not now." She pulled back suddenly. "Can we just be happy for a little while, enjoy being close?"

Grayson, baffled by her circuitous reactions, eased her head back to his chest and stroked her hair.

At least I know the depth of her love. We can build from here.

Chapter 56

Tactical Marcie

Year 18

Grayson finished his scrambled eggs and bacon just as the sun began to peek over the horizon. He looked across the table at Marcie. "Treat your mother with more respect, and now that you have your license, I'll let you drive to the farm and back."

"That's not fair!" She cocked her head. "What exactly does *more respect* mean?"

"Don't play games with me, missy. Be polite, kinder, less argumentative."

"Forget it! You drive."

"Fine. You sit in the passenger seat and listen to my hard rock blaring all the way up and back. Get Maverick and Bubbles ready."

Marcie gave him a dirty look. "You're mean."

"Yep...as a rattlesnake." Grayson dangled the keys in front of her face and grinned. "If I were you, I'd wipe that dirty look off my face and rethink my options. You don't have to feign adoration, but you damn well better be respectful, like you are toward Miss Grace. Otherwise, you aren't going to the farm anymore. Period. Your attitude makes a difference in when you get your own car."

Marcie snatched the keys. "Deal. I don't want a new car. I want the sixty-eight Ford pickup at the farm. I'm a prepper."

"Be nice to your mother, and you might earn enough points to get it. Don't forget to pack your dress for Saturday Vigil."

"Already packed it."

"Sunday, we're going to the Church of Christ service with the chief and Miss Grace."

Marcie gave him a questioning look.

"We're all Christians and worship the same God and have the same Jesus. We go to Mass but should occasionally worship with our Protestant brothers and sisters. It's educational for us and helps bond the community."

Marcie began backing out of the driveway. "I can't wait to ride Bullet. He's the fastest horse in the county."

"When did you start riding horses?"

"About three meetups ago, when I had that sprained ankle and couldn't participate in training. It was Miss Grace's idea. Mr. Ramirez showed me how to put the saddle on Bullet and mount without putting pressure on my bad ankle."

"Oh! Now I know why Austin's been showing up with his horse. Young lady, you'd better not be riding into the woods with that boy."

"We don't! We hide in the barn. Soft hay…you know."

Grayson flashbacked to his teen years and a very pregnant Margaret. "I'll have a special talk with Austin this weekend."

Grayson's concern for her made Marcie feel safe. She appreciated his straightforward advice about boys.

"We just kiss a little. I think he's scared to do anything else." She shrank at the look he gave her.

Grayson was proud of Marcie for her self-confidence, as naïve as it was. It would serve her well when she matured into a full-grown woman. *Why must little girls have to grow up?*

"You'll have to invite him over, so I can lay down the law and show him my muscles and the shotgun I keep behind the door. Boys have one thing in mind, and they better be scared to death of touching my little girl."

Marcie giggled. "You don't keep a shotgun behind the door. Austin's so cute and sweet, and he's a **real** cowboy with real cows."

Grayson was speechless.

"Cat got your tongue?"

"Watch it, missy! So he's more than a passing fancy, someone to share horse rides. You know the rules."

"Yes, sir. I'm not allowed to date until I'm ninety-nine, and when I go on dates, I have to hold an aspirin between my knees."

Grayson nodded. "And wear a turtleneck sweater that grips your ankles. Let's change gears and discuss today's training exercise."

"You've taught me a lot since I became a SET Patriot and I know all about survival and how to use a rifle and a pistol."

"You know about shelter, water, food, security, and you've trained Maverick as a military combat dog. But you haven't participated in tactical exercises since you joined."

"We hunt and you've drilled me on how to move through woods and open areas in stealth mode."

"You don't know about camouflage and concealment or militia operations, like patrolling, raids, and ambushes. You need training and practice in immediate action drills, which is what we're doing this weekend."

"Training exercises will be fun," Marcie beamed.

"Watch your speed and back off that car in front of us."

She slowed down. "How's this?"

"That's better. Keep checking the speedometer and braking distance."

~~~

Grayson and Ramirez waved at Marcie from the gazebo when the group left the lodge for the training area.

"Looks like the classroom instruction is over. Why aren't you participating?"

Grayson sipped his coffee. "I want Marcie to focus on her training, not worry about screwing up in front of me."

Marcie stood at attention in squad formation. It was her first big training exercise as a private in the SET Patriots. Jillian helped her apply camouflage face paint and dress in full kit.

Jillian was pleased that Wayne chose her to oversee the event. She proudly stood in front of the formation. "Sir, first and second squads are prepared for the practical exercise."

Wayne, facing the formation, asked, "What is the general purpose of the exercise?"

Jillian didn't hesitate. "Sir, this exercise puts into action the instructions presented in the classroom pertaining to ambushes, patrolling, and immediate actions when ambushed."

"What are the specific training goals?"

"The first squad will establish an ambush in a wooded area unknown to the second squad. The second squad will practice patrolling techniques along a path that will take them within the ambush kill zone. Patrolling techniques will include individual tactical movements by forward, rear, and parallel security and movement of the main body. The patrol will pass within the ambush kill zone and employ immediate action to counter the ambush."

The men accepted the women as equals when they were in their uniforms and armed, and that made Marcie feel like a grown woman. She was in the second squad and focused on patrolling techniques.

Wayne sent the first squad ahead to set up the ambush before allowing the second squad to begin their patrol.

The second squad moved slowly and alertly through the woods. Marcie felt calm and one with nature, the same as when walking trails with Grayson and her mother. About twenty minutes into the patrol and on top of the world, she stepped into the middle of the ambush kill zone.

Suddenly, a string of firecrackers, heavy blank ammo shots, and Tannerite explosives—set off at a safe distance—sent her into a panic. She froze as though half-awake in a nightmare.

After less than half a minute, Mark blew a whistle to signal cease firing and announced, "Everybody circle-up for the critique."

~~~

Euphoria replaced Marcie's panic. "That was great! I almost peed my pants when they set off the bombs. The firecrackers sounded just like a real machine gun."

Focusing on their new recruit, Mark asked, "What was the main thing you learned from the exercise, Pvt. Fisher?"

"Hmmm. I can't say if there was one main thing. I became confused, not knowing if I should keep going and fight through the ambush, turn into the ambush, or take cover while returning fire. Being scared was spooky, but it was such fun, I can't wait to do it again!"

Mark got in her face and used his drill-sergeant voice to bring her in line with reality. "This is serious business, soldier! If you want to play games, then get yourself some Barbie dolls! When you're here, you kill or be killed! This is not a game! Do you understand me?"

Marcie slumped at attention, her face hot from Mark's scolding, something she'd never experienced.

"I said, do you understand me, soldier!"

"Yes, sir."

"Speak up soldier! I can't hear you!"

Marcie, filled with anger and humiliation, stood up tall and shouted, "Yes, sir! I understand, sir! This is not a game, sir!"

Her strong response knocked Mark off guard, and he almost cracked a smile. "That's good, soldier. At least you remembered your options, but not until after the shooting stopped. In a few minutes, we'll walk through this exercise several times to help you rectify the panic and freezing problem. When on patrol, always imagine you're about to be hit and know in advance what you'll do. Situational awareness is your friend, but a word of warning: training exercises are harmless; in real combat, you must have a warrior's mentality, and that is a serious thing, not a fun game. Without it, you die. When we conduct practical exercises, do something, even if it's wrong. That's the only way to learn the right way. Understand?"

"Yes, sir…and, Mr. Hamilton?"

"What?"

"Thank you for calling me 'soldier'."

"You're welcome, private."

Marcie began to bob up and down with a strained look on her face. "Mr. Hamilton, sir!"

"Yes, Private Fisher."

"Sir, I gotta pee really bad. May I be excused from formation?"

Everyone smiled when Mark slapped his hands together, slid his right arm out to full length, and pointed toward a big clump of bushes. "Dismissed, soldier!"

Chapter 57

The Farm Girl

Year 19

Grayson and Marcie placed Maverick and Bubbles in Grayson's fenced backyard and dropped their backpacks and dirty boots in the mudroom. Grayson sniffed the air. "Something smells delicious."

Shannon was in his kitchen preparing dinner, something new. Thankfully, they'd changed out of their camo gear before leaving the farm, but Grayson still felt defensive. "You won't believe the photos of wild animals we got on our late fall trek into Crockett National Forest," he lied and held his cellphone so she could see the screen. "Look at this photo of Canada Geese in the meadow by a lake. There must be a hundred." He omitted the part about taking the photos on the way home.

"Wow. They're beautiful."

When Shannon's back was turned, Grayson motioned Marcie toward her mother.

Marcie rolled her eyes and plastered on a phony smile. "Dinner smells great...Mom."

Startled, Shannon looked at Marcie closely, her eyes misting. "Thank you, sweetheart. You know, I enjoy our outings. Maybe I should start going backpacking with you guys again, visit the farm too. I'd like that."

"Like what?" they said in unison.

"Visiting the farm with you next time you go. What do you think?"

Grayson and Marcie looked at each other.

"What's with the look?" She studied the guilty-looking pair.

He swallowed hard. "It's weird. We talked about that not long ago. The guys ask about you. It'd be great having you with us. First, we need to get you outfitted."

She turned back to the stove. "I'll need to buy rubber boots for traipsing through cow pies."

"How do you know about cow pies...Mom?"

Grayson grinned at Marcie and held his truck key in the air while Shannon's back was turned.

Marcie stuck her tongue out at him.

"I lived on a farm until I started college. Guess we haven't talked much about my early years."

Marcie glanced at Grayson but couldn't control herself. "You never have time to talk about your early years or any other years for that matter."

"You're right. I'm sorry, Marcie. I've let my work get in the way."

"It wouldn't if you didn't go to those stupid anti-gun rallies."

Grayson cleared his throat. "Marcie, run along and take a quick shower. I'll help your mother with dinner."

Shannon's ire triggered, she retorted. "There's nothing stupid about eliminating guns to save people's lives."

Grayson was tired of running interference. "Go get your shower and change clothes before dinner." Marcie spun on her heel and ran to her room.

He wondered if she would hate her mother forever. Time was running out to get Shannon on their side before the encroaching collapse. "So, we need to plan a weekend camping trip soon."

"I'd prefer to go to the farm, but right now, I have to run to my house for nutmeg."

When the front door closed, Marcie shot into the kitchen. "We can't take her to the farm and I don't want to go backpacking with her again either!"

Grayson's tone made it clear he was tired and his patience stretched thin. "Thank you for being polite for a few minutes."

"She and her dirtball husband messed up my life, and I don't like either of them."

"You're only seventeen. A long time from now, when your mouth and brain catch up with each other, you'll have what it takes to get past those feelings. Like it or not, your mother loves you. I can't make you love her, but if you want to keep *our* relationship healthy, stop the childish rejoinders **today!**"

Her reply was half-hearted. "I'll try."

"No. You'll **do** it. That's like saying 'I'll *try* to be a good soldier.' If you only *try*, others will die. Christian adults don't intentionally cause pain to others. If you want to be a woman instead of a kid, that's what *you* must stop doing to your mother. Respect her right to her opinions and to make mistakes."

"So, what about the farm and backpacking?"

"It's natural for her to be curious about what we do when we're away. She needs to meet the group and know where the BOL's located.

If we have to bug out on foot, she must be in shape, an experienced backpacker, and know the direction of travel. Otherwise, she'll endanger all of us."

Marcie turned his lessons over in her head.

"Do you honestly want your mother dead, never to see or talk to her again? Do you want the responsibility of her death resting on your shoulders because you didn't try to save her?"

She shrugged and replied weakly, "I guess not."

"Sweetie, you were traumatized by something that happened between your parents. That's your business, and I've respected your right to privacy. My business is to love both of you and provide you with security. I can't do that if you continue fighting me. I need your help."

Marcie nodded, then challenged him. "If the SET Patriots decided two years ago to let her visit the farm, why didn't you invite her before now?"

"The time was never right."

"I guess you'd rather play with a barrel of rattlesnakes than be caught in the same room with two girlfriends."

"That about sums it up. You been talking about me with Austin?"

"Who else?"

"Hurry with your shower, missy. I'm ready to eat her delicious-smelling meal."

"I hate to admit it, but she is a good cook."

"And I'm sure you'll tell her how delicious it was. Be nice and I'll convince her to let you drive her Jag to the farm."

Islamic State of America - 14

Cairo Egypt – Time Has Arrived

Year 19

Akeem, Carlos, and Miguel sat and chatted, curious why Imam Omar summoned them from battle. Coming straight from a long hard-fought war in the heart of Angola, they were not current with the political and economic situation in America. They rose when the holy man entered the room.

"*As-salāmu alaykum*, peace be upon you." He kissed each on the cheeks.

"*As-salāmu alaykum,* and upon you peace," they replied.

Imam Omar praised his soldiers. "Through these years, you fought shrewdly and bravely and established Sharia, the law that pleases Allah, in many lands in Africa. You are prepared for the coming battle in America. The time is near."

Carlos stood fearless before the eminent and revered holy man and spoke to him in perfect Arabic. "All praise is to Allah. Everything happens by the will of Allah. We are His servants and carry out His will as given to us by our beloved Prophet Mohammed—peace be upon him."

Akeem praised Carlos. "Well-spoken, my friend."

Miguel spoke with confidence, the same as his brother. "You said, 'the time is near.' Do you speak of America?"

"I speak of all Western Civilization. The infidels destroy their own houses as we speak, work of their own evil hands. Thanks to your efforts, our cells are in position and ready to conduct holy war, *Alhamd lilah*, thanks be to god. It is time for you to return to America and make ready."

Carlos' fervor was unmistakable. "We will conquer the Southwest for the caliphate, for ISA, the Islamic State of America, and you will be our caliph. *Insha'Allah*, god willing."

Imam Omar smiled at Akeem. "You have done well, my friend. He turned to the group. "Tomorrow you travel to Mexico. Make ready to depart. *Allah yahmik*, may Allah protect you."

Chapter 58

Shannon's Epiphany

Year 19

Marcie brought her mother's dark sapphire Jaguar to a stop in front of the farmhouse and jumped out before Grayson and Shannon opened their doors.

Within seconds, Shannon saw Jillian with a large group gathering the last of the fall produce. "What's Jillian doing here, and why are those Houston cops here?"

"I thought you knew she'd joined our organic farming group. The cops are the chief's friends."

"You never mentioned them before. Maybe I should go home."

"You'll be fine. Let's go talk to Jillian." He waved to her while surveying the group for Laura.

Jillian held up a huge cabbage. "Hi, Sissy. Look at the size of these babies! Let's use one to start a big pot of veggie soup."

"Why didn't you tell me you'd be here? What's going on?" Shannon asked suspiciously.

"Chill out. We do a lot of farming and produce some great food. Enjoy your day."

Shannon gave her look only a close sister would understand. "We'll see. The cabbages are beautiful. I should've brought my grungy clothes, so I could help."

Most of the group remained working, but a few came over to say hello. Shannon had questioned many of them on the witness stand. They were polite and shook her hand, but nobody welcomed her.

Grayson grabbed her hand and walked to the knoll where he stood with Joe his first day at the farm.

Ever the lawyer, Shannon analyzed the surroundings. "The pond is beautiful. Why are those shacks in a big circle around this spot?"

"Those are the cabins everyone stays in when gardening and hunting. The center makes a good place for an open fire to socialize."

"I don't see any signs of a fire pit, and you never mentioned hunting. Do they have guns here?" She gasped when she saw the deer carcasses hanging by their hind legs from a big oak tree.

"Some of the guys do."

Shannon tamped down her anger, afraid to ask if Marcie hunted. Her uncontrolled guilt again edged her to the threshold of detesting her decision to accede quietly to Grayson's secret parental entitlements. Listening to the easy banter between Grayson and Marcie on the drive to the farm had triggered it, and she felt it spiraling out of control. Jillian's unexpected appearance added to her irritation and gave her a profound sense of isolation.

"That big thing over there. It's enormous."

"That's the BOL backup solar power station. Commercial power goes out for days at a time here."

"B-O-L?"

"It's a solar power company. Obama didn't invest in it. You know, because it didn't pay off big-time contributors and then go into bankruptcy." His joke didn't amuse her.

She was on full alert. The late November day was cool with a slight breeze, and they were not exercising, but he was starting to sweat.

"What about that long building beside the B-O-L solar?"

"That's the lodge where the group meets to socialize and cook meals from the fresh veggies."

"What about those towers with the wires and antennas hanging on them?" *She has strong Ralph Nader with hints of J. Edgar tendencies.*

"That's Weber's antenna farm. He's a ham radio guy and doesn't have enough space at his home for his hobby."

"Weber? Harold Weber? The cop that made a fool of me in the Delgado trial? On second thought, don't answer that."

She spoke through gritted teeth. "You never told me about a lodge. I suppose you cook venison, too?"

"That and beef, chickens, rabbits. See the herd of cows over there? Chicken and rabbit coops are near the barn."

He attempted to hold her hand as they started back to the group, but she shook loose.

"I don't know what's going on here, mister, and don't try to bullshit me, but you've got my daughter mixed up in something weird. I'll leave it alone for now, but we **will** talk later."

Grayson saw Laura chatting with the group around the baskets of fall vegetables. He scanned for Austin and found him in the gazebo with Marcie. *Might as well get it over with now.* He steered Shannon to the group and covertly watched Laura connect and follow them.

"Hi, Grayson. It's nice to see you." Laura dripped sugar with each word.

"Hi, Laura. How are you?"

"I'm fine. Who's your friend?"

The men enjoyed watching Grayson squirm, but Joe took pity on him. "Come on, guys, these veggies won't load themselves for the drive back to Houston. Grayson, I have a big pot of chicken-veggie soup on low heat in the lodge for the evening social. Check on it for me, please, and get the cornbread started. It's already in the pan, covered with plastic wrap. The fire in the stove has the oven hot by now."

Grayson pulled on Shannon's hand, and she reluctantly followed. "A fire in the stove? You're using a wood-burning stove for cooking?"

Bucko, you're back in the minefield without combat engineers to clear a path.

"Jillian, come help me," he almost begged. He waved for Marcie.

"Austin and I have to help his mother," Marcie yelled to him. She didn't budge until Grayson gave her his you'd-better-do-as-I-say look.

~~~

Grayson stepped out of the kitchen and sat down at the table. "Cornbread's in the oven."

Shannon glared at all three of them. "Who wants to explain what the hell's going on here? And I don't mean with that woman; that's obvious."

"What crawled up your butt?" Jillian asked. "It's our hunting camp and garden club."

"Don't insult my intelligence. Sister-mine, I also grew up on a farm. That garden is big enough to feed an army, and those rabbits and chickens could feed everybody here for a year."

No one spoke until Shannon pounded her fist on the table. "Damn it! Say something!"

Marcie flinched. She'd never seen her mother so riled.

Grayson and Jillian nodded to each other in agreement. It was time.

Jillian took a deep breath. "I'll start. You know Grayson and I are preppers, and this is what we call our bugout location, or BOL. This is where we, *and you*, will come to survive the die-off after the collapse occurs. That's it, plain and simple."

Shannon punched Grayson hard on the arm. "B-O-L, a solar power company?"

"I didn't want to scare you."

"But lying is okay?" Shannon's gaze shot to the ceiling as she struggled to control herself. "What's this *die-off* and *collapse* bullshit?"

Grayson felt himself standing at the urinal again. "Shannon, all indications are that the government is on the verge of bankruptcy. When it happens, there will be an economic, political, and societal collapse, a state of anarchy. Within a few months, ninety percent of the population will die of starvation, disease, and bullets. That's the die-off."

"You're brainwashed. How many times do I have to tell you, 'if we do have an economic downturn, America will recover?' The government has plans to take care of us."

Jillian shook her head. "Remember our little *Fox News* experiment and how mainstream media reporters make fools of ignorant citizens?"

"I'll ignore the fact that you just called me ignorant. You two have corrupted my daughter. You knew how I felt. You had no right—"

Marcie, in tears, stood and turned to Grayson. "I'm sorry." Her voice slightly above a whisper and absent of sarcasm, she spoke directly to Shannon. "You. Are. **NOT.** My. Mother." Jillian followed her out, shooting a disgusted look at Shannon.

Shannon sat at the table in shock. "I've lost everything dear to me: my daughter, my sister, and you, too."

"What?"

She glared at him with fire in her eyes. "That woman is why you come here every month."

"What the heck are you talking about?"

"Don't play innocent with me. I saw how she looked at you. Gotta get your nookie somewhere, huh sailor?"

Grayson was too stunned to speak.

The air hung heavy, like a morgue.

A soft voice spoke from the lodge doorway. "No, Shannon. That's not why he comes here every month. Sorry. I just came to say goodbye before going to work and didn't mean to eavesdrop, but I'm glad I did. He couldn't commit to me and now I know why. You're his special love and the reason he left me to move back to Houston. He's your man, one hundred percent."

The fire in Shannon's heart began to extinguish as comprehension replaced fury.

Tears streaked Laura's cheeks. "I've hated you for years. I came today to get him back, to let him compare us and see I'm the better choice, but that isn't going to happen. He finds something in you that I don't have."

Shannon went to Laura and put her arms around her. "Thank you, Laura. You have no idea what that means to me. I'm sorry for what I was thinking."

Laura whispered something to Shannon, and the two hugged again before she left.

Grayson watched it play out on the stage of his life without him participating. The two women he loved seemed to have laid down their swords.

I've never felt so stupid in my life.

Shannon stared for a lifetime at Grayson. He saw the wheels turning in her head, analyzing and deciding. Once she reached her conclusion and without any indication on her face to reveal its impact on his life, she walked back to the table. He stood and braced himself for another blast of insults.

"We still have unfinished business." She pressed herself against him, wrapped her arms around his neck, and pulled him into a long kiss. "I love you, Grayson Dean. Will you marry me?"

"I thought you were going to…er…I mean…." *Why is the man always wrong?*

"I'll give you a going over, once we're in Vegas on our honeymoon. Reserve the same room at Caesar's Palace and let me know if you need the room number. I still have the key with the number written on it."

"You're not angry?"

"Not anymore. Laura made me realize I have to accept my life as it is. That means accepting that you three will not stop your adventures here. What you're doing is stupid, but it's also harmless. I have to accept that I've lost Marcie until she matures; it's a fact that…." She stopped and looked around. "No! I don't have to accept it!"

"Accept what?"

Her eyes reflected excitement. "Everything is going to be okay. You'll see. Not today, but you'll see very soon. Oh yes, you'll see. So will Marcie."

"I don't know what the hell is going on in that beautiful head of yours, but I think I like it."

She placed her head on his chest and hugged him tightly. "Work with me to put aside our differences, so we can have a happy life together."

Perhaps life experiences that came with age were starting to soften her, too. His heart was lighter and filled with hope. "May I ask what Laura whispered to you?"

"She said you and I are in our forties, and we're foolishly letting some of the best years of our lives slip by us. She's right."

Shannon took a step back and pretended to be offended. "Since you ungraciously didn't answer my proposal of marriage, not a Texas gentlemanly way to behave, drop to one knee and *do* the right thing. You'd better be convincing of your love and devotion to the lady, or she might not accept *your* proposal."

"Will you always be this bossy?"

"Yep. It's in my DNA. You know the rule. If Mama ain't happy, ain't nobody happy. Get with it and make me happy."

Grayson dropped to his right knee and took her left hand just as the SET Patriots, chatting loudly, poured in for supper with Miss Grace and the chief leading the troops. Never had silence grown so loud so fast.

Miss Grace broke the silence. "Son, you don't have a ring, do you?"

"No, ma'am."

She walked directly to Grayson and removed a beautifully crafted, antique, diamond ring from her finger. "This is my grandmother's engagement ring. It's been waiting for someone to love it. It's yours." She bent down, kissed Grayson on the cheek, and stood back.

Grayson took the ring, placed it on Shannon's finger, made a magnificent proposal, and the lady was convinced. He picked Shannon up by the waist, spun her around, and gave her a big kiss.

The group wasn't sure how they felt or how to act. Their nemesis, the ACLU lawyer, was their leader's fiancée. Ramirez, ever wise, and knowing the unpleasant thoughts of the group, took charge. "Guys we just witnessed our executive officer and good friend make a beautiful proposal of marriage to the woman he loves. It brings joy to my heart."

Joe began to clap heartily and move toward the couple. The rest slowly began what turned into a rousing round of applause and congratulatory remarks, followed by lots of handshakes and hugs, except for Jillian and Marcie who, just having entered, stood at the door in shock.

"What the hell did we miss?"

Bright red covered Marcie's neck and face, and fire danced in her eyes when she saw Shannon holding the engagement ring high in the air for everyone to see. "I don't know, but I don't like it, not one bit."

Chapter 59

The Awful Secret

Year 19

"Marcie, your behavior's been appalling. What's going on in that teen head of yours?" Grayson asked. "Since our engagement, your animosity towards your mother has escalated out of control. Don't you want us to get married?"

Marcie gave Shannon a dirty look. "No. I don't! The two of you'll make my life miserable. Until I find a particular relative I've never met and don't know anything about, I **won't** get along with *her*."

Shannon began to tremble. "Please, Marcie, not now."

Grayson's patience slammed into the end of its road and his tone allowed no alternative. "Let's get this out in the open and closed, once and for all. I'm mentally exhausted from running interference between you two, of being jerked around at every turn."

Fear shot through Shannon as she watched Grayson's eyes harden. "It's impossible for us to move forward until the two of you deal with this. It ends today. Now!"

Shannon's naked emotions were ripe with confusion, angst, indecision, and a dozen other reactions rolled into one. She paced like a caged tiger then rushed toward the back of the house, her voice shaking. "Give me a minute."

Grayson paced and Marcie drew herself into a tight ball and sulked, as they listened to Shannon's heavy, heart-wrenching sobs for what seemed an eternity. Occasionally glancing at one another, both with the same questioning thought, then looking away.

She finally returned, dabbing at her bloodshot eyes with a handful of tissues.

"Grayson, please sit down."

"Okay."

Shannon fought to keep her composure, her voice unsteady. "You're right. It's time we talked about this."

She choked and burst into tears again. "Please don't hate me," she spoke to Grayson. "Please tell me you won't hate me."

Grayson stood to hold her, but she motioned him back down.

He gave Marcie a stern glance. "Whatever it is, we won't hate you, Shannon."

Gaining control, her voice still tense, she blotted escaping tears. "I've been guarding a secret. I'm a coward for not telling you both a long time ago."

Marcie gave her mother undivided attention. "Marcie, do you remember what Larry said the night before he left?"

"He called you a horrible name. I don't want to talk about it."

"We have to talk about it if you want the answer you've begged for the last four years."

Marcie's eyes zeroed in on her mother, a tiger poised for the kill.

Shannon studied her shaking hands. "Larry accused me of infidelity."

She looked at Grayson but spoke to Marcie. "As Grayson knows, Larry was right."

Grayson's eyes widened, and he warned her. "Some things are best left unspoken. That's one of them."

Shannon ignored him and turned her swollen eyes to her daughter. "Grayson and I ran into each other at a conference in Las Vegas eighteen years ago. The short story is we ended up in bed together."

"TMI!" Marcie hid her face in a pillow.

Shannon took a ragged breath. "Larry was sterile when we married. I didn't know." She hesitated. "You two do the math."

"You and Grayson? I didn't need to know," Marcie wailed, her tears flowing.

Grayson's surging emotions sent him to his feet. Rubbing the back of his neck, his heart pounded. His brain knotted. His mouth dry, he strangled on his words. "Oh, my God." Tears filled his eyes.

Fear swiftly cloaked Marcie. "Grayson, you're crying…. Mom?"

"You wanted to know, Marcie. Larry admitted that horrible night that he'd secretly had a vasectomy. Do you know what that is?"

Marcie's eyes blinked and she nodded.

Shannon's burst of anger saturated the room. "It's just like the bastard!"

Broiling in heated emotional chaos, Grayson sought verification of what his logical mind told him but was afraid to accept for fear of it not being true. "Are you sure, absolutely sure?"

"Look at her, Grayson. Marcie is the spitting image of you and Amanda, her half-sister. She was born forty weeks to the day after we were in Vegas. Larry and I…were intimate just after I returned home.

Forcing you out of my mind, I missed the connection of her birth to the trip."

Squeezing the pillow to her chest, Marcie, understanding starting to take hold, began to cry softly.

Shannon blew emancipated air through pursed lips. "Sweetie, I swear to you with all my being that the time Grayson and I were together was the only time I wasn't faithful to my husband. I won't make excuses, but I thank God for that night with him. It gave me the two people I love more than anything on this earth. Marcie, like it or not, Grayson Dean is your father."

"Like it? I love it!" Marcie raced to Grayson with loud sobs of joy. He held her against his chest, placed his head on top of hers, and stroked her long red curls.

"Mom, I'm sorry I was so mean!" She pulled her mother into their first family hug. "I have a real family! Does Aunt Jillian know?"

"I think she figured it out a long time ago."

Questions poured from Marcie, ending with, "Will you guys go back to Las Vegas and make me a sister or brother?"

Impulsive, just like her old man.

Grayson could hardly contain himself. "You have a brother—Danny. Well, he's your half-brother. And, you're an aunt; you're Gabriel's Aunt Marcie."

"That's right! I'm and aunt. This is so cool." Marcie couldn't stop moving and laughing. She twirled around the room. "Wait. Oh! Oh!" A small frown formed on her face. "I can't call you 'Daddy.' It's what I called *him*."

"Don't fret over it, sweetheart. Something will pop up," Grayson said.

"Pop! That's it! I'll call you 'Pop.'"

She looked hopefully at him for approval. He flashed back to Daniel's name for him and smiled, making it official.

~~~

At midnight, Marcie calmed enough to fall asleep. When Grayson and Shannon looked in on her, she had her arm around Mr. Purber. They returned to the living room and sat on the couch in quiet contemplation.

His thoughts drifted to the coming crisis. It was only a matter of time before all hell broke loose. He mentally recoiled when the near presence of Carlos Murtadha assaulted his consciousness.

Shannon squeezed his hand and kissed his cheek.

He pushed Murtadha away, relaxed, and put his arm tightly around her, taking great delight in the moment. *It will be okay. We'll face the future without fear and conquer life's challenges as one.*

His innate instincts to provide and protect—passed to him through the DNA of his male ancestors for thousands of years—resettled in his psyche and once again, Grayson Dean was a complete man.

AUTHOR'S NOTE

Thank you for purchasing Islam Rising. I hope you enjoyed reading it as much as I enjoyed writing it. Please consider taking a few minutes to leave a review on Amazon.com. Reviews are important in that, they assist others to determine their potential interest in reading a book.

COMING SOON

Jihad Begins**: **Patriots and Infidels - Book 2 picks up at the point of economic collapse, onset of anarchy, and the beginning of Imam Omar's unholy war against America. The Set Patriots struggle to protect the BOL and local community from overrun by tens of thousands of desperate, starving refugees and attacks by organized gangs and good guys turned bad.

Meanwhile, Grayson Dean and his small crew find themselves walking the 150 miles to the BOL through masses of Houston refugees and bad guys, while being chased by a vengeful Carlos Murtadha.

Jihad Begins is replete with bugging out survival techniques, dangerous encounters with bad guys, romantic interludes, heart-rending life and death decisions, and a host of twists and turns sure to please any fan of post-apocalyptic novels.

BOOKS IN PRINT

Absolute Anarchy, Interactive Study Guide to Surviving the Coming Collapse

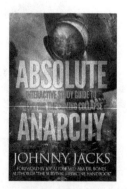

Absolute Anarchy is the most comprehensive prepper study guide ever written. See the proof:

https://AbsoluteAnarchyBook.com

Pay close attention to the Table of Contents

Available on Amazon: *http://a.co/7S809lc*

CONTACT ME

You can find more information on my books and many prepper topics at the following websites. Contact me via Messenger or by clicking on the *Contact the Author* button in the main menu of one of the websites.

WEBSITES

https://AbsoluteAnarchyBook.com

https://NewAmericaBooks.com

https://PrepperSchool.org
(Under Construction with completion scheduled for late 2018.)

FACEBOOK PAGE
https://www.facebook.com/Prepper1944

Written Word

The Competitive Edge

Written Word provides editorial and written services for a wide variety of book genres. Mahala Church works with authors through traditional and online media to promote sales, build credibility, and establish platforms for their work. A Pushcart Prize nominee in 2008, Church is the published author of fiction and non-fiction. Editorial credits include anthologies, novels, and non-fiction books.

Editing manuscripts
Ghostwriting
Developmental coaching for fiction and non-fiction
Blog and social media posts, web articles
Press releases
Marketing tools

For More Information

mahalachurch@gmail.com.

https://www.editwriteteach.com

https://www.facebook.com/mahalachurch

Written Word